W9-BCW-092

THE BODY IN THE CAST

THE BEELER LARGE PRINT MYSTERY SERIES

Edited by Audrey A. Lesko

Also Available in Beeler Large Print by Katherine Hall Page

THE BODY IN THE BOG
THE BODY IN THE KELP
THE BODY IN THE BASEMENT

THE BODY
IN THE CAST

KATHERINE HALL PAGE

ST. MARYS PUBLIC LIBRARY
127 CENTER ST.
ST. MARYS, PA. 15857

BEELER LARGE PRINT
Hampton Falls, New Hampshire, 1999

Library of Congress Cataloging-in-Publication Data
Page, Katherine Hall
The body in the cast. / Katherine Hall Page
p.cm.-(The Beeler Large Print mystery series)
ISBN 1-57490-239-3 (acid free paper)
1.Fairchild, Faith Sibley (Fictitious character)—Fiction. 2.Motion picture
industry—Massachusetts—Fiction. 3.Caterers and catering—
Massachusetts—Fiction. 4. Women detectives— Massachusetts—Fiction.
5. Large type books. I.Title. II.series
PS3566.A334 B653 1999
813'.54—dc21   99-0511851

Copyright © 1993 by Katherine Hall Page

All rights reserved.

No part of this book may be used or
reproduced in any manner whatsoever without
written permission except in the case of brief
quotations embodied in critical articles or
reviews.
For information, address St. Martin's Press,
175 Fifth Avenue, New York, NY 10010
Illustrations by Phyllis G. Humphrey
A THOMAS DUNNE BOOK
An Imprint of St. Martin's Press

Published in Large Print by arrangement with
St. Martin's Press.
BEELER LARGE PRINT
is published by
Thomas T. Beeler, Publisher
Post Office Box 659
Hampton Falls, New Hampshire 03844
Typeset in 16 point Adobe Garamond type.
Printed on acid-free paper and bound by
Sheridan Books in Chelsea, Michigan

I would like to thank Raymond Norman, owner, and Meg Bezucha of Media Gourmet, Jamaica Plain, Massachusetts, for all their advice, and my cousin Elizabeth Samenfeld-Specht for permission to use her delicious Sugar and Spice Cookie recipe.

Thanks also, as always, to my editor, Ruth Cavin.

The quotations that introduce each chapter are from The Scarlet Letter *by Nathaniel Hawthorne, first published in 1850.*

EDITOR'S NOTE

The Body in the Cast includes, at the end of the story, five full recipes from Faith Fairchild's (fictional) cookbook, Have Faith in your Kitchen, *as well as a number of descriptions in the text of the way Faith makes some of her delectable dishes.*

For my brothers, sisters, and their families:
David and Barbara Page; Ann and Ron Page-Roose; Sheila and
Manny Pologe.

PHYLLIS G HUMPHREY

CHAPTER 1

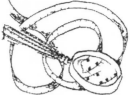

The page of life that was spread out before me seemed dull and commonplace, only because I had not fathomed its deeper import.

ALEFORD, MASSACHUSETTS, WAS REELING—LITERALLY. Not only was an actual Hollywood movie crew in town filming a modern version of *The Scarlet Letter* but Walter Wetherell had abruptly resigned from the Board of Selectmen, igniting a fierce three-way contest for the vacant seat.

And, as if these were not enough, Town Meeting was in session, with all its attendant intrigue: loyalties and grudges handed down from one generation to the next; back-room political maneuvers; and immediate front-room protests. Never before had the dismally bleak month of March seemed so bright. March—when the possibility of a crisp white snow-fall was greeted with about as much enthusiasm as another tax increase from Beacon Hill. March—when only the young, or perennially foolish, talked about smelling spring in the air and the imminent arrival of daffodils. March—whether accompanied by lions or lambs, a month to get through.

Over at the First Parish parsonage, the Reverend Thomas Fairchild and his wife, Faith, were adapting themselves to the newest member of their family, Amy Elisabeth. It had been Baby Girl Fairchild for about twenty-four hours following her birth the previous September as Tom and Faith battled it out, albeit with velvet gloves. Faith had counted on a dramatic pose in the hospital bed, fresh from her labor, to win the day. It didn't. She was forced to give in on Sophie, with all its sweet little French schoolgirl connotations, but rallied to demand that Tom abandon Marian, after his mother. A nice woman, to be sure, yet what would Faith's own mother, Jane, have to say? The remote and absurd possibility that Faith might be forced to have another baby to keep both grandmothers happy had presented a singularly grueling specter at the moment. For a while, it appeared agreement might be reached on Victoria, or Victoire (Faith persisted), but both parents eventually concurred that it might not be clear whose victory and over what, since it wasn't even clear to Tom and Faith themselves. Faith's escape from a crazed kidnapper in a French farmhouse during the fourth month of pregnancy? Or, Faith's suggestion, the whole less than enjoyable experience of childbirth itself? A memory any number of friends had assured her grew dim with time. And this had proved to be the case—somewhat. Ben's birth three and a half years earlier had receded to a far distant shore, then instantly crashed forward into total recall the moment her water broke.

They had finally settled on Amy, but Faith perversely decided to hold out for the French spelling, Aimée, to almost a bitter end. It was only when Tom sang "Once in Love with Amy" for the hundredth time, firmly declaring Ray Bolger wasn't immortalizing an Aimée, that Faith gave in. She pulled her last punch and salvaged the European s instead of z in Elisabeth, and the family turned to more important things like nibbling the baby's toes and wondering how fingernails could be so tiny.

Faith Sibley Fairchild had not always lived in Aleford, a fact she no longer blurted out insistently when introduced but that she nevertheless managed to subtly work into the

3

conversation—such was the increasing wisdom that age, and life in a small village, conferred. She had grown up in Manhattan, established herself as one of the hottest caterers in town as an adult, and reluctantly left after she realized the sole way she could have her cake and eat it was to move north, marry Tom, and make sure she had a decent stove.

The institution of the ministry was not foreign to her. Both her father and grandfather were men of the cloth. It was this familiarity with parish life during her formative years that made her swear an oath with her sister, Hope, one year younger. Neither would marry men working for any "higher authority" than someone with a name on the door and a Bigelow on the floor. The girls went so far as to avoid dates with Matthews, Marks, Lukes, and Johns for a time, until this became counter-productive when Hope fell for a particularly attractive bond salesman named Luke at work. Still, she married a Quentin, an MBA, not an MDiv, and lived up to her side of the bargain. It was Faith who fell from grace when she met Tom, sans dog collar, at a wedding she was catering, not realizing he had performed the ceremony until it was too late.

Almost five years had passed. Faith had become a bit more used to Aleford and Aleford to Faith. However, she still suffered frequent longings for the sound of taxi horns blaring, the sight of blue-and-yellow Sabrett's umbrellas protecting spicy dogs and kraut, and the aroma of Bergdorf's fragrance counters. You could take the girl out of the city, but you couldn't take the city out of the girl. Her stylish New York clothes and penchant for Woody Allen movies were no longer hot topics for the early coffee and muffin crowd at the Minuteman Café. If she was talked about, and she was, the conversation now tended toward her knack for both finding corpses and subsequently solving the crimes.

But old habits die hard in places like Aleford, and stalwarts like Millicent Revere McKinley, a descendant of a distant cousin of Paul Revere and the pillar of the DAR, Aleford Historical Society, and WCTU, regarded Faith's sleuthing abilities as child's play compared with Millicent's own encyclopedic knowledge of the life and crimes of every Aleford inhabitant for the last fifty years. This knowledge was gleaned in a variety of ways, the predominant being her daily hawkeyed observations from a perch in the front bay window of ye olde ancestral Colonial house, happily located directly across from the village green and with a clear view down Battle Road, Aleford's main street. No, *Miss* McKinley, thank you, was not interested in Faith's supposed abilities pertaining either to detection or cuisine. Millicent clung to her initial impression; to do otherwise would have suggested uncertainty, or worse—whimsicality—and she chose to dwell on the peccadilloes of a person from "away." Her attitude was made manifest by audible sighs, especially where two or three were gathered, followed by the words "Poor Reverend Fairchild."

When Faith reopened her catering business, Have Faith, after Christmas in the former home of Yankee Doodle Kitchens, Millicent added, "And her poor neglected little children" to the litany, smiling a gentle, mournful smile before moving on to the next audience.

"Honestly, Tom, I should be used to her after all this time, but she still gets under my skin," Faith exploded one evening after the neglected children had been read to, cuddled, and generally spoiled rotten before drifting off to sleep. "It's a Gordian knot and I'm all thumbs. If I hadn't started the business again and had stayed home all day

5

with Amy, dear as she is, I'd be a crazy woman by now. Or let's say crazier. On the other hand, working makes me feel guilty about leaving her, even for short periods. And I know the house is suffering."

"I'd rather have you sane—or are we saying saner? Besides, you've done everything you can to be with Ben and Amy as much as possible." Tom looked around the living room from the depths of the large down-cushioned sofa, a comfy legacy bequeathed by one of his predecessors. "The house looks fine and so, Mrs. Fairchild, do you." Faith was conveniently near and he drew her into his arms.

"I suppose you're right," she said contentedly. "Anyway, the flowers help." Faith had placed pots of bright tulips and freesia she'd forced, so as to distract the eye from whatever might be out of place or in need of cleaning. It was a trick she had learned from her Aunt Chat: "Put plenty of flowers around, keep the silver shiny, and no one will ever know how many dust bunnies are under your bed."

While letting some of the housework slide, although she was managing to keep the bunnies from reproducing at too rapid a rate, Faith did everything guilt-ridden moms everywhere do to minimize the time away from the kids. She may even have gone overboard, she'd thought on more than one occasion, longing for a moment alone. It was getting hard to remember the last time she'd had a shower more than three minutes long, and a soak in a perfumed tub seemed like a chapter from somebody else's life.

Yankee Doodle's premises had needed some remodeling, so Faith had had a carpeted play area installed at one end of the huge space, complete with jolly jumper, playpen, shelves for toys, and a small table and chairs.

Most days, the baby came to work with her. Just as the books said, second child Amy Elisabeth was easier, settling placidly into two long naps and food at reasonable hours, except for that very early morning demand for mother's milk—now! Ben was at nursery school through lunch and spent the afternoon with Faith or, when she was pressed, in day care with Arlene Maclean, mother of Ben's beloved friend, Lizzie. Arlene also took Amy at times. Arlene didn't smoke, wasn't noticeably psychotic, and, if Lizzie was proof, knew what was what in the Raising Nice, Obedient, Yet Interesting Children department—a department Faith still felt much less familiar with than, say, Better Dresses at Bloomie's.

It had been an enormous amount of work starting the business in the new locale, far from her former suppliers and staff. She'd been discouraged almost to the point of giving up when Niki Constantine, a young Johnson and Wales graduate fresh from washing pots at Biba's, one of Boston's culinary shrines, strode confidently in to be interviewed for the job of Faith's assistant. Niki had grown up in nearby Watertown. Her parents still operated a bakery there. She nibbled all day, tasting constantly, and never seemed to put an ounce on her wiry frame. Her tight, short black curls had a few streaks of premature gray and she brought an air of serious professionalism to the job that matched Faith's own.

They soon became a team: two ambitious, hardworking women who were often convulsed in laughter, as when Niki presented Faith with a tray of spectacularly fallen individual soufflés Grand Marnier, declaiming in solemn tones, "They just couldn't keep it up." Niki also tended to answer "Food is my life" in a deceptive deadpan to most queries.

So, all was well, or at least this is what Faith

7

optimistically told Tom, and herself, whenever she returned home at the end of a particularly long day. Amy was benefiting from having a contented mom, not to mention the purees of artichoke hearts and spoonfuls of *pâté de foie de volaille avec champignons* the baby gobbled down with significantly greater gusto than she brought to Gerber's fare. Ben was the same, munching chocolate madeleines and milk as his after-school snack. And there were stretches when Faith wasn't working much at all and packed the kids up for enriching trips into town or dragged them along on much-neglected parish calls. She was, after all, a minister's wife. And she knew her duties.

The first inkling that movie people were coming to Aleford had been in December, shortly before Christmas, when a tall, thin young man in an olive Joseph Abboud suit and slightly darker topcoat had showed up at Battle Green Realty and asked the startled owner, Louisa May Talcott (her mother had read *Little Women* over seventy times), whether she could show him some houses. December was a slow month and Louisa May had been engrossed in the latest Charlotte MacLeod mystery when the sleigh bells on the door jangled. She'd looked up, to find her own distorted reflection in the sunglasses her caller had donned against the novel glare of white snow. Politely removing his shades, he explained he wanted to rent a small Cape Cod house, authentic if possible, located on several acres, preferably with lots of trees. It was the work of a moment to drive him out to the Pingree place, a two-hundred-year-old Cape. It had the requisite light-obscuring windows, low ceilings, and small, drafty rooms. The house also abutted a large stretch of conservation land complete with forest, streams, a bog, and several picturesque tumbled-down stone walls. Delighted with the house and its setting, the stranger revealed he was Alan Morris, the assistant director on a new Maxwell Reed movie. Alan shot countless rolls of film, took copious notes, and left a check that turned the visions of sugarplums dancing in Louisa May's head into more palpable goodies under the tree: a laptop computer for husband, Arnold; Nintendo for little Toby; and the cashmere twin set from Talbots she'd long desired for herself.

The Pingrees went to Paris.

The advent of the movie people had occupied center stage throughout December and into February. Aleford dubbed itself L.A. East as it watched the progression of various individuals arrive to scout locations, arrange permits, rent a house for the director, who did not like hotels, and book blocks of rooms for everyone else at a Marriott in nearby Burlington—Aleford itself had but one hostelry, which boasted only three bedrooms. (You did get a mighty delicious breakfast thrown in.) Everything had to be in place well before the March shooting date. But all this, even the helicopter flying low over the conservation land, was firmly relegated to the wings once the news of Walter Wetherell's resignation got out.

While some residents of Aleford had been known to take an interest in national and state politics, particularly during presidential and gubernatorial years, it was local elections that gripped the hearts and minds of the majority. Balloons did not tumble down from the ceiling, nor did smiling, well-groomed red-white-and-blue-clad families grace a podium when candidacies were declared. But this did not mean there wasn't plenty of hoopla. It merely took a different form. Perhaps a small, discreet notice in the town paper, the *Aleford Chronicle,* or, better

9

still, a letter to the editor, which didn't cost anything. Then as things heated up, there would be larger ads listing the names of those who endorsed the candidate. Properly studied—and there were few Alefordians who were not adept at the art—the names revealed more about the candidates than any debate or position paper. Once the ads appeared and everyone had figured out who was representing whom, bolder measures would be taken. The tops of cars sprouted signs precariously anchored by bungee cords and the space between front and storm doors filled up with fliers describing the candidates' records all the way back to things like "Winner of the Fifth Grade All-Aleford Spelling Bee."

Campaign mores were as invariable as the flag raising every morning on the green.

In the late fifties, someone had passed out ballpoints with his name emblazoned in gold ink on each and every one, but the general opinion was that he'd gone a little too far—for which he was resoundingly defeated. In a gesture of defiance, or remorse, he moved closer to Boston, where his flamboyant style presumably found a more congenial home.

The first fireworks in the current election had started in February, before any of the candidates were announced.

"Why in tarnation Walter Wetherell thinks he has to resign just because he's having some sort of pig valve put in his heart is beyond me," police chief Charley MacIsaac told Faith one particularly chilly day. He'd formed the habit of dropping in at the caterers now and then for a cup of coffee, and Faith was glad to have him. She missed their morning colloquies at the Minuteman Café. She'd been afraid she'd get woefully out of touch when she went back to work, until Charley had solved the problem. Not that he was a chatterbox, but she could usually work the conversation around to what she wanted to know. She didn't even have to try this time. Charley was more than ready to spill his guts.

"I didn't know you were such an ardent supporter of Walter's. I thought you two were at odds over widening Battle Road," Faith commented.

"We are, were, whatever. Somebody's going to get killed on that road. It cuts straight through to Route 2A and if he had gone there at rush hour like I asked, he'd have seen what I was talking about. All his talk about preserving the quality of the community—it's really because it so happens his cousin lives over there. More like preserving the quality of Bob Wetherell's front yard," Charley fumed.

"Then I would have thought you'd be happy Walter is resigning. You might get someone who agrees with you."

"And I might get somebody who doesn't. But I will get somebody I don't know, or maybe do know, which could be worse. And what's sure is, whoever it is, it will be someone who'll be asking a million dumb questions—and the meetings are long enough as they are. No, in this case, I say take the devil you've learned to put up with."

"You just don't like change, Charley. Besides, the poor man can't be expected to perform a selectman's duties while he's recuperating from major heart surgery."

"People pamper themselves too much these days. If there's anyone to feel sorry for in all this, it's the poor damned pig."

Chief MacIsaac was echoing the opinion of most of the town, and for a while Winifred Wetherell did her shopping in Waltham at the Star Market instead of the Shop'n Save. And rather than going to the town library, Walter read all the books he had at home that he'd been meaning to read but didn't actually want to.

11

The identity of the first candidate to file remained a secret for only the five minutes it took town clerk Lucy Barnes to lock up the office and walk briskly down the street to the Minuteman Café. It had been a slow week for Faith and she was actually present at the historic event. She was sharing a table with Pix Miller, her close friend and next-door neighbor, and Amy, the latter delightedly finger-painting with corn muffin crumbs and spit while securely strapped into her Sassy seat.

"There I was, not expecting a thing, when I saw a shadow at the door," related Lucy breathlessly.

Faith knew the door well. She'd copied the list painted on its frosted glass and sent it to her sister, Hope, upon arriving in Aleford as a new bride. Under TOWN CLERK'S OFFICE in impressive bold script, it read: DOG LICENSES, MARRIAGE INTENTIONS, BIRTH CERTIFICATES, DEATH CERTIFICATES, VOTER REGISTRATION, ELECTION INFORMATION, ANNUAL CENSUS, BUSINESS CERTIFICATION, RAFFLES, FISH AND GAME LICENSES, MISCELLANEOUS. It was the last item that had caused Faith the most amusement. What could be left? she wondered.

The town clerk had the attention of the entire café.

"Before I had a chance to even think who it might be, the door bangs open and it's . . ." Lucy paused; it was her moment. "Alden Spaulding. 'I'm going to be your new selectman,' he says, bold as brass, as usual. 'Give me the papers.' I hadn't expected a please or thank you, and it's a good thing I didn't. Anyway, what are we going to do?"

It was a call to arms.

Alden Spaulding had few friends but some grudging admirers, whose comments took the form of, "Whatever else you may say about Alden, you have to admit the man knows what he's about"—local parlance for "knows how to make a buck." While in his twenties, forty years before,

12

Alden had taken his inheritance and put it all into what was then the novel idea of a duplicating service. Over the years, he had expanded his offerings and locations, becoming one of the wealthiest men in the area. He was the proverbial bridegroom of his work, remaining unencumbered by a wife and family; swooping in without prior notice at one of his branches to see what the laggards were not doing at any time of day or night.

Politically, he was a rabid conservative, so far right as to be out in left field. This would not have been a problem in other election years, but it posed a major difficulty this time around. Aleford's Board of Selectmen was composed of five citizens. Since anyone could remember, putting said recollection somewhere shortly after the Flood, there had always been two liberals, two moderates, and a conservative on the board. Walter Wetherell had been one of the moderates, the swing votes. With two conservatives, the historic balance of power would be altered and, what was worse, would put all the town's major decisions in the hands of the remaining, tie-breaking moderate, Beatrice Hoffman, who could never quite seem to make up her mind.

Chief MacIsaac groaned audibly. If Spaulding was elected, the new cruiser he hoped to get the town to buy as a replacement for the barely operable 1978 Plymouth Gran Fury currently doing duty would be a 1995 or 1996 by the time Bea made up her mind, because of course the vote would be two to two. He could hear her now: "We mustn't be hasty. This decision is too important to be made in a cavalier fashion." *Cavalier.* Many's the interminable meeting he'd wished someone, dashing or not, would ride in on a big black horse and carry Bea off. That was another thing. They would be meeting continuously, since one session would be ending as the next was called to order. Why the police chief had to be at these things was beyond him, but the forefathers had decided, maybe two hundred years ago, that the law had to be present, and no one was about to change it now.

"Obviously someone has to run against him—and soon. We can't let him remain unopposed." Faith spoke firmly, confident in the knowledge that no one expected *her* to run—not because as a wife, mother, and businesswoman she obviously didn't have a free moment to work the crowds, but because she had not lived in town the requisite thirty or so years and/or was the product of several generations of Alefordians.

Her stirring words, however, did not have a galvanizing effect on the group in the café. Everyone assumed a studied lack of activity and even nonchalance as they looked out the window, toward the ceiling, anywhere save in the direction of Faith's eye.

"Well, perhaps no one here"—the room relaxed and people dared to sip their coffee once more—"but we have to make an effort to find someone. Any ideas?"

Pix would normally have felt compelled to volunteer, except for the fact that her husband, Sam, had declared heatedly that if she took on one more thing, he was going to incorporate himself and the children as a charity and make her head of the board of directors to force her to stay home at least one night during the week. She did have an idea of someone else, though.

"What about Penelope Bartlett? She's never been on the board, and I can't imagine why not."

"Perfect," cried Lucy Barnes in delight. "No one is more dedicated to Aleford than Penny, and she has so much good common sense. I'm sure she'd do a fine job."

Perfect, declared Chief MacIsaac, in what Faith would have sworn was a parody, were he given to such things.

14

"Alden will be running against his half sister, someone who hasn't spoken to him in twenty years or so. Should be fun."

"I didn't know Penny Bartlett was Alden Spaulding's half sister," Faith said to Tom that evening as he got ready to leave the house for a session of Town Meeting. He'd been an elected Town Meeting member since he'd arrived at First Parish. He thought it would be a good way to get to know Aleford and its inhabitants. Besides, Fairchilds always sat at their local Town Meetings, guarding their seats and passing them down as lovingly as they did their season's tickets to Celtics games at Boston Garden.

"You really should ask someone else for the details, but I think Alden's mother died when he was about seven or eight and his father married Penny's mother, who was much younger and a neighbor, in rather indecent haste."

"Probably needed someone to cook and do the wash," Faith said.

"I don't think so. He was comfortable, as we New Englanders like to say, and could have hired any number of housekeepers."

"'Comfortable,' which means something akin to rich as Croesus. No, he wouldn't need to cut costs. Maybe he wanted a mother for little Alden. Then again, given the evidence of their offspring, it's probable that the first Mrs. Spaulding wasn't up for the title of Mrs. Congeniality and he may simply have wanted a pleasant spouse."

"Possibly. Penny's mother, his second wife, died long before I came here, but there are plenty of parishioners who remember her, and I've always heard her mentioned with great affection. No one mentions Alden's mother. Since Alden's father was active in the congregation and Alden, too, in his own inimitable way, I'd imagine she must have attended, although perhaps she was an invalid of some sort."

Faith thought they ought to get off the subject of the Bartletts. Alden's participation in the congregation, along with a decent-sized pledge, took the less welcome form of line-by-line sermon critiques and objections to the amount of money spent on social concerns. He seemed to regard his tithe as an entitlement.

"What's on the agenda tonight?" she asked. Faith had no desire to attend Town Meeting, yet she liked to know what was going on. It made the old Tammany Hall look like a Brownie Scout troop.

"The library budget. I could be late, very late. Our friend Alden, who is maintaining a very high pre-election profile these days, has submitted an alternate resolution calling for drastic cuts in staff and hours. He wants the library closed weekends and Wednesdays. The rationale for this being that people read too much and should be out getting some exercise instead, which costs the town nothing. Oh, and he wants to eliminate the library aides and have patrons reshelve their own books when they return them."

"I know we have to cut, but this is ridiculous. Surely no one will vote with him."

"I wish I could be certain. There's a strong feeling in town that spending is out of control, and a sizable contingent sees Alden first and foremost as a successful business manager. These are the people who will vote with—and for—him. Enough philosophizing. We need someone who knows dollars and cents-type stuff. We *do* have to cut the budget, but not with a machete."

"Have fun. I don't envy you." Faith kissed her husband and sent him off with his shield. She only hoped he would not come home on it.

16

Aleford had resolutely resisted the blandishments of the local cable television franchise. No one could see the point of paying perfectly good money for extra television channels when they already had more than they wanted to watch. Yet when the company offered to broadcast Town Meeting on its local access station, quite a few heads were turned. No more sitting in the hard seats up in the balcony of the Town Hall, straining to hear what the members below were debating. No more listening to embarrassing stomach rumbles, as no food was allowed in the hall. The cable TV proposal had come up at last year's Town Meeting and lost by a whisker. But with the added incentive of the election—the company had promised to film candidate's forums and live ballot counting—it was sure to pass this time, unless Millicent McKinley could rally a few more Town Meeting members to her camp. The cable proposal, she declared, was one more example of the moral turpitude rapidly creeping into all aspects of everyday life. It was positively indecent to think of such a hallowed tradition as Town Meeting being broadcast to people who might be doing Lord knows what as they watched. She had heard of homes where a television was actually in the bedroom! If someone wanted to know what was going on at Town Meeting, he or she could go to Town Hall just like all the elected members. It was a question of simple equilibrium, she stated. Though people weren't too clear what she meant by the phrase, it sounded good and they didn't doubt her sincerity.

Faith had waited up for Tom and he *was* late. She'd been reading M. F. K. Fisher's *The Gastronomical Me* in bed and got up to get him something to eat when she heard the car pull into the driveway. She'd been stunned when she first learned that they had to sit all those hours without any form of nourishment. "An awful lot of people chew gum," Tom had told her. "Sometimes I look around and feel like I've been put out to pasture with a herd of malcontented cows."

"I'm almost, but not or quite , too tired to eat," he said, collapsing at the kitchen table in anticipation.

Faith was mixing beaten eggs, chopped green onion, crisp, smoky bacon, and Parmesan cheese into some spaghetti she'd cooked earlier and set aside. She poured the mixture into a frying pan with some hot olive oil and spread it out to form a large, flat mass. "Did Alden's amendment win?"

"Praise the Lord, no, but he got more votes than I would have expected. I think I'll pay a call on Penelope tomorrow and add my voice to the swelling chorus urging her to run. She looked slightly confused and blushed a couple of times when people passing her to go to the john or whatever leaned down to whisper in her ear. I'd say the campaign to get our Penny to throw her bonnet into the ring is on with a vengeance."

"Nice to know you're not getting too involved in all this, darling." Faith smiled at him as she deftly slid the golden brown frittata onto a plate and flipped it back into the pan to cook on the other side.

Two days later, Penelope Bartlett entered the race, which came as no surprise. The surprise was James Heuneman's appearance at the town clerk's office and his demand for nomination papers the same afternoon.

This time, it was Millicent who carried the news. Faith was beginning to think she should put some tables and chairs in her catering kitchen, since so many people seemed to regard it as an outpost of the Minuteman Café. Millicent was ostensibly there to get Faith to sign up to work on Penny Bartlett's campaign.

18

"A spoiler, plain and simple. James Heuneman knew that Penny intended to run!" Millicent bit down viciously on the large oatmeal raisin cookie Faith had the good manners to offer her with a cup of coffee.

"Won't he take votes away from Alden rather than Penny? He's a businessman of some sort, too, isn't he? I would have thought he represented the same constituency."

"He's a lawyer, not that it matters. What he'll do is take votes away from both of them and in all likelihood win. People who think Alden is a little beyond the pale but has some good ideas regarding fiscal matters will vote for James, and people who think Penny is nice but a bit too liberal—not to mention being a woman—will vote for Heuneman, too. That's why we've got to do everything we can to help her get elected. I'm putting you down for leafleting and telephone calls. I don't expect you to hold up a sign with all the children you have." Millicent made it sound as if Faith was the old woman in the shoe or some other wanton.

"But surely, being a woman—and the sole woman to have won the Bronze Musket Award twice in one lifetime should help her in this day and age." The Bronze Musket Award was given annually to an Aleford citizen who had contributed above and beyond the call of mere duty to the well-being of the town. Recipients were held in special regard, and any citizen given the choice between the tasteful embossed Bronze Musket plaques and the shiny Oscars of the impending Hollywood invasion would not hesitate for a moment to snatch the former.

"This day and age is not so different from that day and age as you may think, Faith. Remember, nobody knows what you're marking on your ballot in the voting booth, and you can say anything you want afterward. It's my

19

opinion the vast majority of the electorate, even in Aleford, still isn't sure about women in office."

Millicent was a constant source of amazement. Faith had never suspected this feminist streak, but upon reflection, it made sense. No one believed more ardently in the power of women, especially as personified by Millicent McKinley, than the lady herself.

"What about Bea Hoffman?" Faith asked. "She got elected."

"She ran unopposed, remember? And the men in town probably figured one female on the board wouldn't make much difference—but two! Why now we're getting dangerously close to a majority!"

"Do you think that's why James is running?"

"Absolutely not. That's about the one thing I am sure about in this election. His wife is an active member of NOW and the Heunemans are the ones who got the recreation department to start the girls' soccer program. James is one of the coaches. No, I can't figure out why he wants to run. It's a complete mystery. He's such a Milquetoast—which could be another reason some people would vote for him. He won't open his mouth, just vote with Bea and keep the board balanced."

Faith had a sudden irrational image of the board as a giant seesaw with slight James Heuneman, pale-faced, his dun-colored hair receding ever backward from his often-furrowed brow, high in the air on one end and Beatrice Hoffman, large, pigeon-breasted, and given to brightly colored poplin shirtwaists, stuck on the ground at the other.

"Well," Faith told her visitor as she fetched the dough that had been rising, gave it a firm punch, and started to knead it—hoping her actions might suggest work to do and a "mustn't keep you" exit line from Millicent—"Tom and I are happy to do whatever we can to help Penny get elected. She has done so much for the town, particularly the children. I still find it hard to believe there would be anyone who wouldn't vote for her."

"Fortunately, she lives in North Aleford, too," Millicent remarked, taking another cookie and, as Faith told her husband later, showing absolutely no inclination to get on her broomstick.

"Why is that fortunate?" Faith gave the dough a resounding smack.

"You know what they're like up there. Then again, how could you? Not being from here, I mean. I don't like to sound catty, especially about my neighbors."

The "especially about my neighbors" part was right, anyway, Faith thought.

"But there is a tendency for the residents of North Aleford to feel they're a teensy bit better than the rest of the town. It's one of the oldest sections—not as old as mine, of course, but old—and the houses are impressive, covering the hill the way they do. Then, of course, they have their own residents' association, which we *have* to make sure endorses Penny. Remind them how she got them their playground on Whipple Road. Alden lives up there, too—in his father's house. When Penny got married, she moved several streets away and has stayed in that house, even after her husband died. To be sure, no one thought for a moment she'd move back in with Alden. Poor Penny. She has been widowed for a long time. It was a real love match. She's always said she could never find anyone like Francis."

Faith had been to Penny Bartlett's house on several occasions. It was a large Victorian that contradicted Faith's prior association of Victorian houses with crowded, dark rooms, memories of antimacassars and aspidistras still

21

haunting the corners. Penny's house was filled with light. There was stained glass, plenty of odd-shaped windows, and gingerbread trim, but the Bartletts had cleared away the huge trees and monstrous shrubs shadowing the house and let in the sun. The house was painted a warm buttercup yellow, with deep green, almost black, shutters and white trim.

She wanted to ask Millicent why it was a foregone conclusion that Penny wouldn't move back in with her brother. It obviously had something to do with why they didn't speak to each other. Millicent rarely responded to questions, though, preferring to be the recipient of information and choosing what she would share. But the woman had wolfed down two of Faith's cookies and a large mug of coffee. It was worth a try.

"Did Penny and Alden have some sort of quarrel? I've heard they don't speak to one another."

"Yes, I believe I have heard something like that. To be more precise, Faith dear—and it is so important to be precise, don't you agree?—Penny doesn't speak to Alden. He's constantly making outrageous remarks in her presence. Howsomever, these things are all ancient history, and we must concentrate on our present goal."

Effectively shut out, as well as reprimanded, Faith could only think to comment, "It's a shame Penny never had any children. She's so wonderful with them."

Millicent looked down at the counter. "Francis Bartlett had some sort of plumbing problem," she said vaguely. Doling out this information as a sop for witholding the rest?

Now how on earth did she find that out? Faith almost found herself asking Miss McKinley, maidenly reticence not withstanding, but to her relief, Millicent stood up abruptly, brushed the crumbs off her plaid Pendleton suit,

22

put on her gloves, and said, "I can't sit here all day chitchatting, my dear." And she left with one last parting glance of annoyance in Faith's direction for having wasted her time, diverting her from her mission.

Faith put the loaves she'd formed to rise again. All in a row, the rounded mounds looked like a series of low foothills. That reminded her of North Aleford. She was well acquainted with the way certain residents of this area of town regarded themselves. Maybe it was living on a hill, like Beacon Hill. Did people who looked down on the rest of the town eventually come to look down on them in other ways? Something about being top dog, top of the heap, king of the hill?

She thought wearily of working on Penny's campaign with Millicent, apparently the self-anointed campaign manager. The election was to be held March 26. If, as she hoped, she got the contract to cater the movie shoot, she'd be in the midst of the job and Tom would have to bear the brunt of the campaign responsibilities. She felt more cheerful. It was true that politics made strange bedfellows, but seldom ones who kicked half the night and hogged the blankets as much as Millicent did.

Faith had catered for shoots in New York, and she was quick to get her name in to Alan Morris. He arranged to come by the kitchens for a tasting later that week on one of his flying visits through town. Faith was ready for him.

"Great," he said, referring perhaps both to the attractive lady in front of him and the mouthful of warm pizzette with pears, brie, and caramelized onions (see recipe on page 310) he'd just swallowed. Faith had let her shining blond hair grow longer over the winter and now it grazed her chin in a simple blunt cut. She'd diligently lost the weight she'd put on in pregnancy, and at thirty-two, she

23

caused as many heads to turn as she had at twenty-two, a fact that, while diminishing somewhat in importance over the years, still didn't bother her in the slightest. After the initial shock of that milestone birthday, her thirtieth, she was enjoying being thirtysomething and firmly believed the best ten years of a woman's life were between thirty-nine and forty, which gave her something to anticipate.

Alan was now speedily devouring a plateful of spinach lasagna with a three-cheese béchamel sauce, while keeping a close eye on the medley of Have Faith desserts beckoning from the counter next to him: flourless chocolate cake with raspberry coulis, a steaming fruit gratiné, and crisp dark molasses spice cookies (see recipe on page 312). He smiled. "Max is really going to be happy." From the relief in his voice, it was no secret that keeping Max happy was Alan Morris's most important job.

Max was Maxwell Reed, the director of the film. At fifty-two, he was both a legend and an enigma in Tinseltown. Known as the "New Jersey Fellini," owing to his origins as the son of a wealthy shoe manufacturer from Montclair, Reed made obscure but critically acclaimed films, often in black and white. While he was the subject of a shelfful of biographies and critical studies in Europe, he'd received little recognition in his native land. He took great pains to make it clear this bothered him not at all, but the word on the street was that he needed a big commercial success to keep attracting backers. And the movie about to be shot in Aleford had to be it. No matter how much Vincent Canby and *The New York Times* loved it, if it didn't do at least $9 million in wide release the first weekend, Reed would be yesterday's news for the foreseeable future and could watch his films move from "New and Recommended" to

"Cult" in the video stores.

Mercurial, with mood swings so rapid that a sentence could start on an up note and plunge two words later to despair, Max Reed had attracted a group of actors, actresses, and crew who slavishly followed him from film to film, deeming it an honor to work with the master. He rewarded their loyalty with his, making film after film with the same individuals, often playing roles himself, yet never duplicating an effect. His most famous film, *Maggot Morning,* cast his constant companion, the beautiful Evelyn O'Clair, as an elderly homeless woman. She won an Academy Award for best actress and went on to other roles, keeping herself available, however, for Max's films. Speculation was that fresh from her sizzling triumph for another director in *Body Parts,* Max wouldn't be hiding Evelyn's attributes under any bushel baskets or behind shopping bags the way he had quite literally in *Maggot,* as it was called in the trades.

Maxwell Reed was also known for his obsession with security on the set. Often the actors themselves didn't know the name or plot of the movie they were shooting until it was released. He'd broken with custom this time and let it be known he was making a modern reinterpretation of Nathaniel Hawthorne's *Scarlet Letter.* The name of the picture was *A.* He'd also hired two actors who'd never appeared in any of his films previously but who were box-office magic. Over Ty Nants and Evians at the Polo Lounge, heads were nodding just perceptibly— Max was desperate indeed. If he pulled it off, the same nods could later be translated as "I told you so."

The first ringer was Caleb "Cappy" Camson, star of the phenomenally successful TV series "1-800-555-1212" when he was a teenager, later making a graceful transition to films. His tanned, well-developed physique, thick, dark,

25

always slightly touseled curls, and deep brown eyes with the requisite gold flecks guaranteed any movie in which he was cast at least initially large audiences. Cappy had been in the business long enough to know his limitations and ventured from romantic comedy only for a comic romance. But nobody turned down the chance to work with Max Reed—not even Cappy. He'd modified the curls and agreed to less flattering makeup in order to play the role of the tormented young minister, Arthur Dimmesdale.

Max's other orthodox move was to cast Caresse Carroll as Pearl, Hester Prynne's daughter. Eight-year-old Caresse would be playing a major role; it could be a stretch, but Caresse was a pro down to her toenails. At age four, she'd nagged her mother, Jacqueline, into auditioning her for commercials. "I can do that," she'd said, and hadn't looked back. She was the child of choice for a whole string of space alien and horror movies. "It may not be art, but I'm working," she told her mother at six. Currently, the trades labeled her "America's Sweetheart for the Nineties" after her gutsy portrayal of a little girl who saves the family split-level after her parents lose their auto-plant jobs by forming a recycling company that ends up employing most of the town. Caresse didn't have Shirley Temple's dimples or curly hair. In fact, her features were a bit odd—straight, silken white-blond hair and large aquamarine eyes that Caresse was able to fill with tears, flash with fear, or twinkle with delight depending on the script. But it was her smile that was instantly recognizable to millions of Americans. Warm, engaging, it was the kind of smile that, well, gosh darn it, made you just have to smile right back. An eminently bankable smile.

Casting her as Pearl months before, Max planned to use Caresse's pale luminescence to personify the name. The child was a metaphor, he told Caresse and her mother, for the essential innocence of Hester Prynne's act, a jewel beyond price to be worn proudly at her mother's breast, next to the scarlet letter of her supposed shame. Hester herself was Everywoman and Pearl, Everychild. Jacqueline and Caresse nodded solemnly when he'd related this to them in his office early in the fall. Neither had the faintest idea what he was talking about, yet, whatever it was, they both had no doubt Caresse could do it.

Max knew Caresse was older than Hawthorne's Pearl, but audiences might find it hard to believe a three-year-old could discourse as eloquently as he'd planned on the meaning of life and existence of God. The director had told his assistant, Alan, that Hawthorne's book was a canvas—a masterpiece—to which they would essentially be adding brushstrokes, such as increasing Pearl's age.

Sitting silently in a chair next to Max since the Carrolls' arrival was Evelyn O'Clair, who would, of course, play the role of Hester Prynne. Max had cast himself as Chillingworth, the older husband who returns after a long absence to find his wife the outcast of the community for the adulterous conception of a child. The director had felt a little awkward explaining all this to Caresse. He wasn't used to children, although he would have to be, since Evelyn was about to give birth, fortunately well before the picture started.

Caresse was getting bored with the meeting. It was a pretty cheesy office, no bar or any evidence of snacks—not even an entertainment system. Just a big desk, a couple of chairs, a couch, and walls that must have been newly painted, since the smell of the stark white paint filled the air. The only thing hanging on them so far was a large calendar. He had a window, though, and a

27

basket of fruit.

Her mother had been the one who was hot to do the movie and was being totally spastic about how lucky Caresse was to work with Maxwell Reed. Caresse herself wasn't so sure about the project. To begin with, the script sucked, a real downer. She'd even tried reading the book but couldn't get past the first page. Her taste in literature ran more to *Sweet Valley High,* but she knew it wouldn't make a major motion picture. She tried to quell the feeling that accepting this role might not have been the best career move by concentrating on the fact that she would be acting with big names for a big name. Caresse looked over at her mother, who was gazing at the director with open adoration. Caresse felt sorry for her. She needed a man. Caresse wouldn't be surprised if the last time Jacqueline had had sex was when she'd conceived her daughter—with whom, Caresse didn't know. It was the one thing Mom would never discuss.

But definitely Jacqueline wasn't getting any. Not that Caresse was anxious for some old fart to enter their lives and start telling her what to do. She'd trained her mother to know her place, and truthfully, Mom didn't really understand the Business.

Enough was enough. Caresse Carroll turned on her famous smile, tossed her shining hair away from her face, and interrupted Max's convoluted explanation. "Don't worry, Mr. Reed, I know all this stuff. See you in March."

"Call me Max," he replied, and the meeting came to an end.

Evelyn had not said a word—not even *good-bye.*

CHAPTER 2

Crime is for the iron-nerved . . .

UNTIL THE CALL WENT OUT FOR EXTRAS, ALEFORD wasn't sure what it thought about having all these movie people around. There was some surprise at finding neighbors who had affected an attitude of only mild interest now camped out so as to be first in line. But this place had been resolutely claimed by one of the most uninterested of all, Millicent Revere McKinley.

"Maybe she needs the money. The pay is astonishing," related Pix, who had rushed to Have Faith's kitchens to report the news.

"Sure, like Imelda needed shoes," Faith retorted. "She just wants to be where the action is, like most of the rest of Aleford, and the greater Boston area, from what I hear."

"Well, how often does a movie get made in our own backyards? I'd try out myself, except I get stage fright painting scenery."

"Why don't you reconsider my offer? Then you'd be on the set every day behind the scenes."

"But, Faith, how could I possibly work for *you?* You know what I'm like in the kitchen."

Pix's family was used to having emergency microwaved frozen dinners whenever something inexplicable happened to the tuna-noodle or hamburger casseroles that composed the normal Miller bill of fare.

"I keep telling you. You wouldn't have to do any cooking. In fact, I wouldn't let you do any cooking. I have other people to help me, most especially Niki." She waved toward her assistant, who was covering a stack of paper-thin sheets of phyllo dough with a damp towel to keep them from drying out while she spread melted butter lavishly over the one in front of her. "What I need you for is that steel-trap mind of yours—bookkeeping, ordering, counting forks and napkins."

Pix's face was contorted by a mixture of emotions: Could she? Should she? Would she? She fidgeted about on her long, shapely legs. Pix was an attractive woman with short brown hair, but she tended to downplay her natural gifts with drooping skirts and ancient pullovers.

"I'll think about it," she promised.

"No," Faith said with surprising firmness, "You've been saying this to me for months. You've talked to Sam, talked to the kids, probably even talked to the dogs." Besides Mark, a college freshman, Samantha, a junior in high school, and sixth-grader Danny, the Miller household included a large number of golden retrievers. "I'll give you until tomorrow morning, and if I don't have an answer, I'll have to start advertising the position. We start the movie job in less than two weeks."

"Okay," Pix agreed.

"Okay what? Okay you'll give me an answer or okay you'll do it?"

"Okay I'll do it," Pix mumbled bravely.

After Pix left, Niki asked Faith, "What do you think made her agree? I've been pretty sure she wouldn't after going back and forth all this time. Do you think it's the chance to be on the set?"

"Maybe, but I should have been tougher weeks ago. She's wanted to do it all along. I think she's been afraid of

30

messing up—and when you work for a friend, that's a pretty scary thought. Anyway, she'll be fine, and deep down—I hope—knows it."

Niki put a generous spoonful of the walnut pesto and ricotta filling she'd made at the top of a strip of the dough before deftly folding it like a flag. They were restocking the freezer with several varieties of phyllo triangles for hors d'oeuvres.

"I'm glad Pix is going to be here. She reminds me of the room mother I had in third grade."

"She probably *was* the room mother," Faith said. "I don't think there's a town in this area code and beyond that doesn't know to call Pix Miller when they need a volunteer. She's still running the preschool PTA, and her youngest will be shaving soon. Much as I admire what she does, and thank God she'll keep on doing it, I'm going to like handing her a paycheck."

"Mrs. MacDonald!"

"Mrs. MacDonald what?"

"That was the name of my room mother. I used to elbow other kids out of the way so I could hold her hand on field trips, and I would put myself to sleep at night dreaming about being one of her freckle-faced kids. She used to make great devil's food cakes." Niki's normally sharply contoured face softened as a wistful smile crossed her lips.

What was it about Massachusetts, Faith wondered, that caused its adult population to wax nostalgic about their childhoods at the drop of a beanie? She'd never noticed this tendency in New York—except maybe in someone who'd grown up in the Bronx.

"I'm not saying she might not have been swayed by the movie job. We're talking about Pix now, Niki, not your sainted Mrs. MacDonald."

"Who wouldn't? I'm pretty excited myself. Cappy Camson. Close your eyes and think of him in those Calvin Klein ads." Niki's sharp edge returned.

"I can do it with my eyes wide open," Faith laughed.

"He wouldn't have been my choice to play the minister, especially a Puritan. I don't remember the book much except for Hester and her red letter, but wasn't Dimmesdale sort of a nerd?"

"That's how I'd recalled him, too, but I reread the book when I heard about the movie, and it's not a bad role for Camson. Maybe he's a little too healthy-looking, but he should be able to portray a man torn between passion and conscience. And Dimmesdale was described as handsome even the same color hair and eyes as Camson has. I wonder how Reed's going to interpret the character. He has to create something different to keep people from expecting Cappy to get the girl."

"Chillingworth was the villain, right? Wasn't he a minister, too? Maybe I have him confused with Dimmesdale."

"You do. He was a doctor, well versed also in the ancient arts of alchemy." Faith rubbed her hands together, leaned over the simmering stockpot on the stove, and looked wicked in what she judged to be a fair approximation of the doctor at his cauldron of henbane and the like. "He arrives in Boston on the same day the Puritans have put Hester and her baby on the scaffold for show-and-tell, only she won't reveal the name of the father. Chillingworth joins the crowd and indicates that she shouldn't recognize him, which she already had instantly because of his ugly face and the fact he had one shoulder higher than the other. He was much older than she was, and she had married him back in England after her parents died because she had no one else to turn to and he had some sort of mesmerizing effect on her. Except she did tell him she didn't love him. After that, he decided they would emigrate, and he sent her on ahead. But then he was shipwrecked, captured by Indians, and whatever else could delay someone in those days before car phones, leaving her on her own for two years. She and Arthur Dimmesdale fell in love. The rest you know."

Faith took a tray covered with the phyllo triangles and put it in the freezer. When she returned, Niki picked up where they had left off.

"It's coming back to me. Roger Chillingworth moves in with the Reverend, right? And sucks his blood or something—and in the end, Dimmesdale is so eaten up with guilt, he tells all."

"Sort of. Roger Chillingworth moves in with the minister to try to cure the illness we all know is not the common cold, but remorse and shame. The doctor's convinced the young man is hiding something, which he is. Meanwhile, Roger also haunts Hester, who makes a fair living doing exquisite needlework, and tells her his mission in life is to discover the man who has cuckolded him. If she warns her lover, Chillingworth will kill him or worse when he does find out. Hester ends up keeping more secrets than the chemists at Coca-Cola, since she, of course, still loves Arthur. But she is not at all ashamed of what they've done. It was a pure act before God, and her fellow townspeople are the ones with the problem. Maxwell Reed may very well be onto something. It really is a very modern story. Hester manages to convince Dimmesdale she's right, or maybe his flesh is weak, and they decide to run away together, except Chillingworth discovers what ship they're sailing on, and the minister realizes he has to confess to everyone. He literally bares his bosom, revealing, some of the crowd swears, the letter *A*

33

branded in his flesh, and thus escapes his tormentor, Chillingworth. He dies in Hester's arms."

"I can't wait to see the movie. If it's anywhere near as good as your synopsis, it's Oscar time."

Still in the mood, Faith mused, "It does offer a director like Maxwell Reed a lot. Hester is a great character. Hawthorne suggests that as an outcast, Hester derives from the scarlet letter some strange power to see what people are truly like, as opposed to how they present themselves. But it's also a curse—she sees evil everywhere, like the husband in Hawthorne's short story 'Young Goodman Brown.' " Faith was having fun. American Literature 101 was coming back in full force. "Then there's Pearl, trading insults at the age of three with the goody two-shoes village children and exploring theological issues with her mom. And the governor's sister. I forget her name, but she's later executed as a witch, Hawthorne tells us. She keeps asking Hester and Dimmesdale to go dance in the forest with her. Marta Haree is playing the role and she should be terrific."

"I read in *Parade* magazine that she's into fortune-telling and tarot cards. Maybe that's why Max picked her."

"She's been in almost all his movies, but this casting does seem particularly apt. Caresse Carroll is a little old for Pearl and she doesn't look anything like the description in the book—the scarlet letter come to life—but Reed must have his reasons," Faith mused.

"I'll have to read the book this time, not just the Cliffs Notes. Sorry," Niki said, correctly interpreting Faith's expression of disapproval, "we weren't all English majors in the making, and as I remember, it was assigned just when we were busiest at the bakery—the week before Greek Easter."

34

"It's not as though it was a long book, Niki, like *Love Story* or one of your other favorites."

"Can it, boss."

Niki liked working for Faith.

Two weeks later, the staff of Have Faith climbed into the canteen truck Faith had rented for the duration of the shoot. The movie crew took a break in the middle of the morning, and the truck was filled with a variety of hot and cold drinks, several kinds of muffins, fresh fruit, and bagels with various spreads. Later, lunch would be served, also on location, but inside a heated tent. The crew would return to the Marriott for dinner, where Alan Morris had arranged for Max to watch the dailies. Faith would provide dinner only if they were doing a night shoot.

In addition, the caterers were responsible for the craft services table, which would be kept stocked round the clock with essential snacks such as pretzels, M & M's, fruit, granola bars, Twinkies, soft drinks, and oceans of coffee. This would be set up permanently in the barn in case of inclement weather. Pix had agreed that keeping it supplied would be something she could handle. "I just have to think what I put in the kids' lunch boxes—the days I'm a good mother and thinking nutritionally and the days when the bad mother throws in a Ring-Ding because the bus is at the door."

As Faith ran over all the plans the night before, she told Tom it was a job that posed a unique challenge, even though it was a relatively small shoot.

"How so?"

"Well, most of the crew is pure California by way of Manhattan, so this means they know what pastrami is supposed to taste like, but they're still going to want their sprouts—plus, there will be macrobiotic types who want only sprouts. Then the people they've hired locally aren't going to want either. They think 'low-fat' is some sort of Madison Avenue gimmick to sell things that don't taste very good."

"Which is partly true," Tom interrupted. "The cheese spread we had last week at the Millers' that Pix was so excited about, because it was so good for us, tasted like wallpaper paste—not that I've sampled that delicacy myself. Although there was a boy in my first-grade class who ate paste. You know that thick, gloppy white kind. The teacher had a big jar of it. I wonder what happened to him. Probably won a Nobel Prize."

"More likely owns a chain of stationery stores," Faith said. Native nostalgia again. At the moment, she was not in the mood for reminiscences of Tom's beloved Norwell school days. If he was to be believed, his childhood in this hamlet on the South Shore, about forty miles south of Boston, was a cross between Christopher Robin's Hundred Acre Wood and Tom Sawyer's Hannibal, Missouri. Normally, her husband's stories fascinated her. Growing up at the same time in the same country, they might as well have been living on different planets, for all the similarities in upbringings. But tonight, her mind was on the present, not the past.

"I'm not worried about the logistics or that everyone won't find something they want to eat. I'll have a good hearty soup each day for the New Englanders and plenty of fresh veggies for the rest. It's going to be interesting to see how the whole thing plays out."

"A play within a play? And if you add what they're going to do to poor Nathaniel's masterpiece, yet another play within that."

"I thought you liked Reed's movies."

36

"I do, but I also like *The Scarlet Letter*—and for starters, Hester Prynne was a brunette."

"Typical," Faith countered. "If he wasn't filming a New England classic, you wouldn't feel so protective. And in any case, you can't fool me, Thomas Fairchild. I know how star-struck you are. Play your cards right and I'll let you come and stuff some pita bread someday."

It was true Tom was a movie buff, but his torches were lighted by Garbo, Dietrich, Colbert, and the like. Still, Faith was sure he wouldn't mind getting a closer look at Evelyn O'Clair, blond tresses or not.

"I would like to see how they film a movie, and I'm not planning to be in the crowd scene with the rest of Aleford. Even if I wanted to, it wouldn't be worth the flak. Half the town would applaud my participation in a community event, half would have me abandoning my congregation for the siren call of the silver screen, and half would say I was stuck on myself."

"We'd better get some sleep, darling. Your halves don't add up. Anyway, tomorrow's going to be a long day for me and I don't know what's on your ecclesiastical plate. Besides, as soon as we close our eyes, our little bundle of joy will be calling for her morning snack."

"Think we could train Ben to feed her, now that she's taking a bottle? You know, give the lad a sense of responsibility."

"He would be responsible all right—responsible for restoring the natural order of things to a house with only one child."

Faith honked the canteen truck's raucous horn at what had to be an out-of-state driver, despite the Massachusetts plates. A native would have known that a posted twenty-five mph zone meant the local police chief had some extra signs lying around going to waste and the posted speed was in no way meant to be taken seriously. Making a sharp left onto River Road, toward the shoot, she smiled as she remembered the conversation the night before. It wasn't that Ben was a little monster. He might not even be terribly jealous; he had been known to let Amy grab his finger in her mighty clutch. Ben had just liked things the way they were and saw no need to change. There was some logic to his thinking. Why rock the boat?

The truck was what was rocking now as they reached the Pingrees' long, rutted driveway. By the time they finished filming, the combination of heavy usage and possible heavy March downpours would require all-terrain vehicles. Maybe Alan Morris would have it paved before then. He seemed to pave the way for most things.

Faith had come out several days earlier to talk about where to set up and had supervised the erection of the tent the previous afternoon, so she knew what the place looked like. She was not prepared, however, for the army of trucks, trailers, people, wires, and equipment that filled the New England landscape. She pulled up to the barn, which was a good distance from the house, and stopped. Alan had told her they would be shooting interior shots to begin with and that the noise of her arrival wouldn't disturb them. A short time later, the crew took its break. For the next forty minutes, the staff of Have Faith was frantically filling orders.

"A large tea, no sugar, and cream, not milk," demanded a voice accustomed to being obeyed. "And one of those muffins—warm, but not hot."

"Corny!" cried Faith in sudden recognition.

"Cornelia," the voice replied automatically, and its owner pushed aside several underlings to get a better view of the individual using the much-loathed moniker of her

38

adolescence.

"It's Faith. Faith Sibley, only I'm Fairchild now. Your old Dalton friend. My company is catering the shoot."

"Faith! Of course, how delightful to see you. So you decided to be a cook." Having pushed Faith firmly "downstairs," Cornelia added a hasty, "So much catching up to do. Perhaps a word tomorrow? Today is just too-too." Her eyes conveyed the enormity of her responsibilities—responsibilities that words could not begin to describe.

"What is your job on the film?" Faith asked. She wasn't going to let Corny get away without learning this vital piece of information.

"Max's production assistant," responded her old schoolmate in a tone of voice, similar, Faith later told her sister, Hope, to the one an apostle might have used to describe washing Christ's feet or passing Him the matzos at the Last Supper.

Faith was tempted to reply, "Oh, a gofer?" after the "cook" business, but they were grown-ups now, so she had to be satisfied with saying, "That's terrific, Corny—oops . . . Cornelia. See you tomorrow, then."

And with that, Cornelia took her statuesque self away to minister to her master's needs.

Cornelia Stuyvesant had been in school with Faith since kindergarten and came from an old-money New York family, as her name implied—or rather, declared. She had always been an athletic girl and played a fierce game of tennis—also a fierce game of lacrosse, a fierce game of field hockey, and so on. She moved beautifully, with the confidence good health and a healthy portfolio supply. She had never bothered much with her appearance, still sporting, Faith noticed, the same shoulder-length brown hair cum headband of yore. Yet the tortoiseshell glasses—

in the past, usually held together with a paper clip at the side—had been replaced somewhere along the line with contacts. Slim-hipped, flat-chested, tall, Cornelia was made for Armani, but she stuck resolutely to Brooks, with an occasional wild fling at Lauren.

Of course the first thing Faith wanted to do when she got home later that afternoon was call Hope, one class behind them in school and possessing a seemingly inexhaustive memory for detail. But what with baths, supper, quality time for Amy, Ben, and Tom, it was nine o'clock before she was able to pick up the phone to call her sister.

Hope came through with flying colors. Faith wouldn't have been surprised to discover her sister had a right frontal Rolodex implanted in her brain. In this instance, however, Hope's recollections went beyond where Corny lived, family income, phone number, and what she had worn to the 1974 Winter Cotillion.

"She hated you, Faith. How could you forget that?"

"Don't you think *hate* is a little strong? I do remember some friendly rivalry, but hate?"

"Come on! She started the Faith Sibley Hate Club in second grade and even made up membership cards, but she could only get poor, sad Susan Harvey to join—you know, 'I'll buy you an ice cream if you'll be my friend' Harvey—and when everybody sided with you, it simply made Corny madder. Then the teacher heard about it and made her apologize in front of the whole class. I don't know how you lived to reach adulthood."

"I do remember that! Maybe I've just wanted to forget it all these years. But Corny seems to be in a good place now and I'm sure that's all in the dim, dim past."

"What's dim is you, sis. Corny was always the green-eyed monster personified. What about the time in ninth

40

grade when you took her boyfriend away and she set off a stink bomb in the bathroom and told the headmaster she saw you do it."

"She really wasn't cut out for that type of thing—too transparent. You could always tell when she was lying. Her face would get all red."

The scene in the headmaster's office flashed on a screen in front of Faith's eyes and she blinked, protesting to Hope, "Besides, she had no reason to be jealous. I didn't take her boyfriend away. Bobby Conklin never even looked at her. She just told everybody they were an item."

"Anyway, be careful, Faith. Think of Corny's famous temper as one of those inactive volcanos that suddenly erupts and wipes out a village or two with no warning. On the surface, she may look like a reasonable adult—and sure, she has a good job. Being a production assistant on one of Reed's movies is something people would kill for. Still, I'm sure you were the last school chum she wanted to run into—during this lifetime, for a start—and puffs of telltale steam may start to escape."

"You're waxing very metaphorical for a business major. And I think you're exaggerating more than a tad. It was all years ago. She was quite cordial, and we're going to get together tomorrow. It will be fun to find out all about everybody in the movie. And I'm going to make a conscious effort to avoid calling her Corny, which was not the greatest nickname. Parents should think of these things."

"Speaking of parents, her mother hated you, too. How could you forget Corny's birthday party when Mrs. Stuyvesant—"

"Enough!" Faith shrieked in protest. Sometimes Hope's memory was a little too good.

As she hung up the phone, Tom mumbled, "Who or

41

what is Corny?" from his side of the bed, where he'd been drowsily reading Paul Tillich.

"An old school friend who's working on the movie. Her real name is Cornelia."

"Were you and Hope the only ones at that school to have normal names? What was with those people—Buffy, Kiki, Dede, Muffin?"

"Well, dear, they'd already used up the good names for the dogs," Faith countered archly, and turned off the light.

It wasn't until the following week that Cornelia and Faith were able to get together. Faith had reluctantly risen a little earlier to give herself some leeway to change her mind a few times about what to wear for the reunion. Sure, she'd told Hope bygones were bygones, but that didn't mean she wanted to be caught in last year's hemlines, no matter what Anna Wintour said about anything goes.

She settled on a charcoal Anne Klein knit turtleneck, an oversized matching cable-knit cardigan, and black wool crepe pants. Serviceable *and* chic. She was going to be working and so it wouldn't do to show up in silk. Over this, she'd wear her gray-and-white large-checked blanket coat today, instead of the Eddie Bauer down parka she'd reluctantly adopted as the indispensable, albeit ungainly, mainstay of her Aleford winter wardrobe. And she was still usually cold. Corny looked her best in jodhpurs and the like, Faith remembered, and had worn something similar the other day. Faith already had a million questions for her, starting with what Maxwell Reed was really like. But she'd phrase it in such a subtle way that Cornelia wouldn't realize it was a question she'd been asked hundreds of times before.

Alan Morris had introduced Faith to the director the

first day, and Reed had come into the tent for lunch once; other times, he ate from trays reverently fetched by one of the PAs. The day he ate with the crew, faithful Cornelia at his side, he'd complimented Faith extravagantly on the meal, adding that if he wasn't careful, he'd gain a lot of weight in the next few weeks. "But of course I won't be," he'd said in chagrin, then turned away with sudden intensity—as if he'd finally realized how he wanted to end the film and had to write it down before he forgot.

During the shoot, Amy was spending mornings with Arlene Maclean, where Faith picked her up after lunch, taking her back to work for the afternoon. She didn't want to bring the baby in the canteen truck, and what if she suddenly started screaming during a scene? Not that Amy was much of a screamer, more of a mewer, but motherhood had taught Faith one or two things, the most important of which being that all children are innately unpredictable. It wasn't anything to do with nature versus nurture. It was fact.

There was a baby on the set—or rather, two. Pearl as an infant was being played by twins from Natick, pretty pink-and-white babies who were even more docile than Amy. "The mother must sedate them," Faith told Niki, "the old 'gin in the milk' trick." Whatever the cause, little Hillary and Valerie Phillips—" 'Hill' and 'Valley' we call them," Mrs. Phillips, warming up a bottle between takes, confided to Faith—were perfect.

Evelyn and Max's baby was, by coincidence, exactly the same age as Hawthorne's Pearl at the start of *The Scarlet Letter*—three months. But little Cordelia was installed in a lavish nursery with her own nanny at the house Max had rented for them in North Aleford. Faith wondered who had picked the baby's name: Cordelia, King Lear's good daughter. It would be interesting if it had been Max's

43

choice. Another thing to ask Corny.

"You look awfully natty for ladling out soup, sweetheart," Tom noted as he helped Faith bundle the two kids into what seemed like thirty or forty pounds of outerwear. "Trying to land a part in the film?"

"I arranged to meet Cornelia for coffee after the break. She has some free time this morning at last, though she'll probably cancel again to impress me with how indispensable she is. It's what I suspect she was doing last week."

It had not escaped Faith's notice that what Cornelia mostly seemed to do was run around getting things for Maxwell Reed, like endless bottles of his favorite Calistoga water, cold but not chilled, and boxes of imported glacéed fruits to nibble. The other production assistant working directly for Max, Sandra Wilson, was vying with Cornelia for the title of head handmaiden, and seemed to have the edge, since she was also Evelyn O'Clair's stand-in. There was no way Cornelia qualified for that. Sandra was eerily like Evelyn, although the poor man's version-no makeup; dressed in old jeans and T-shirts, except when they were checking the lighting. Then she emerged from the chrysalis costumed and cosmeticized, but still no O'Clair.

"Oh yes, your old school friend. I can see the two of you getting all misty over those happy golden years," Tom said mockingly. He knew very well how eager Faith had been for those golden years to pass as she sat and gazed out the windows of her Dalton classrooms at the teeming sidewalks below, infinitely more exciting than the Missouri Compromise. *Arma, virumque, cano,* or whatever else was being imparted within the walls. Cornelia had chafed at the bit, too, but mostly for the day to end so she could ride one of her beloved horses in Central Park.

A few hours later, Faith and Cornelia, gingerly holding

44

hot cups of strong black coffee, were walking slowly across the large field in front of the Pingree house, toward the woods. Cornelia hadn't canceled; however, she had informed Faith sternly it would have to be a "working coffee." She was rechecking locations for the scene where Hester waits for Dimmesdale in the woods and they decide to run off together.

"He's a genius, pure and simple."

It was immediately clear that the challenge for Faith was not going to be getting Cornelia to talk about Maxwell Reed but getting her to talk about anything else.

"I've always admired his films, yet—" Faith wasn't allowed to finish her sentence. It could even be difficult to say anything at all, an unusual situation for Mrs. Fairchild.

"This is the third film I've been fortunate enough to work on, and I wouldn't dream of doing anything else. You must try to imagine, Faith dear, what it's like to sit and listen to him discuss his work." Corny's tone clearly implied that imagining would be all Faith would be doing.

Faith resolutely finished her earlier thought.

"This film seems a little different from the others—casting Cappy and Caresse. How do you think having such big names is going to affect the film? His other pictures have always been, well, a little like watching extremely good home movies shot by someone you know slightly.

Faith realized her choice of words—*home movies*—had not been the best, but oddly enough, Cornelia's face glowed with pleasure.

"That's what Max says! He would be happiest just walking the streets with a small video camera and capturing those moments no one else notices. Of course the public would never understand. But I don't think *A* will be any different from the others because of the

45

casting. It's not an Evelyn O'Clair, Cappy Camson, or Caresse Carroll picture. It's a Maxwell Reed." The pleasant expression vanished with the acerbic tone of her voice.

They'd reached one of the brooks that crisscrossed the conservation land. The relatively warm weather had melted some of the ice and the banks were covered with mud. It didn't look very inviting, and as a spot for a romantic tryst, it ranked close to the tundra during a spring thaw. Corny loved it.

"Exactly what Max wants for the scene where Hester and Arthur renew their passion!" she enthused.

"I don't remember any mention of their making love—and wasn't Pearl around during the forest scene, too?"

"Faith, Faith," Cornelia chided, "this is Max's interpretation, not Nathaniel Hawthorne's." Whoever he might be, Faith silently finished for her.

Cornelia was off and running. "Reality is an illusion as far as Max is concerned. Last night, he told me, 'The world is a defiance of common sense.' I treasure those words—and the fact that he has always been able to confide in me about his work."

René Magritte treasured those words, too, Faith recalled. There had been a review of an exhibit by the artist in last Friday's *New York Times* and Max must have seen it, as Faith had. It was possible the words entered his subconscious and he truly believed they were his own thoughts. Or not. But Corny believed and Faith wasn't about to mention any feet of clay. It was enough that Faith herself was suffering feet of mud—her new Cole-Haan boots were encrusted with the stuff.

"I think I have to get back and check on the lunch preparations," Faith said as Cornelia eyed the mucky path ahead with interest.

"I should be getting back, too," she said, abandoning the path not taken with a perceptible sigh. "I'm supposed to be helping Evelyn with her lines this morning."

"That must be fascinating." Faith would have been happy to spend time listening to Evelyn O'Clair's slightly husky, velvet voice try out various readings.

"Nothing fascinating about it," Cornelia complained. "The woman can barely remember her own telephone number. I can't imagine what Max sees in her. Actually, I can imagine, but he certainly doesn't talk to her!"

She suddenly lowered her voice, although the only potential eavesdroppers were a few gray squirrels and a solitary crow motionless on a tall pine.

"You may have heard that Evelyn took a long vacation in Europe last year?" Faith hadn't, but she nodded encouragingly, "Well, she was in Europe, only it wasn't for a vacation."

Faith didn't need Corny's long pause to indicate emphasis. Her voice had underlined the words sufficiently. It would be on the final for sure.

"It wasn't?" she asked obediently.

"No, she was at a spa, if you know what I mean."

Faith was pretty sure she didn't mean sixteen glasses of water a day and a seaweed wrap. "Was it alcohol or drugs, or did she have some other kind of breakdown?"

"That would be telling," Corny said, smugly fastening every button on her unbared breast with annoying swiftness.

This was good gossip, but Faith knew there would be no more. The moment had passed. Preoccupied, Cornelia stomped steadfastly back toward the set, obviously thinking how much better a consort she would make. More like the virgin queen, Faith reflected. Anyway for now, and quite likely forever, Miss Stuyvesant would have

47

to be content with the crumbs from Evelyn's table.

They were both surprised to see Max himself at the canteen truck with Sandra Wilson and some of the rest of the crew, instead of sequestered in his trailer or on the set as usual. They were laughing and it was obvious from their good humor that the morning's shoot had been successful.

"Mistress Fairchild—Faith, if I may—whatever these are, they are wicked and as addictive as . . . well, let's merely say addictive. You are going to have to cater all my films," Max called out.

Faith was inordinately pleased. It was nice, of course, when the Ladies Alliance at First Parish praised the tiny buckwheat walnut rolls she filled with thin slices of Virginia ham and a touch of honey mustard, but to hear it from a famous person—this was something else again. She just might have to become a Maxwell Reed groupie herself, no matter whose quotations he cribbed.

Cornelia had immediately insinuated herself into the group around the director, and from the way she regarded Sandra, her fellow PA, it was apparent to Faith that Evelyn O'Clair was not the only fly in the pancake makeup so far as Corny was concerned.

They were all diverted by the arrival of Caresse Carroll with her mother literally following at her heels. Caresse was running, and when she stopped, planting herself firmly in front of Max, it was clear it wasn't the exercise that had brought roses to her cheeks, but annoyance —a lot of annoyance.

Caresse was very, very angry.

"Who the hell do you think you are kicking me off your stinking movie! Do you think I wanted to work for an old weirdo like you!" she shrieked. Her whole body was rigid and the only part moving was her lips. She looked like the

48

little girl she'd played in *Adopted by Aliens* after they'd snatched her body.

Her mother put her arm around Caresse's shoulder, attempting to lead her away, whispering something that sounded like "Now, dear, it's not worth . . ."

"Get away from me!" Caresse rudely pushed her mother, sending her almost tumbling to the ground, and without pausing for breath continued her tirade. Jacqueline Carroll had tears in her eyes.

"We have a contract, mister." Caresse took a step forward and was shaking a tiny finger that threatened to become a fist at Max. "And you'd better remember that or you'll be sorry!"

"Are you finished?" Max asked quietly. He didn't look at all disturbed, yet the words were menacing in their steeliness. He might just as well have pulled a whip from his coat pocket and snapped it in the air. Caresse stood still, openmouthed, but not for long.

"No, I am not. Fuck you! And fuck the whole movie!"

"Are you finished?" he said in the same voice, a voice that belied his casual stance. He folded his arms across his chest. The cast and crew remained frozen in position. Nobody wanted to miss this scene.

"I'm waiting. Are you quite finished?"

Caresse hadn't said a word.

"Good. Now then, I have no idea who told you you were off the film. You're not. It's true I have been rethinking a few of Pearl's scenes and we may use the infant in some where we had originally thought we would use the older child. But nothing, I repeat *nothing,* has been decided."

"Bullshit," Caresse said, looking Max straight in the eye. "Bullshe-it." She drew the word out and walked over to her mother. "Come on, Mom, we're outta here. If he wants me, he can call my agent."

"Much as I admire the exit, I can't let you do it, Caresse." Max approached Jacqueline and softened his tone, "Believe me, Mrs. Carroll, I don't know how the rumor started and I will find out. Caresse is listed on tomorrow's call sheet and I want her to rehearse with Marta after lunch. Please let's not allow this misunderstanding to get out of control."

Caresse had continued to walk off after Max's first words, and now she called back to her mother, "Mom! Are you coming or not?" Jacqueline gave Max an encouraging nod and murmured, "I think she's a little overtired"—that time honored apology of mothers everywhere.

"Yeah, like Nero's ma said when he played with matches, 'The child simply needs more sleep,'" whispered Niki to Faith, who thereupon had to walk away to recover her composure. She took the opportunity to make a visit to the "honey wagon," as the toilets were quaintly called. She passed Marta Haree, who had been watching the whole scene from a distance. There was no mistaking the sardonic amusement on her face, and Faith thought Marta was someone she'd like to get to know better. Certainly the woman was extraordinary-looking. Her fine red frizzled hair surrounded her head like a Pre-Raphaelite aureole. Her face was pale, with mostly delicate features— high cheekbones, a pointed chin, almond-shaped green eyes. The exception was her nose: large, slightly crooked, dominant. It was hard to tell whether she was heavy or the bulk was an illusion created by the many layers of clothing she affected—trailing gypsylike garments in bright colors. Surely Marta Haree was a stage name, but it suited her. There was something a bit secretive—and seductive— about her. She didn't mix with the other actors, spending her time alone in her trailer or with the director. Like her weight, her age was difficult to calculate. In some of Reed's movies, she played octogenarians; in others, ingenues. Faith put her somewhere in her late forties or fifties and decided there was more than a trace of Magyar in Marta.

Returning to the catering tent to put the final touches on the black bean soup and other things on the menu for lunch, Faith passed Max and Evelyn, arm in arm, deep in conversation. They stopped when they saw Faith and Evelyn smiled engagingly. "Could you prepare a tray of something delicious for me to eat in my trailer, dear? I missed the morning break and I'm absolutely ravenous." It was difficult to imagine calories put to better use, and Faith told her she'd see to the tray immediately.

"Thank you. One of those nice little PAs will be along to get it." Evelyn bestowed yet another smile on Faith and then continued to stroll with Max. They picked up their conversation when Faith was almost out of earshot. His words were muffled, but Evelyn's were piercingly clear. "I'm tired of telling you, Maxie. I don't care what you want. Once and for all, *I* want her off the picture."

Back at the tent, Faith quickly put together a tray for Ms. O'Clair: a large, steaming bowl of black bean soup topped by a dollop of sour cream and fresh chives (see recipe on page 308); some of the buckwheat walnut rolls with ham that she'd missed; a salad; and a ramekin of crème caramel, along with Evelyn's drink of choice—Perrier mixed with diet Coke. As Faith worked, she thought about the fragment of the conversation she'd overheard. Caresse obviously was "her." But why did Evelyn want her off the picture, especially at this stage of the game? Wouldn't any objections she'd had have been made when Max was casting in the first place? Maybe she hadn't heard "Never act with children or dogs"—or

51

hadn't believed it. Whatever her opinion had been earlier, she was certainly definite now. Faith added a small bud vase with a single pale pink rose, a damask napkin, and appropriate cutlery. She knew from past experiences that catering to the stars meant exactly that.

The tray dispatched, Faith, Niki, Pix, and the rest of the staff turned their attention to preparing for the stampede that would arrive shortly—not before Pix had voiced her irritation with little Miss Carroll, however.

"You know what I think about spanking," she said. Faith nodded and quoted, " 'A parent out of control means a child out of control.' " Pix had taken some sort of parent-awareness classes at Adult Ed in between pierced lamp shades and folded star patchwork tree ornaments.

"But," continued Pix, and it was a momentous but, "this child needs someone to turn her over his or her knee and if I see her push her mother again, it's going to be mine, no matter how much money America's Sweetheart makes." Having disposed of the problem of Caresse, Pix turned her attention to counting napkins, knives, forks, and spoons.

Besides the soup, there were individual tomato and onion quiches, couscous with grilled vegetables, a salad bar, assorted breads, and a savory whole pastrami keeping warm under the lights, which made it look all the more appetizing—not too fat, not too lean. Mr. and Mrs. Sprat would have had a tough time deciding.

"Stations, everyone," Faith called, and she tied back the tent flaps. The heaters made the inside a cozy contrast to what was yet another typically "brisk" New England March day. People were beginning to straggle across the Pingrees' lawn in search of sustenance when a call for help stopped them dead in their tracks.

"Fire!" somebody screamed. "Come on!"

52

Everyone, including the caterers, rushed off in the direction of the house. The clapboard would go up like the kindling it was. Faith grabbed one of the fire extinguishers she had on hand and shouted over her shoulder for someone to get the other one.

Once outside, they realized everyone was running toward the barn—the site of the fire made obvious by the thick cloud of black smoke billowing from the open door. It was mass confusion with a touch of mass hysteria. Two crew members—stuntmen, Faith discovered later—grabbed her extinguishers and disappeared into the smoke. The breeze spread the harsh odor of the fumes over the watching crowd. In what seemed like several hours but was in reality no more than twenty minutes, the stuntmen and the others who had gone in immediately with extinguishers from the set emerged. They looked none the worse for wear, except for smudged faces, shiny with sweat and tears from the smoke.

"It's all over, folks. Oily rags. No damage, Max," one of them reassured the director, who was hastening toward them.

"How did it start?" he asked.

"Your guess is as good as mine. Maybe somebody sneaking a smoke."

Maxwell Reed had a hard-and-fast rule about smoking on the set—anywhere. He was fanatic on the subject. Not everybody was able to live with it, and the stalls in the honey wagon smelled a lot more like Luckies than Lysol.

"I hope not," Max said grimly, his eyes raking the group still assembled outside the barn. When he reached where she was standing, Faith felt instinctively guilty—for what, she knew not.

"It's out now, and that's the important thing." Alan Morris moved quickly to douse these new flames. "Let's eat, everybody."

It was out. And out before both bright red Aleford fire engines tore into the yard, sirens blaring, carrying a full complement of the Aleford Ancient Order of Hook and Ladder Volunteers. Screeching to a halt behind these came the ambulance. Bringing up the rear, the chief's venerable police car sputtered to its own inimitable stop.

Faith hurried back to the tent to put out additional food.

"More mouths to feed," she instructed the staff, adding to Niki and Pix, "You know they're all kicking themselves for missing the action, and you can be sure they're not going topass up the chance to hobnob on the set now that they're here." She looked into the soup tureens. There was plenty and it was steaming hot. "And, to be fair, they can't leave without checking things out, which just might have to take all afternoon. We can grab Charley later for coffee and doughnuts. I'd like to know myself how the rags caught fire."

"Is this the Faith Fairchild version of 'inquiring minds want to know' again?" Niki asked. "I've heard stories about you. I'm sure it was a cigarette. You know they all go into the woods to smoke. It's a wonder we haven't had a forest fire."

"You're probably right," Faith agreed. "But why is it always a pile of oily rags? Do you keep oily rags around? I don't. What do *you* do to get them oily, anyway? If you were being terribly crafty and refinishing furniture or working on your car, why not throw the rags away? It's not as though you'd wash them and use them for oily things again. No, it all seems so—well, so convenient."

"You've obviously put a great deal of thought into the problem of oily rags and I'm sure you'd prefer a straightforward fire of suspicious origin in this case, but if you'd ever looked in the hayloft of that barn, you'd have seen there are piles of all sorts of junk, including oily rags created by God knows who for what purpose."

Tucking the thoughts of what Niki was doing in the hayloft and why she, Faith, hadn't checked it out herself into a corner of her mind for later consideration, Faith got ready to serve the returning crew. "It looks like our purpose is coming in the door."

They were followed by the Aleford brigade about thirty minutes later. Which is why Police Chief MacIsaac, Fire Chief O'Halloran, and their cohorts eagerly slurping down Faith's soup and clamoring for seconds in amiable company with the director, cast, and crew of *A* were all there to witness Evelyn O'Clair's possibly last dramatic entrance.

Clutching her stomach and moaning, she staggered into the tent. "I've been poisoned!" she cried. Then she vomited violently and collapsed.

CHAPTER 3

But who can see an inch into futurity beyond his nose?

IF ONE HAS INDEED BEEN POISONED, HAVING A LARGE number of trained rescue workers and an ambulance close at hand may be regarded as something more than a happy coincidence. Evelyn O'Clair had been damned lucky indeed.

But not poisoned.

Or rather, not poisoned in the classical, even conventional sense. It wasn't strychnine or arsenic. Not even digitalis—admittedly difficult to cull from the abundant foxglove still slumbering under the earth surrounding the old house.

It was Chocolax, a digestive aid, and it was in the black bean soup—a medium that unfortunately intensified the drug's effects. In addition, a substantial amount of a liquid laxative sold over the counter for use before certain X rays had been added.

"Why didn't anyone say anything!" wailed Faith when Charley MacIsaac stopped by early the next day to bring her the ill tidings in person. He had had a bad night himself after yesterday's lunch and was not in a good mood.

"We all thought it was some sort of new fool concoction of yours, that's why. And it wasn't bad. Just kind of unusual. Besides, there was so much smoke in the air, nobody could taste much of anything."

Tom and Ben had departed for their respective morning activities—sermon writing and Play-Doh—and at least one of them wanted to switch. Amy was asleep.

Faith had offered the chief some breakfast, but he had declined with unaccustomed haste. He opted for the sofa instead of the large Windsor chair, his usual choice. His face was a study in contrasts: affection for the woman sitting next to him struggled with animosity. Faith watched in alarm.

"Charley! You know I wouldn't have put a laxative in any soup I'd made, especially Chocolax, which must bear no more resemblance to real chocolate than Styrofoam to meringue. That means somebody else put it in. The question is, who and when?"

"All right, let's start from the beginning." Affection triumphed and Charley managed a weak smile. He took a small, creased spiral notepad from his jacket pocket, along with a sharp number-two yellow Dixon pencil. Faith expected him to lick the tip before commencing to write, and he did.

"When did you make the soup?"

"Wednesday afternoon."

"And it sat in your refrigerator until you brought it to the set yesterday?"

"Yes, but . . ."

"Hold your horses, Faith. Now who besides you and probably the Reverend has keys to the place?"

"Pix and Niki, but . . ."

"No spares hidden under the mat or in a flowerpot?" he asked doggedly.

"Charley, I'm trying to tell you something! Nobody could have put anything into the soup at the kitchen. It was fine when we arrived at the set, because I tasted it to check the seasonings when we first heated it."

57

"All right, now we're getting somewhere." The chief gave her a baleful look, suggesting that she had hitherto been throwing sand in the gas tank of justice. "When, as near as you can remember, did you do the tasting?"

"It was before we heard the fire alarm, and that was about quarter after twelve. We normally serve lunch at twelve-thirty, and I was watching the time pretty closely."

"So let me get this straight. The soup was fine before the fire broke out."

"Yes, which could mean the fire was set to get us out of the way while the soup was doctored. Sorry, poor choice of words."

"All the soup was in one big pot?"

"No, there were two tureens. We serve from two stations so the lines go faster."

"I'm sure they kept the samples separate, but, in any case, everyone who had the soup got the runs, so they both must have been tampered with."

Faith had not been ill, nor had the rest of the Have Faith staff, since they normally ate after everyone else. After Evelyn's pronouncement, nothing passed anybody's lips. No, it was only the cast and crew of *A*, the entire fire department, and both police and fire chiefs who had been felled.

Something was nagging at Faith. Something was wrong, besides what was so obviously wrong—that person or persons unknown had deliberately set out to destroy her reputation and business.

"Charley, wait. Whoever dumped the Chocolax in the soup had to have done it earlier, because it was in the portion on Evelyn's tray and we sent that to her trailer before the fire."

"But after you tasted it?"

"Yes. Just after. I remember thinking how good it was,"

58

Faith declared staunchly. It *had* been good—she'd used hickory-smoked ham hocks for flavor, plus two kinds of onions and a touch of dry sherry before pureeing it all into a smooth liquid.

Charley looked tired. Up and down all night perhaps? "Then what we have here is a situation where someone comes into the tent in broad daylight and empties God only knows how many packages of the stuff into two soup pots in front of you, Niki, Pix, and the rest of the bunch."

"Plus a dozen or so crew members who needed to eat early or were waiting for trays. I admit it is impossible."

"Yet it must have happened that way."

"We would have noticed, believe me. Even if someone palmed the stuff and dropped it in the soup while we weren't looking, he or she would have to have stirred it to mix it in and then have repeated the whole thing at the other table."

Charley looked glum. When more than a minute had passed, Faith tentatively asked the question that had been on her mind since he'd told her what had happened.

"Are you going to have to close me down?"

"I'm supposed to. You know the law as well as I do, probably better.

"Yes, except this was not a result of the caterer in question's actions. I mean, we're not talking salmonella chicken or spoiled mayonnaise here."

"Sort of what I said to the Department of Health."

"And they said?"

"They agreed—after a while. But whether the movie people still want you . . ."

"It would be perfectly understandable if they didn't. I just don't want to be shut down. You can't imagine how grateful I am to you, Charley." Faith would have thrown her arms around the chief, but he wasn't the hugging

59

kind.

Charley still had the notebook out. He was thinking out loud. "A fire and food poisoning—all within the same hour. Could be one of those movie people is some sort of lunatic. You ever notice any of them behaving more strangely than the rest?" Charley took it for granted all of them were demented in some respect—otherwise, they wouldn't live in California. Faith had observed this regional chauvinism in Charley, and other Alefordians, on numerous occasions. New York City was the worst. Make no mistake about that, but L.A. was definitely in the running.

"No, I can't say I've seen anyone wandering around talking to lampposts. The only slightly maniacal outburst was an eight-year-old girl's, and she's merely spoiled." Faith then gave Charley an account of Caresse's temper tantrum, which was accompanied by noises from Amy's room, indicating she was up and ready for company. The first soft babbles became increasingly puzzled syllables, then finally insistent crying as Faith ignored her—hoping to finish the story before tending to her child.

"Get the baby, Faith, before she blows a gasket. I have to check in at the station and see what's going on there before I head over to the Marriott."

Amy's cries had become one long antiphony.

"But I still have so many questions. At least tell me if the fire was set or an accident."

"You have questions! Some things never change." Charley looked more cheerful than he had all morning. "All right. We don't know if the fire was set or not yet. We don't know why someone wanted to close down the set of *A, B,* or whatever the hell the name of this thing is. And we don't know why Evelyn O'Clair was so much sicker than anybody else. Okay?"

60

She who must be obeyed would soon rocket right out of the crib. Faith called, "Coming, sweetie. Mommy's coming," and turned to start up the stairs. "Thanks, Charley. For everything. And let me know what's happening."

"Sure, Faith." Police Chief MacIsaac let himself out the front door and got into the cruiser—if you could call it that, he reflected dismally. He'd bring Patrolman Dale Warren along while he questioned everyone at the Marriott. The kid saw a lot of movies. And he hadn't eaten any soup.

Amy stopped crying the moment her mother entered the room, and as Faith changed her diaper and put on a fresh set of clothes, she positively beamed. Faith's mood, however, did not match her easily placated daughter's. The business of who had put the Chocolax in the soup had to be cleared up, and cleared up quickly. Rumors in the catering business traveled faster than the latest chili pepper craze, and if word got out that there had been a food poisoning episode at Have Faith, she'd be lucky to be catering snacktime at Ben's nursery school. Certain food purveyors who would leap at the chance to stick a knife or even a fork in her back came to mind with frightening speed.

She took the baby into the kitchen and packed some zwieback and other baby goodies into her gargantuan diaper bag. Faith was upset and had to talk to Tom—in person. After bundling Amy into her L. L. Bean Baby Bag, she grabbed her own jacket and headed across the yard and through the ancient cemetery that separated the church from the parsonage.

At least no one had died in the incident, she reflected, looking at the slightly askew slate tombstones with their lugubrious messages from the glorious beyond—such as

61

Daniel Noyes's pithy 1716 epitaph: "As you were, so was I/God did call and I did dy." The sun had not managed to pierce the gray cloud cover overhead and the ground was frozen. There hadn't been any snow, but the remnants of last summer's green carpet of grass, so very green in the burial ground, crunched underfoot.

Tom was slightly surprised to see Faith, flushed and obviously agitated, at his office door. She rarely ventured into this part of the church, whether from lack of interest or fear of being added to a committee, he was still not quite sure.

"Is everything all right, honey?" he asked anxiously.

"No," she replied, peeling off Amy's layers and looking around for a place to deposit her. Tom was not the tidiest person in the world. His office consisted of a large rolltop desk, several bookcases crammed with books, two wing chairs, one Hitchcock, and piles and piles of papers and more books on the floor, said chairs, and any available surface. A four-drawer file stood to the right of his desk and held church stationery, extra hymnals, and prayer books. "I know exactly where everything is," he'd protested to both his wife and the church secretary, earnestly imploring them not to touch a thing. "I have my own system."

Faith refrained from her usual comment. Before slumping into one of the wing chairs, she removed a stack of the yellow legal pads he favored when composing his sermons, written in longhand. "These are my computer," he often said, wiggling his fingers. Too precious for words, his wife had told him on more than one occasion, and an unlikely affectation for a man whose state-of-the-art high fidelity system required a degree from MIT to operate.

"What's happened?" he said, reaching for the baby, who proceeded to treat his lap as a trampoline, delightedly bobbing up and down in his grip.

"The reason everyone got sick yesterday was a superabundance of Chocolax and some other laxative in the black bean soup."

"Faith, this is terrible! Are they going to suspend your license?" Tom knew the repercussions almost as well as Faith.

"For the moment, no, and the rumors will die down, I hope," Faith said in a voice that belied her words. "But what's got me is, who would do such a thing and why? Was it directed at the film people or me?"

"My guess would be the cast and crew, and perhaps Evelyn O'Clair in particular. You just provided a happy medium."

"There's something else . . . There's no way anyone could have put the stuff in the soup without being seen."

Faith recounted the timetable, and Tom had to admit he was stumped, too.

"The only thing that makes sense is that the stuff was added to Evelyn's soup and the soup in the tent at different times. I'm convinced the fire was set to get everybody out of the way. But we're right back at who and why again."

"So, what next? Are you going to get in touch with Alan Morris to see if you still have a job?"

"I have to, although I'm not looking forward to it. Charley said Max wants to start shooting again tomorrow. They kept Evelyn at the Lahey Clinic for observation overnight, but she's all right now. That's another thing I don't understand. Why was she so much sicker than anyone else?"

"Body weight, maybe. Or a greater concentration of the stuff in her particular serving. Nerves. Maybe all three."

Faith stood up. "I know you're busy, darling, and I'll be

going. I just needed to be with you. I think I'll call my old friend Cornelia and see if I can find out which way the wind is blowing."

"Apt choice of words." Tom grinned and folded his wife and daughter in a warm embrace. "Need me anytime you want."

"I feel much better—and madder. Believe me, I'm going to find out who's responsible. You don't go fooling around with a woman's livelihood—not to mention the suffering all those people had to endure."

Tom knew his wife well enough to know which fueled her anger more at the moment. It wasn't that she had a hard heart—merely certain priorities, bordering on maybe a touch too much self-interest. "I may have been slightly spoiled as a child, you know," she had told him shortly after their wedding in a moment of early marital candor. "Oh, really?" He'd only just managed to keep a straight face.

Faith trudged back home, her heart lighter but her chest heavier. It seemed Amy was getting larger by the hour. Her birth weight had doubled to fourteen pounds. When Faith strapped the baby in the Snugli now, she sensed the day would soon come when she'd fall face-forward as gravity and the baby joined forces. And if she fell forward here in the yard, she noted ruefully, she'd be covered with the slippery, moldy leaves they hadn't managed to finish raking last fall.

The message machine was blinking frantically. Both Niki and Pix had called to find out what was going on. There was nothing from Alan Morris or anyone else connected with *A*. Faith made brief calls to her two assistants to tell them what she knew—or rather, didn't know—and asked that they get in touch with the others. Then she called Cornelia and invited her to come over for lunch.

"Well, I don't have much time. Max has asked me to work on part of the script with him, but I might be able to squeeze a quick bite in. It would be faster if you came here. There's a little restaurant not far from the hotel called The Dandy Lion. Do you know it?"

Faith did. It was opposite the huge Burlington Mall and provided decent salad, soup, and sandwich-type fare amidst a forest of ferns populated by the high-tech Route 128 computer crowd that favored it as a watering hole.

Arlene Maclean and even Faith's old standby Pix were both out, so Faith was forced to take Amy along to the rendezvous. With luck, the baby would lapse comatose in the stroller, as this was close to her normal postprandial naptime. A more probable scenario was alert wakefulness in a new and exciting place. Faith had packed a bushel basket of toys and various foodstuffs to keep the infant involved while her mom pumped Auntie Cornelia for information.

After all, what were old friends for—especially old friends like Cornelia? Faith had no problem reassuring herself as she drove down Middlesex Turnpike onto Mall Road, where the restaurant was cosily tucked into a minimall with a panoramic view of vast parking lots.

Cornelia was waiting at a table in the main dining room and looked slightly askance at the baby. She favored Faith with an air kiss and waved dismissively in Amy's direction, wafting away any thoughts Faith may have had of baby worship as a way of getting Corny to spill the beans, black or otherwise.

"I've already ordered. I suppose you want to talk about yesterday." Cornelia was using her best head counselor's voice to come straight to the point, and it suddenly occurred to Faith that her friend thought she was to blame

65

for the disaster.

"Corny," she gasped, "you certainly don't think I or any of my staff had anything to do with everyone getting sick!"

"You did prepare the food, Faith dear," she said, fixing Faith with a stern eye that continued the thought.

"But I didn't put Chocolax in the soup!"

Now Cornelia appeared surprised. "Chocolax. Did you hear this from the police?"

Obviously, the news had not reached the Marriott, or Cornelia, at any rate. Charley MacIsaac had not told Faith to keep it a secret, so she supposed the news was for public consumption.

"Yes, from our chief. He said it was Chocolax, loads of it, and another liquid laxative." Since hearing the method, Faith assumed the police were asking around at such places as Aleford's own Patriot Drug to find out whether anyone had made suspiciously large purchases of it lately. She was so busy with this thought and with rooting around in the diaper bag for Amy's plastic keys that it was a moment before she realized Cornelia hadn't said anything. She looked up. Corny had a puzzled look on her face and was staring off toward the other dining room—the one Faith preferred because of its fireplace and smaller, more intimate size.

The waitress arrived to take Faith's order, and by the time this had been accomplished, Cornelia's expression was almost back to its usual imperturbability.

"What is it? You know something, don't you?" Faith pressed. She wasn't about to miss this opportunity. Not with her business at stake, as well as enough curiosity to decimate the greater Boston cat population.

"The laxative, the Chocolax. Evelyn takes it by the handful." Cornelia was almost whispering.

"What on earth for?" Faith asked, then quickly said,

66

"You mean . . . ?"

"Yes," Cornelia replied. "She throws up, too. It's one of the reasons she was at the clinic in Switzerland."

At that moment, the food arrived. Faith stared at the burger with Boursin, salad to one side, she'd ordered. Cornelia hadn't picked up a fork, either. It all looked so robust, a trickle of fat and blood oozing from the rare meat. She was being ridiculous, Faith told herself, apparently at the same time Corny told herself the same thing. They grabbed their utensils and took two large bites of lettuce.

"An eating disorder. The poor woman. Is this common knowledge—or is it only because you're close to Max that you know?" Faith went from sympathy back to the main point rapidly. She hoped her not-so-subtle flattery would produce results. It did.

"Of course I knew about it before other people," Cornelia preened, "although by now it's old news. But surely Evelyn wouldn't put it in her own soup?"

Exactly what Faith was thinking. Still, it may not have been in Evelyn's soup. She bent down to pick up the toy keys that Amy had thrown on the floor for the tenth time, ecstatic as always with the game of "Fetch, Mommy, Fetch." Evelyn might have taken the Chocolax before lunch. Then why had she gotten so sick? It couldn't have been suggestibility—everyone else getting sick. Her dramatic entry had preceded the onset of the others' symptoms. But if she had taken some and it was also in the soup, that might account for the severity of her attack. Faith bit into her hamburger ruminatively. One thing was sure: Everyone working on *A* knew where to go to get plenty of yummy Chocolax. Or did they? She swallowed hastily.

"Did she keep the laxative in her trailer or at the

67

house?"

"In the trailer—at least that's where I've seen the stuff. She thinks Max doesn't know, so she wouldn't have it at the house, where he might find it. "Cornelia's face crumbled into the kind of pout it had assumed in earlier years when her father had said she couldn't have a new pony. "They share the master bedroom suite."

"But Max does know?"

Cornelia nodded. Her mouth was full.

Faith continued to think out loud. "What do you think? Does someone have a grudge against Max—or the crew in general?" She was eager to get as much information from Cornelia as possible before her old classmate ran off to save the movie or, more likely, to put in an order for more cases of Calistoga water—and before Amy tired of the stroller. The baby was beginning to eye her mother's lap with increasing determination.

Cornelia looked decidedly uneasy. In fact, Faith realized, she'd been uneasy and tense since Faith's arrival. Of course, this could be attributed to the events of the day before and a night Cornelia had complained about venomously to Faith, the caterer, on the phone. Yet it was also possible she was hiding something, or someone.

"Everyone loves Max, or even if they don't exactly love him, they're thrilled to be working with him. I can't imagine that this is directed against him." Cornelia paused. "Unless it was Caresse. Little Miss Wonderful is far from his greatest fan right now. Her agent should have told her Max often writes people in and out of his movies once he starts shooting. There's no need for her to carry on the way she is."

Faith didn't care much for the child, but if Maxwell Reed was planning to cut her role, it would be a bitter blow and one that wouldn't do anything to enhance her career. Cornelia might be onto something. Putting a laxative into everyone's food was a very childish thing to do. And precocious Caresse probably knew about Evelyn's cache. Caresse. It all added up, except for one thing. When did the merry prankster do it?

Another thought occurred to Faith. "Has there ever been trouble of this kind on Max Reed's other films?"

"No," Cornelia answered fiercely, "certainly not. Oh, well, the usual tricks, especially at the end of a shoot when everyone's nerves have been getting a little frayed. One of the PA's found a lot of plastic maggots in her coffee during *Maggot Morning*, thought they were real, got hysterical, and quit. Then, of course, there were plastic maggots everywhere. And sometimes people prepare joke versions of certain scenes. However"—she squared her shoulders, shoulders that needed no pads—"the individuals who work on his films are professionals.

"Now, I'd love to stay and chat with you all day"— Cornelia was up and flinging some money on the table "but I've stayed too long already. Take care of the bill, will you?"

Another kiss kiss, a vague good-bye to little whatever, and she was gone.

"You know she didn't leave enough," Faith told her daughter, who obligingly blew a few spit bubbles in agreement.

She paid the bill and once again prepared herself and her child to meet the elements. It would be simpler, she'd told Tom her first winter in Aleford, to get sewn into a kind of quilted all-weather cocoon in October and emerge as a rank butterfly in May than constantly getting in and out of layers of clothing day and night.

She wheeled the stroller toward the door, then, attracted by the warm smell of the burning logs in the other room, turned the corner to look at the fire. The logs were crackling in the fieldstone fireplace and the occupants of the tables lingering over coffee seemed to appreciate the ambience created. Two patrons at the table farthest from the door were not looking at the fire or Faith. They were gazing into each other's matchless eyes, gems of sparkling sapphire blue meeting deep puddles of liquid brown velvet.

It was Evelyn O'Clair and Cappy Camson.

No reason why two cast members shouldn't get together for lunch, even if one of them has just gotten out of the hospital. No reason at all. Faith filed the picture the two made for future reference. Her system was every bit as efficient as her husband's, and, like Tom, she really did know exactly where everything was—usually.

This time when Faith returned home after picking Ben up at school, there was a message from one of what she and the rest of the town customarily referred to as the "movie people." It was Alan Morris and he asked her to call him back at her earliest convenience. That could be a few weeks, she thought as she tried to listen to Ben's tale of some playground inequity, gave both children something to eat, and finally settled them—Amy playpen-bound—in front of a tape of "Thomas the Tank Engine." The British had managed to make the series so didactic, a mother could almost feel she was advancing her children's moral development instead of parking them in front of the TV.

Alan Morris was in and, from the sound of his voice, happy to hear from her.

"The police chief said he had spoken with you, so you know what caused the uh . . . problem yesterday," Alan said delicately.

Faith wasn't sure what she was supposed to say. Beg for

her job back, asserting Have Faith's noninvolvement? Commiserate with the assistant director, who, she recalled, had come back for seconds? But would saying she was sorry suggest blame?

"Yes, he told me," was the best she could come up with at short notice.

"Max is, as you might expect, quite furious about the whole affair," Alan continued.

Furious at Faith in some way? Furious at fate? She stuck with the tried and true. "Yes, I can imagine," she replied.

"Of course, he's not angry at you. He adores your cooking. Obviously, you and your staff had nothing to do with it."

Did his voice rise slightly at the end of the sentence? Was it a question? Was he fishing for reassurance? Faith knew what to say now.

"*Obviously*. And I'm so glad you recognize this. I would hate to think you believed we were in any way responsible. And I'm sure you know the Department of Health has come to the same conclusion."

There was relief in his voice. "Max is convinced it was a practical joke gone wrong and that whoever did it is too embarrassed to come forward. The fact that all this came at once—someone smoking in the barn and the, uh, food incident—is simply a bad coincidence. These things happen when you put a lot of people together under pressure. But any delay like yesterday's means money down the tube, and the producers are already nickel and diming us to death. Max has instructed us to put the whole thing out of our minds. We are continuing to film as if nothing happened."

That's going to be quite a trick, Faith thought.

"Now," he continued, his calm, ever so slightly theatrical voice even calmer, "the reason I called was that

71

we'd like Have Faith to continue to work with us."

Faith felt an enormous load lift from her mind. Until it was gone, she hadn't realized how heavy it had been. Even though she'd sensed from Alan's tone during the call that this was where they were heading, it wasn't until he actually said the words that she could allow herself to take a deep breath.

"So, see you bright and early tomorrow morning. Max wants to shoot the dawn scene—the one that I spoke to you about last week—on the village green. He's been waiting for the right weather, and tomorrow the sky should be perfect."

"We'll be there," Faith promised happily.

"And remember, none of this ever happened."

So *you* say, she thought as she hung up the phone. You may have decided to believe it was a joke, but I'm still not laughing.

The whole town was learning more than it thought it would ever care to know about the way movies are made, and if it all didn't make sense at first, it was beginning to make even less by now. Millicent, who Faith suspected had taken out a subscription to *Variety*, was expounding on the craft as the caterers arrived in the pitch-dark before dawn the following morning.

Miss McKinley was responding acidly to a fellow Alefordian's comment that he couldn't see why they didn't just start at the beginning and go to the end instead of jumping around in the script, this being the way *he* would do it—in a logical manner.

"The director has to shoot out of sequence to take advantage of the weather and lighting conditions when they go on location. And not all the actors can be on the set all the time. Now today, Max has worked everything out with the director of photography, the gaffers, and the best boy." She continued with the air of one who expected to be sitting next to her new best friend in one of the front rows at the Dorothy Chandler Pavilion some day soon.

"The gaffers, of course, carry out the cameraman's lighting plan—they're those people setting up all those lights and reflectors." She gestured grandly toward the crew. They were attaching various forms of lighting to the trees and on poles surrounding the large wooden scaffold that had been erected in the middle of the green, with the flagpole to the left and First Parish directly behind. Huge mobile generators were parked nearby and the greenskeeper and crew were busy burying the last of the wires and replacing the grass with new sod.

"The best boy is the chief gaffer's assistant," Millicent determinedly continued. She was not about to waste all the time she'd spent looking this stuff up in the reference room. Her audience had diminished, however, basely abandoning her for the hot coffee, fresh raised doughnuts, and fruit muffins that Faith had brought.

About fifty extras were dressed in their own dark-colored overcoats, hats, and gloves, as instructed. *A* was being filmed in modern dress, but looking at her neighbors, Faith thought not a few of the outfits failed to qualify. Millicent's serviceable black coat was definitely prewar—and which war was open to debate.

Alan Morris walked over to them. The stars and the director were presumably in their behemoth RVs lined up at the curb, getting into their roles or catching a few more winks. Several of Aleford's finest were on duty and, by their frequent yawns, perhaps not convinced the extra pay was worth having to get up so early.

"Good, good. Everyone looks fine. And remember, all you have to do is mumble. Something like 'apples and oranges' usually works to produce the illusion of conversation. You won't be miked directly. Then the women, where are they?"

Five women stepped forward, Millicent, Penelope Bartlett, and Audrey Heuneman among them. They were all carrying their good pocketbooks and looked as if they were either going shopping in Boston or to a funeral.

"You will be directly below the scaffold where Hester and Dimmesdale will be standing. On cue, you are to point to the sky and cover your mouths, like this. Don't exaggerate it too much. And don't point until the plane is out of sight and we only see the letter."

Alan had sketched the scene out for Faith when he told her about the early-morning shoot, Max had hired a skywriter to position an enormous *A* in puffs of red smoke above the scaffold where the minister is joined by Hester after he'd spent the night standing there alone in shame, delivering a lengthy soliloquy encompassing everything from the inevitability of alienation in modern society to the Vietnam War as a metaphor for adultery—the cuckolding of a nation. It was Cappy's big scene. They would shoot his speech back on the lot in L.A.

Max wanted a clear, bleak day and hoped to get a shot of the letter drifting down between two large leafless maples until the burning capital *A* was over Hester's and Dimmesdale's heads as well as to one side of the American flag, which Max hoped would be caught by the breeze. The flag joined to the letter in the sky symbolized the hypocrisy of the country's public morality, and the staid townspeople gathered below in judgment would later be revealed as secret adulterers, embezzlers, even murderers.

It was starting to get light and Faith could make out the faces of the other extras. They were beginning to learn what she already knew from past experience—that making

74

a movie was perhaps 90 percent waiting around in boredom, and a 10 per, cent adrenaline high. She'd tell Millicent and Penny to start toting their knitting bags.

Maxwell Reed appeared, and for a moment no one recognized him. The director had disappeared and Roger Chillingworth had taken his place. It wasn't that Reed had put on a wig or substantially changed his appearance, other than removing his glasses. It was the sense of evil he projected, darting malevolent looks back toward the crowd over his slightly deformed shoulder. In accord with the modern-dress costuming, he was wearing shapeless gray sweatpants and a loose gray sweatshirt. He spoke to no one and moved quickly to Alan Morris and the director of photography, who were positioned under the scarffold.

The sun was rising, but it was not bright. It cast a tepid light over the green, unable to penetrate the shadows left by the night.

"Let's make a movie," Reed shouted into the stillness, and everyone hastened toward him. Evelyn appeared from somewhere and took off a heavy sable coat, which she handed to her dresser before mounting the stairs to the platform. She wore a gauzy white dress with a large pink fleshlike letter *A* pinned over one breast. The other was not quite hidden by the layers of cloth and the nipple was prominent in protest at the freezing cold. Cappy Camson followed, and he at least was dressed warmly in a black turtleneck and tight jeans. Faith had to remind herself it was a serious allegorical reinterpretation as it became apparent that there was nothing between Cappy and his Calvins. Caresse joined the group, scowling. Max was going to shoot two versions of the scene—one with infant Pearl; one with child Pearl. Caresse had a scarlet velvet party dress on, richly embroidered with gold thread, lace on the collar and cuffs.

Max stood in front of the crowd below and fixed his eyes on the three figures above him. Faith couldn't see his expression, but from the response of the actors looking down at him, he must be acting very well indeed. They all looked absolutely terrified.

Alan Morris shouted, "Stand by! Quiet on the set." And everyone stood like statues while the plane sputtered overhead, producing an elegant script letter *A*. A loud buzzer went off.

"Roll sound."

"Camera."

"Speed."

The clapper/loader stepped in front, holding the arm of the clap slate up: A SCAFFOLD SCENE. TAKE ONE. SOUND TAKE ONE.

The arm banged down. It sounded like a shot in the morning quiet.

"Just like in the movies," Niki whispered to Faith.

"Action!"

The crowd commenced murmuring. Dimmesdale and Hester held hands. For some reason known to the director, Pearl lay down at their feet as the scarlet letter drifted to the exact spot Max had wanted and the women gasped and pointed. Dimmesdale and Hester looked up, then lay next to Pearl. Roger Chillingworth climbed up the ladder to the scaffolding and stood over them.

"Cut."

"Cool 'em off."

The lights went out. Evelyn's dresser rushed forward with her coat and Caresse's mother with one for her daughter. Max spoke to Alan and went to his trailer. Evelyn and Cappy disappeared into hers.

Huge fans on derricks were brought in to blow the

76

remnants of the red smoke away. Everyone crowded around the coffee urns, then came the call: "All right, people, again and then with the baby."

And they did it again. Then again with the baby. Then again with Caresse, and this time Max had everyone freeze, not hard to do, until the wisps of smoke had floated off into the increasing morning brightness.

"We've lost the light," he shouted to Alan, "but we got it." There was an audible sigh of relief and everybody started talking.

"How's the campaign going, Penny?" Faith asked when what she hoped would be the next selectwoman on the Aleford board came over for some food.

Penny looked tired for a moment. "It's going fine, dear. Of course I never would have gotten involved in all this if everyone hadn't pushed me so hard, and they swore they'd do all the campaigning, but they can't very well speak for me. I've never drunk so much coffee in my life, although it is fun getting to see everyone's living rooms."

Coffees to meet the candidates were the mainstay of Aleford electioneering.

"I know what you mean," Faith agreed. "It's always nice to take a walk at night when people's lights are on and you can see in."

She firmly believed there was nothing voyeuristic about this natural tendency to check seating arrangements and where people kept their books and objets d'art. If they didn't want onlookers, they should pull the drapes.

"Will you be at the debate on Monday?"

"Tom and I wouldn't miss it for the world."

The League of Women Voters was sponsoring a candidates night at the junior high and supporters of all three candidates planned to turn out in full force.

Penny thanked Faith for the doughnut and, as she

77

turned to go, walked straight into the arms of her half brother, Alden.

She backed away without expression. He grinned wickedly and, pointedly not addressing her, said to the person next to him, "Have you noticed some older women tend to be a little unsteady on their pins?"

Penny flushed and left without saying anything in return.

"Give me some more of that java," he ordered Faith. "Could be a little stronger."

But you couldn't, she retorted silently. She wasn't surprised he was one of the extras. He always seemed to be playing a role of some sort. At times, he was the quintessential New Englander, walking his pure-bred Labrador in the early morning, scorning an overcoat or muffler. Then there was the hard-bitten businessman complaining about profit margins and the interference of the government. He could be hail fellow, well met—or more often, "I'll say what I want to whom I want." During a parish call, Faith had been amused to see him trot out the deep thinker, casually motioning to Stephen Hawkings's *A Brief History of Time* placed conspicuously on the coffee table next to the latest book by A. N. Wilson, a life of Jesus Christ. When Alden left to get them a thimbleful of the second-best sherry from the kitchen, Faith picked up both books and was not surprised by their pristine, obviously unread condition.

He was playing his curmudgeon role now, or perhaps this was the real persona. He'd put his campaign button on after the shoot—SPAULDING, THE ONLY CHOICE— and took the cup of coffee with a mumble that could possibly have been a thank you by a gymnastic stretch of the imagination. Buttons, bumper stickers, and posters were sprouting up all over town. Alden was putting quite

78

a bit of money into his campaign, and Faith wondered why he wanted the seat at this particular time. He'd never run before and there had been plenty of opportunities.

He took several doughnuts and remembered he was running for office. "Shall we see you at the debate, Mrs. Fairchild? Although I don't flatter myself that you are one of my supporters, I would hope the Reverend has kept an open mind."

Really, the man was so offensive, it was hard to think of an adequate rejoinder that would not wind up as headlines in the tabloids: REV'S WIFE TELLS ONE OF THE FLOCK TO F—

Her thought was interrupted and, as it turned out, Faith didn't have to say anything at all.

The steaming-hot coffee urn went flying off the end of the table along with a tray of doughnuts, muffins, cream, and sugar—flying off to make a direct landing on Alden Spaulding's outstretched left arm. He screamed in pain and rage.

Faith ran around the table to his side; he'd collapsed onto the grass and people were running toward them to see what had happened.

"Quick," she called, "someone get the ambulance over here. I think he's been burned."

"You damn fool woman," the victim shouted, "I'm not burned. You've broken my goddamned arm, is all, and I'm going to sue you from here to Sunday!"

Faith looked around. By some miracle, the urn hadn't opened. No coffee had spilled out, except from Alden's own cup. His thick dark tweed coat, jacket, and the longjohns no doubt below had protected his arm from the heat, but not from the weight, of the heavy metal urn. There go my insurance premiums, she thought dismally.

"It had nothing to do with Faith," said a distinctly cool

79

voice. "In fact, it was no one's fault but yours, Alden, for having the misfortune to be standing in the wrong place at the wrong time." Audrey Heuneman joined the group gathered about the prone figure of her husband's political opponent, but she did not crouch down to his level. "Someone bumped into me and I hit the table," she stated matter-of-factly.

The EMTs were loading Alden onto a stretcher after he declared himself unable to move in no uncertain terms. It was not an easy job. Alden was a large individual, one who might have been called a fine figure of a man in the nineteenth century, when twelve-course dinners did not signify excess. In the twentieth, he was constantly advised by his doctor to cut down and didn't.

"Then I'll sue *you*," he roared.

"Fine," she said. "Only you'll have to prove malice aforethought."

Looking at the expression on Audrey's face, Faith had the feeling that might not be so difficult. It also explained at long last why James was running. Obviously Audrey Heuneman hated Alden Spaulding with every bone in her body.

Still swearing vengeance on somebody—he'd gotten around to the film company by this point—Alden was lugged off and the crowd on the green melted like snow in May to spread the news.

There were times, Faith told Tom over dinner that night, when her sojourn in the Big Apple seemed pretty dull compared to Aleford's day-to-day dramas.

Tom was less interested in what turned out to be Alden's minor injury than the filming of the scene on the green.

"It sounds like a brilliant effect—the letter in the sky at

80

dawn."

"It was amazing," Faith recounted. "The letter drifted down perfectly every time. It was as if Max had some sort of remote control."

"I don't get the jogging outfit, though. What's that supposed to represent?"

"Well, Chillingworth is supposed to be some sort of medical researcher who's been away in the Middle East and Hester has moved to town while waiting for him to come back. Maybe the clothes are meant to suggest he's in good shape? Or maybe Max wanted him to look like Everyman, and around here, Everywoman." Jogging suits seemed to be the approved apparel for anything from dropping your kids off at school to a dinner party, Faith had noted disapprovingly when she'd arrived in the suburbs. She did own a sweatshirt—a gift from Tom's family the Christmas after they were married, with FAIRCHILD NUMBER EIGHT stenciled on it—but had yet to complete the outfit.

"Maybe he doesn't want the clothes to distract the viewer, although Evelyn's might."

"Definitely, and you should see her scarlet letter, Tom, it's slightly obscene. It looks almost alive, as if it's made out of flesh."

"There is a danger in updating the story. Hester Prynne wouldn't be an outcast in today's society. She'd be asked to join a support group and neighbors would come round with booties and casseroles."

"And on what planet is that perfect little village? Come on, think what the response would be here if an attractive married lady moved into town, spurned all attempts to be drawn into the Newcomers Club, Friends of the Library, even shut the door on the Welcome Wagon. Then got pregnant! The first thing that would happen is that

81

Millicent would circulate a list of every man she'd ever seen drive in that direction, then everybody would get nervous about whose husband it might be, and finally, and forever, they'd ignore the harlot—except for those hushed-voiced 'I think you should knows' whenever someone who wasn't familiar with the story was around."

"Maybe you're right, honey. But I like to think the best of people. It goes with the trade. Now is there any more of this lasagna left, or did those movie people scarf it all down?"

The movie people had finished most of the three-cheese vegetarian lasagna Faith had offered as one of the lunch choices, but there was plenty of bread and salad, she told her husband, proffering as consolation another glass of the 1988 Caymus Napa Valley Cabernet Sauvignon they'd opened.

"There's lots of apple crisp (see recipe on page 311) for dessert, though. The crew seemed to be avoiding sugar shock today. They'd all been pretty keyed up about getting the shot right and I think they were high enough on that afterward."

"Lucky me," said Tom. His lanky frame seemed immune to the vicissitudes of sugar, starch, and fats. His sole problem since he was a kid had been filling himself up. Faith put a large bowl of the fragrant hot apple crisp in front of him and added a generous scoop of vanilla ice cream, which promptly oozed over the apples in a warm, delicious sauce.

The children were both asleep. The house was blessedly silent. She kissed the top of her husband's reddish brown hair. He smelled good, not like shampoo, but a clean soapy Tom smell all his own.

"Don't take too long, darling," she said. "I'll be upstairs."

The next morning in church, Faith's mind was wandering as usual. She still hadn't convinced the Ladies—no one could remember to call it the more politically correct Women's—Alliance that cushions with an actual filling as opposed to the ancient slabs of thin cloth presently lining the pews would be a worthy fund-raising project. No, they kept insisting on eminently more worthwhile projects such as helping the homeless, AIDS sufferers, and battered women—and Faith concurred. The only good thing about the cushions was that they kept you alert. It was impossible to get too comfortable and doze off.

Well aware of how numb certain parts of her body were getting, Faith kept half an ear on the order of service so she'd know when to stand up, while she thought some more about the food poisoning and the fire. Further conversations with Charley had done nothing to help. He'd questioned everyone involved and the police were still stuck with both opportunity and motive. He was leaning toward Reed's "practical joke gone wrong" theory and bluntly suggested that Faith do the same. Faith had tried to cast her eye about while on the job the day before, but she had gotten too busy to give it much thought—which is why it was inappropriately occupying her mind now.

Cornelia had said that "tricks" like this hadn't happened before, although she wasn't exactly objective. There were no chinks in Maxwell Reed's armor, as far as his devoted page was concerned, and that included his set. Faith thought Alan's comment about people under pressure was more accurate. It just happened to be Faith's soup.

Faith had noticed on the calendar this morning that it was going to be a full moon and she hoped that wouldn't

83

cause any more high jinks among the lotus eaters.

Her attention was caught by the lector reading the second lesson. It was Penny Bartlett and she was reading from St. Mark, chapter 10, the section on adultery. It was an apt passage for these red-letter days. Mark was pretty specific about the do's and don'ts of it, but Penny read swiftly on, her voice slowing only when she got to the part about "how hard is it for them that trust in riches to enter into the kingdom of God!" By the time she reached the camel going through the eye of a needle, it was apparent to the entire congregation she was addressing her half brother, fixing him with a steely eye and quoting the words by heart with unmistakable emphasis. He looked straight back at her and glowered.

It was a positive relief to stand up and start singing, although the first line of the hymn—"When the world around us throws all its proud deceiving shows"—was a bit too apt for comfort. A few voices faltered on the high notes and there were more throat clearings than usual. Faith knew the title of Tom's sermon, "Material Men and Women: How Much Is Too Much?" and so the whole thing made sense to her, but what did Penny have in mind? Campaign spending, business ethics, a quarrel over their father's will?

Faith settled back into the pew and prepared to listen to her husband talk about what constituted riches. She was willing to bet Alden wouldn't agree.

"Get the cards, Marta."

"Oh, Max, not tonight. I'm tired. Besides, we just read them Wednesday."

"A lot has happened since then."

"That's true and the moon is full tonight, so the power will be strong."

84

She got up, went to the bureau in the hotel room, and took a small intricately carved wooden box from the top drawer. Max sat down in one of the chairs by the window, in front of a low table. Marta placed the box carefully in front of him and drew open the drapes. Strong white moonlight streamed over the room and Marta turned off all the inside lights, except for one next to the table. She sat opposite Max and said, "Open the box." She preferred the querent to handle the cards as much as possible, transferring whatever vibrations he or she was carrying around to the pack. Max unwrapped several layers of bright silk and silently handed her the cards that were inside the package.

She looked through them and selected one. "I still see you as the King of Swords. All right?" He nodded and she placed the card face up on the table.

"Do you have the question firmly fixed in your mind?" Marta asked.

"Yes," answered Max, closing his eyes.

"Then shuffle the cards and cut."

Max shuffled several times with great deliberation, then hesitated before cutting the deck. With an almost defiant gesture, he quickly cut and leaned back in his seat.

Marta turned up the top ten cards, placing them in a pattern around the court card.

"What do you see?" he asked with a slight smile. "Anything different?"

"You're always too impatient. Don't rush me." Marta's face was anxious.

He leaned forward and scrutinized the cards. By now, he knew their characteristics as well as she did, but he couldn't interpret them.

"The Knight of Swords again—and the Chariot."

"Hush, Max, the cards often repeat."

Marta looked intently for several more minutes, then

85

pointed to the first card and intoned, "The Five of Wands covers him. He is involved in competition and struggle."

The film, Max thought. The card pictured five young men fighting. He'd be happy to have so few adversaries.

"The Four of Cups crosses him. He is weary and discontent. It is a time to rest in life's race."

"The Wheel of Fortune is beneath him. He has had much good fortune in his past. There have been times of plenty and times that were lean."

I know this. Max knew not to interrupt the reading. Get to the future, Marta.

"The Six of Cups is behind him, happy memories and possibly a friendship are moving out of his sphere, leaving a space for new ones."

Or not, Max reflected pessimistically.

"The Nine of Pentacles crowns him. There will be wealth for him far ahead."

"Solitary wealth!" Max blurted out. "I know that card!"

"Shhhh." Marta reached over and stroked his hand. He slunk back against the chair cushions.

"The Queens of Wands is before him."

Max's face brightened. It must be Evelyn. The Queen of Wands was a blonde. What other blondes were there? Or rather, other blondes who counted.

"The querent fears the Knight of Swords, the brown-haired youth who brings or takes away misfortune."

"The Two of Pentacles represents those around him. He is balancing many factors."

A balancing act. His whole life was one long balancing act. The cards never lied, he thought.

"The Chariot carries his hopes. He would like to achieve greatness."

Marta stopped speaking and looked at the last card, the outcome, with the director.

"The moon is strong tonight, Max. It was inevitable."

"And the other night, the same damn Moon card?"

Marta reassembled the deck.

"I know what it means, remember. Perils, deception, and secret enemies."

She sighed. "It depends on your question. The Moon can also illuminate your path and lead you away from danger."

"Do you want to know my question?" he asked.

"I think I know, Max dear."

"I wonder if you do."

CHAPTER 4

It is a curious subject of observation and inquiry, whether hatred and love be not the same thing at bottom.

THE AUDITORIUM AT PRITCHARD JUNIOR HIGH WAS packed and the highly partisan audience a bit more rowdy than was usual at Aleford public gatherings. At the moment, the stage was empty except for four gray metal folding chairs and a long table on which four glasses of water, a full pitcher, and a microphone had been placed.

Supporters of the three candidates waiting in the wings had had to choose between front-row seats and sitting en masse. The Alden Spaulding contingent opted for proximity and tried to snare as many as possible in the choice location close to the stage, elbowing their neighbors in a determined way. Penny Bartlett's fans went for unity and were occupying a block of rows under the balcony in the center of the room. The Heuneman forces had rallied undecidedly to the left-rear and front rows. Very few in attendance were uncommitted, and Faith wondered aloud to Tom why they had all bothered to come when everyone's minds were already made up.

"You shouldn't assume everyone is so firmly decided. I, for one, intend to listen with an open mind to all three candidates"—Tom paused and then just before his wife could jump on him, he continued—"then vote for Penny."

"You see, everyone is decided. We're only here because we're all afraid the opposition might outnumber us."

"Usually true, sweetheart, but I think in this election there are really quite a few people who have not made up their minds. If it was simply Penny against Alden, the choices would be clear, yet James is a dark horse. I don't know where he stands on a lot of things myself, and I've known him since I arrived in Aleford. Then, last but not least, let's not forget the entertainment value an event like this affords the town. Who could stay home, even to watch 'Murphy Brown,' when you have the opportunity to see your fellow citizens going at it hammer and tongs live?"

The candidates were taking their places. Peg Howard, the reference librarian at Aleford's Turner Memorial Library and president of the League, was calling the crowd to order. Whether it was because the audience was eager to hear the speakers or because of Peg's intrinsic association with silence, everyone immediately shut up.

"I'd like to welcome you all here tonight on behalf of the League of Women Voters and explain the format. Each candidate will have seven minutes to introduce himself or herself, then I will ask several questions prepared by the League. After that, you will have an opportunity to ask questions from the floor, and finally each candidate will have five minutes for a closing statement. Please refrain from any applause or vocal demonstrations, as it merely wastes our time." Peg looked sternly at the rows directly in front of her. Faith had no doubt the librarian would move to eject any miscreant from the hall and take away their borrowing privileges for a week.

Alden Spaulding was making quite a show of cradling the cast on his left wrist with his right hand. Faith was sure the wrist wasn't broken and that he had somehow intimidated the doctor into putting a cast on in a bid for sympathy votes. Audrey's remarks had eliminated any possibility that Spaulding would sue the caterers, but with everything that had been happening lately, Faith was jumpy and would have preferred to see the wrist bare, or in an Ace bandage at most.

"Now, James Heuneman will begin as he drew the highest card."

Peg passed the mike to James and he seemed a bit confused by its appearance for a moment. Admittedly, it was vintage, a twin of Edward R. Murrow's "London Calling" one. James managed to elicit a high-pitched squeal with his first word, then delivered a fairly bland speech about the importance of democracy in action and preserving the town for future generations. It took a total of three minutes. He handed the mike back to Peg with a smile of obvious relief.

"Thank you, Mr. Heuneman. Now Penelope Bartlett will present her remarks."

Penny took the mike easily, like the true club woman she was. Faith was surprised she wasn't wearing a hat and gloves, but she had put on one of her good flowered silk dresses and her handbag was sitting squarely between her feet, sensibly Cobbies-clad. She took the full seven minutes to touch on several subjects. A brief, and modest, description of her own qualifications—Wellesley '49, her volunteer work, years in Town Meeting—then proceeded to a description of the problems Aleford was facing with diminished resources and a population that was growing most rapidly in the over-sixty-five and school-age categories. "Two wonderfully entertaining groups," she declared, "but one like as not on a fixed income and the other with none. Which means we have to find ways to be fair to both. We'll need to reopen one of the schools we closed when enrollments were down, yet we can't let our older friends turn the heat too low or start eating one meal a day less as a result."

Faith couldn't imagine life being sustained with the heat turned any lower than it was in the majority of Aleford households, whatever the age of the occupants. In fact, it seemed the older they were, the more insistent they were on flinging windows open in December to let in some fresh air, or firmly shutting off the furnace in April because it was spring, come what may. Economizing by cutting down on food was another matter, and she knew from Pix and her Meals-on-Wheels work that malnutrition due to a lack of money was a big problem among the elderly.

Penny had barely finished—leaving, Tom whispered to Faith, a warm, fuzzy feeling, like one of the kids' blanket sleepers—when Alden seized the mike with his good hand and, without waiting for Peg's introduction, launched into his speech—or rather, attack.

"My good friends, here you see exactly what is wrong with us and why, if you'll pardon the expression, Aleford is going to hell in a hand basket."

90

Alden was opting for slightly less than the full treatment. Profanity, yes, but genteel, even folksy profanity.

"Now let's start with Mrs. Barlett's ill-advised, and I do not use these words lightly, notion of reopening schools left and right." He took a sheath of papers from his suit pocket and rustled them importantly in front of the microphone, startling James Heuneman, before quoting to the penny how much it would cost to reopen even one school and how much the town would lose in revenue from the current tenants, a computer-software development firm.

"If you elect me your selectman, I will not spend one cent to reopen these schools. We have no idea whether this trend will continue." He eyed the audience, as if to say, And it better not.

Faith poked Tom in the ribs. "If we have another baby, we'll have to answer to Alden . . ." "A pretty good reason," he mouthed back, and she was sorry she'd made the comment. Tom came from a long line of large families—to Faith more than two children fit the category—and was eager to maintain the tradition.

"The whole thing can be solved with a little ingenuity. That's what this town is lacking these days. Yes, a little ingenuity and belt tightening. Mobile classrooms can fill the bill nicely for a few years and then we can sell them to some other school system."

"Trailers!" Faith gasped to her husband, who nodded grimly.

"Four walls are four walls, and what happens inside them depends on the teacher, anyway. That's what all the research the fellows at Harvard—oh, pardon me—the fellows and gals, say."

Alden really was wicked. He'd probably picked up one

91

issue of *The Harvard Educational Review* and now would cut its findings to suit his cloth. Faith was suddenly nervous. "We'd better give some more money to Penny's campaign," she murmured. "You bet your sweet ass we will," he muttered.

Tom, from the evidence, was even more nervous.

Alden finished with a flourish. "Everywhere I go, I see the quality of small-town life deteriorating, and this was not why I put on our great country's uniform and laid my life on the line. We've got to go to war again and fight against the spendthrift mentality represented by my opponents here. I know you will help me in the struggle. Together we will succeed!" He smiled ingratiatingly and passed the microphone to an obviously annoyed Peg Howard.

"What war was he in?" Faith asked Tom. "Korean?"

"No war. National Guard. But to be fair, he stayed in a long time."

"Who wants to be fair?" Faith remarked, then decided to curtail her remarks. Millicent, in the next row, had turned around, and Faith didn't want to see a finger on those pursed lips.

Round one was over and Alden had definitely won, on shock value alone. He was at one end of the table. James sat between him and his half sister, which most of the audience knew was no accident.

Firmly in control of the microphone and protocol once more, Peg asked the questions prepared by the League. The candidates' replies contained few surprises, and the heat in the auditorium supplemented by all the warm bodies in the audience combined to make Faith very drowsy. She was having trouble keeping her eyes open and had resorted to pinching herself to stay awake. Even putting the finishing touches on the menu Alan Morris had requested for a surprise birthday party for Max Reed the next night failed to capture her attention, but the first question from the floor catapulted her into a state of total alertness.

It was asked by Daniel Garrison, sporting a gigantic Spaulding button, befitting his dual role of best—and some said only—friend and campaign manager.

"My question is for Mrs. Bartlett," he began suavely. "Would you not agree that it is absolutely necessary to have the trust and confidence of the entire community in order to serve on the board?"

"Yes, of course." Penny seemed puzzled about where the question was going, as was a sizable portion of the audience.

"You would agree that a member of this board, the most important single unit in governing the town, must be like Caesar's wife, let us say, and thus above reproach?"

Penny's face grew stern and her no-nonsense reply made it clear she thought the question just so much hollow campaign rhetoric, paving the way for a paean to Alden's own lofty qualifications.

"Mr. Garrison, could you get to the main point and leave Caesar's wife to Caesar? If you want to discuss accountability, I am more than happy to address the issue."

"I'm delighted to hear that, Mrs. Bartlett." He pronounced her name as if it was an alias. "Then you will not mind disclosing certain financial transactions made by you and your late husband, particularly regarding those reported on your state and federal income tax statements in 1971?"

There was an immediate buzz in the audience, followed by absolute silence. Faith reached for Tom's hand and whispered in his ear, "What is this? Alefordgate?"

Penny did not retreat. Faith's admiration for the woman doubled, if that was possible. Had she been attacked in such a manner, Faith's inclination would have been to hoist her loaded pocketbook and bean both Alden and his slimeball friend.

"Mr. Garrison." Penny smiled gently. She shook her head slightly in sorrow for someone led astray by bad companions. "I think this town knows me well enough after all these years to trust me. I have always been forthcoming, and my late husband was the same. I find your question inappropriate."

A real lady. Right down to her mother's wedding pearls and the slim gold band from Shreve's on her left ring finger, worn thin from years of constant wear.

It was this last article of jewelry that Faith noticed Penny began to twist after handing the microphone back to Peg. It was the sole outward sign the question may have disturbed her.

Dan Garrison tried to ask a follow-up question, but Peg was quick to cut him off. "Thank you, Mr. Garrison, we'll get back to you if there is time. However, I see many other hands."

After this beginning, the rest of the questions seemed tame, even the heated exchange between Alden and one of the PTA presidents over the use of mobile classrooms, which ended with the good lady red with frustration, exclaiming, "Why am I wasting my breath? You just don't get it and never will!"

The order for the closing statements had also been predetermined and Alden was last. After expressing his thanks in a similar manner to his opponents, he chose to use the rest of his time to discourse on the importance of trust.

"Public office is not sought lightly. Representing one's

fellow citizens is a sacred duty. Therefore, I find it extremely unsettling that Penelope Bartlett has refused to level with all of us tonight. She was given the opportunity to answer a specific question regarding her participation as a taxpayer and she avoided the issue. I don't know about you, my fellow Alefordians, but her response has made *me* nervous. Can we have someone in our highest office who presents a mere part of the picture? Is this the type of leadership we need in these difficult times? I leave it to you."

Alden pushed the microphone past James and toward the moderator, but it didn't quite make it. As Penny passed it on, it was impossible not to notice that her hand was shaking.

"What in heaven's name is he talking about?" Faith asked Tom fiercely. Peg had thanked them all for coming and everyone was assuming the burden of their winter overcoats. There was no longer any need to whisper, but Faith's seemed the only voice raised, and several people turned to look at her.

"I have no idea, honey. I can't imagine Penny or Francis Bartlett being involved in income tax fraud. But the scary part is, I also can't imagine Alden making an accusation without something to go on."

"I know. Insinuation is one thing, yet this is a direct challenge, and if he didn't have at least some sort of evidence, it would mean the end of his own bid for the seat."

Millicent was steaming up the aisle, scattering people, jackets, mufflers, and gloves to the left and right of her.

"Obviously, we'll have to issue a statement. The man is abominable! To even suggest such a thing! Poor Penny. She'll want to set the record straight as soon as possible, no doubt."

However, Penny most emphatically did not. Joining them in the lobby for coffee and cookies, she looked more than a little tired, but she was completely resolute.

"It's no one's business. I told that Daniel Garrison that people in Aleford should certainly trust me after all these years, and that's all I'm going to say. I will not start digging through Francis's and my old papers to please Alden and his crowd. No, Millicent, I know what you're going to say, but this is my decision."

Faith had never heard anyone say no to Millicent, and when it became apparent that lightning would not strike nor the earth open, she decided to follow suit.

"I think you are taking the right course, Penny. It's the desperate tactic of a desperate man. We should be encouraged, actually. If they have to resort to things like this, it means they must certainly think they'll lose."

"You don't know what you're talking about," Millicent snapped. Penny might be off limits, but the minister's wife wasn't—especially since it wasn't Miss McKinley's church. "Of course I'll abide by whatever Penny wants to do. She's the one running, after all, but people are going to talk."

"People have always talked. Now let's get some food before it's all gone." Penny took Millicent's arm and marched her over to the refreshments, prepared to mingle and drink yet another cup of coffee.

In bed that night, Tom agreed with Millicent.

"It would be much better if Penny cleared up whatever this is and issued some sort of statement to the *Aleford Chronicle*. Alden planted a seed, and in the kind of political soil we have around here, we are talking kudzu."

Faith nestled close to her husband and debated whether their marriage would withstand putting her cold feet against his warm legs.

She had decided both Tom and Millicent were right, but she wasn't about to admit it. "I think people will admire Penny's stand. There's entirely too much invasion of privacy when people run for office. She'll be admired for choosing a loftier path."

"You mean a lonelier path."

"And this from a man in your business," Faith chided as she slid her feet from the polar regions they were occupying to her husband's side of the bed.

"Faith!"

"So when can I see them all on 'Larry King Live'?" Niki asked late the following afternoon after Faith and Pix had thoroughly discussed the debate and its possible repercussions. "Your campaign makes the national stuff seem as dull as dishwater."

Pix, Faith, and Niki were packing everything up to take to Maxwell Reed's rented house in preparation for the evening's birthday party. According to Cornelia, Max would be completely surprised, particularly as the cast and crew had already presented him with a large cake in the shape of the letter *A* at lunch.

The dinner party was a select one—the principals, including Caresse and her mother; Alan Morris; Max's two production assistants, Cornelia and Sandra; the cinematographer, Max's close friend and longtime associate, Nils Svenquist; and the two producers, Kit Murphy and Arnold Rose, hitherto holed up in a suite at the Ritz-Carlton in Boston, biting their nails to the quick. Max allowed no one, but no one, on the set while he was working.

Faith had asked Alan what Max's favorite dish was.

"His mother's meat loaf, but don't try to copy it. Only

97

she can make it, I understand."

Although Faith didn't, she had nodded, anyway. Meat loaf? What kind of favorite dish was that?

"So what you're saying is, he's more of a meat and potatoes man than say sushi and angel hair pasta?"

"You got it."

Accordingly, Niki was now covering two impressive crown roasts of lamb from Savenor's new market on Charles Street with a coating of mustard, garlic, bread crumbs, and crushed juniper berries. No one had answered her Larry King question. Faith was busy peeling Yukon Gold potatoes, which would be boiled with whole cloves of garlic, the cloves removed, and mashed with basil, butter, and a mixture of warm cream and milk. Pix was making lists.

"Come on, you guys. Lighten up and talk to me. We have plenty of time. What's with this Alden Spaulding— and did any of you check to find out if that's his real name? Alden Spaulding. Give me a break."

Faith laughed. "Sorry, Niki, my mind was wandering."

Wandering to the sorbets they'd prepared to go along with the cake Alan Morris had insisted he would provide. He also said he'd take care of the wine, and Faith hoped it wouldn't be California Cooler.

"Alden Spaulding is his real name. Probably with something old and familial in the middle. And it's true, last night did make history in Aleford. The first out-and-out negative campaigning."

Pix finished her lists with a last definitive stroke of her pen. "You know what politics are like around here, Niki. It's not that there haven't been innuendos—and even dirty tricks—in the past. But no one has ever made such public accusations before."

"Have you ever heard any rumors about Penny and her

husband's finances?" Faith asked Pix. Pix was twenty years younger than Penny, but both their families had lived in town "forever."

"Never. The only gossip about Penny has been her feud with Alden, if that's the right word. They don't speak to each other."

"Millicent says Penny doesn't speak to Alden, not the other way around."

"She's splitting hairs. I don't know who's not talking. I just know they don't—and haven't ever since I can remember. And to answer your next question: I don't know why."

"Too bad it wasn't a real debate," commented Niki. "Would they have addressed all their remarks to the moderator?"

Faith was busy thinking again, and this time the sorbets had figuratively melted away. Tom had told her that Penny's husband had died around 1971—the time of the tax returns in question. It didn't take Sherlock Holmes to connect the two events. Even Watson would have tumbled to it.

Pix seemed to be reading her mind. "Penny has been a widow for so many years. She was about the age I am now when her husband died."

"And what would you do, Mrs. Miller?" Niki asked mischievously. "Carry your sainted husband's memory to the grave?"

"First of all, my husband is no saint, thank goodness, and no, I would not. I'd rather remarry than spend so many years alone. That is, if I could find someone halfway decent who wasn't interested in a nubile woman your age, Niki. You know—men get distinguished-looking and women get old."

"I told you not to read that Germaine Greer book,"

Niki chided. "Besides, I don't believe it's true. Look at you. Look at Faith."

They looked at each other, both in what they thought of as their prime, Pix from ten years further down the road than Faith.

"Ah, youth." Faith sighed. Had she ever held such opinions?

"Chill, Faith. I don't mean to suggest you two are antiques—maybe collectibles." They laughed. "Anyway," Niki continued, "how about you? What would you do if the Rev were suddenly called to his Maker?"

"We're going at the same moment, sweetie, so the point is moot."

A few hours later, Faith stood surveying the table in front of her, set for twelve. She'd selected a dark red and gold paisley cloth and brought her own gleaming silver. The china the caterers used for formal dinners was off-white, with a thin gold band. Food looked good on it and it matched all decors. She'd also filled the room with candlelight and flowers—alstroemeria, lilies, and boxwood in large bouquets tied with sheer gold ribbon on the sideboard and Sheraton card table against one wall; small single flowers in bud vases scattered on the table. Nothing with any scent, though. Nothing to interfere with the food. She took one last look and turned the dimmer switch on the brass chandelier lower. The glow was reflected in the large mirror that hung between two long windows and made the room seem larger than it was. The heavy damask drapes softened the dark landscape outside. The room was ready for these players, who, in fact, needed little help in transforming wherever they were into a stage set.

The house that Alan Morris had rented for Maxwell

Reed and Evelyn O'Clair was a beautiful central-entrance Colonial. It was a faithful reproduction, which gave it the advantage of a state-of-the-art kitchen, luxurious bathrooms—Faith had peeked at the master bedroom suite when she'd been in the house alone in the morning—and a dependable heating system. Faith checked the living room. The fire in the fireplace was burning nicely and the rest of the room was toasty warm, too, thanks to said system. She'd been to too many Aleford gatherings where the guests huddled together in front of the fire, avoiding figurative snowdrifts a few feet away. In this room, she'd placed masses of spring bulbs—pots of red tulips, purple hyacinth, and white freesia. Their fragrance, mixed with that of the burning logs, was not overwhelming—a whiff of spring in the midst of winter.

The fire reminded her of the fireplace at The Dandy Lion and of Cappy and Evelyn. It should be an interesting night. She hadn't seen too much of either of them. They usually ate in their trailers, but her glimpses of Evelyn and remarks the crew had dropped reinforced Faith's initial judgment that this was a prima donna for whom the line "All the world's a stage" could well have been written. She was always on—and always aware of her audience.

Faith walked back through the dining room. She wouldn't be waiting on the table herself, but there was a very convenient pass-through, which she lifted a few inches as she went into the kitchen: better air circulation.

In contrast, the kitchen was a whirl of activity. Niki had started to mash the potatoes. Tricia, an Aleford friend who had helped Faith unmask a murderer several years earlier, was now providing occasional aid of another sort. Tonight she would serve and clean up. At the moment, she was busy arranging chocolates from Lenôtre in Paris, Max's favorite, on several plates. They'd been flown in that morning, Cornelia the faithful factotum informed Faith when she dropped them off, handing the boxes over like so many bars of gold bullion—which was not far from the cost.

Tricia's husband, Scott, also an old acquaintance of Faith's and one who could give Cappy Camson or Tom Cruise a run for his money in a Better Than Average Looks competition, was on hand as bartender. Tricia and Scott had been married last spring and their reception at the Byford VFW hall was one Faith would never forget— for the great band and the trays of American cheese and bologna roll-ups.

"No wonder it costs so much to go to the movies," Scott commented. "Did you get a load of this stuff?" He pointed to the cases of wine, whiskey, and liqueurs that had been delivered during the afternoon.

"And that's not all." Faith waved him over to a second refrigerator in the pantry and opened the door. Magnums of Dom Pérignon nestled on the racks, waiting to be popped. "Max likes champagne. Good champagne."

Scott grinned, "So don't I."

Faith was used to the local colloquialisms and knew what the negative meant. She gave him what was supposed to be a stern look.

"I just meant that maybe an opened one will happen to be left over after they've rolled on out of here." He liked helping Faith occasionally. It made a change from his day job in an auto-body shop. "On second thought, I don't want Tricia getting used to it. She'll never go back to Bud."

Faith laughed. If Tricia wanted champagne, she'd get it. She wasn't a bossy person—Scott wouldn't care for that— but things she wanted had a way of happening—like a real

102

wedding, not a justice of the peace, and the latest, house hunting.

The staff looked attractive and professional in black trousers, white tuxedo-front shirts, a black tie for Scott, a black rosette for the rest. Faith made a bow in the direction of her profession and wore traditional checked chef's pants, altered to fit by a clever little seamstress in nearby Arlington. At the moment, everyone also wore long white aprons with *Have Faith* emblazoned in small red script on the bibs.

The kitchen door swung open. It was Alan Morris. Faith was surprised. She hadn't heard a car pull up.

"The producers are due any minute," he announced excitedly. "Nils is stalling Max over at the Marriott, pretending not to like the camera angle on the dailies they're watching. Evelyn's upstairs getting changed. We came together in her car and I think all four wheels were off the ground most of the time." It was obvious his breathless state was not entirely due to anticipation, but fear. Faith had heard about Evelyn's penchant for fast sports cars; a red Mercedes convertible had been rented for the Aleford shoot. "You can plan on serving dinner in an hour and a half."

This was what Faith had been waiting for—a timetable.

"Fine. Tricia and Scott will be in the hall to take coats and drink orders. We'll start serving the hors d'oeuvres as soon as the first guests arrive."

"It's going to be great. Max doesn't have a clue." Alan was as excited as a schoolboy. Apparently, it wasn't often that Max was in such a position, and Alan, for one, was enjoying it.

Thirty minutes later, Max walked through the front door, still arguing with Nils, who had made some excuse to come along. Nobody jumped out from behind the furniture, but the effect was the same. He was well and truly surprised—and touched. The nanny had brought Cordelia downstairs to show off, and Tricia reported in the kitchen, with a trace of possible wishful thinking, that the baby was absolutely beautiful. They all had a chance to confirm this when the nanny bustled in soon after to demand her dinner tray and to warm a bottle. Cordelia was beautiful. She seemed to be Evelyn's sole creation—a soft down of golden hair covered her head and drifted over her brow, where it met a pink-and-white porcelain complexion, and deep blue eyes. Pure O'Clair. Faith felt a sudden pang of longing for her own sweet baby girl, bundled in Carter's, not Baby Diors, as this exquisite creature was, but with her own inimitable Amy face. Maybe they'd decide not to shoot on Saturday and she'd have a chance to play with her kids.

Tricia was taking another tray of hot phyllo triangles and mushrooms stuffed with chorizo sausage out to the living room. "Scott says he's going to need some more champagne and another bottle of scotch soon." Faith headed for the pantry, saying, "Tell him to meet me in the dining room." Tricia nodded, carefully pushing open the swinging door. She was terrified of smacking into someone. Normally unflappable, she was unhinged a little by the evening's proximity to so many celebrities.

Faith stood in the dining room, listening to the happy buzz of conversation and the crackling fire. Someone, probably Alan, was keeping it going. Scott walked in, took the bottles, smiled ingenuously and said, "You should see the outfit on Evelyn O'Clair. I wish I could spray-paint that good! I thought they used all sorts of trick photography to make them look like this on the screen, but she's even sexier in person. I wouldn't throw her out of—"

104

"Be quiet, you lecherous old married man, or I'll tell on you." Faith hustled him back to his post.

She'd get a look at the dress later from the pass-through. The men were all in black tie, Tricia had told them immediately, awestruck—"and nobody's even getting married!" she'd exclaimed. Max, of course, had arrived in his perennial work attire, corduroy pants, a denim work shirt, and a baggy Irish fisherman's sweater. He'd raced upstairs and replaced the sweater with an incongruously elegant burgundy velvet smoking jacket—Evelyn's birthday gift.

Faith hoped they wouldn't linger too long over their drinks. She'd allowed an hour. Alan had stressed it was to be an early evening. Work would start again promptly the next morning at 7:30. But Tricia reported that no one showed any signs of moving toward the dining room. The catering staff was used to changes in schedule. The only problem would be the lamb. It would be a crime to serve it overdone.

At last, Tricia appeared to say that Alan had announced dinner, and described what had been going on.

"They insisted on keeping the baby downstairs and the nanny didn't seem too happy about it. Cappy Camson tried to get her to have a glass of champagne, but she said, 'Not while on duty, sir,' just like a cop. He must be nuts about kids. He's been playing with the baby all this time, making funny faces, and Evelyn O'Clair is laughing her head off. In a very ladylike way, of course." Scott followed behind her with the drinks tray and as many of the dirty glasses as he had been able to squeeze on. Faith told him to return discreetly for the rest, since they'd be having coffee and liqueurs in the living room after dinner, then to come hack and pour the champagne.

Everyone was seated and Faith opened the pass-through

to hand Tricia the plates of steaming butternut squash soup that Niki was ladling out and garnishing with toasted pine nuts. A basket of warm, crusty spiced corn sticks sat at either end of the table.

It was a festive and attractive-looking group. Evelyn was sitting down, and if her bodice was any indication, the red satin of her dress might have been applied with a spray gun. Her hair was piled on top of her head, all the better to show off a necklace and earrings with diamonds in the Gibraltar range compared to most rocks. Cornelia was in red, too, but a deep maroon velvet. She was wearing her grandmother's garnets, Faith noted, and looked, well, like Cornelia. Marta had diverged from the scarlet theme and glistened softly in layers of silver gray silk, Caresse wore the party dress she'd worn as Pearl and was the only person who appeared bored. Her mother, sitting across from her, looked anxious and immediately drank some of her champagne when Scott poured it. Caresse was more than a full-time job, Faith imagined. Jacqueline Carroll looked very elegant in an emerald cashmere knit. Her dark hair was lustrous, loosed from its usual French twist. Faith saw Max regard her appraisingly in the candlelight. She half-expected him to pull out a lens from his pocket to see how the frame looked.

Candlelight—kind to both men and women; but more than candlelight had to be responsible for Sandra Wilson's transformation. She'd squeezed in a visit to Makeup and Wardrobe. If Faith hadn't known who it was, she never would have recognized her. Her fine blond hair seemed to have doubled in volume and deepened in color to a rich, shimmering honey tone. It was artfully disarrayed, brushing her naked shoulders. Her dress, what there was of it, was a strapless gold sequined sheath. Her carmine lips were almost too red—suggestive of a Transylvanian repast. But the whole effect was stunning, and Cappy, sitting next to her, was in danger of ignoring his hostess at the head of the table to his other side. A danger Evelyn quickly and firmly averted by engaging him in conversation.

Arnold Rose stood up, glass in hand, "A toast—to Max, the most brilliant director in the business. Happy birthday!"

Everyone stood up and repeated, "Happy birthday," the sentiment unmarred by what Faith was sure was Caresse's deliberate overturning of her chair as she rose. Then Cappy called out, "Speech! Speech!"

Max debated with himself for a moment, then looked at the expectant faces around the table, groaned dramatically, and grinned. "If I must."

"You don't fool us for a minute, Maxie, you old windbag," Arnold said affectionately.

"A phrase has been running through my mind since we started shooting. It's something Napoleon was supposed to have said: 'What a novel my life is.' " Max paused dramatically, then continued, the cadence of his words measured, even stately. "I look at myself—at us—and think, What a movie my life is. I can't remember not looking at the world through a lens, so to speak, then running the rushes all back in my mind. Everything I see, everything I do is part of the script, and you, my friends, are forever in the cast. On-screen and off."

He held his glass high above his head, "To all of you, I am profoundly grateful." He drained his glass but did not sit down. Scott quickly filled it again, and in the brief interim, Max seemed to take on some of his Chillingworth character. He raised his glass, not high but outstretched toward Evelyn at the opposite end of the table, then quoted his muse in a voice that was low and pregnant with

107

meaning, like the doctor's, "Hawthorne wrote, 'In most hearts, there is an empty chamber waiting for a guest.' In my heart, that chamber is full. To you, my love. Now let's eat."

Everyone laughed. The solemnity was over. It was a typical Max moment—pathos to bathos in sixty seconds. They sat down, started to eat the soup, and the dinner was launched.

Faith closed the pass-through, but not completely. Niki raised her eyebrows, commenting, "Tricks of the trade?" She was sautéing walnuts for the brussells sprouts. It wasn't a vegetable known to cause dinner guests to stand up and cheer, but with the walnuts and the French *huile de noix*—walnut oil—dressing, the aroma alone made instant converts.

After ceremoniously showing Max one of the succulent crown roasts, Tricia and Scott served the table. It was all going beautifully.

Too beautifully.

Alan had either turned out to be an oenophile after Faith's own heart or had received remarkably good advice. They were drinking a 1970 Léoville Las Cases, a Médoc, with the lamb—a lot of it, Scott remarked after returning to the kitchen for yet another bottle.

In vino veritas, and the producers were the first to start, tongues loosened.

"Maxie, Maxie," Kit Murphy began in a slightly wheedling tone, "what would it hurt for Arnold and me to come out just for one day to see some dailies, maybe visit the set, schmooze with the crew?"

Max's face clouded slightly.

Arnold jumped in. "We're not talking interference. We're not talking reporting back to the studio. We're only talking interest, Max. We're interested."

Before Max could answer, Caresse, fortified by several tumblers of Coca-Cola, announced, "If you're so interested, you might be interested to know I'm off the picture."

"Caresse!" her mother admonished. "You know this isn't true."

There was a pause as everyone waited for Max's response. When it became apparent that he wasn't going to say anything, preferring to help himself to the large bowl of mashed potatoes left on the table and taking a generous swig of wine, Kit spoke up,

"She's right, isn't she, Max? You know the publicity has already gone out. And we agreed—these guys, Caresse, Evelyn, Cappy, they're 'the money,' remember. . . ."

"Look, whose picture is this? And so long as we're reminiscing, let's not forget about the artistic-license clause."

"We haven't forgotten about it, but what's going on?" Arnold Rose's voice was a whole lot more threatening than Kit's had been. A fascinated kitchen staff gathered close to the pass-through. They could hear every word and, by bending down low, could peer in. Arnold and Kit reminded Faith of good cop/bad cop. She wondered whether it was their standard modus operandi.

"Nothing's going on." Max's voice was studiously casual. "I've changed a few scenes, used the baby more, but Miss Carroll is not out of the picture. And, as her charming mother said, she knows it," he added.

"But I'm out of here. Come on, Mom." Having stirred up her hornet's nest, Caresse was bored again. MTV was a whole lot better than this.

"Sweetheart. It's not polite to leave before dessert." Jacqueline sounded wistful. Maybe she didn't want to miss the cake.

109

Caresse was at the dining room door. "Oh, Mom, for God's sake, we'll stop at Friendly's if you want. The food is a whole lot better, anyway."

In the kitchen, Scott grabbed at his chest and pretended to pass out. Faith thought of Pix's words. "Spare the rod and spoil the child" had never seemed more apt.

"Let her leave if she wants to." Evelyn's dismissive tone gave way to parody. "I'm sure the poor child is merely overtired and overexcited."

Jacqueline did not fail to recognize the allusion, and flushed.

Alan reassured her, "Don't worry about it, Jackie. We'll see you on the set tomorrow morning. I'll get your driver."

He then strode into the kitchen so quickly that the caterers had to scramble madly to get away from the pass-through to other locations. As the door swung completely in, they presented an impassive, uninterested front. "Mrs. Carroll and Caresse are leaving now," he said to one of the chauffeurs who was sitting in the breakfast nook with the others, playing cards. The man jumped up immediately and went out the back door. Alan spoke to Faith: "Could someone help them with their wraps? And several glasses could use touching up."

"Certainly," Faith replied, reaching for a decanter of the Bordeaux she'd prepared and handing it to Scott. Tricia went to fetch their coats. Alan's presence in the kitchen reminded Faith that he had neglected to tell her where the cake was. They had searched high and low but hadn't turned up a crumb.

"I haven't been able to find the birthday cake."

"Don't worry"—he smiled secretively—" it's all set. You just put out the plates with the sorbet and leave room for the cake. We'll be bringing it in from the den."

110

"This must be some cake," Niki commented after he'd returned to the table. "Little Caresse is going to be sorry she missed it."

Scott had returned and was eating a piece of lamb with his fingers. "I don't think 'Little Caresse' is ever sorry, but I'd love the chance to try to make her be."

Faith was looking through the pass-through again. It was time to clear the plates from the main course. The unpleasantness had apparently been swept under the thick Oriental rug and everyone was talking to his or her neighbor. Cornelia's unmistakable voice rose above the others. She was expounding on the influence of Hegel on Sergei Eisenstein to Cappy Camson across the table. "The triadic process is so obvious in *Ivan the Terrible*," she said. "Thesis, antithesis, synthesis—it's positively riveting." Cappy nodded amiably. He had moved his chair closer to Evelyn's. Sandra Wilson had left the table—the powder room? Faith felt as if she was watching a play or a movie. The next act was about to begin. Marta stood up and took Caresse's empty seat beside Max, placing herself between him and the two producers. Faith was sure she was not misinterpreting either the ironic glance Marta gave Cornelia in passing or the intent of Ms. Haree to act as a buffer between her director and producers.

The Parisian chocolates had been placed on the table and Max thanked Cornelia. "I know the Stuyvesant touch." She colored almost prettily and looked about to note her rival's reaction, but Sandra had still not returned. Faith was waiting for a signal from Alan to serve the sorbets—a trio of apricot, Granny Smith, and black current. She opened the hatch a little farther. Cappy and Evelyn were deep in conversation. Max, protected from the demands of his producers by Marta's bulk, cast his eye absently around the room. His gaze came to rest on

111

Evelyn at the opposite end of the table. He watched her for a moment, then spoke to Nils, next to him.

"Nils, I haven't seen Evelyn all evening. Trade places, won't you? I want to hold her gorgeous hand, and you can tell Cappy about the town hall scene for the hundredth time, so maybe he'll get it right."

Faith couldn't see Evelyn's face, but Cappy did not seem overly thrilled with the change in seating or the director's caustic remark. The actress got up and moved next to Max. He greeted her with a kiss and whispered something in her ear. Then he threw one arm around her shoulders and left it there.

Alan Morris had also been absent from the room, and upon entering, he came directly to the kitchen.

"It's time! "he announced. "I'll need this young man here to help me with the cake, and perhaps you'd like to cut it, Faith. The meal has been superb and I know Max will want to thank you."

Faith was a little puzzled. Niki was right, this really must be some cake. She went to get a knife, then followed Alan and Scott out of the kitchen. Tricia started the sorbet. The glasses for red wine were removed and replaced with flutes filled with more champagne.

A moment later, the table was startled into silence at the sound of music. Solemn music. Religious music. Chants from the *Bay Psalm Book*. Then Alan and Scott wheeled a dolly in with an enormous cardboard cake on it. Slowly, the top lifted off and Sandra Wilson dressed as Hester Prynne in period clothes emerged, her head bowed and her hands clasped together at her waist. A huge scarlet letter was pinned to her breast. She stood demurely as the music continued. Everyone smiled politely. Suddenly, with one swift motion, she knocked the sides of the cake down, tore the letter from her dress, flung it at Max, and proceeded to execute a very professional striptease as the taped music changed to one of the sexiest renditions of "Happy Birthday" anyone had ever heard since Marilyn Monroe sang it to JFK. The room exploded in applause and laughter.

Then as it became apparent that Miss Wilson intended to go for broke, the reactions changed. Faith found herself spellbound. The contrast of Hester's chaste under-garments and Sandra's explicit performance was both funny and a turn-on. Scott was grinning from ear to ear, as were the other men. Kit Murphy was chanting, "Go, Hester, go." Max himself shouted, "Yeah, baby!" every once in a while. Marta sat with a neutral smile; Cornelia openly scowled and reached for a chocolate. It was difficult to read Evelyn's expression. She seemed to have drawn the curtains. Annoyance? Pity? Sandra was getting close to the end. It was hard not to be impressed by the woman's great body, and Faith resolved to increase her own work-outs once the shoot was over. Alan moved out of the shadows and handed Sandra two lighted sparklers. She was down to a red G-string and two red pasties in the shape of A's.

Definitely not your ordinary Aleford dinner party.

Sandra wriggled over to Max, said a final happy birthday, and planted one on him—a long one. He emerged breathless and laughing again. Her red lipstick was smeared all over his mouth. Her grabbed her for a repeat. Alan placed a conventional cake with candles before the director, gloating over the success of his surprise.

"Alan, you old son of a bitch, you!" Max remonstrated jokingly.

"Make a wish, Max." It was Marta.

He blew out the candles and Faith served the cake. The

113

sorbet had melted into pools of purple, orange, and pale green.

The next day on the set, Faith felt as though the night before had been a dream.

Alan had obviously been waiting for the truck and as soon as she got out, he asked her to set up a table with plenty of coffee and snacks at the bottom of the meadow near the woods.

"We're shooting a test of the forest scene today," he said, literally rubbing his hands together in anticipation. "With Sandra standing in for Evelyn." He didn't say anything about the party.

Cornelia followed at his heels. In this case, Faith did not expect accolades, or even a comment. She assumed Cornelia would prefer to forget the whole night. What Sandra had placed on Max's plate made Faith's fellow alum's chocolates look like last year's Halloween candy.

"Max wants a couple of cans of Jolt cola. I assume you've got some," she demanded.

Faith always stocked plenty of this super-caffeinated drink on shoots.

"Is that all he wants—nothing to eat?"

"Yes, he's . . ."

Faith finished for her. "A little hung over?"

"Absolutely not," Cornelia retorted. "He's just not very hungry after all that heavy food you prepared. I wasn't hungry myself this morning."

"Does anyone else want anything? Cappy, Evelyn?"

"Lady Evelyn has just fired her hairdresser—again. When I saw her, she was yelling for someone to give her a shampoo, so I doubt she needs food, and I haven't seen Cappy. just get me the soda. Please."

Cornelia adjusted her coat and shook her hair back, like

a dog that's come in out of the rain. She obviously felt much better.

"Must be going. So much to do to stay on track. We're shooting the forest scene today. The weather is perfect, Max says."

She was gone abruptly before Faith could say, "Have a nice day."

Not that the day was nice. Max's idea of perfect weather seemed to run to overcast gray skies. But in this instance, he was staying close to Hawthorne. Faith remembered the forest scene well. She'd gone over it again after Cornelia's description of Hester and Dimmesdale's roll in the moss. The day was "chill and somber." What sunshine was around retreated before Hester's steps, and her precocious child, Pearl, remarked that the sunshine must not love her mother. It was a sensual scene in the book, but they had kept their clothes on. Faith wondered how all this was going to be handled.

She went back to the tent to help with the unloading and asked Pix if she would take charge of getting the table set up near the woods. She told Pix and Niki about Cornelia's request for Jolt cola.

"We'd better have a lot of the stuff handy," Niki said. "You should have seen how much booze they put away, Pix. And I wouldn't be surprised if the esteemed director is tired, besides being hung over. From the way he was looking at Evelyn, he definitely had plans for after the company left."

It was also the way Cappy had been looking at Evelyn, Faith remembered. The dress had been sensational and when she'd stood up to move to Max's side, Cappy, who could have just about anybody he wanted in Hollywood—or anywhere else, for that matter—had been positively drooling. Who says clothes don't make the woman? Faith

115

repeated one of her favorite adages to herself with the vaguely uncomfortable feeling she'd be editing an almanack soon.

Pix was back almost immediately for another urn of coffee. "Everyone is freezing despite the lights and portable heaters. Especially Cappy and Sandra! This is going to be some movie! They're writhing around on some sort of astromoss next to the brook, stark naked. I saw them when I went to tell Alan the table was set up. They must have body makeup on, because they look perfect. Or maybe they are perfect." Pix had come to terms with her cellulite years before, yet she still found it hard when someone else appeared not to have any. "And they're shiny. The sweat of passion. Faith, you have to sneak up and see this."

So Max was going for nudity. *A* was going to be an X.

For a moment, Faith held back. It was without question prurient interest, but then she couldn't resist. It wasn't so much to see the scene as to see the scene—how everyone else was reacting and what they were doing. If she got caught, she could say she had to discuss something with Alan. What a convenient person he was, always around when anyone needed him. Always around. It occurred to her that she had no sense of what he was like, except as the fixer. Was he content to play second banana to Max on into the sunset, or did he aspire to a directorship himself Cornelia seemed to hold him in some contempt. A location scout. Faith was sure there was a whole lot more to the man.

She started up the path and circled around back of the lights to a grove of trees overlooking the brook. Sandra, wearing a ratty old fake fur coat, was sitting in a chair, waiting for the next shot. Cappy was in a Ralph Lauren duffel, talking on a cellular phone. Max was standing still, looking at them. Evelyn was nowhere in sight. Caresse was arguing with her mother. "I'm not in the scene again until later. Why do I have to stand around watching this gross stuff?" Max tuned in to their conversation.

"By all means, go back to your trailer and we'll call you. We may not even get to it today, so there's no need for you to stay out here in the cold."

Caresse had the surprising decency to thank him, and her mother beamed as they left.

They got ready to start up again and when the clap board came down, the action really did start. The minister in his jeans and Hester in her filmy white dress sat motionless on the green carpet. Hester spoke: "We have done nothing wrong. Before God or anyone else." It was obviously Reed's deathless prose, not Hawthorne's.

Dimmesdale took her hand. "But I must leave. You know that."

Hester nodded and stood up. "You will not go alone. I will make you very happy." At the word happy, she reached to her shoulders, undid some fastenings, and her dress dropped to the ground, taking the scarlet letter with it. Faith was so transfixed by the moment that she almost forgot to stay hidden behind the trees. Sandra in her body makeup looked like a goddessAphrodite. The whole crew seemed to be holding a collective breath. The forest was completely silent. Not even a breeze swayed in the trees whose bare branches were beginning to swell slightly with buds.

Faith looked at Max. He was in his Chillingworth makeup and costume. There was a smile on his face and he was nodding, then as Dimmesdale removed his clothes and drew Hester down to the ground, Max looked irritated. He seemed about to stop the scene, but didn't. It could be that it wasn't going the way he wanted. Or it could be that he was staying in character.

For some reason known to the director, Marta Haree as Mistress Hibbins was positioned on the other side of the brook in her bright gypsylike clothes. She was beckoning to them, slowly waving her arms. As the two began to make love, she called out triumphantly, "I will see you in the forest tonight!"

The rest of the players looked merely interested, or, in the case of Alan Morris, entranced.

"Cut!" Max screamed.

Faith realized she had to get back quickly. Max might decide to break for lunch now. She ran back toward the meadow, when suddenly she realized she wasn't alone. Someone else was moving among the trees. Moving furtively.

Whoever it was didn't want to be seen.

CHAPTER 5

Yet, if death be in this cup, I bid thee think again, ere thou beholdest me quaff it.

IT IS NOT EASY FOR AN INDIVIDUAL TO CREEP ABOUT the forest on little cat—or more aptly, squirrel-feet when hitting two hundred pounds on the scale represents some weight loss. Therefore, it was only a matter of moments before Faith identified the creeper as Alden Spaulding. His efforts to escape detection by hiding in a grove of slender birches was ludicrous. She walked rapidly to his side,

118

greeting him heartily, not from any desire for his company, but rather to find out what he was up to.

"Alden! Out for a stroll? You didn't pick the best day for it."

He seemed flustered and was hastily trying to fit something into the pocket of his overcoat at her approach. He closed the flap and kept his pudgy hand over the object from the outside. It made a bulge that was difficult to identify. What on earth was the man doing?

"Harumph"—Faith had never actually heard anyone say this and was delighted—"Mrs. Fairchild. Yes, I am out to get some air. Often walk this way. It's conservation land, you know. Open to everyone." He glared at her.

Faith was enjoying herself. It was nice to watch him squirm for a change. She knew, of course, why he was there, and she tried to push aside the thought that it was also why she was there. Somehow Alden had found out about the nude shots, or he'd gotten lucky. Whichever, this particular conservation tract was far from Alden's house. He would have had to drive. Getting some air, indeed.

"I would have thought you'd favor Simond's Woods. Isn't the entrance at the end of your road?"

"Sometimes people like a change." He had regained his composure, and nastiness. "Take the election, for example. Come March twenty-sixth, you'll see some big changes in town. Now, good day. My regards to the Reverend." He stomped off in the direction of the main road, where he must have left his car.

"Good-bye," Faith called after him. "Interesting running into you." Nothing would induce her to say *nice*. And it had been interesting.

Alden Spaulding creeping about the woods. Alden Spaulding, the creep! He had made certain feeble, off-color suggestions to her when she'd first arrived in Aleford, before he knew she was married to his minister. And he was one of those men who always stand too close to women. Faith invariably took a step backward when he came near her.

She retraced her steps back through the woods. No, Alden was no latter-day Thoreau. The mysterious object was probably a pair of high-powered binoculars. All the better to see you with . . .

Pix and Niki were both waiting at the table. No one else was around and apparently Max hadn't called a break yet.

"So?" they asked in unison.

"As the lady with the golden retrievers said, 'This is going to be some movie,' " Faith concurred.

"Maybe I can get a peek," Niki said. "There isn't much of Cappy unknown to his adoring public after those ads, but the real thing is something else again." She rolled her eyes. "Mama wants to see those buns!"

Faith burst out laughing. Niki was always falling in and out of love. Her latest was getting an MBA at the Harvard Business School, but Niki had cheerfully assured them he was the type you didn't bring home—much, much too eligible. "In my family," she'd said, "what you do is invite the guys with tattoos who had five o'clock shadows in third grade, then when you finally have someone you want, they're so relieved, they'll welcome anyone who's even related to someone with a job."

Niki continued to enthuse about the film. "One of the crew just told us that this afternoon they're going to shoot from a helicopter. The idea is to go slowly from a close-up of the lovers to a panorama of the whole countryside."

Faith didn't recall a shot like it from Max Reed's other films and it could be very effective—the camera virtually

120

rising into the sky over Hester and Dimmesdale until they disappeared in an extra-long shot of the bleak New England landscape. The helicopter was already big news in Aleford.

"This must be why they're shooting with Evelyn's stand-in this morning. Checking the lighting, positions."

Pix and Niki started to giggle. "Can't practice those positions too much," Niki gasped.

"You two are impossible! Pix, what would Sam say?"

"Which one? Husband would be thrilled; daughter would say—no, make that would go—'Oh, Mother.' This seems to be the extent of her conversational repertoire lately—at least with me."

Faith wasn't looking forward to either of her children's adolescence, although the Miller teens appeared fine, even fun, to a nonfamilial eye. She changed the subject. She had almost let Alden the nature lover slip from her thoughts.

"I wish we could use this somehow in the campaign," Pix said after Faith described her chance encounter, "but I can't think how." The campaign was constantly in mind.

"What a lech! It's disgusting. The man must be sixty at least!" Niki exclaimed.

"His age is not the disgusting part, you ignorant child," Faith was quick to retort. So forward-thinking in everything else, Niki and her cohort aped all their predecessors and ran headlong into the "anyone over thirty" roadblock.

"I know, I know," Niki conceded, "but would *you* want to go to bed with him? Probably has drawers stuffed with inflatable party pals."

"To borrow an expression of Ben's, Yuck." Faith recoiled.

She and Niki left Pix to return to the final lunch

121

preparations.

"Why are they shooting with Evelyn's stand-in and not Cappy's?" Faith wondered aloud. "He must have one."

"You've got me," Niki said.

"Unless Cappy wanted to do it." Sandra's striptease the night before might have been too tantalizing to resist. Or maybe Cappy just wanted to rehearse—a rehearsal falling into the category of "It's a tough job, but *somebody's* got to do it."

The crew seemed even more wired than usual. The medallions of pork with winter vegetables and pans of *spanakòpeta,* a Greek spinach and feta cheese phyllo dough pie, disappeared in record time. No one lingered over coffee and dessert. It was obvious that today's shoot was proving more energizing than any amount of Jolt cola. The principals all ate in their trailers and their trays, too, came back early. Everyone, it seemed, wanted to get back to work.

Alan Morris motioned to Faith. He had come to lunch later and was one of the last ones in the tent. She sat down across from him. He was scraping the last bit of the spinach pie from his plate.

"There's plenty more. Would you like me to get you another piece?" Faith asked.

"No, thank you. I've had two already. You are really a fabulous cook and I wondered if you could help us out tonight. Max is going to be looking at some of the rushes from the last few days in private at the hotel. Do you think you could bring over some desserts, coffee, whatever, for a nosh around seven o'clock? He'll have had dinner at home. I hate to ask you after all your work last night, but we won't be late."

"Certainly," Faith replied. "He liked that cookie assortment the other day at lunch, didn't he? I can add some pastries, fruit, and a crème brûlée if you want."

"Sounds perfect. And, by the way, Max doesn't want too many people to know about the screening. He isn't asking everyone, so . . ."

"I won't say a word," Faith promised.

Tom wasn't thrilled at the idea of Faith's overtime, but he sensibly held his tongue. The shoot wouldn't last much longer and he planned that his marriage would. Faith could have asked Niki or someone else to go, but she was intrigued by all the secrecy. Besides, she'd never seen dailies screened. Maybe they would let her stay.

When she arrived at the Marriott, Alan Morris was waiting for her and swiftly ushered her into the room they were using. The hotel had set up a table and there was someone to help her unload the car. Unless they planned on serving themselves, she would be seeing the footage.

It was a select group—only Max; Nils Svenquist; Marta; Cappy Camson; Max's stand-in, Greg Bradley; some of the lighting crew, and Alan. Everyone settled into comfortable chairs, their plates heaped high with goodies. What a civilized way to watch a movie, Faith thought. Whenever Tom and she went lately, it seemed that either the seats were left over from the days when theaters had stars on the ceilings and organ music or the entire population of Aleford High noisily surrounded them.

The lights went out and the film rolled. Faith wasn't surprised to realize it was today's takes. Max must have paid a premium to get the lab in Cambridge to process them so fast. Was it to check out the expensive helicopter shots, or for some other reason! Faith had her answer almost immediately.

Sandra's face filled the screen, and before long, her body. The takes were repetitive, but it didn't matter. Each one was totally captivating. No one said a word.

The camera was in love with the young PA. It was difficult to believe this was the same person scuttling about anonymously, clipboard in hand, behind the scenes.

On-screen, she became the embodiment of desire. The final effect was in no way pornographic, but erotic—and more. Her expression conveyed a sadness, an awareness that the lovers were destined to remain forever apart. There was no sound, only the images. It was so powerful that Faith wondered whether Max might dispense with the dialogue in the final version, as well. Sandra's performance seemed to inspire Cappy. The minister's face continued to register nuances of his guilt and torment, even in the midst of passionate joy. At the end of one of the takes, the camera moved away from the couple and shot a close-up of the letter pinned to Hester's discarded dress.

"I was playing here, Max. You can think about it. Maybe too obvious, I don't know. But the girl—she's brilliant," Nils remarked. The footage continued. "She's—"

Whatever else he had intended to say was cut off as the lights were flipped on and a figure who had slipped unnoticed into the dark room ran toward the director, shrieking, "You bastard! You goddamned bastard! You thought I wouldn't find out! Just going over to the hotel to talk to Nils!"

It was Evelyn O'Clair. She was dressed in tight black jeans and a red suede jacket with Joan Crawford shoulder pads. Her hair was pulled back in a low ponytail. For an instant, her outstretched hands and long fingernails threatened Max's face. There seemed no way he would avoid carrying the marks of her wrath.

She dropped her arms to her sides. "No, I'm not going to hurt you. Not now. Chillingworth with scratch marks."

124

Her voice had changed completely. She was the tragic queen. Injured dignity. "Some of us are professionals. Some of us play by the rules. What do you want, Maxie? You want to make porno flicks. Go ahead. Use her. But finish this picture first. You're filming me now."

Max put his arms around her and spoke softly, but his words were audible. Everyone in the room remained motionless.

"Sweetheart, you're leaping to conclusions . . . the wrong conclusions. You came in at the beginning, the morning takes. I only used her to get things set up for the afternoon, your takes. We're going to see those now. The real thing."

True or not, his words seemed to have the intended effect on Evelyn, at least partially—or maybe she wanted to see her footage.

"Let's have something to eat and then see the rest," Alan suggested. Everyone stood up gratefully and refilled their plates. Cappy Camson joined Max and Evelyn. He seemed to be adding to Max's reassurances. Faith heard someone say, "She's just a PA."

The lights went off again. Evelyn's chair was between Max's and Cappy's. When the rushes started, from her position directly behind them, Faith could see Evelyn was holding hands with both of them.

Faith was curious to see the contrast between the two actresses, but before the nude scenes, Alan came back to the table and whispered to her that she could go home.

"I promised not to keep you late, and this could go on for quite a while. I'll make sure the hotel locks the room."

Faith was disappointed, yet it was clearly a dismissal.

"Thank you. We'll pick up our equipment in the morning."

"Thank *you*. Everything was delicious, as usual. Good

night."

"Good night."

On film, Evelyn was standing up, about to drop her dress. This footage included sound, and her rich inflections added to the sensuality of the scene. Sandra Wilson might have the body, but she didn't have the voice.

When Faith got into her car, her disappointment soon turned to relief. She hadn't realized how tired she was. She drove down Mall Road and turned onto Middlesex Turnpike toward Aleford. She'd be home in ten minutes, and in bed in twenty. With that comforting thought, she let her mind wander. Was there some reason Alan hadn't wanted her to stay? He'd been sitting on the other side of Max and the director had leaned over to say something to him just before Alan had come back to Faith. Was it Max's idea that Faith leave? Maybe he didn't want anyone to see the "real" scenes until the movie was released. Or maybe he didn't want her to witness another kind of scene. Or maybe he, or Alan, simply thought it was getting late and that since they really didn't need her, she could go home.

Evelyn had certainly been ripping—or delivering a fine performance. If you were good—and she was—you could create a role to suit the occasion, then play it to the hilt. Which was it tonight, Evelyn the woman or Evelyn the actress? Holding hands with both men added an element of intrigue—and humor—to the part. One thing was certain: Evelyn O'Clair wasn't doing Hester Prynne.

Faith pulled into her driveway, found the strength to hoist the garage door, and ten minutes later was sinking into slumber beside her almost-oblivious mate.

The next day, Thursday, whether because of the

126

associations or because the sun was trying to break through the clouds, Max abandoned the forest scene and decided to do an interior shot. Sandra was in her jeans again, running around trying to locate a bolt of sheer drapery material that Max wanted pinned on the walls of the Pingrees' dining room, now Hester's prison cell.

Cornelia was stalking around in high dudgeon. She seemed to invite inquiry and Faith was happy to comply. The movie production was intriguing beyond all expectations.

"Sandra"—Cornelia's voice dripped with scorn—"has managed to lose an essential prop and we can't shoot, can't even arrange the lighting until she finds it."

Faith felt sorry for the PA—from the Follies to folly, *sic transit gloria mundi.*

The fabric was still missing at lunchtime. Faith was back in the catering kitchens with Ben and Amy when Pix returned from her post at the craft services table.

"They finally found the fabric. It was in the barn, which seems like a strange place to put such easily soiled material. And Sandra swears she didn't, but people are pretty annoyed with her, anyway. Max decided by the time they got the room the way he wanted it, it would be too late to shoot, so he sent everybody except a few people home."

"Did anyone say anything about Saturday?" Faith was thrilled to have the job, but she'd love a real day off. They didn't shoot on Sundays; only that was not a day of rest in the Fairchild household.

"No, not yet, but why don't you take the day, anyway? Niki and I can handle lunch with the rest of the staff."

Faith was tempted, except too much was at stake. The Chocolax crisis was still fresh in her mind, though the birthday party's success and subsequent repasts had

127

virtually erased it from everyone else's. She was beginning to agree it had to have been Caresse. Nothing else made sense. She'd love to have some time alone with the child to find out how she did it, but that wasn't going to happen.

"It's sweet of you, but they're not going to be filming here much longer and I think I'd better stick around."

The following day, Faith was around even more than she had been before. They were all set up to shoot inside the house, which turned out to be providential. It was Max's favorite weather, cold and gray, but the cold was freezing cold. Shooting outside would have been cruel and unusual punishment, although unusual was not out of keeping with *A*. Cornelia crisply delivered a message from the assistant director asking the caterers to set up plenty of coffee, tea, and things to eat in the kitchen so people wouldn't have to go down to the barn.

The crew had redefined the Pingrees' small dining room into a surreal landscape, swathing the walls and furniture with the gauzy off-white fabric. A straw pallet had been arranged in one corner next to the cold fireplace. A period chair and cradle stood by the prisoner's resting place. Lights had been placed outside the diamond-paned windows and now they were working on the inside, covering some of the exposed beams with what looked like aluminum foil to create the effect Max wanted. Nils was everywhere, as was Max. Cornelia, as was her habit, scurried around looking busy. Cappy had checked in—and Evelyn—then they left to take a walk.

Faith felt once again as though she was watching a play from her position in the butler's pantry, which separated the dining room from the kitchen. And in a way, she was. Setting the stage. It was fascinating. She never failed to be impressed by the magic that transformed a room with piles of equipment, drapes held in place with safety pins, and groups of people at the perimeter into an intimate, isolated, realistic moment on the screen. She knew what would follow to create the illusion—the editing, which Max had frequently declared in print was as important a process as the filming itself. "The footage is his clay and Maxwell Reed is a master potter," Faith had heard a film critic say on the radio.

Sandra was talking to Max now. She had a clipboard and, as usual, her entire attention was focused on the director. To be near a genius was to be a bit of a genius yourself, Faith supposed. Certainly that was what Cornelia conveyed. PAs—and the rest of Max's devoted crew—ate, drank, and lived the movie.

Faith moved back into the kitchen to check on her supplies. Everyone else was at the tent getting lunch ready.

Alan came into the room and asked for some coffee. "Black, and I hope it's strong. Not that I need it to keep me awake. Nobody could fall asleep during this take." He rubbed his hands together in anticipation, apparently a habit. Faith could well understand why Max kept him as his assistant on picture after picture. Alan never seemed down. His constant phrase to Max after the innumerable glitches that arose during a typical day was, "Don't worry. Be happy. We'll handle it." It never failed to provoke some kind of smile from the director.

"Max sees it as a pivotal scene, Hester and Roger's first meeting alone after many years. The doctor has been called in to attend to the baby, who is having convulsions, mimicking Hester's own frenzied state." Alan put his cup down and put his thumbs together to frame the picture he was seeing in his mind. "Man and wife. They stare at each other for a moment. Later, we'll superimpose a shot of

129

them in the same positions back in England—a younger Hester reluctantly wedding Chillingworth. Then the whole thing will turn like a kaleidoscope and we're back in the present, the baby screaming."

"I remember the scene," Faith said. "Chillingworth gives Hester some medicine to give to the baby, then hands her a dose of noxious herbs for herself."

"And she has to decide if she trusts him enough to drink it." Alan took a large swallow of coffee. "It's a great moment. We're going to shoot first to check the lighting, using the stand-ins, so you can come in and watch if you like."

"I'd love to," answered Faith. Then she added, "It's been fascinating watching the progress of the film." Maybe if she showed an active interest, he'd let her stick around even more.

"You'd better be careful. This business can get in your blood. Look at me. I was headed for medicine when I met Max, had finished my first year of medical school. Of course, I'd always been addicted to films and the theater—from both sides of the footlights. I picked up some rave reviews for college performances. You never know where life may lead you. Anyway, enough profundities. It'll be about ten minutes. I'll call you." Alan finished his coffee and left.

Faith made another pot and decided she didn't have time to check on lunch preparations. Tom kept telling her she was going to have to learn to delegate more, and maybe he was right. She had in New York, but her staff had been with her a long time. Still, Niki knew what she was doing and they had steered away from anything remotely resembling black bean soup. Today there was pasta—penne with a choice of two kinds of sauce—a spicy linguica sausage with tomatoes and yellow peppers or a

130

broccoli pesto. They'd also made a variety of *tortas*, the usual salad bar, breads, and rare roast beef for the meat eaters. She rapped the wooden table and said a silent prayer to Escoffier in defiance of both reason and her spouse's oft-repeated ridicule of such shibboleths. But such practices had worked so far—everyone on this shoot liked the food, as they had on every other one she'd catered. She'd known excellent companies that had been fired merely because one of the stars didn't like the choices one day or a fanatic had detected white sugar in the granola. Maybe she should run over to the tent—just for a second.

Alan Morris stuck his head in the door. "We're ready to start," he said, then disappeared.

Faith took off her apron, went into the dining room, and found a place in the corner, well out of the way.

Nils and Max were silently pacing on opposite sides of the set, then at some unspoken signal, both men met and gave a nod to start.

Sandra was in full makeup, wearing a duplicate of Evelyn's gauzy costume, but the Totally Hair Barbie look of the other night was back to lank locks. She looked tired and not a little pathetic. Max's stand-in took his place by her side.

"Let's try it, people," Alan called. "Stand by."

Faith had assumed there wouldn't be any dialogue, since they were interested only in the lighting; however, she supposed Max wanted to see how the whole thing played—like the forest scene. The filming started and Chillingworth handed a pewter cup to Hester Prynne.

"Drink it! It may be less soothing than a sinless conscience. That I cannot give thee. But it will calm the swell and heaving of thy passion, like oil thrown on the waves of a tempestuous sea."

Sandra took the beaker reluctantly. Faith didn't blame her. Her husband's words might seem reassuring on the surface, yet his tone was that of one bent on revenge.

The lighting was extraordinary. A few seconds ago, Sandra had looked pale and wan. Now she appeared bathed in a sensuous, rosy luminescence, bosom heaving with conflicting emotions. Chillingworth reached over and slowly traced the letter at her breast, circling close to her nipple, clearly visible through the fabric. She flinched at his touch, then stood up, took a step toward him, raised the cup to quaff the draft in one swallow, and . . .

"Cut! Cut!"

"Cool 'em."

Sandra put the cup on the wooden mantelpiece and blinked. She was back and she didn't even have a glass slipper as a souvenir.

"It's fabulous." Nils executed a little jig. "Following the montage, the scene will continue to seem like a dream sequence, even in the present. Pure genius, Max."

Max was smiling like the Cheshire cat. "Yeah," he said, drawing the word out, "I think it's going to fly."

Alan rushed over. "I'll get Evelyn. I assume you want to shoot now."

"You assume right." They bent their heads together in further conversation for some minutes, then Max walked over to Sandra, who was sitting down in the chair, and said, "That was beautiful, honey. Evelyn couldn't have done it any better herself."

Faith looked uneasily over her shoulder to be sure the lady in question wasn't about to walk in on this, but she was nowhere in sight. It had been a powerful scene, and for a few seconds, Faith had completely forgotten where she was, where they all were. It was Hester's jail cell hundreds of years ago. She began to fully appreciate what

132

this movie could be Max's masterpiece.

The director left the room to hasten things along. Faith, still caught up in the moment, stayed where she was. Five minutes later, Max was back, but without Cappy and Evelyn. He went over to Sandra, who had remained seated, and bent down to speak to her. He straightened immediately and beckoned to the other PA. "Cornelia, Sandra isn't feeling very well. I think we'd better call a doctor."

Faith moved to the center of the room. Max had shifted to one side and Sandra was completely visible. Her face had assumed a bluish cast and her eyes were terrified. She appeared to be having trouble getting her breath, taking rapid, shallow gulps of air. She tried to speak, but no words came out. She began to cough, then that stopped abruptly and she brought her hand to her throat, as if trying to force the words out and air in. Faith ran over to her and felt for her pulse. It was hard to find.

"Don't call a doctor," she shouted to Cornelia. "Call the fire department; they'll bring an ambulance."

Sandra's face felt as cold as the weather outside, despite the warmth the lights and people had created in the room. Her eyes closed and she would have toppled from the chair had Faith not caught the young woman. Faith sat on the floor, Sandra cradled on her lap. She seemed to weigh less than Ben. One hand clutched the pewter cup she had placed on the mantel a few moments ago. It was empty.

Faith shouted one final instruction. "And call the police. The state police, too."

Had the town of Aleford replaced its ancient cruiser, Charley MacIsaac would not have lost precious time changing a tire on his way to the Pingree house and would have been there to warn Detective Lieutenant John

Dunne of the Massachusetts State Police that it was likely he would encounter his old friend Mrs. Fairchild once again. As it was, Dunne walked onto the movie set and confronted Faith center stage, not merely with a finger in the pie but up to her elbows—with her arms around the victim.

Sandra Wilson was not dead, yet Faith had known immediately something other than fatigue had to be responsible for the woman's pronounced symptoms. One of the crew had brought a blanket and reached for the empty cup that had fallen from Sandra's hand as he was covering her.

"Don't touch it—please!" Faith said. The man had looked mildly surprised and drawn back his hand.

Time had stopped, but Faith's mind was racing. If there had been something in the cup, it might be best to try to get Sandra to vomit. But with some poisons, this was the worst course of action, doubling their effect. Poison—she was using the word.

Sandra's breathing was shallow and slow. Her chest, incongruously clad in Hester's flimsy costume, barely moved. The scarlet letter that had looked so sensual a few minutes ago was now a mere piece of brightly colored cloth.

Faith kept her fingers on the woman's pulse. Her wrist felt limp and flaccid; her body draped across Faith like one of Amy's soft dolls.

At first, the room had been as still as the figure drawing every eye, then Max cried out, "Shouldn't we be doing something? CPR, for God's sake!"

Faith had decided they better try it, even if it did cause the girl to throw up. Then they heard the ambulance siren.

"Let's wait," she said. "The EMTs will know what to

do."

Dunne had followed on their heels and immediately took up all the available space in the cramped room in much the way that Alice had the White Rabbit's house after nibbling a cookie. It was always a shock to see Detective Dunne the first time after an interval. Faith remembered he was large, but not so large—and with a face that could only be cast, to put it politely, in "character" roles. His curly hair, cut close to his head, was grayer than the last time she'd seen him. His wardrobe as bespoke as ever. Today he wore a heavy camel's hair topcoat against the cold. He took charge immediately. Sizing up the situation with one rapid glance, he motioned the EMTs forward and instructed Detective Sullivan, at his side as usual, to rush the cup to the lab. As he left the room, Sully whispered something in his boss's ear.

Relieved of her burden, Faith stood up. Detective Dunne said, "I probably know the answer to this one, but it was your idea to phone us, right?"

Faith nodded. "It seemed like too much of a coincidence for someone to be saying lines about poison in a cup, then immediately keel over. And what with the business with the black bean soup—"

Dunne interrupted her with an explosive, "More soup! After that guy turned up headfirst in your bouillon, I'd have thought you'd stay away from the stuff!"

"You know perfectly well there was nothing wrong with my bouillon and the same—"

This time it was Maxwell Reed who broke in.

"Would somebody in charge like to tell me what the hell is going on here besides a discussion of Mrs. Fairchild's menus? And what is this about her soups?"

The detective lieutenant answered icily. It was his show

135

now and he'd decide what was going on and when.

"I am Detective Dunne of the Massachusetts State Police. We were called by the Aleford police. Mrs. Fairchild worked with us on an investigation last year, and in the initial stages, there was an incident with some soup. The coincidence struck me. Now why don't you tell me who you are and I'll try to figure out what's going on here."

Faith was flattered. John Dunne had actually said she had worked on an investigation. This could mean he was beginning to regard her as other than a nuisance and a pest. It could also mean he wasn't. After all, he hadn't said *helped,* although without her, corpses would still be piling up in the neighboring town of Byford.

"I'm Maxwell Reed." The director appeared to think his name was sufficient introduction, and he was right.

"And who was the young woman we've just carted off to Emerson Hospital?"

"That is one of my production assistants, Sandra Wilson. She has been working extremely hard and I'm sure they will discover she simply needs some time to rest."

Dunne didn't respond. He walked around the set, threatening cameras, lights, and even the fabric pinned to the walls.

"*The Scarlet Letter.* I've heard that's what you're filming, so the cup means this was the scene in Hester Prynne's prison cell where Roger Chillingworth gives her something to calm her down."

Faith was impressed. She knew that John's upbringing in the Bronx, across the river from her own in Manhattan, had been unusually literary. His mother was devoted to English poetry—witness the name. Apparently, Mom had revered the Concord Renascence crowd, as well.

"Yes," replied Reed. "We were using the stand-ins to test the lighting before shooting with the principals. But Miss Wilson didn't drink from the cup. We cut before that point."

Reed's stand-in, Greg Bradley, who also worked as one of the grips, spoke up. "She did after you stopped shooting. Said she was very thirsty."

"What was in the cup?" Dunne asked. It was a simple question, but Reed seemed to draw a blank. Faith knew the answer.

"Diet Coke and Perrier. That's what Evelyn O'Clair likes to drink," she added after noting Dunne's arched eyebrow, a habitual gesture that emphatically did not make him look like Cary Grant.

"Hmmm," he said, "Detective Sullivan told me it smelled like booze."

Someone gasped and everyone looked surprised. Sandra a secret drinker? Or Evelyn?

Dunne was about to speak again when Chief MacIsaac, Evelyn O'Clair, Cappy Camson, and Marta Haree all showed up at once.

Evelyn, wrapped in her sable coat, was almost hysterical. "What were all those sirens? We heard them in the woodsand what are the police doing here? Max! What's happened?"

The room was ready to burst.

Dunne answered, "I was just about to say that we don't know whether anything has happened here. Sandra Wilson passed out and is now being treated. Until we hear from the hospital, we only have Mrs. Fairchild's intuition to go on." He managed to make her hunch sound extremely dubious and Faith began to think she might have been overoptimistic about his attitude.

"Yesterday was the Ides of March, you know," Marta

commented in a voice filled with foreboding.

"Yes, but Sandra wasn't stabbed and we're not doing Shakespeare, Marta!" Max was annoyed. He looked angrily at Faith. "What is *she* doing on the set?"

Alan stepped forward and said something sotto voce to Max, who struggled with himself for a moment, then calmed down—the whole process vividly enacted on his face.

"Detective Dunne, I am sure you will understand that we need to get on with what we're doing here. I can't have a whole crew just sitting around on their hands. It gets to be very expensive. Producers don't like it, especially my producers."

"Of course I understand. As soon as we get word from the hospital, you can all get back to work." Dunne's tone suggested he liked movies as much as the next guy.

"But this could take hours!"

"I'm sorry. However, since there is the possibility that there was something in the cup that shouldn't have been, until we hear otherwise, we can't disturb the room." He waved his hand vaguely in Faith's direction.

He might just as well have said it out loud, Faith thought bitterly: If you want to blame anyone for all this, blame little Mrs. Fairchild, your soon-to-be-ex caterer.

"The cup!" Evelyn's voice rose to a wail. "My cup! What was in my cup!" She'd taken off her coat and was wearing her Hester costume. Faith had had to look twice to be sure it wasn't Sandra miraculously risen from her hospital bed.

Max put his arm around Evelyn. She'd detached herself from Cappy, to whom she'd been clinging like a limpet, and crossed over to Max's side as soon as she entered.

"Nothing! Nothing was in the cup. Maybe some liquor. Somebody did it as a joke. Hester with bourbon on her

138

breath—something like that. Everything's going to be fine. Why don't you go back to your trailer and lie down for a while until this is all sorted out?"

"I'm not going back there alone! Something's going on here! I want a bodyguard, Max. I told you I should have one!" She began to sob. She looked absolutely terrified.

He put his other arm around her. "Nothing is going to happen to you. Nothing has happened. Just some mix-up. I wouldn't let anything or anyone hurt you. You know that, darling! How about if Marta goes back with you? Just until I can come?" He looked over Evelyn's head, now buried in his shoulder, at Marta, who nodded and moved toward them.

Max addressed Dunne pointedly. "I assume we're free to leave the room."

"Certainly, but, for the time being, not the property."

After Marta led the distraught actress away, others left—in search of a breath of air, perhaps, and also to get away from the eidetic images hanging about of Sandra prone on Faith's lap—and the cup.

Max looked glumly after the retreating figures and said to Alan, "Oh well, we were going to have to break for lunch soon, anyway." The remark reminded him of Faith, and he seemed about to say something to her she'd rather not hear. She was hastily following the crowd out into the frigid March morning when Dunne called after her, "Don't go too far, Mrs. Fairchild. I want to talk to you."

Faith ran to the tent to tell Niki and Pix what was going on—or rather, what had happened. The news had preceded her and they were waiting anxiously by the entrance.

"Faith! One of the crew said Sandra drank from a cup that was a prop and passed out! Do you think someone has been playing tricks again?" Pix asked.

139

ST. MARYS PUBLIC LIBRARY
127 CENTER ST.
ST. MARYS, PA. 15857

"I don't know. But whatever was in the cup acted extremely quickly and she seemed in very bad shape." Faith suddenly realized she had to sit down or she'd fall down. Her knees had buckled out from under her at the memory of how rapidly Sandra's skin had cooled and her heartbeat slowed. Someone was talking.

"Put your head between your knees." It was Pix with typically useful advice, although Faith had long ago decided she'd have to be in extremis to assume such an ungainly position.

"I'm okay. And I'll be a whole lot better when we hear that Sandra is."

But they didn't.

As they were serving the first of the crew, Dunne strode in, took Faith aside, and said, "She's dead. Now come with me and tell me everything."

CHAPTER 6

Death was too definite an object to be wished for or avoided.

FAITH WAS STUNNED. THE THOUGHT THAT SHE SHOULD have started CPR or done something else nagged at her. Her nose got stuffy and she felt the tears come. She stuck her hand in her jacket pocket and found a blue crayon but no tissue. It made her cry harder. Dunne reached into his pocket and pulled out a fine Irish linen handkerchief with his initials discreetly embroidered at the border. She took it silently. It smelled faintly of bay rum.

She wondered where they would be able to talk and followed him into the house—an hour ago crawling with movie people, now crawling with police. She noted the familiar yellow plastic crime-scene ribbons and the plethora of cameras as they passed the dining room. She followed Dunne up the narrow, twisting stairs to the second floor and into the front bedroom. It was being used to store equipment and the only place left to sit was on the floor or on the large four-poster. Charley MacIsaac, who was behind Faith, immediately claimed the end near the pillows. Dunne sat next to him and Faith perched at the foot of the bed. The lyrics to one of Ben's favorite songs, "Ten Little Monkeys Jumping on the Bed," immediately leapt to mind and she could hardly keep herself from chanting, "And the little one said, 'Move over, move over.'" She restrained herself by focusing again on the tragedy. It wasn't difficult to push nonsense aside in the face of incomprehensibility.

"What made you think Sandra Wilson had been poisoned?" John got straight to the point.

"I'm not really sure." Faith tried to explain the feeling she had as soon as Max had said Sandra needed a doctor. "Maybe it's left over from the other night. The whole thing was pretty strange." She described Max's birthday party in detail. Charley's eyes opened wide and the detective lieutenant allowed himself one of his thin-lipped little smiles. "A Hester Prynne striptease. Wait until they hear about this down in the Zone. It could replace 'All Nude College Girls.'"

Faith continued. If she thought out loud, maybe things would get clearer.

"It's very hard to tell what's normal on a movie set. I

mean, there's obviously a lot of tension about time and not going over budget. Then the actors all have a lot of anxiety about their roles. In some cases, whether they're doing it right; in others, whether they've got enough to do. And you have all these egos that need caressing, which reminds me. Caresse Carroll." She told them about the child's tantrum and fears about being off the picture. She and Charley filled Dunne in on the black bean soup incident.

"I don't see how the two events can be connected, yet they have to be. And the fire. I'm sure it was set to get us out of the tent while the Chocolax was put into the soup, although it still leaves the question of Evelyn's soup, That was served before the fire. But tampering with food—twice in less than a week. Even if the first incident gave someone an idea, there has to be a link."

Dunne shook his head, in agreement. "Do you know who was responsible for filling the cup?"

Faith had been dreading the question. "Yes. Me. That is, the prop man came into the kitchen before they started shooting and asked me to fill the cup with diet Coke and Perrier. I did and he took it back to the dining room."

"Charley, you want to go down and find the guy? Ask him what he did with it after he left the kitchen."

"It probably sat on the mantel the whole time. That's where it was when I came in later," Faith told them.

"Makes sense, but let's get him right away."

Charley left and Dunne speculated: "It sounds to me like somebody wants to shut the production down. I wonder if Sandra's death wasn't an accident. Too much of whatever was put in the alcohol, or something she was allergic to. The idea was to have another poisoning where nobody actually got hurt, although from what Charley has said, everyone suffered." He looked pointedly at Faith.

"You could be right," she said. "I think what I'm trying to say is that there's been an unusual amount of tension on this set compared to others I worked on. I've been chalking it up to Max's unorthodox methods—and his personality. We've all been waiting for a display of his famous temper. Evelyn isn't exactly laid-back, either." She told him about the forest scene shoot and subsequent drama enacted at the Marriott, then returned to her previous point. "In retrospect, I think the other night was Evelyn's ego run amok, no doubt an everyday event. Stars with their noses out of joint are pretty common on movie sets. People work around it, ignore it. But the strain in the air on *A* has been more than that."

"Any ideas who would want to stop the filming?" Dunne asked.

Faith thought for a moment. "No. In fact, it would be detrimental to everyone I can think of—the actors, Max, crew, producers."

"What about the studio? Isn't there some sort of insurance money they collect if the movie isn't finished? Could they be in trouble?"

"Maybe, but this is supposed to be a blockbuster with an all-star cast and the cachet of Maxwell Reed as director. It's slated for a wide release at Christmas. They stand to make a whole lot more money if the picture is finished. Besides, and maybe I'm being naïve, I can't imagine they'd go to such lengths to get the insurance money."

"Unless somebody was overextended, shall we say. Like one of the producers. The track, women, high living."

Faith tried to fit Arnold Rose into the picture. Or Kit Murphy, lounging in someone's pink satin boudoir, her filmy negligee carelessly tossed to one side, next to the marabou feather trimmed high-heeled mules she'd kicked off before lowering the lights and finishing the

143

champagne. The champagne was right, but the rest . . .

"No, the producers—and they've been with Max for years, like almost everyone else seem as anxious as anyone to get the picture made."

"A disgruntled crew member?"

"Possibly. And he or she could be responsible for the soup, too, but other than run-of-the-mill grousing about lack of sleep and cold weather, I haven't heard any complaints. Working on one of Max's pictures is a credential people in the business fight to get. Caresse has been the only outspoken malcontent."

"What about Caresse?"

"I suppose it's possible. She's hardly led a normal childhood—whatever one is." Faith tried not to get distracted. She spent a lot of time these days thinking about this topic in the hopes of saving Ben and Amy hours on the couch, not to mention fees that could be put to better use, such as sending aging parents to the Caribbean or the south of France in some far distant winters.

"Putting the laxative in the soup seems like something she would do out of spite—she was really furious at Max and could easily have grabbed a dozen or so boxes from Evelyn's stash, but she wasn't even on the set today. This scene involves infant Pearl, represented by very docile twin baby girls."

Faith looked out the window. The dull gray sky framed by the ball fringe on the Pingrees' white Priscilla curtains threatened rain, or worse—snow. When had she stopped greeting the first flakes with the delight Ben did? Sometime in April her first year in Aleford? She was getting old and her bones felt creaky, or maybe it was just from sitting on the four-poster, which seemed to have a mattress stuffed with corncobs. There was such a thing as

144

too much authenticity, and people with period houses often veered dangerously close to the line.

"We'll start someone checking on what Miss Carroll and her mother were up to this morning. Anyone else missing from the set—that is, any of the principals?"

"No, I was surprised to see Marta, though. I didn't think she was involved in this scene, except you never know with Max. He's taken a pretty free hand with Hawthorne."

"Reed said Sandra Wilson was one of his production assistants. Did you see her other than at the party and on the set . . . know her at all?"

"Not really. She'd come to request a tray for Max, Evelyn, or one of the other actors at lunch or a snack at other times, and I'd see her when she ate, usually with Max's stand-in, the guy who said she drank from the cup. We'd exchanged pleasantries. That's all. She struck me as somewhat shy, although her performances were anything but. She seemed totally devoted to Max—following him around with her clipboard and watching him starry-eyed when he was busy with someone else, that kind of thing." Faith was glad she hadn't known Sandra better. It was easier to deal with her death in a vacuum, without the knowledge of parents, sisters, brothers, happy years growing up in wherever.

"What about the male stand-in? Were they romantically involved?"

"I don't know. Though I hope so, because if she was in love with Max, it was pointless."

Faith saw Sandra's glowing face again as she emerged from kissing Max after the strip. There was no *if* about the young woman's feelings for the director. She sighed. Life was monumentally unfair.

Having reduced God's cosmic joke to a single sentence,

145

she debated with herself what to tell Dunne about Cornelia. Cornelia had been on the set, of course. Glowering in the corner during the stand-in shooting and strangely quiet and immobile during its aftermath. Certainly she was jealous of Sandra, but she wouldn't do anything like this. Tamper with one of Max's sacred props! Never!

Dunne eyed her suspiciously. Faith found it almost difficult to meet his gaze.

"Are you sure you've told me everything? Do I have to give you the speech again?"

The speech, Faith knew from experience, consisted of stern reminders that this was a murder investigation, not a Sunday School picnic, etc., etc., etc. Certainly it was a murder investigation, and investigate was exactly what she intended to do.

She crossed her fingers behind her back, something of a reflex, and said, "Of course I have."

Anyone peering in the lighted windows of the parsonage later that evening would have been rewarded by a picture as wholesome as apple pie, or, since it was Faith, *tarte tatin*. Mother was at the sink washing pots. Baby Amy was swaying contently in her wind-up swing and little Ben was drawing pictures across the table from Father, who was reading the newspaper—yesterday's, since it was Tom. He never seemed to have time to catch up and yet could not bring himself to take his wife's suggestion and skip a day. An acute observer might have noticed the slight frown on Mother's face as she attacked the broccoli and orecchiette pan with a scouring pad. And Father seemed to be reading the paper uncommonly fast—as if nothing could engage his attention for long. He flung the pages to one side and directed his attention to his son.

"What are you making? It looks like a very nice car. Good job, Ben."

Ben shook his head. "It's our house, Daddy. See all the bushes in front, and here's Superdog to save the day!" Ben finished his explanation in song. Grown-ups just didn't get it.

Superdog or man, woman, girl, or boy was what they needed about now, Faith reflected. Someone who would go directly to the heart of the matter and solve it in the name of truth and justice. She was so enmeshed in this fantasy that when the doorbell rang, she called out to Tom, "I'll get it," half-expecting to throw open the door and see someone of steel in blue tights and a cape.

The cape part was right—and the steel—but the person before her was wearing hose of an indeterminate brown, presumably to blend with the putty tweed suit and olive green Alpine cape she wore against the cold night air. It was Millicent. If not Superwoman, possibly a cousin. Faith felt oddly relieved to see her and wondered why.

"Millicent! Come in. We're all in the kitchen. Have you eaten?"

This last was automatic with Faith, and as she took Millicent's cape, she mentally surveyed the contents of the larder. They'd finished the pasta, but there was some good smoked trout pâté and . . .

"Of course." The idea that, number one, she might arrive unannounced at someone's house for dinner was as preposterous as, number two, that at well past six o'clock she would not already have dined. "I've come to talk to Tom," she said, promptly quelling any misconceptions Faith might have had about Millicent's intent.

Faith was puzzled. She had assumed Millicent was there to pump her about the events on the set. Sandra Wilson's death had been old news in Aleford an hour after the fact.

147

The phone had been ringing all afternoon and Faith was keeping an ear cocked for it now. Once again, she didn't know whether she had a job or not. She assumed the filming would be suspended for a while, but what after that? And here was Millicent. If she didn't want to talk about the murder, then what?

Millicent followed Faith into the kitchen and graciously accepted the offer of a cup of coffee. Tom cleared some space at the big round table and pulled out a chair for her next to Ben.

"That's a very nice house, Benjamin," she said with her "children's smile" firmly pasted into place, "but why is the dog in the sky?"

"It's Superdog!" Ben chortled. He liked Millicent for some odd reason known only to himself.

"Oh," she commented, then turned her attention to the Reverend. "I'd like to pick your brain, Tom." She looked about the kitchen as if seeing it for the first time and not happy then. "Perhaps your study?"

Remembering the profusion of papers that had sprouted like mushrooms after a rainy spell, Tom hesitated. Good wife that she was—and she intended to store away the points—Faith immediately said, "Oh, it's so comfy in here. Stay where you are. I have to put the children to bed now, anyway."

"So soon?" Millicent's voice rang with insincerity. "Good night, then, dears." Amy beamed over Faith's shoulder and Ben gave her a big kiss. Millicent absently waved in their direction. As Faith left, she caught the first words: ". . . a desperate situation and getting worse. We . . ." before the door swung shut.

Upstairs, the Fairchild children were washed, brushed, drained or diapered, and in their sleepers so fast, they barely had time to protest. Faith grabbed *Goodnight Moon*, which she knew by heart, and got to "Goodnight noises everywhere" before Ben could put up any token resistance to a "baby" book. It was short and it was good. She kissed him and sternly asked him what would happen if he didn't go to sleep immediately.

"A bad day tomorrow," he said promptly.

"You got it. Now go to sleep so you'll have lots of energy for playing." Sometimes it worked.

Amy was another matter entirely. She needed milk and a few verses of "Dream a Little Dream of Me," the Mama Cass version, not the Louis Armstrong one. Tom usually took care of that. Faith tucked the baby into her crib and was not fooled for a moment by the heavy-lidded drowsy smile her daughter gave her. She knew she would be back, but maybe she'd at least have enough time to find out why Millicent was downstairs monopolizing Faith's husband.

As she entered the kitchen, it suddenly occurred to Faith that perhaps Millicent had wanted a confidential chat with Tom as the Reverend Tom. This had not entered her thoughts before, because Millicent was a Congregationalist, as were her mother and father before her and theirs before them and so and on and so on—like the catsup bottle's label of a picture of a lady holding a catsup bottle with a label of a picture. . . .

Faith shook her head. It had been a long day.

Could it be possible that Millicent had come seeking advice for a personal problem, one she didn't dare confess to her own spiritual adviser? A secret sin? A burdened conscience?

Not. The spry elderly woman with the Mamie Eisenhower bangs who smelled discreetly of Dierkiss talc purchased by the boxcar load in 1958 may have had secrets—mainly other people's—but the only sin she would ever admit to was the original one, and that was the serpent's fault.

Millicent paused in what had evidently been a long harangue. Tom looked tired and did not hide the relief from his eyes when he saw Faith.

"Come join us, honey. This concerns you, too."

"It concerns every man, woman, and child in Aleford," Millicent clarified.

Faith poured herself a cup of coffee. She wasn't going to be able to sleep tonight, anyway. She grabbed the cookie jar and put it in the middle of the table, noticed Millicent's cup was empty, and went back for the pot. She also got Tom a tall glass of milk, although at this point, she was sure he would have preferred something stronger. But scotch didn't go with chocolate macadamia nut cookies, and even if it did, the prospect that Millicent would have him figuratively, if not literally, enrolled in AA by morning thoroughly discouraged the idea. Faith could hear her telling one and all, "His hands positively shook, my dear. He *needed* the drink."

"Are you talking about the murder?" Faith asked now that they all had something to consume, always the top priority.

"The murder? Oh, you mean that movie person? Sad." Millicent's tone suggested murders and movie people went together like a horse and carriage and that if one would insist on pursuing such a career, one got what one deserved.

Faith was momentarily taken aback by Millicent's callousness—and also lack of interest. This was the woman who a few short days ago was ready to give Angela Lansbury, Jessica Tandy, Kate Hepburn, and any other actress over a certain age a run for her money. Yet, having moved from behind the footlights for the nonce herself, Millicent the extra had obviously passed on to other

150

things—more important things. And she hadn't known Sandra Wilson. None of them had.

"No, we're talking about the election." You silly goose, Faith finished for her.

"Has something new developed?"

Tom summed things up. "The Spaulding forces have started an old-fashioned whisper campaign against Penny. The kickoff was Daniel Garrison's leading question at the debate Monday night. Since then, it's been what I predicted. Penny—and Millicent—have had the unpleasant experience of walking into public places and immediately stopping all conversation."

Faith knew the experience well.

"People are saying, 'Where there's smoke, there's fire,' and that Alden wouldn't have brought the whole thing up if he didn't have something very specific in mind."

Faith sincerely doubted anyone, even in Aleford, had said, "Where there's smoke, there's fire," but she didn't question the intensity, or the potential viciousness, of the whispers.

"What does Penny have to say about all this?" she asked. "Is she still refusing to issue a statement?"

"Yes, and that's why I'm here. She won't say anything, and Tom has got to make her."

No wonder her husband looked weary.

"But Millicent . . ." Faith thought she'd give it a try. She was married to the poor man. "How can Tom possibly do this? If Penny doesn't want to talk about it, that's her business."

"It is not," Millicent shot back in no uncertain terms. "Penelope Bartlett is running for office in our town and she has a responsibility to respond. Besides, she's going to lose the election if she doesn't."

This put a different light on the matter. Faith saw Ben

151

and Amy tripping gaily off to school in what would amount to a trailer park, with forty children in a class and no books. No art or music. These were "frills." She found herself wishing, as Pix had, that they could use the encounter in the woods against Spaulding somehow, but it might backfire. Alden would claim he was exercising his constitutional right to walk freely in the town-owned wild, and his supporters would agree, making sure one and all heard that the minister's wife had a very dirty mind.

But they had to do something. They couldn't let Alden win!

"Tom . . ."

"I know, I know. It's a heck of a dilemma, Millie." Tom and Charley MacIsaac were the only ones privileged to use the treasured childhood nickname. Faith envisioned her with iron gray pigtails on the playground, turning the double dutch jump rope faster and faster as her little playmates skipped to her tune, "Too fast, Millie! Too fast!"

Tom took another cookie. "If you can't convince Penny to clear the air, I don't know who can. I agree it would be better if she did write a letter to the paper or put out a flier, and I'll tell her, but . . ."

A thought struck Faith. "Maybe there is nothing. Maybe this is just campaign dirty tricks." Aside from what made sense in terms of an Alden Spaulding campaign, Faith was sure Millicent, of all people, would have known everything about Penny's blameless past.

"I wish it was." Millicent sounded almost pathetic. "Lord knows, I've tried to think what it can be—and it is something. I've known Penny since we were children, and she couldn't tell a lie to save her life. I asked her straight out if there was any truth to what they were saying, and all she would say was, 'Don't ask me that.' Oh, there's something all right."

"Could you figure it out from what they said the other night? What was the year they claim the taxes were fraudulent?"

"The Bartlett's taxes were never fraudulent!" Millicent spoke as if Faith had started the rumor.

Faith protested. "I'm not agreeing with them! I'm simply trying to remember what they said!" She looked to Tom for support. No wonder he was tired. She began to toy with the idea of leaving to check on the baby, but there was still the possibility she might miss something. Tom was notoriously bad at remembering conversations.

Millicent was somewhat mollified. "The Spaulding campaign is alleging that Penny and Francis did not report 'certain financial transactions'—I believe those are Mr. Garrison's words—on their state and federal tax forms for the fiscal year 1971."

Miss McKinley, on the other hand, could repeat conversations from thirty years back word for word.

"Nineteen seventy-one, about twenty years ago. Do you remember anything that might have happened to the Bartletts then? Did they seem to be in any financial difficulty?" Faith was fishing, but if Penny wouldn't tell them what was going on, they'd have to figure it out themselves.

"Francis was dying. It was a terrible strain on Penny. He had cancer of the liver and was in a great deal of pain. I used to go and sit with him to relieve her. She didn't have a nurse until the very end. That was in the fall of 1972."

Tom wondered aloud, "Do you think something could have been overlooked during his illness? They could have forgotten to report some income, but how would Alden have found out?"

"It's possible. Barry Lacey always did their taxes. He did mine, too, until he passed away. Playing tennis." Millicent raised an eyebrow as if the CPA had been *en flagrante*. "If they had missed something that year, he would have straightened it out for Penny the next. It's also extremely unlikely that Alden would ever have had access to the Bartletts' tax records."

"Unless he saw something on somebody's desk or went into somebody's file. Did this Mr. Lacey do his taxes, too?" Faith had visions of Alden, a stocking pulled over his pudgy face, with a flashlight.

"Barry did everyone's taxes," Millicent said smugly, not needing to add the "anyone who was anybody," since it was in her voice.

"Then Alden might have picked up on something and tucked it away for future reference, say to blackmail his sister. Was this when they stopped talking, too?" Faith thought she had the whole thing neatly tied up.

"No, that was earlier. I think when their father died, but they were never close even before then."

"Could they have quarreled over his will?"

"I doubt it—and that we would have heard about since everybody knew Jared Spaulding divided the bulk of his estate equally between the two of them. Penny's mother died when Penny was in college. Jared seemed to have a penchant for fragile women." Millicent was slightly disapproving. To be once a widower was bad enough; twice was close to profligacy. She continued. "In any case, Penny would never have bickered over money."

Faith knew what Millicent meant. It would have been beneath a lady like Penny, but then Francis Bartlett made a good living, and having money made it a whole lot easier to be noble about said commodity.

Millicent was positively loquacious on the subject of

Penny and her half brother, especially in light of her closed lips the other day when Faith had been asking the very same questions.

"I never thought of Penny and Alden as brother and sister. They weren't really raised together. Alden is seven years older than Penny and he was mostly at boarding school and the university (this meant Harvard, Faith guessed) when she was growing up. Then when he came home to live, she was at school. She married Francis shortly after she graduated from college. It was such a lovely wedding—in the Wellesley chapel. Sue Hammond caught the bouquet . . . and how we laughed. Poor Susan. Not the most winsome girl, but would you believe she was engaged before the year was out!"

Faith knew once Millicent got going, it would be impossible to change the course of the speeding locomotive that passed for conversation back to the matter at hand. She interrupted quickly and firmly.

"So, what we know is whatever the Spaulding campaign has on Penny happened when her husband was very ill and that's about all, except, as brother and sister, Alden and Penny were pretty distant." Faith had already connected Alden's accusation with Penny's husband's death, but the rest was new.

Millicent nodded. Tom followed suit, nodding several times and seeming about to put his head down on the table. It was time to hear the baby, bless her little heart. Faith jumped up. "I think that's Amy. I'll just run up to make sure she hasn't kicked her covers off." Tom took the hint. "No, you stay here, sweetheart. I'll go." Now, would Millicent take it, too? It was their lucky day—or, more probably, she didn't feel like sitting in the kitchen with Faith while waiting for Tom to come back.

"I must be going," she said over the Fairchilds' feeble

155

protests.

At the door, having swirled her heavy cape around her shoulders, imperiling the light fixtures, she addressed Tom in the familiar tones of a woman not to be trifled with lightly or otherwise. "Tom, I expect you to deal with Penny. The deadline for letters to the editor of the *Chronicle* is Monday. That gives you two days."

"I'll do my best," Tom promised. He knew it was pointless to object.

"Thank you for the coffee and that very rich cookie, Faith," Millicent remarked politely. Any increase in her cholesterol level would, of course, be laid at Mrs. Fairchild's door.

After Millicent left, Tom and Faith looked at each other.

"I don't know whether to laugh or cry," he said;

"Maybe both? Laugh now and then cry later when Penny Bartlett doesn't budge an inch."

"I know." Tom sighed. "But what could I do? By the way, you didn't really hear Amy, did you?" He had folded his wife in his arms and they were talking nose-to-nose.

"No, both cherubs are blessedly sound asleep. I had the intercom on. And from the look of you, it won't be long before you join them."

"But not immediately."

Faith smiled. Suddenly, she wasn't tired at all.

The next morning, Faith wandered around the house, changing sheets, energetically attacking the dust bunnies, and in general trying to keep herself occupied.

"I feel fragmented," she'd told Tom at breakfast. "Yesterday, I held a dying woman in my arms, who it now appears was a murder victim. Then Millicent assigned you the thirteenth labor of Hercules. I start to try to figure out

156

who might have killed Sandra Wilson, then my mind jumps to what was going on with the Bartletts in 1971."

"Why not think of something altogether different? Like me," Tom had suggested.

"Don't tell me you're feeling neglected!" Faith had protested. After all, he was still smiling.

"No, no," he'd reassured her hastily. "Not at all. Think about some new recipes or the state of the union or anything you want."

And so she'd played with Amy, enthusiastically applauding her sluglike wriggles across the floor, which would become crawling one of these days too soon. Faith found that Amy's babyhood seemed to be whizzing by at an alarming rate, whereas Ben's had progressed at a more petty pace. Maybe it was because this was the last child—*definitely*.

When an exhausted baby had allowed herself to be sung to sleep, Faith had dragged out the vacuum cleaner. But without the baby, all her attempts to keep fragmentation at bay failed. She found herself longing for Amy to wake up and Ben to come home from his friend's house. Before either occurred, the phone rang. It was Charley MacIsaac.

"Before you say a word, I don't know a thing. Or not much. You were right about the cup. The propman went straight from the kitchen and put it on the mantel—where it sat, available to everyone and his cousin, the whole time. Dunne's still questioning some of them over at the hotel, and, if you can believe it, they're all having a conniption fit over how much money the movie is losing."

Faith thought sadly of how short-tempered everyone had been with Sandra when she'd misplaced the fabric for the walls. In death, she was causing even greater inconvenience. Did anyone connected with the film actually remember the person who had been killed, or was the budget so almighty? From what Charley was saying, he seemed to be wondering the same thing.

"But Max can't really be thinking that they can just go on shooting as if nothing happened."

"According to John, he can and is. Wants to get everybody back on the set immediately."

"What about the poor girl? I assume her family has been notified." Faith hadn't wanted to know too much about Sandra, but the temptation to round out the picture was overwhelming.

"Didn't have much family. Mother dead and no father to speak of. Grew up in Southern California. Her roommate from Los Angeles is on her way and she's pretty broken up. I talked to her. Wants the studio to have a memorial service. According to the guy who saw her take the drink, all the studio wants is to forget her."

"I'm sure they can't afford the bad publicity." Although, as she spoke, Faith remembered what an agent friend had told her once: "There is no such thing as *bad* publicity." People who might have avoided *A* as highbrow and boring would flock to the movie because of the murder.

"Dunne wants to talk to you some more. He has the idea you aren't telling us everything." Charley sounded both weary and wary. He knew Faith.

"That's ridiculous she said firmly, and after they hung up, she promptly dialed her sister. Even though it was Saturday, Faith knew where Hope would be.

Calling Hope at work was not something she did often. For one thing, it was hard to get her. For another, when she did, she had to contend with Hope's office voice and manner, which suggested that while she was delighted to hear from her sister, the interruption had just blown a $30 million deal.

158

But the situation was serious.

Miraculously, Hope's equally workaholic secretary, Bryan, put Faith through immediately, and while Hope did not sound chatty, she did inject more ore than usual warmth into her greeting. She'd seen the papers.

"Not again, Fay!" Happily or unhappily, Hope was the only one who called her this. "How on earth do you end up with all these stiffs? *A* is the movie you're catering, right?"

"Yes, and I don't exactly go looking for 'stiffs.' " Faith was about to chastise Hope for her insensitivity. This had been a person. Then she reminded herself that Hope had never even set eyes on Sandra. She tried to continue speaking and realized she was about to cry. A bright, beautiful young woman was dead and Faith hadn't been able to do a thing to save her. An expendable PA with dozens of others eager to take her place.

"Fay, *Faith,* are you okay? I'm sorry. That was really stupid and insensitive. Tell me what happened. I have loads of time."

Faith was sure she didn't, but she told her everything, anyway.

"But I didn't call you about all this, or at least I don't think I did. The thing is I haven't told the police about Corny—her temper. And she was terribly jealous of Sandra, especially at the birthday party. Yet I can't believe Corny would murder her. It would make more sense to murder Evelyn."

As she said that, the penny dropped and she realized what it was that had been in the back of her mind since yesterday. It was Evelyn O'Clair's cry, "My cup!" They really hadn't explored the very distinct possibility that Evelyn and not Sandra was the intended victim. Which could make Cornelia a suspect.

159

"Oh, Hope, what am I going to do? I suppose I'll have to tell Detective Dunne about Corny, but this is not going to look good in our class notes."

"Don't worry. Corny wouldn't kill anybody, except maybe you. She likes to watch her victims sweat, and from what I understand, once you've killed someone, that is unlikely. Sorry, I'm being a jerk again."

"No, it's all right. I mean, I'm all right, but what you say is true. And I'm pretty sure our dear Cornelia was responsible for the missing bolt of fabric that turned up in the barn—a missing prop, for which Sandra Wilson, the dead woman, was blamed."

"Now that sounds more like our old chum. She likes to get other people into trouble. Lord forbid she should get into trouble herself."

Faith felt a whole lot better. She decided it wasn't necessary to tell Dunne about Corny's rotten disposition. Difficult as she might be, Cornelia was a kind of friend.

"You should have seen her the night of the party. It was tragic. And what is Corny doing in the glitzy movie business in the first place? She should be living in New Canaan with three kids by now and twice as many horses."

"Agreed, but you know how stubborn she is. If she's decided to worship Maxwell Reed, it's till death do us part."

Faith felt a distinct chill. She thought of that odd saying, Someone must be walking over my grave.

Hope was asking after her niece and nephew. It was a relief to talk about teething and Ben's worship of a nice safe hero—Barney, a six-foot, cuddly, purple *Tyrannosaurus rex*.

Dunne didn't call until late in the afternoon. Faith hadn't left the house all day and was feeling not simply restless but cross. Tom wouldn't be home for dinner, and for a fleetingly insane moment, she wished she had a cardboard package of macaroni and cheese to whip up for Ben when he returned from the Macleans'. It was over in an instant, yet she was still shaken when the phone rang.

"Well, we decided to let them start filming again on Monday. At least we'll know where they are, and that's about all we do know about the case. Unless you know something you, ahem, forgot to tell me?" Dunne's gravel-like Bronx accent softened with faint hope.

"Sorry, no, but something did occur to me."

"Yes?"

"That whatever was in the cup was intended for Evelyn and not Sandra."

"It occurred to me, too. Pretty much right away, which merely gives us twice as much to sort out. We did find out that the kid was in the hotel with her tutor at the time and the mother was in town shopping. At Filene's Basement, she says, and she has a bag to prove it, but no slip. She left that on the counter. We're trying to find someone who remembers her."

Faith had never been to Filene's Basement. The idea of pushing and shoving for clothes did not appeal to her. Besides, she'd heard that most of the fabled bargains were last season's. But she knew enough about the venerable Washington Street institution to place Dunne's odds of finding a salesclerk who remembered Jacqueline Carroll at about forty to one.

But Caresse, at least, was eliminated. Faith was glad. The little girl might need to turn over several new leaves; still, at least she wasn't the bad seed. Murder was horrible, but a child murderer was particularly monstrous.

"By the way, what was in the cup?"

"Perrier and diet Coke, as you said, plus a lethal

161

combination of rum and chloral hydrate."

"Chloral hydrate! Isn't that a sedative? How could that have killed her?"

"By itself, it wouldn't have. At least she'd have had her stomach pumped before it did, but with the rum chaser and her body weight, it did the job. The fact that she was an asthmatic and smoked helped. Somebody knows a lot about drugs, a lot about Sandra, or was just lucky."

"Plus, it would be easy to get. No doubt everybody on the set is taking something to get to sleep—and to wake up."

"Exactly."

"John, could I have done anything?"

"No, not unless you had had a bottle of ipecac in your pocket and given it to her immediately, and even then it probably wouldn't have helped. Besides, you didn't know what was in the cup, and if it had been Drano and you'd made her throw up, you'd have killed her."

Faith was relieved, but she knew she would never get over the remorse she felt—the *if only.*

"Stop thinking about it," Dunne said when she didn't respond. She was getting this advice from all quarters lately.

"You don't happen to know if I still have a job, do you?" she asked, determinedly changing the subject.

"Actually, I do." He paused for a tantalizing moment. "You do. We told them we would prefer to keep all personnel the same, including the caterer."

"John, that's wonderful! I can't thank you enough." Once again, Faith was relieved. Even though they'd have a late night tonight getting ready and she'd have to do her part at home, since Tom was out.

"It's not a totally disinterested act. Without getting involved—and I want to stress this . . . God knows why I

162

think it might help—you can keep your eyes and ears open."

They were a team again.

At least Faith thought so.

Suddenly, she found she was feeling more energetic. It was still early. She could take the kids over to the kitchens. She called Pix and Niki, who agreed to meet her there. They could get virtually everything set for Monday. During the past week, Faith's crew had worked as efficiently as usual. She was sure they wouldn't have to do much now besides get organized and assign jobs. The freezer had been amply stocked and she'd go back the following day to bake.

Pix had been a godsend. Her organizational abilities were phenomenal. Besides taking over the books, she'd worked out schedules for everyone. Have Faith was beginning to resemble the proverbial well-oiled machine, perhaps olive-oiled in this case—the good kind, extravirgin, first cold-pressed from Lucca.

Faith's initial stop was the Macleans'. As the books put it, Ben had trouble with "transitions" and so raised holy hell when he saw his mother arrive to take him away. Faith characterized it rather as an understandable unwillingness to leave a good party for plain old home. Whatever it was, it was a nuisance. She managed to get him away with a contradictory combination of threats and promises. He was somewhat quieted by the prospect of playing at the kitchens for a while. Amy beamed quietly throughout. It wasn't her turn yet.

Pix and Niki had already arrived by the time the Fairchilds walked in. It took a few minutes to get the kids settled, then Faith joined the other two women, who were looking through sample menus for ideas.

After a while, their talk drifted away from ratatouille

163

and chicken pot pie—Faith made a delectable one with a puff pastry crust, lots of chicken, and a creamy sauce with a touch of sage. But the conversation did not turn to the subject uppermost in Faith's mind. Pix was much more interested in talking about the town elections than the murder. She wasn't sure she even knew who Sandra Wilson was, she'd told Faith when Faith had originally brought the news. It wasn't that Pix didn't care; it was as with everybody else, Sandra had not made much of a lasting impression—at least so far as Faith could tell.

"March twenty-sixth is only nine days away! If we can't clear the air, Alden is certain to win. I'm getting so mad about all this. Every time I see him in the center, I want to break his other wrist—if the left one really is. Sam and I have our doubts."

"Me, too. But I'm not so certain Alden's a shoo-in. What about James Heuneman?" Faith tended to overlook him, as did most of the Aleford electorate.

"He's not mounting much of a campaign and will probably take votes away from Penny, not Alden."

"Won't people see him as a compromise candidate?"

"People don't want a compromise candidate. They want one who stands for something definite."

Faith told them about Millicent's visit the night before. Pix was elated.

"If Tom can't convince Penny, then nobody can." Faith half-expected her friend to break out into one of her old high school cheers: "Tom, Tom, he's our man! If he can't do it, *nobody* can." She'd be willing to bet that Pix could still turn a mean cartwheel, too.

"Millicent is sure Penny is hiding something, because she's not good at deception. Millicent referred to their girlhood days and said Penny never could tell a lie."

"*Their* 'girlhood days'!" Niki rolled her eyes

164

expressively. "Millicent Revere McKinley has got to be at least three days older than water. She *wishes* they shared their girlhood days." Niki was not a big fan of Ms. McKinley's, finding the lady's habit of dropping by to nibble more than a tad annoying. "Let her hire us if she wants to eat up all our food," she'd told Faith.

When Pix and Faith finished laughing, Pix said, "Millicent has, let us say, an air of permanency about her, but I'm sure she and Penny are contemporaries—give or take a few years."

"Say ten or twenty," Niki retorted.

Faith sent everyone home after all, it was Saturday night—and soon was locking the place up, bound for home and hearth herself.

Both children dined unfashionably early and by 6:30 Faith was harboring hopes of a hot bath and early bed— for herself.

She was startled by a knock on the back door and even more surprised when sixteen-year-old Samantha Miller, carrying a pizza box—a rare sight in the Fairchild household—walked into the kitchen.

"Hi, Mrs. Fairchild. Reverend Fairchild called and said for me to tell you that you're to go straight upstairs and change your clothes. Leave the kids to me. You're going out to dinner." She plunked the pizza box, presumably her own repast, on the table and eagerly lifted Amy from the windup swing. Sam was one of those teenage girls who doted on small children. Pix vacillated from thinking it was a lovely trait to worrying that it would provoke ideas of early motherhood. Sam's oft-stated intent was to be a marine biologist, marry at twenty-five, and have her kids by thirty, but in her mother's worrying mode, Pix made frequent references to the best-laid plans, and so forth. Faith's money was on Sam.

Intrigued, and impressed that her husband had been able to find a sitter on a Saturday night, truly an act of God, Faith ran upstairs to get ready. Tom walked into the bathroom as, still damp from a shower, she was putting on her makeup.

"What's going on?" she asked as he grabbed her from behind. She turned to meet his embrace. A moment later, he answered, "What's going on is, I am taking my beautiful wife to dinner. You—make that we—need a night out."

"What a terrific idea! Where are we going?"

"Claude's. So put on a nice frock and get a move on. You know Sam will take care of everything."

"This feels like a fairy tale," Faith said as she rummaged hastily through her closet, pulling out a fawn-colored soft suede tunic by Michael Kors. It was her favorite dress this season and she always felt very sexy in it, sliding it ever so slightly off one shoulder.

"And the nice part is, you don't have to kiss a frog to get the prince."

As she finished her makeup, Faith thought what a relief it was to talk nonsense.

Chez Claude was a short drive away in Acton. Claude Miquel, the chef, who owned the restaurant with his wife, Trudy, had been one of Faith's discoveries soon after moving to Aleford. The Parisian had come to Acton by way of Chez Pauline on the rue Villedo and Maison Robert in Boston. Now, in a cozy restored farmhouse, he did a superlative job cooking the traditional dishes he knew best.

Over a glass of kir in one of the smaller dining rooms, the Fairchilds were having their usual discussion of which favorite to order.

"We know we want the onion soup, the gratinée, first," Faith declared, her mouth watering. It was the perfect choice for a cheerless winter night. She had never tasted a better one, even in France. Claude topped his rich onion-laden stock with several kinds of cheese melted over a thick slice from one of his crusty baguettes.

"The *pâté de maison* is so good, too, though. But you're right, the soup is perfect for tonight. Are you in the mood for meat or fish?"

"Definitely meat. I want to discuss something with you. It seems crazy, only I can't put it out of my mind, and I need hearty, chewable food."

"Ah, Mistress Fairchild. I thought something ailed thee." Tom had been rereading Hawthorne, too.

The kir and the glowing copper colors of the pleasant country French decor in the room were making Faith feel quite mellow.

"Not as bad as all that. Just an idea. How about going all out and splitting the Chateaubriand?"

"But then we'll miss the duck à l'orange."

"Tom. We live in Aleford. We can come back."

"Béarnaise sauce it is and a bottle of Côtes du Rhône."

I should be thinking quite creatively before the night is out, Faith said to herself.

The steaming soup arrived and as Tom stuck his spoon in eagerly, he said, "All right, let's have it. It was partly to give you a chance to talk that I engineered this whole thing. What's been going on lately has been strictly *pas devant les enfants.*"

An undergraduate year in France had left him permanently in love with the country and prone to French phrases and Franglais—all of which had increased due to their recent sojourn in Lyon. A sojourn that did have its rocky moments, but by concentrating on memories of

167

certain meals, certain people, and the light on the hills in Provence, those other moments had taken on pebblelike proportions—most of the time.

"And partly by a lust for Claude's cooking," Faith added.

"*Certainment, mon petit chou.* So, what's up?"

"I can't stop thinking about Sandra Wilson. I know it's irrational, but I feel responsible. I owe it to her to find out who did it."

"It's not irrational to wish you could have saved her, but it is to think you have to track down her killer. Be sensible, Faith."

"But none of this has been sensible. Since I started this job, I've felt as if I've been watching a movie of a movie. Even before Sandra was killed. It's been a very strange, sort of disassociated sensation. Today, especially, I began thinking how blurred the boundaries between life and art are. I know I'm beginning to sound like a sophomore who's just discovered Joyce, but where it's led me is to wonder if the answer lies in the fact that some of the people in the film are forgetting to put aside their characters when they wipe off their makeup."

Tom reached for Faith's hand. His bowl was empty. He was contemplative, "Many actors and actresses find themselves living their parts after the camera stops—particularly in roles that require great intensity. It's got to be confusing, and maybe after a while it is hard to remember which face is the mask. Do you have anyone special in mind?"

Faith's answer was vinous stream of consciousness.

"There are, or were, two Hesters, and at first I thought it was Hester/Evelyn he was obsessed by. There was the way he looked at her—at them—at the dinner party, and there's no question that he's enormously protective of her.

It's Max—or rather Roger Chillingworth. Sometimes I can't tell where one leaves off and the other begins."

"What do you think this means?"

"It's all confused, because now I'm beginning to think the cup *was* meant for Evelyn. Max didn't ask her to the screening the other night. He seemed entranced by Hester/Sandra. Except he still seems very jealous of Cappy. When he saw him with Evelyn at the dinner table, Max made her move. Then when they walked in together after Sandra had passed out, he looked unbelievably angry. Of course, he was upset at the situation and at me for suggesting the call to the police. Evelyn went over to him immediately, almost as if she was afraid. She immediately assumed the poison was meant for her."

"So you think Max or Roger, whatever, put the chloral hydrate in the cup?"

"He stopped the shooting just before Sandra took a drink. That way he could have been sure Evelyn would drink it. Or thought he was."

Trudy Miquel appeared and showed them the succulent piece of meat, beaming as she presented the platter for their approval. It was done to a turn, a very short turn. They oohed and aahed appropriately. After she left, they resumed their conversation.

"What you're suggesting is that Max wanted to replace Evelyn with Sandra, both because he was jealous of Cappy and because he was besotted with Sandra."

"I know it sounds farfetched. But I think the two women are merged into one Hester in his director's mind—and he's in love with both. Two aspects of one character. And he's split, too. The director wants the best for the role, which might be Sandra. The actor—Chillingworth, the jealous husband—wants to get even with his wife for her adultery. The result is the same. A

169

potion—remember it wasn't normally a lethal dose."

"It's not impossible. Jealousy and ambition are powerful motives, yet why would he sabotage his own movie?"

"Maybe he merely intended to scare Evelyn. Give her a warning. Or make her just ill enough so Sandra would have to take her place. Or maybe he can't help himself. And there's another thing."

The food arrived, postponing further speculation. The moment the waitress left, Faith took a sip of wine and said, "What if Cordelia isn't Max's child? What if she's Cappy's and Max has just found out? It really would be like *The Scarlet Letter*." She waited for her husband to stop chewing and put a dollop of the béarnaise sauce, redolent with tarragon, on her plate.

"Do you know that Cappy and Evelyn even knew each other before? Other than as box-office draws?" Clearly Tom thought the whole thing was extremely speculative.

"No, but Cappy spent a lot of time at the party playing with the baby, and the baby doesn't resemble Max in the slightest. Then there was that time I saw them together at The Dandy Lion, right after Evelyn got out of the hospital. And she held hands with both Cappy and Max at the screening." As she listed her evidence, she had to admit it was far from an airtight case.

Tom was shaking his head. "One lunch does not an affair make usually. Nor does holding hands qualify as foreplay, especially in the presence of a room full of people." He poured himself some more wine. "It would make a good novel—Max could film it instead and poor Nathaniel could stop spinning in his grave. Sometimes life does imitate art—how's that for sophomoric?—but I can't believe that Maxwell Reed is this crazy. He stands to lose too much: his movie, the love of his life, and the clincher—possibly many, many years in prison."

"I suppose you're right, although think of the contrasts between the two men. Cappy is closer to Evelyn's age and certainly more conventionally good-looking. Much more."

"Maybe Evelyn is interested in other than a pretty face."

"Other than hers?"

"Maybe not," Tom conceded. "And it is an extraordinarily pretty face. I didn't see the footage, but I can't imagine that Sandra Wilson could hold a candle to Evelyn O'Clair. Both ladies, I might add, completely outclassed by my own wife. My own overly inquisitive wife."

It might be time to move on to another subject, although Faith knew this one would continue to claim front row center. But for the moment, Tom's last remark had been happily diverting. She sighed and soaked up the last bit of sauce from her plate with a piece of bread.

"Now, what shall we have for dessert?"

Cappy Camson had opened the drapes in his Marriott room, but what moonlight there was did not penetrate the night fog and his windows were well above the lights on Cambridge Street. Unable to sleep, he'd rolled out of bed and deliberately hadn't turned on the lamp by his side. He slumped in the room's one armchair, the darkness suiting his mood.

He stretched his feet out on the small table in front of him and wondered how he had ever gotten into this mess.

Stardom was something that had happened to him. He hadn't pursued it and, he told himself, he wouldn't miss it. But she was attracted by all the phony charisma. He didn't kid himself. She would never have been interested in Caleb Camson from Oklahoma City. And was she even that interested in Caleb Camson from Laurel Canyon?

He stood up, walked across the room, and opened the small refrigerator the hotel kept stocked with whatever he might want day or night. The light shone weakly and he stared at his bare feet with sudden repugnance. His tan was almost gone. He took a can of V-8 juice and went back to the window.

He was obsessed. And this had never happened before. All these years. All those women. He'd always been able to erase his current favorite from his mind and concentrate on his work. Until now. Now all he could think of was how her incredibly smooth flesh would feel pressed close to his. He was haunted by the smell she exuded, the perfume of her hair and something else, something that didn't come in a bottle. How was he going to finish the film without exploding? He rested the half-empty can on his thigh and noted without surprise that he had a hard-on.

At times, he wished he had turned Max's offer down. He had been flattered and excited by the idea of playing against type. But he knew he'd do the same thing all over again. Cappy was nothing but honest—with himself.

CHAPTER 7

I pity thee, for the good that has been wasted in thy nature!

IN CHURCH SUNDAY MORNING, ALDEN SPAULDING appeared decked out in a campaign button the size of a turkey platter, which Faith thought was in very poor taste. If Alden wanted a bully pulpit, let him get one of his own.

She was sure the Lord agreed with her.

After the service, Alden worked the crowd at coffee hour: pressing the flesh, mixing and mingling. In contrast, Penny left after a scant cup. Alden appeared to find her departure telling and was quick to point it out to several of those around him.

"I'm afraid my dear sister doesn't seem to have much time to talk about the burning issues that confront Aleford. Perhaps," he said sarcastically, "she has another engagement."

Faith pulled Tom away from an earnest discussion of who really wrote the Dead Sea Scrolls. "You've got to do something about Alden! Or at least make him pay for airtime."

"Darling, I can't ask a man to leave his own church, whatever I may feel about his uncharitable behavior."

"At least go over there. Maybe your ministerial presence will shame him into going, or at least behaving better."

"I doubt it, but I guess it's worth a try."

Faith watched Tom's black-gowned figure move through the crowd. "If he can't do it . . ." ran through her mind and she seriously contemplated a cartwheel or two in front of the astonished congregation. She was ready for a sabbatical. If the clergy could take them, surely spouses qualified, as well.

After half an hour, she went downstairs and collected Ben and Amy from Sunday school day care. It was freezing out again and she had no trouble convincing Ben to race. Encumbered by Amy, she lost, much to her son's delight. He crowed, "I won! I won!" over and over in a typical almost-four-year-old manner as she struggled with her keys and finally opened the door to the warm kitchen. She stripped off their snowsuits quickly and turned her attention to the stove.

In a moment of brotherly love, Ben was teaching Amy to bang on pots, and when the phone rang, Faith had to divert them with raisins and Cheerios, respectively, so she could hear.

"Hello, Faith. It's John. Did you pray for me?"

"Yes, I think you were covered in the collect for grace. But surely this is not the sole reason for your call?"

"No, and I may be sorry—a phrase I seem to say a lot around you—but I'd like you to look at the footage of the scene they shot just before Sandra drank from the cup."

"I'd love to! When do you want me to come?" Faith had been thinking about the scene. She knew the cameras had been rolling when they were checking the lighting. It was unlikely that they had recorded a mysterious hand pouring something into the cup, yet they might have caught something in the room that would trigger an idea.

"We've got the film, of course, so it can be anytime. I don't want to take you away from Tom and the kids today, so how about tomorrow morning?"

Oh, take me away, Faith wanted to beg. She was dying to see the shots, but with Tom plus three parishioners due for Sunday dinner any moment and the rest of tomorrow's food for the shoot to prepare, she had to agree. They arranged to meet around 7:30 A.M. at state police headquarters, which would still give Faith time to get to the set before lunch. She quickly called Pix and Niki, then turned her attention to the "chicken every Sunday" type of meal she was preparing, this version a nicely browning roaster with slices of garlic tucked under the skin and stuffed with chopped red peppers, onions, golden raisins, and bulgur moistened with butter and a little vermouth.

The following morning, Faith was ushered into a darkened room by a stalwart young state police officer

174

who bore a vague resemblance to Dudley Do-Right about the chin. John Dunne and Charley MacIsaac were both waiting for her. No popcorn, but Charley had a bag of Munchkins that he offered around. John took four and Faith politely declined.

Dunne got up and stood by the projector. "There isn't any sound. They weren't recording."

"It was to test for lighting," Faith said, "but they did say their lines."

"Yeah, you can see that." He flicked a switch and first there was a long black leader, then the Pingree dining room sprang onto the screen, only it wasn't the dining room at all. It was a room out of a dream, totally a creation of the imagination. There was no suggestion that the white fabric floating about the walls was held on by pins or that about twenty people were just out of the frame. A soft light suffused the interior, leaving the periphery in shadows. After lingering on the room as a whole, the camera moved in for a close-up of Hester/Sandra. She looked absolutely terrified. Her eyes were abnormally large and fixed straight ahead on Roger Chillingworth, whose back was to the camera. Slowly he turned, revealing a small table that held his bag and the cup into which he had poured his healing draft. Either Greg was no actor or the role specified that Chillingworth's face be devoid of expression. As Faith gazed transfixed once more by the film, she suspected the latter. The doctor's lack of expression as he encouraged Hester to drink was particularly menacing. Hester/Sandra seemed to shrink inside herself and, trembling, took the cup. Her husband reached out and traced the scarlet letter on her bosom. She flinched, then stood up with an almost defiant look, raising the cup to her lips. The scene ended abruptly and once more they were looking at a dark screen.

It had been horrible watching Sandra Wilson's last moments in what it now appeared was almost a snuff film. Faith felt ill.

"Anything?" Dunne's voice asked quietly. He must have seen the film before, probably many times, but there was sadness and shock in his tone.

There was no question. Without the distraction of sound, it was her face, her presence that dominated. As Faith had realized at the Marriott screening, the camera was enamored of Sandra. She was destined for stardom, and the same subjective camera had almost recorded her death.

Faith closed her eyes and thought. Nothing came. Nothing she could put in words. She had to see it again.

They ended up watching it three more times—and repetition did not lessen the impact—before Faith said, "Enough."

"Let's go to my office," Dunne suggested, and the three left the room.

"You got any coffee?" Charley asked. It was the first time he'd spoken since offering the doughnuts.

"Sure not so good as Mrs. Fairchild's, but it does the job."

They settled into Dunne's cramped office, which was filled with file cabinets; a few chairs, not of the same period; and a battered wooden desk, conspicuous for the absence of any pictures, memorabilia, or personal items save a Gary Larson calendar. The coffee did indeed do the job, if the job was to unclog a drainpipe. Faith hastily put hers down after one exploratory swallow. Charley was made of sterner stuff and determinedly made his way through the cup.

"What did you see?"

"Something I didn't pick up on when I was actually in the room. There were so many people and so much going on that I didn't really focus on Sandra's face, just on the overall effect of the scene, which is both terrifying and very sensual."

Charley and Dunne both nodded.

"When I saw it today, it seemed that she looked more frightened than I remembered. Her pupils were enormous—and when I was holding her, waiting for the ambulance to arrive, they were like pinpoints. Which must have been from the chloral. Also, in the film, you can see she was shaking all over. When the camera moved in for that tight close-up, I even thought I could see goose bumps on her arm. It seemed more than the part called for and I wonder if she was afraid for real—or it could have been something else."

"Like what?"

"Like drugs!"

"Same thing struck us. Nothing turned up in the autopsy, but she may have been experiencing some kind of withdrawal. Or, as you say, she could have been afraid of something."

"Or someone," Charley contributed, crumpling up his cup and making a shot into the wastebasket that Larry Bird would have admired.

"I'm wondering why she drank from the cup. From the look on her face, the most natural thing would have been to get the hell out of there. Unless it wasn't someone on the set upsetting her, but an incident that had happened before the scene."

"Did you see her come in?" John said.

"No, I was there earlier, watching from the butler's pantry, and she was already in the room with Evelyn and Max. I remember thinking that she seemed to be trying to stay out of their way. She was in costume and stood by one of the front windows. It was a contrast to her usual spot—at Max's elbow, ready, willing, and able. The rest of the crew was bustling about putting up the fabric and doing whatever. Then Cappy Camson came in and asked Max if he had time to stretch his legs. Max told him to check back in an hour and Evelyn said in that case, she'd go for a walk, too." As she recounted this, Faith debated whether to tell them her Maxwell Reed/Roger Chillingworth theory, but she decided now was not the time. She needed to work on it some more.

"You've been a help, Faith." Dunne leaned back in his chair, taxing the frame to its limits with his own.

"I don't see how," she replied.

"You confirmed my own initial impression. That the girl was afraid. This means that someone may have been threatening her, subtly or not so subtly. She may have stumbled onto something that someone wanted kept secret."

"And from her reaction, the threat occurred close to the time she died. When I'd seen her before—when she was standing by the window, there wasn't much of any expression on her face. Maybe she was wiping the slate clean to prepare for her role."

"Great. We're beginning to narrow things down. We've been able to piece together most of her last morning and we'll concentrate even more now on anyone she was seen in conversation with during the time immediately before the camera started rolling. Starting with the other stand-in. He would have been there the whole time and she might have mentioned something to him."

"Let me know what you find out."

"Maybe." Dunne smiled. It always reminded Faith of a child's drawing, lopsided and raggedy. Not a pretty sight.

She was only slightly miffed. "Well, I have to get to work, if you two gentlemen will excuse me." She'd learn more about Sandra Wilson's death on the set than by sticking around police headquarters not drinking their coffee and not consuming the cardboard sandwiches from the machines in the hall that would comprise lunch.

"Thank you." Dunne stood up and both he and Charley followed her out into the corridor. "I mean it. And, Faith, keep in touch."

Maybe he'd give her a badge someday, Faith thought as she started up the Honda and drove toward Aleford. A tin one.

While Faith did not assume a deerstalker and magnifying glass, she nevertheless felt vetted by Dunne and arrived at the set shortly before the morning break, ready to detect whatever might come her way. It didn't take long. Cornelia was one of the first to seek sustenance from the canteen truck, and during the few moments they were alone, she uncharacteristically told Faith how afraid she was.

"You've been pretty chummy with the police. What do they think? Is it some crazed serial killer going after PAs?" Her voice shook and, from the bags under her eyes, it was clear she hadn't been sleeping soundly.

"That seems very unlikely," Faith reassured her, although the whole thing was extremely unlikely—a thought she kept to herself. "I can't imagine you are in any danger." Trying to make light of the situation and alleviate Corny's fears, she added, "Just stay away from pewter cups."

Cornelia stiffened. "I've been watching what I eat and drink for quite a while," she said pointedly, and Faith flushed. The black bean soup incident had been eclipsed

179

by recent events to the point where Faith had almost forgotten it.

"Or it could have been that someone was after Evelyn. At least this is what Evelyn thinks. She's been in constant hysterics since Friday. Max had to call her shrink in L.A. to see if he could calm her down. Of course she won't drink any Perrier and diet Coke."

This didn't surprise Faith. Evelyn would probably avoid the mixture for the rest of her life, for much the same reason that Janet Leigh didn't take showers after *Psycho*.

Cornelia continued to whine on. "But why anyone would want to kill her, especially before the movie is finished, I can't imagine."

Practicality—and loyalty to the project—were firmly intact and Cornelia's words reassured Faith that Ms. Stuyvesant might hate Ms. O'Clair passionately but was not a murderer. Hope had been correct in her assessment of Cornelia's personality. She wouldn't even jaywalk when they had been kids, let alone commit a major felony.

"What does Max think?" Faith asked quickly as she saw some of the rest of the crew approaching. She suspected Corny's tell-all mood wouldn't carry over to another occasion.

"It's been devastating for him, of course. He is so sensitive, and for Sandra to do something like this . . ." It was clear that despite any fears Cornelia may have expressed, deep down she was sure it was all the dead woman's own fault. "He called a meeting at the Marriott when we got back and announced he would do everything in his power to keep the movie on schedule and you see he has. Other than that, he simply won't talk about it. Too, too traumatic."

Faith wondered whether Max had said anything about the person who had been killed at the meeting. Watching

180

the laughing crew reach for muffins and put in coffee orders, it was beginning to seem as if the earth had swallowed up Sandra without a trace. Faith also tucked away a thought that something other than trauma might be responsible for Max's reluctance to discuss Sandra's death—something like guilt.

Faith had felt distinctly superfluous when she'd first arrived from police headquarters. Niki, Pix, and the others had preparations well in hand. Now with lunch in full swing, it was clear how capable those hands had been. Everything was going beautifully. Normally on shoots, the talent ate first, but on *A*, everyone ate together. Maybe because it was a relatively small company, many of whom had worked together before. Whatever it was, they were amiably consuming large bowls of Italian vegetable soup with several varieties of crusty foccacio. The meat entrée was Swedish meatballs (see recipe on page 309) served over egg noodles, a prized recipe from a friend's Norwegian mother. When Faith called them Norwegian meatballs, no one knew what she meant, so with a silent apology for ignoring what she understood were time-honored national differences, she bowed to custom. Whatever they were called, they were fantastic.

The crowd was thinning out and she noticed Greg Bradley sitting by himself at a table, nursing a cup of coffee. She quickly poured one for herself and went over.

"Do you mind if I join you?" she asked disingenuously. "I have to get off my feet for a moment."

"Sure. It must be quite a job, feeding all of us. I can't even boil an egg—and I don't want to learn. I'm happy to let people like you do the work, and you certainly do a great job." His plate was conspicuously empty.

"Thank you." Faith was touched by his appreciation. She tried to figure out how to direct the conversation

181

toward Sandra Wilson in a tactful manner.

Greg Bradley was roughly the same shape as Max, even down to the paunch, and his coloring was similar. But his face did not display the quixotic changes of temper that were Max's stock-in-trade. The grip/stand-in had been invariably easygoing every time Faith had seen him, except during the frantic moments before the ambulance had arrived to take Sandra away.

Before he could leave, Faith plunged in. The direct approach was often best, she found. "It's hard not to think about Friday. I felt so helpless."

"Me, too." His voice dropped.

"Was Sandra a close friend?"

"Almost." A shadow crossed his face. "This was the first time she'd worked with Max, and I've been around for several pictures. She was totally star-struck on our great director. Don't get me wrong. I think the man's a genius myself, but let's say I was waiting for the effect to wear off a little. Waiting in the wings."

"It must be hard for you to go about your business now."

"A little. Although work keeps me from thinking too much. The whole thing just doesn't make any sense. Who would have wanted to harm Sandra? I was going to take her into town next week. It would have been her twenty-first birthday."

Faith hadn't realized the girl had been so young.

"She came from here. Born in Boston—bred in the USA, she'd say. Her mom moved around a lot and I don't know what the story was with her dad."

"Did she want to act?"

"Not in the beginning. She'd talk to me for hours about all the technical aspects of filming. She wanted to go to school and make her own movies. Like a lot of us. Then after Max asked her to be Evelyn's stand-in, she began to talk about acting. You saw the footage. She was a natural, something that doesn't come along too often in this business."

Faith had another question she had to ask. "Do you think Max returned her affection?" She couldn't think of the right way to express her thought, but he understood.

"Was he sleeping with her, you mean? Maybe. You have to understand that during a shoot, a lot of everyday rules get turned upside down. Maybe it's true all the time in this business. Anyway, if he did, it didn't mean anything to him, but a hell of a lot to her. Now, I have to get back or Max will have my hide. Let's talk some more another time. I miss her very much."

It had been more than she expected. Much more. It was difficult to turn her attention to work when she kept hearing Greg's words, "I miss her. . . ."

Faith had nothing to report to Dunne, except her brief conversation with Greg. The police no doubt knew how old Sandra was and where she was born, and probably that Greg had been interested in her. Still, it was something. No one else had even mentioned Sandra's name. She could tell him about Cornelia's fears, only Faith wasn't entirely sure she wanted to introduce the subject— although she was sure Corny had had nothing to do with it. If Faith wanted to maintain credibility with Dunne and be the recipient of whatever tidbits of information he might fling her way, she couldn't very well say she'd had certain suspicions of her old classmate but now didn't. It was to maintain this tenuous position that she decided to call him after she got back to the kitchens. He told her they had known Sandra's age and birthplace but not that Greg hoped for a relationship with her. Dunne then said

Faith needn't bother to call again unless she had something to tell him, quashing her hopes of code names and check-in times but leaving her free to chart her own course.

The phone rang as Faith was leaving to pick up Amy and Ben. It was Alan Morris. No chance for any discussion of Friday's tragedy, however. It seemed it was business as usual.

"Max wants to shoot the town hall scene tomorrow night—and it could go all night. We'll start as soon as it's dark, so we'll need supper and then stuff to eat for the duration."

Faith said, "No problem." Aleford would be elated. This was the last scene for the extras and it was a cast of thousands, not to be confused with Mark Antony's welcome party for the queen in *Cleopatra*.

The Aleford Town Hall was what had sold Alan Morris on Aleford as a location, even before he'd seen the Pingree house. It didn't remotely resemble the architecture of Hester Prynne's day. It didn't remotely resemble the architecture of any day. It was a conglomerate, or, as some liked to put it, a "bastardization," if only to have the chance to say the word out loud, Faith suspected. The central portion was a basic Federalist domed red brick building with columns rising from several flights of treacherous stairs, now happily supplemented by a ramp. Another generation had added neo-Gothic wings to either side, complete with turrets and stained glass. The coup de grace was a Bauhaus addition, or "Bow wowhaus"—same people as "bastardization"—extending out the rear toward the parking lot. It took the form of a long, low building with plate-glass windows that was supposed to function as the police station, only neither Charley nor his predecessor would budge from their present quarters. They shared space with the town clerk, who had also refused to move, and if it was cramped, it was preferred for the privacy it availed. The "new addition," as it was still called, served as space for various town activities, most recently the Gentle Gymnastics class for senior citizens led by Poppy Wagner, a remarkably limber septuagenarian.

It was Dada. It was Nouveau. It was retro and, above all, Alan Morris had known immediately, it was Maxwell Reed. The large hall with its 1920s Maxfield Parrish-like murals of important events in United States history, site of Town Meeting for well over a century, would be perfect for the tribunal scene Max had extrapolated from the original book.

When the stagestruck extras took their seats the following night, no one was thinking how hard and uncomfortable they were or that they might get hungry. They were too intent on Alan's words as he described the scene for them against a backdrop of cast and crew finishing preparations. Cornelia was very much in evidence, standing by with her script and, for some reason, a stopwatch around her neck. She was Morris's Greek chorus, nodding vigorously as he spoke, an occasional "Yes, exactly" escaping from her lips.

Once again, Alan explained, Reed planned to mix past and present events, dissolving from one to the other until time itself became completely obscured.

"All of you are gathered to hear a proposal for a new youth center, spearheaded by Reverend Dimmesdale, Cappy Camson. Evelyn O'Clair—that is, Hester—unable to resist seeing him, creeps into a seat in the rear of the hall. She's wearing a long black hooded cloak as a disguise. On no account is anyone to turn around or pay any attention to her, even those next to her. It's as if she

185

wasn't here, remember. But Dimmesdale sees her immediately, knows who it is, of course, and memories of their shared passion befuddle his presentation. He is meeting her for the first time. They are making love."

Alan was going off into some private screening room of his own.

"Finally, he imagines that she is coming toward him as he pulls down a flowchart. She will actually be walking down the aisle at this point, but again *only* Dimmesdale can see her. He blinks and she vanishes. Roger Chillingworth gets up on the stage. He announces he will donate ten thousand dollars to the fund in honor of 'men like Arthur Dimmesdale.' Now you react. Clap, whistle, stomp, whatever, until you see this light go out"—he pointed off camera—"then stop immediately. We're going to run through all of it a couple of times before we shoot, so don't worry. After the applause, Dimmesdale tries to refuse the honor, then Hester reappears and walks back to her seat. This time, she is visible to everyone. As she goes by the stage, Chillingworth looks from the minister to his wife and realizes with full force what he has suspected all along—that Dimmesdale is Hester's lover. When Hester passes each row, you will stand up in turn and silently point at her—like this, with your right arms."

He stretched his arm out full length and pointed his finger. "As she passes, you turn slightly to keep pointing at her, still without saying a word. When she reaches the door, Pearl—Caresse Carroll—rises from one of the chairs and stands behind her mother. Hester kneels and Pearl silently puts her hands over her mother's eyes, then you'll hear the director say 'Cut.' That's it. Any questions?"

Millicent raised her hand, her right arm stretched out full length.

"Yes?"

"Are you sure you don't mean that those of us seated on the left side of the aisle should point with our right hands and those on the right side with our lefts? If you're striving for symmetry, as I understand Mr. Reed often does."

Alan Morris looked terribly flustered.

"I'll have to ask the director." He left hastily, pointing in the air first with one hand, then with the other.

Millicent sat down to general, unspoken acclaim. The pride of Aleford. Gave those movie people something to think about, bet your boots.

Alan returned after a few minutes.

"Mr. Reed likes the concept and we'll go with it. Does everyone understand the change?"

Of course they did. They all knew their rights from their lefts and especially which side they were on.

"All right, let's break for ten minutes, then come back and try it out."

Millicent Revere McKinley made for the rear of the hall swiftly, decisively slicing through the crowd shuffling to its feet like McCormick's reaper through a field of ripe wheat. Seconds later, she was in the basement of the building, swinging open the kitchen door.

The town hall's basement was legendary, even for Aleford. Some swore that there were tunnels from Civil War days, used as part of the Underground Railroad. Others said the tunnels were a legacy from a Prohibition-era board of unsavory selectman, but this was thought to be sour grapes on the part of the descendants of those not elected to said board. There was always some desultory talk at Town Meeting time about hiring someone to break through the backs of a few closets and rooms to find these tunnels, but nothing had ever come of it. Others doubted the existence of these tunnels, period, and thought both uses apocryphal, yet they did not deny the Byzantine

187

nature of the existing hallways and rooms, many without any electricity. There was also a smaller hall, Asterbrook Hall, with a stage that was often used for the less ambitious productions of the Aleford Thespians; several bathrooms of varying vintages; and a large kitchen. Have Faith had received permission to use this facility, and the entire staff was busy preparing the buffet to be served in the cavernous marble-tiled first-floor entry, the scene of other soirees, Faith surmised after discovering an ancient, and nonfunctional, dumbwaiter.

It was into a frenzy of steaming pots and piles of freshly cut sandwiches that Millicent sailed, blithely disregarding all agenda save one.

"Faith, where's your husband?" she demanded, implying both that Faith was amazingly lucky to have a husband and that said husband was dangerously close to being stricken from Millicent's Christmas card list.

"Why, he's home. With his children, our children." One had to be precise with Millicent. "Is anything wrong?"

"I thought he was going to talk to Penny, and just now upstairs I asked her if she'd seen Tom Fairchild lately and she said she had in church, which sounds to me as if Tom is forgetting our agreement!"

Your agreement, Faith amended to herself, saying out loud, "Tom has tried to talk to Penny. He called her on Saturday, but she put him off. She told him she couldn't discuss anything relating to Alden's charges with him or anyone else because they involved things that happened a long time ago and were private. She didn't accept our invitation to Sunday dinner, either—not that we wanted her to say anything more. We just wanted to show our support." This should satisfy Millicent, although Faith was sure it wouldn't.

It didn't.

"I expected more from Tom," she said sadly. "He has such a good reputation around town."

For what? Faith wondered. Wringing confessions out of unwilling parishioners? Getting people to do things they didn't want to do? Maybe this last was partly true. When the church needed volunteers, people tended to cross the street if they saw him approaching with that disarming smile of his.

"Well, it can't be helped. I must go back upstairs. Such a lot of fuss over standing up and sitting down. You would think we were imbeciles."

"I'm sorry." Faith found herself apologizing. Millicent had that effect. "Perhaps Penny is right and the town will simply have to trust her. In any case, we'll find out in less than a week from tonight. Right here again."

"He's up there, of course." Faith was a beat behind and realized Millicent meant Alden, not the Almighty, when she added, "Couldn't wear the foolish buttons on his suit, but it's written all over his face, and there are some stupid enough to listen to him. Pushing one another out of the way to be near him. Like a boy with a new toy they want. Fair-weather friends. I don't know what they're doing living here."

For Millicent, Aleford was the land of the brave, the true, milk and honey all in one.

"I'll see you at supper. Break a leg."

Either Miss McKinley had never heard the old stage adage or she chose to take it literally. Scowling, she went out the swinging door marked IN.

"Phew," said Niki. "You'd better call Tom and tell him to sleep with a pistol near his pillow."

"He usually does, Faith said sweetly.

189

It was a very long night. Max wasn't happy with anything and they did the whole scene and then parts of the scene over and over and over again. He tried having them all point with their lefts, then their rights, then every other person left and right, then randomly. After that, he was upset with Cappy's reaction to Dimmesdale's offer and had the young actor do take after take. Marta Haree was on the set, although not in the scene, and Max spent time between takes talking to her and to Nils. Marta was draped in her trademark scarves and wearing several large crystals on a chain around her neck.

During one of the breaks, Faith saw Penny in the milling crowd in the entryway and asked her how things were going. The candidate looked startled. "Oh, you mean the film?" She laughed at herself. "It's rather nice just to have to sit down, stand up, and point."

"I see what you mean," Faith commented. "You don't have to think about much."

"Exactly—and these days, that's a relief."

Faith seized the opening. "Penny, I know Tom talked to you, and probably the whole town has by now, but I'm very worried Alden might win. Don't you think you would improve your chances if you could at least give a hint about his allegations?"

"I'm sure it would improve my chances, and I know how important this election is, especially to young people like yourselves with children in, or almost in, the school system. But I would be betraying a trust, and there's no way I can ask the individual for permission. He's dead. In any case, I didn't mention it when he was alive and I certainly won't now. I'm sorry, my dear, we'll just have to take whatever comes. Perhaps James will win."

"What's that?" The candidate, accompanied by his wife, wandered over. "Talking about the election?" James did

190

not seem overly interested and took several sandwiches from the stack of smoked turkey, chutney, and thinly sliced sharp cheddar they'd prepared. From the crumbs on his plate, Faith guessed he'd also been sampling the lox and scallion cheese spread on dark rye. With a glance at Penny, Faith hastily replied, "Not really."

Penny's words had convinced her. Apparently, whatever this involved concerned the late Francis Bartlett, and it was certainly wrong to try to persuade a widow to violate her late husband's trust—however curious one might be. As she moved a bowl of curried coleslaw within James's reach—it went particularly well with the turkey—Faith puzzled briefly over Penny's reference to not saying anything while he was alive. This sounded as if she knew something that Francis hadn't known she knew. Faith was a bit in awe of women like Penny. They seemed mostly to be in books. She herself was hopeless at keeping big things from Tom. Little things were another matter, of course, but something major—and this had all the earmarks—was another issue entirely.

Nobody had said anything for several minutes, although Audrey Heuneman looked as though she might. Faith, uncomfortable with lengthy silences, however short, filled the gap, "We were merely talking about the voters deciding what they will—and in less than one week."

That unleashed Audrey's thought. "He thinks he's going to win, you know." From her venomous tone, it was clear she did not mean her husband, James. "But he's wrong. Dead wrong."

They heard the buzzer to return to the set. Faith was left to clear away the crusts and empty the dregs. The crowd had already consumed the vats of creamy New England clam chowder she'd prepared—though a fiercely loyal daughter of Manhattan, she drew the line at

191

chowder: no tomatoes. But there was plenty of everything else. It was two o'clock in the morning.

At 3:00 A.M., the legs on one of the tables decided to give way. While Pix, Niki, Scott and Tricia Phelan, and the rest mopped up the debris, Faith went in search of another table. When she had been in the basement previously to check out the facilities, the custodian had told her there was a supply room filled with folding chairs and tables if they needed them, behind Asterbrook Hall.

She opened the door of the first room leading from Asterbrook Hall and found it filled with old scenery and props. Another door proved to be a large walk-in closet, the repository of everything from Bicentennial souvenir mugs, "Aleford Then, Now, and Always," to what appeared to be some sort of truss. It was time for a town hall tag sale. Probably make a fortune. Mulling over what at this late hour seemed like a phenomenal idea, Faith turned a corner and entered a hallway that led back toward the new addition and a stairway to the main floor. It was dark, and groping for a light switch was proving fruitless. She could, however, see a dim glow around another corner. If she remembered correctly, it was the location of a bathroom—something that at the moment assumed priority over finding a new table, as she realized it had been many hours since the last pit stop. She walked rapidly toward the light, her eyes adjusting to the dimness. There was a door just before the corner. If her memory served her, it was the door to the bathroom.

It didn't. It was the fabled storage room, and as she entered for a better look, she tripped on a rolled-up carpet next to a pile of scrap lumber, probably left when the addition was built, and almost landed flat on her face. Her hands broke her fall, but her shoe went flying. She stood up. Everything was where it was supposed to be.

192

She turned back to retrieve her shoe, flicking on the lights, and realized that what she had stumbled over wasn't a carpet at all.

It was a body. The body of Alden Spaulding, with the back of his head caved in.

The cast on his left wrist was a dead giveaway.

CHAPTER 8

By thy first step awry thou didst plant the germ of evil; but since that moment, it has all been a dark necessity.

FAITH'S FIRST IMPULSE WAS TO RUN AS FAST AND AS far away as she could, but after several deep breaths, she knelt down to check for Alden's pulse. Her heart was beating so loudly and rapidly that it took a moment to confirm her initial impression. Anyone suffering a blow to the head like this would most certainly be dead.

Alden Spaulding was no exception.

She stood up and took a couple of shaky steps farther into the room. What to do? The moment word got out upstairs, the entire town would stream down, hopelessly obliterating any clues for the police. Clues. She looked around.

There were the tables, plenty of them, and stacks of folding chairs. Two of them were opened in the middle of the room, next to a table with a slide projector that faced a blank wall. Faith held her hand above the projector, careful not to touch it. It was still giving off some heat.

Alden and company had apparently been watching slides. It was an odd time for such entertainment. She was willing to bet the show hadn't been "My Trip to Parrot Jungle," but she hadn't a clue as to what it could have been. The only thing on the table was the projector. Unless the box of slides was in one of Alden's pockets, it had been taken by his assailant.

Nothing else in the room seemed out of place and there was no sign of a blunt instrument or other weapon lying by Spaulding's side—she assiduously kept her eyes off the region at the back of the head. His hands were not clutching a torn garment or strands of hair. No crumpled slips of paper. No sign of any struggle at all.

She turned off the lights—her prints were already on the switch—and closed the door. It was unlikely that anyone else would happen by until she could get to the police, but then three people had already been in this out-of-the-way spot in the last half hour.

As she walked toward the stairs, she noted that the door to the parking lot, a bit farther down the hall, was shut. But the button in the middle of the knob was out. It was unlocked, which could mean that someone had exited very recently. Unfortunately, this being Aleford, it could also mean that it hadn't been locked in the first place.

It was while Faith was contemplating the door that the lights went out.

Just one sound: *click*.

The basement was totally dark—and totally silent. The only noise was the pounding of her own blood in her ears. There wasn't even a slight rustle to indicate that another human being stood a few feet away.

She stiffened in terror and cautiously backed toward the wall as quietly as she could. Her flattened palms pushed hard against the rough concrete. If someone was going to rush out in attack, at least her position would be changed. She forced herself to think coherently; to think rapidly. She had three choices: she could run back the way she'd come and chance getting waylaid in the labyrinthine corridors; she could bolt for the door and race outside to the front of the building; or she could make a try for the stairs, possibly encountering the murderer. The only light switch she knew of for sure was around the corner by the stairwell. She cursed herself for not having gotten away at once. The whole thing had seemed so improbable, she hadn't felt in any danger, just sickened at the sight of the corpse.

There was the barest suggestion of movement. Faith was not sure she'd even heard anything. Alternative number four—staying where she was and being killed—moved prominently to the top of the list. It was madness to hesitate for even a moment more when someone was stalking her, armed with whatever had killed Alden and ready to repeat the act—this time in darkness.

The lights in the parking lot decided her. Whoever it was must have seen her, but she had seen nothing—so far.

She sprinted across the hall and threw open the door. The bitter cold night air was as welcome as a day in June, and she did not stop to look over her shoulder, running as fast as she could to the front of the building and tearing up the stairs.

Inside the front entryway, she stopped, panting slightly. She was safe. She'd made it.

The mess from the collapsed table had been cleaned up and her staff was presumably downstairs preparing replacements. It still didn't make sense to alert everyone. Instead, Faith went into the corridor circling the auditorium and soundlessly opened a door. She had to get in touch with the police.

195

Patrolman Dale Warren was having the time of his life despite the late hour. Normally, he had trouble staying awake for the ten o'clock news, let alone "The Tonight Show." They'd needed an officer of the law on the set in order to use the town hall, and to Dale's surprise, the chief hadn't wanted the plum assignment for himself. All night, the young policeman had watched in fascination as Maxwell Reed shot take after take after take. And they were going to shoot again tomorrow night. He'd never been so close to even one movie star, and to top it all off, he'd been addressed by Cappy Camson, who'd asked him if the time on the large Roman numeral clock facing the stage was correct. The patrolman was able to answer in the affirmative without hesitation. His own second cousin, Norman Warren, was responsible for winding it and seeing to its inner workings. He couldn't wait to tell Norm that none other than Caleb Camson had been asking about what Norm thought of as "his" clock.

It was this dream of glory that Faith abruptly dispelled, tiptoeing over to his post and grabbing him by the arm. "You've got to come with me right away!" she whispered urgently in his ear. "Do you have your gun with you?"

Dale Warren was one of Faith Fairchild's devoted partisans, yet as he looked into her agitated face, he had but one thought: The woman was nuts. Out in the corridor, when she breathlessly told him that Alden Spaulding's dead body was lying in the basement below and they had to hurry before the murderer got away, the patrolman was actually a bit afraid of her. So it took a moment to readjust his never swiftly running thoughts when they went down the stairs into the hallway, lighted once again, opened the storeroom door, and were presented with the fact.

"It's Mr. Spaulding. He's dead!"

Faith nodded. She'd known Dale since she moved to Aleford. "Yes," she said patiently, with only a slight impulse to scream, "that's what I've been telling you." She continued to spell it out for him. "The lights were off when I left. I mean, someone turned them off after I found the body, so whoever it is must have escaped when I did and is long gone. You'd better stay here while I call Charley. He'll probably call the state police, too."

Dale straightened his uniform and swallowed hard. His Adam's apple bobbed like a Macintosh in a washtub on Halloween. What a night! The movie—and now this!

Faith had to borrow a dime from Dale and went back up,stairs to the front of the building to the phone booth. As she dialed MacIsaac's number, she marveled at the detachment she felt. It was as if some other Faith was doing all these things and the real Faith was watching, too shocked to react. The real Faith's hair was still standing up on end with fright, and if she started to shake, she'd never stop.

Charley answered on the ninth ring.

"Charley, it's Faith. You have to get down here! I'm at the Town Hall and I'm afraid Alden Spaulding has been murdered. His body is in the basement in the new addition, near the door to the parking lot."

"If this is a joke, I'm not laughing. Do you know what time it is?"

"Charley! It's no joke. The back of his head is all bashed in and the man is dead! Dale is standing guard."

"Don't let anyone near the body. In fact, don't say anything to anyone until I get there." Chief MacIsaac spoke quickly, and from the way his voice changed volume, Faith imagined he was already struggling into his clothes while cradling the phone beneath his chin.

"Okay. And, Charley, hurry up!"

197

Convincing the chief had convinced her. The two Faiths slid back together and the situation smacked her full in the face. There was a corpse downstairs, still warm. She had been minutes, maybe seconds, away from witnessing the crime. Fear elbowed its way back center stage and she had to force herself to go back down the corridor, descending the rear stairs to wait for Charley.

It wasn't long before the chief appeared and took charge.

"Poor Alden," he said sadly as he surveyed the remains. "Not too many people liked him, but I didn't think even his worst enemy would have done something like this."

But his worst enemy apparently had, Faith thought. The question now was, Who out of the many contenders qualified for this dubious distinction?

"I called John," Charley added. "He's on his way with the CPAC crew from the DA's office." The Crime Prevention and Control unit, the first sifting and recording.

"Are you going to announce it upstairs?" Faith both wanted to watch the crowd's reactions and to be on the scene when Detective Lieutenant Dunne arrived. If Charley got moving, she might be able to manage it.

"Better do that now. Don't want them going home to bed."

Faith followed Charley into the auditorium. The interruption brought a stream of angry shouts and a few obscenities from Max, Nils Svenquist, and the crew until they saw it was the police chief. The audience looked puzzled. Charley walked onto the stage and stood next to the director and Cappy Camson.

"I want everybody to stay calm and stay put. There's been an accident, a very bad accident, and Alden Spaulding is dead."

A buzz went through the crowd and they weren't mumbling "apples and oranges." Several people half-rose in their seats. One woman yanked at her husband's coattails and he hit the back of the chair with a loud crack.

"We're waiting for the state police, then we'll figure out what we need from you. Believe me, I'm just as eager to go home as you are."

Millicent stood up. Not for her the mere rules of mortal men.

"Chief MacIsaac, do you suspect foul play?"

Charley looked resigned, "Yes, Millie, we do."

She nodded, making clear her unspoken, "I thought as much."

"Then I think you will find your task made easier by the fact that the time is recorded when each take is shot. You will also be able to eliminate some of us as suspects." Here Millicent paused and raked her fellow citizens with a glance, making even the innocent feel guilty as charged. "When you view the rushes, it should be possible to determine who was here and who was not at any given moment." She sat down.

Despite the cinematic jargon, Charley got the idea. Millicent was right—of course. Faith was standing near the director of photography and heard him murmur to an obviously upset Alan Morris, "Once again the camera records a tragedy. I think we are shooting the wrong film, my friend."

Once again. But what possible connection could the deaths of Sandra Wilson and Alden Spaulding have? It was apples and oranges.

She left Charley to deal with more questions and reactions, including a plea from Max that they be allowed to continue shooting, since they had to stay there anyway, and went back down to what was becoming an increasingly familiar spot. She'd check in with her staff after talking to Dunne.

The detective was already there and it was hard to read his expression. It wasn't surprise, since Charley must have told him she'd called. It was more like resignation. He turned to Ted Sullivan, who, like his boss, appeared to be able to leap from his bed into his clothes without a wrinkle or a yawn. Whereas Faith was pretty sure Chief MacIsaac still had his pajamas on underneath his rumpled tan corduroys and well-worn parka—not for him the kind of blade-sharp creases in Dunne's navy pinstriped suit trousers.

"We don't need to take Mrs. Fairchild's prints. They're on file from the last time, and the time before that."

"They'll be on the doorknob of the storeroom, on the floor where I fell, and on the light switch in the room. Oh, and on the knob of the outside door. I had to get out quickly," Faith offered. "I didn't touch anything else except his right wrist—I was trying to find a pulse."

Sully had been bending over the body and was now watching while the pile of lumber was photographed.

"Not too difficult to grab one of these as you follow the guy to the door and bean him."

The detective lieutenant agreed. "We'll know for sure when we get the lab report. Now, Mrs. Fairchild, why don't we sit down and you can tell me all about it?" A flash went off and Dunne winced. Maybe he was more tired than he looked.

Faith's own adrenaline was beginning to ebb. "There's coffee in the kitchen and I'd like to check in. My staff may not know what's going on, since they're in the basement at the other end."

"Sounds good. Lead the way."

Again, Faith went back upstairs to the passageway

skirting the auditorium. Dunne stopped and looked in the open door from the rear. It was controlled bedlam: lots of noise but little movement. Charley was engaged in a heated discussion with the director and his assistant. People in the audience were shouting to neighbors across the room. A stringer for the *Aleford Chronicle* was desperately begging Patrolman Warren to let him use a phone. The scoop of the century and he couldn't report in.

"Jesus." Dunne looked amazed. "The whole town's here!"

"Didn't Charley tell you?"

"He said they'd been shooting a scene, but no, he did not say that every man, woman, and child in Aleford was in it. I've got to call and get more help."

On the way, Faith told him about Millicent's suggestion. It would have been safe to pass it off as Faith's own idea—and it would have been eventually—except this was the kind of lie she didn't tell.

The kitchen with its warmth and deep-seated associations welcomed her like a mother with a glass of milk and plate of freshly baked chocolate-chip cookies after school. Not her mother, but some mother.

From their lack of concern, it was clear that word had not filtered down to the Have Faith staff. She filled them in while Dunne helped himself to coffee and several dozen sandwiches.

"I don't believe it," Pix stated firmly. "I just don't believe it! How could he!"

This was a new slant on the matter and redefined the whole concept of blaming the victim. Pix was treating the murder as Alden's ultimate campaign tactic—"He would do anything to get elected," her unspoken conviction.

The detective brushed the crumbs from his hands. He

201

had come in wearing soft gray suede gloves, carefully removing them when he ate. Faith always thought he looked like a wedding guest who had taken a wrong turn when he appeared at an investigation.

"I'm afraid I'm going to have to ask all of you except Faith to come with me upstairs. We're going to need everybody in one place. She'll be joining you as soon as I finish talking to her."

Oh, so no special treatment, Faith surmised while he was gone. She was to provide her information, then meekly join the rest of the herd. He was back soon.

"Now, Faith, for the love of God—and I know you do—will you please explain to me how it is you have managed to turn up with another body?" John perched on one of the high kitchen stools, creating an impossible balance that threatened at any moment to spill its top-heavy load onto the linoleum.

"One of our tables broke and I remembered the janitor had told me there were some others in a supply room behind Asterbrook Hall, so I went to look. I didn't find the right closet and so I kept going down toward the new addition. Then"—no maidenly blushes for Faith—"I had to go to the bathroom, and I remembered there was one there near the stairs. I opened a door, but it wasn't the bathroom; it was the storage room. I didn't notice Alden until I tripped over him. I thought he was a carpet."

Dunne was writing it all down in his Filofax. It was a new one, Faith noticed—brown instead of black calf.

"Did you hear anything while you were looking for this room?"

"No." Faith thought hard. "The old part of the building makes a lot of noises—creaks and groans—but nothing out of the ordinary. No cars pulling up or raised voices."

202

"And obviously you didn't see anything."

"No, not until I found Alden. But somebody was there. The lights in the hall went out shortly after I found the body."

Dunne looked up, startled. "Jesus, Faith! You might have been killed."

The thought had crossed her mind.

"Whoever it was was more intent on avoiding recognition. Lucky for me."

"Lucky!" John seemed about to say more, then picked up his gold Cross pen again and said evenly, "Charley tells me Spaulding was running for the Board of Selectmen. You're not crying, so he wasn't a friend, but you must have known who he was."

Dunne lived in a much larger town. Despite his years in the area—far away from his beloved Bronx—he still had not caught on to the nuances of places like Aleford. *Of course* she would know Alden Spaulding.

"He was a parishioner—which reminds me, I haven't called Tom—and even though this was the only time Alden had run for selectman, he was involved in all sorts of Aleford institutions: Town Meeting, Chamber of Commerce."

"What did he do?"

"He owns . . . owned COPYCOPY."

Dunne let out a soft whistle, just like the cops on TV. "So he was worth a pretty penny."

"Nothing was pretty about Alden, at least so far as I'm concerned, but yes, he was extremely wealthy."

"We'll get back to your biases in a minute. First, who do you think will get the money? Wife? Kids?"

Faith hadn't thought about who would benefit. She did so now, aloud.

"He never married, and if he had any kids, someone,

203

probably Millicent, would have spread the word. The only relative I know of is his half sister, Penelope Bartlett. His father remarried after his mother died and they had Penny. She's about seven years younger. But the two didn't get along, so Alden may have left his estate to charity."

She stopped short at visions of a new roof for First Parish. She had been forcing herself not to think how relieved she was that Spaulding was very definitely out of the race for selectman. This happy new prospect was testing all her powers of restraint. One didn't jump up and shout for joy when someone died, particularly in such a manner. No matter how one might feel deep down inside. Faith's conscience shook its finger sternly. She was glad it was on the job.

"Penny is upstairs, if you want to question her. She is one of the extras. It's possible she may know the provisions of his will. Some of the property may have been in trust from her father and goes to the next of kin."

"I'll speak with her," he said, then moved on to another subject. "What do you make of the slide projector? Was the guy some kind of photography buff? The slides are missing, by the way, so unless this Spaulding was demonstrating the art of hand shadows, we can assume the murderer took them."

"I've never seen him with a camera or heard him talk about an interest in photography."

Dunne wrote it down. "Now, before I go, tell me quickly why you disliked him so much. Aside from your comment, it's written all over your face every time you say his name."

"Well, to start, he was selfish, mean-spirited, and extremely aggravating." All those endless calls to Tom complaining about picayune things—a sentence in the sermon, a wrinkled choir robe, a charity being supported by the Ladies Alliance. This last was actually not a small matter and had had the congregation in an uproar. He'd objected to their fund-raising for safe houses for battered women; said they should have the houses for men. He was really totally crazy. Here was a new thought.

"You know, he may possibly have been more than a little crazy. He used to have furious temper tantrums and was extremely paranoid."

"All very helpful," Dunne said, "and I want to talk more, only I've got to get upstairs." He got off the stool and walked toward the door. Just before opening it, he turned around and faced her with a look close to the old parental "Can you look me straight in the eye and say that?" one.

"Faith, I like to think you would have told me right away, but I'll ask just to make sure. Do you have any idea who would have wanted to kill him?"

"No, not kill him in fact. Figuratively, more than half the town, especially during this election. His personal attacks on his sister's character were beginning to get to people. But bash his head in? No, I can't think of anyone."

And it was true. Tempting as it was to think that someone had killed Spaulding to prevent his election, no one in either opposing camp filled the bill. Not Penny and not Millicent. Pistols at dawn on the green would be more Millicent's style. She'd never sneak up behind him. She'd want him to know what hit him. And the Heunemans—impossible. James looked to be one of those New Englanders whose reverence for life was such that he even eschewed ant traps. No doubt Audrey was the same, or was she? What about her remark—was it only a few hours ago?—that if Alden thought he was going to win, he was

205

wrong? Dead wrong. And what about knocking over the coffee urn the day they were shooting on the green? What was it Freud said about there being no such thing as accidents? No, it was impossible. Besides, tonight the people around her would know right away she was missing from the scene. Still, when they looked at the film, they'd have to check every empty seat. Besides Alden's.

On the way upstairs, she mentioned this again to John.

"They've been shooting steadily since the break. It should be possible to tell who's missing by comparing the frames, as well as to estimate the time of death."

John agreed. "Very handy—we don't usually have someone with a camera around before the crime."

This reminded Faith of one of many unanswered questions. "I wonder why Alden left for his slide show during the shoot?"

"Maybe he was looking for the little boys' room, opened the wrong door like you did, and just happened to have some slides in his pocket."

"Or he'd arranged to meet someone." Faith was exploring all avenues.

"On second thought, why don't you go home now?" Dunne suggested pointedly.

Sure, run along and miss everything.

"That's all right. I'm really not tired. I'll give Tom a call and join you inside."

"Whatever." Dunne was walking rapidly away toward the auditorium, leaving his aspiring partner in the dust. She phoned home, told a barely conscious and totally astounded Tom what had happened, then followed Dunne's footsteps, carefully positioning herself just behind his line of vision. She'd decided not to inform Tom about the lights going out until she could tell him in person. It might have disturbed his rest.

Cornelia got up from the folding chair near the stage, where she'd been sitting clutching her clipboard, when she saw Faith and walked over to her side. She was visibly upset. "What kind of place do you live in! Every time we turn around, somebody else is getting killed!"

"Believe me, it's not an everyday occurrence." An everyweek occurrence lately, however. Faith was tempted to be more cutting with her old classmate. Oddly enough, it seemed important to defend the honor of what was now her hometown, except Corny was so uncharacteristically rattled that Faith decided to exercise tact. It was due for a workout, anyway.

"I know how upsetting this must be for all of you," she told Corny, "and everyone here feels the same way. It's totally inexplicable. But both Detective Lieutenant Dunne and Chief MacIsaac are extremely capable and I'm sure things will be straightened out soon. Why don't you sit down again? I think Detective Dunne may have something to tell us."

Corny was only partially placated. "I still say this is a very weird place. I'd feel a whole lot safer in Central Park all by myself, wearing Mother's jewels at midnight!"

It was hard to disagree when there was a corpse literally below their feet.

Dunne and Charley were deep in conversation. Maxwell Reed kept trying to interrupt and the detective was waving him away like an unwanted puppy. Finally, Dunne turned to the director and said, "Look. We know you have a movie to shoot. We know how much money you're losing. We know you're famous. But we have a very dead person downstairs. The second cadaver to appear in connection with your endeavor, and it's my show at the moment, so sit down and shut up. Please," he added with one of his monstrous smiles.

207

The director did. Next to Alan Morris, who proceeded to meet Max's furious remarks with what Faith presumed were sympathetic murmurs, guaranteed to calm Reed down while remaining in total agreement. It was a gift.

Caresse and her mother were at the end of the row. It was hard to establish who was comforting whom. Caresse's head was on Jacqueline's shoulder and she was patting her mother's hand. Both looked fearful and close to tears.

Faith was surprised when Marta Haree approached her. "You are the one who found him, yes?"

Was it a guess or had she overheard Dunne and MacIsaac talking?

"Yes, I did."

"It is a horrible thing, murder. Cutting off a life before the appointed time. To find the victim must have been terrible also. I'm sorry, although perhaps he was not a close friend?"

Faith found herself answering, despite her surprise at the question. "No, he was not really a friend at all, although I have known him some time."

Marta looked into Faith's eyes. "Then it's not necessary for you to become involved, which is fortunate. Sometimes people become involved in journeys better not taken." She spoke firmly, each word distinct.

For an instant, Faith was tempted to ask the woman where her crystal ball was. It was definitely strange.

Marta turned to go back to her seat, her crystals clinking faintly. She smelled slightly of sandalwood. "You are a wonderful cook, my dear," she said with a smile.

Faith didn't know whether to break out in the chorus of "Bibbidi-Bobbidi-Boo" or whistle the theme from the "Twilight Zone."

Just then, John spotted Faith. She wondered whether

he was going to make her go home, but, to her surprise, he crooked a finger and beckoned her closer.

"Charley can't find Spaulding's sister. Take a walk around and see if you can spot her. If not, I'll make an announcement."

Faith surveyed the hall carefully. Everyone was clad in the same kind of monochromatic clothing they'd worn for the scaffold scene. She looked down each row. Penny had softly curling short hair-brown mixed with a substantial amount of gray. She might have removed the glasses she normally wore for the shoot, and her ruddy complexion, the result of walking her Irish terrier, was shared by most of the hale and hearty Alefordians in the audience. The hair was the best bet, but it was nowhere in sight.

Millicent was sitting next to an empty seat, an aisle seat, and Faith was sure that must have been where Penny had been sitting, but Dunne had said he would make the announcement, so she didn't ask Millicent whether she'd seen Penny.

"She doesn't appear to be here," Faith reported, ardently wishing it could be otherwise. Why would Penny leave after Charley's explicit directions?

Dunne got up onstage and everyone quieted instantly.

"Would Penelope Bartlett come forward, please?"

The only movement was that of people craning their necks' to look for Penny.

Millicent stood up. She and Dunne were old friends.

"She's not here, Detective Lieutenant Dunne." Millicent believed in using full titles. "The victim was her half brother, so naturally she was very upset. She's gone home."

"Thank you, Miss McKinley."

John Dunne would have leapt off the stage if he had been seventy or eighty pounds lighter and a few feet shorter. He got off as rapidly as possible and told Chief MacIsaac to get over to Penelope Bartlett's house posthaste.

He noticed Faith again and this time he did tell her to go home.

"All we're doing is taking names and asking if anyone saw Alden leave the room. So go home. Straight home."

Dawn was beginning to streak across the horizon as Faith pulled into the parsonage driveway. She was very, very tired, and she endangered several of the Canadian hemlocks that made up the hedge separating the Fairchilds from the Millers before she stopped the car in front of the garage door. She was too exhausted to open it.

Upstairs, Tom awoke as soon as she came in the room. Normally, it took the alarm and his wife's gentle shaking to rouse him.

"Stay where you are. I'll be right there," Faith told him. She was soon resting in his arms beneath the duvet, incredibly happy to be where she was. Incredibly happy to be alive. As she told Tom what had happened, she allowed herself to feel the full impact. There had been a death. Another death. The violence of the crime and her own brush with danger jolted her into wakefulness.

"What do you do when someone you don't like gets killed? It's been horrible all night." She'd been glad the dimly lighted room had obscured the full extent of Alden's injury. It wasn't Technicolor; it was black and white.

"We do the same thing we do when anyone dies. We pray for them. We may not mourn them in the same way. That's only natural, darling, but we pray."

Tom's words were comforting. There were times when it was very handy to have a minister for a husband, and Faith began to get drowsy again.

"I'll take care of everything. You try to fall asleep," Tom told her. She already was.

When Faith opened her eyes, it was almost noon. The phone was ringing. She jumped out of bed, forgetting for the moment that Tom must be home. It was answered on the fourth ring, which proved he was indeed downstairs and the children must be nearby, hence the delay. She grabbed her robe and went nobly to his rescue.

"*Mommee!*" Ben shrieked, "Amy keeps bothering me!"

It was hard to figure out how, since the baby was in her infant seat, peacefully batting at a toy bar with pastel-colored bunnies and other mutants of nature.

Child Number Two occupied for the moment, Faith turned her full attention to Child Number One. It was the ever-present threat to this position that she suspected was really bothering him. She picked him up and kissed the top of his head. His hair smelled like baby shampoo. Tom must have bathed him. Ben hugged her tightly and she hugged him back. She'd been missing both kids terribly.

"Honey, she's so little. She doesn't even know what bothering is." But she'll find out, assured a voice from within. "Show me what you've been doing. Have you had lunch yet?"

Ben wasn't sure. Tom shook his head from his position by the phone, where he was engaged in a remarkably one-sided conversation.

"Do you want to help Mommy make toasted cheezers?" The chance to reduce a slab of cheddar to crumbs with the cheese slicer was always a winner, and Ben nodded enthusiastically. "Amy can't do it. Amy can't do anything," he happily explained to his mother, who was getting out some sliced ham and tomatoes to add to the sandwiches.

211

Tom hung up and came over. He wrapped his arms around his wife and said, "Boy, am I glad you're awake. The phone has been ringing all morning. That was Millicent." He raised his eyebrows. "Our friend regards last night's incident as some kind of divine retribution. Her first words were, in fact, 'Isn't it wonderful for the town.' "

"I don't think it's that she's insensitive—well, maybe she is—but in this case, it's simply the old McKinley tunnel vision at work. She sees the goal, her goal, and nothing else."

"You may be right. At the moment, she's looking for Penny."

"What! You mean she didn't go home after leaving last night?"

"She may have gone home, but she wasn't there by the time Charley got there."

"Maybe she decided not to answer the door."

"They thought of that. Charley knew Millicent had Penny's spare key and went back to the Town Hall to get it. Millie insisted on going back with them to make sure Penny was all right, but she was gone. Millicent had some idea we knew Penny's whereabouts, and you know how Millie is. The more I said I didn't have a clue, the more she seemed to think I had secreted Penny in the attic."

"There's certain to be a lot of publicity. Maybe Penny wanted to avoid it. She's definitely of the "a lady only appears in the newspaper three times: birth, marriage, and death" school. Given the way she felt about Alden, it doesn't seem as if this is a crazed grief reaction."

"It's troubling, whatever her reasons. And speaking of publicity, you're in great demand—we've heard from every newspaper, TV, and radio station on the East Coast. Charley's holding a press conference at three o'clock, so maybe you can get away with a statement there."

"Good idea." Faith removed the nicely browned sandwiches, slightly oozing with the melted cheese, from a large cast-iron frying pan, cut them in half, and arranged them on a platter. She poured milk in a pitcher and set both on the table. All this publicity wouldn't hurt business. Her conscience immediately snapped to attention. What kind of person could even think of something like that!

When she got back from delivering her brief statement about finding the body, it was almost five. Amy was up from her nap. Ben had stoutly refused one, Tom reported. Both Fairchild men looked beat.

"Why don't you lie down before supper and I'll read to Ben?" Faith suggested. "There's some chili and I'll make a salad. Nothing much."

"Sounds wonderful. All of it. Don't let me sleep too long, though. I have a ton of work to do. Nobody mentioned anything about when they would release the body for the funeral, did they?"

"No, but Alden's lawyer from Boston was there. You could call him."

Tom nodded.

"Oh, I almost forgot, two other things," Faith told him, "They've issued a description of Penny statewide and asked that anyone seeing her contact the police."

"The poor woman. What can be going on?"

"Everyone is as puzzled as we are."

"And what's the second thing?"

"Alden was killed with a piece of wood from the pile of old lumber in the storeroom, so it may not have been premeditated—unless the murderer was extremely familiar with the Town Hall's basement."

Tom, his eyes drooping, was clearly not as fascinated by

213

all this as she was.

"Go to sleep, sweetheart, and we'll talk later when the kids are in bed."

After they had finished eating, it was time to tuck Ben and Amy in. When Faith came back downstairs, Tom had started working. She decided to leave him to it. She had work of her own. She got one of his yellow legal pads and sat down at the kitchen table.

Alan Morris had been at the press conference, representing the movie company, and Faith had feared he would avoid her. In a way, she had once more brought the production to a screeching halt. Instead, when the press left, he had greeted her warmly, expressing concern over her gruesome discovery and asking whether she was all right. She'd thanked him, then wondered if she should ask him about plans for the shoot. Were they going to continue and, if so, would her services be required? The police hadn't said anything and Alan's own statement to the press had been a short expression of sympathy for the victim's family. Just as she started to say something, he did. She let him go first.

"Evidently, the police have decided there is nothing to be gained by keeping us captive in our hotel rooms, so we're going to be shooting again tomorrow night. With that area in the basement roped off and an officer at every door, I'm told. Will you be able to supply the same sort of provisions?"

Faith had assented emphatically. And she'd be sure they brought their own extra tables this time.

They would have all day tomorrow to get ready and maybe even sneak in a nap, since it would be a late night again, she thought as she began to make a list on the paper in front of her.

It wasn't a shopping list.

Somewhere, somehow, there had to be a connection between the two deaths besides their occurrence during the shooting of *A*. If she wrote down everything she knew, that connection might become clear.

She folded a sheet in half and neatly labeled one column "Death One" and the other "Death Two." Approaching the whole thing as a kind of social studies report helped. These were events, not people. The first thing to determine was who was present at both times. This neatly enabled her to eliminate all of Aleford save her own catering staff and self. The day Sandra died, there had been no extras around. She had to assume the cast and crew were the same at both, except for Caresse. She hadn't been on the set during the prison cell scene. But everyone else who was at the Town Hall had been.

So where did that leave things? Plenty of suspects, yet no apparent motives. She let her imagination roam free over the landscape of her mind. What possible connection could Sandra have to Alden? They were an unlikely couple, although Alden might have harbored certain fantasies. Besides, Sandra was so besotted with Max that she wouldn't look at Greg Bradley, certainly a more suitable choice than portly, pretentious Alden. Maybe Sandra was Alden's long-lost illegitimate daughter and she was blackmailing him. But Alden hadn't been anywhere near the set of *A* when she died. His presence, even before, to doctor the drink, would have been noted. And, if he'd killed her, then who'd killed him? Sandra's mother, a possible avenger, was already dead. According to the police, Sandra's closest connection had been her roommate, who was in California at the time, and Greg Bradley had not given Faith the impression of an impassioned lover. His relationship to Sandra had been mostly wishful thinking.

But was it so improbable to assume that Alden had been on the set when she died? He'd certainly been there, lurking in the woods, during the shooting of the forest scene. Alden with his binoculars. Faith hadn't actually seen them, and she suddenly realized she'd been barking up the wrong tree. It wasn't a pair of binoculars that Alden had been trying to hide, but a camera. Alden *had* had an interest in photography—"art" photography. Now where did this take her?

If the slides he was showing at the Town Hall were nude shots of Sandra, who would have been there watching with him? The most logical choice was Sandra. He might have tried to blackmail her in some way with them. But she was dead.

Faith decided to approach the subject from another angle: timing. She scribbled away. The neat columns had long gone by the board. Alden had not been killed during a general break, which meant it couldn't have been anyone actively involved in the scene being shot. One of the townspeople would have been able to slip away, but this didn't link up with Sandra's death. Were there any cast members peripheral to the scene? She made a note on a separate page to ask Dunne, who was no doubt going over the footage and might let her have another peek.

She started to gnaw on the pencil eraser, then got herself a large ruby cornice pear instead. It was a juicy one and she stood up to eat it over the sink. Her meanderings had touched upon Sandra's mother, which reminded Faith that neither victim had had many family ties. This was invariably the first place to look for a perpetrator, since every third grader knew from constant repetition on TV and in the press that you were much more likely to be bumped off by blood than water.

The pear finished, she rinsed her sticky fingers and sat

216

down again, the sensation that she wasn't getting anywhere increasing steadily. Her interesting but admittedly tenuous theory about Max/Chillingworth did not apply to Death Two, unless—going back to the purported photos—Max was enraged by Alden's voyeurism. Yet unless Max had some well-concealed reason for wanting to sabotage his own film, she was forced to eliminate him from her suspects. But it could be someone else wanting to sabotage the film. Someone who had it in for Max or one of the other actors?

She thought of Alan Morris, the ever-present, loyal assistant director. He seemed devoted to the movie, and especially its director; however, it was possible he was secretly jealous of Max and resented all the credit Reed got. Certainly, Alan worked incredibly hard. Maybe the one line he got on the screen wasn't enough. Maybe he wanted to move up. He'd been in medical school and might have known Sandra was asthmatic.

She went back to Alden and Sandra. What in their past lives could have connected the two? They lived a continent apart, but she had been born in Boston. Or was it something completely separate in their pasts that led to their deaths happening coincidentally close together? Was Alden's a copycat crime? The two methods were so different: one quite subtle and obviously premeditated; the other brutal and impulsive.

She wrote "Find out more about Alden and Sandra's past" on the page with "View footage." Her head was starting to swim. She had two possible leads. It wasn't much.

Then she added: "Alden on set last Friday? Saw something? Blackmail?" If this was true, she could put Max, Alan, and virtually everyone else at the Pingrees' back in the running. She thought about what Greg

Bradley had said: ". . . a lot of everyday rules get turned upside down." Maybe a lot of those rules got broken, as well.

What else? There was the question of the soup. It had never been answered. Was it safe to assume Caresse added the Chocolax in a moment of pique, or was it some kind of rehearsal for Sandra's poisoning? She made a note to suggest to Dunne that he press the little girl—oh so gently, of course—to confess to her prank.

She tried to picture a piece of blank paper. Someone had once told her this was a way to cure yourself of insomnia—or trigger something you were trying to remember. It seldom worked for Faith in either case, not that she'd had much trouble sleeping since Ben was born. The problem was staying awake.

The sheet stayed snowy white, then a single word appeared: *suicide*. "Suicide," she wrote down. Not Alden. That would have been quite a feat, but Sandra. There was the slim possibility she had been despondent enough over her hopeless crush on Max to want to kill herself. Or drugs may have been involved. Faith needed to think it through some more.

Tom came out to the kitchen in search of nourishment.

"What are you up to, honey?" he asked.

"I thought if I got something down on paper, I might be able to make more sense out of all of this."

"And have you?"

"I've written a lot, but it's mostly gibberish." Faith was disgusted.

"Well, you can't expect to solve a crime sitting at your kitchen table." Tom was sorry the moment the words left his mouth. "Not that you're involved in solving these." He had been understandably very upset about Faith's near tête-à-tête with Alden's murderer.

"Why don't I make you a big sloppy sandwich with the entire fridge in it and we can talk."

"Swell," said Tom. "I know when I'm being side-tracked. But be sensible, Faith—and haven't I said this before recently?—you have two kids to think of, and me, by the way."

"Don't worry, love, you won't be stuck with them."

"That's not what I mean and you know it." Tom was clearly not in a jovial mood.

He seemed to feel better after starting to consume a bottle of Samuel Adams Boston Lager and the sandwich of roast beef, red onion, broiled peppers, tomato, lettuce, Swiss cheese, and mayo on sourdough bread his wife set before him. They talked over the various possibilities on Faith's list, but the combined Fairchild forces didn't get much further than she had alone. They were about to give up and go to bed when the phone rang.

"I'll toss you for it," Tom suggested.

"No, I'll get it. You had to deal with all those calls this morning. Besides, I'm curious to find out who could possibly be calling at such an unfashionably late hour. What is it? Almost ten o'clock? It can't be anyone from Aleford."

Faith wasn't to know where the call came from.

"Faith Fairchild?"

She didn't recognize the voice. Whoever it was had a heavy cold.

"Yes," she replied, ready for a fund appeal.

"Keep your fucking nose out of other people's business."

"Who is this! Hello! Hello!"

The line went dead.

She hung up and immediately dialed the police. Charley was on duty. She realized she was shaking. The

219

voice—she couldn't be absolutely sure whether it had been a man or a woman—had sounded so venomous. The warning was clear.

Charley said he'd be right over and would get in touch with Dunne. Faith went back to the kitchen. It seemed as if she had been gone for an hour. Tom was still contentedly munching.

"Who was it, honey?"

Faith's call to Chief MacIsaac had calmed her down. The last thing she wanted was to upset Tom, but it was inevitable in this particular situation.

"It was a crank, an obscene phone call. Whoever it was told me to mind my own business, essentially."

"Faith! I knew it! We have to call the police!" Tom looked stricken, the remains of the sandwich in his hand suspended between his plate and mouth.

"I've already called and Charley is on his way. Honey, don't worry. Nothing is going to happen to me." Faith knew she could take care of herself. It was harder to convince her husband.

Charley was more agitated than usual, and as they sat debating the ways someone could disguise his or her voice, Faith realized the chief's mind was elsewhere.

"Charley, is something more bothering you? Because if it's just the call, please trust me. I know it was a warning and I'll be careful. Very careful."

"I hope so. You're right. The call was the last straw, but frankly, I'm worried sick about Penny. No one's seen hide nor hair of her since last night after I announced that Alden was dead."

"I wish we could help you, except we haven't heard a thing, either. Millicent's been calling, too. She thinks Tom is hiding Penny."

220

There was a short pause.

"And of course he's not." MacIsaac's expression turned the statement into a question.

Faith hastened to defend her husband, who appeared startled.

"Charley! First of all, Tom is a man of a very high quality of cloth, and they don't do things like that, unless the Nazis or whatever are at the door. And second of all, why on earth would he—we hide Penny? And why would she need to hide? Do you think she's in some kind of danger?"

"You tell me. We searched the house from top to bottom today. Every time I opened a closet, I got the willies, the way things have been happening around here." Faith thought she detected a sigh. More garrulous than was his wont, Charley kept talking.

"Nothing's going right. All those people, and not one saw Alden leave. Too busy stargazing. And he's the only person missing from the audience on the film."

"This is a really tough time for you. I hope you'll drop by whenever you want," Tom offered.

"Thanks, I will. Oh, and you can have the funeral on Friday. I told the *Chronicle* and they managed to get it into tomorrow's edition. Maybe Penny will show up."

The chief was not the only one in Aleford who had the willies. Ever since Alden's body had been discovered, the entire town was looking over its shoulder. Doors that had been kept on the latch for centuries acquired shiny new dead bolts. Children were cautioned to come straight home from school, and hosts and hostesses of social gatherings planned for the weekend found themselves facing a night of TV. No one wanted to be out after dark. Penelope Bartlett was the constant topic of conversation.

The woman had simply vanished from the known

221

world.

The baby was crying. Why didn't that woman shut her up? She was certainly getting paid enough, and with her English accent and starched uniforms, she looked like the real thing. A costume. You could be anybody with the right costume. No one knew this better than Evelyn O'Clair did. Makeup and costumes; smoke and mirrors. It was all an illusion. Her whole life.

Why couldn't the damned nanny keep the baby quiet! Probably didn't want to spoil the kid, but she'd been told more than once that when Evelyn was home, she didn't want to hear a thing.

She reached forward and turned on the gold-plated hot-water tap. It wasn't like her bathroom at home. That was made up of three rooms, one opening into another, culminating in the largest, which had a pool-sized tub made of marble, with malachite inlays, overlooking the ocean through dramatic floor-to-ceiling windows. But this setup wasn't bad. At least it had a Jacuzzi, and the rose carpeting gave the room a warm glow. She leaned back on the inflatable pillow and let her thoughts drift. The perfumed water steamed slightly.

For a moment, she recaptured the calm she'd felt before the baby started screaming. It was quiet. Then the noise started up again. She stood up in annoyance and got out. The water splashed onto the carpet and she reached for her robe, ready to tell the nanny off. Where the hell was Max? It was late. He'd said he'd be home hours ago. He would have taken care of it. Would have picked up the baby himself. He adored her. Had named her. Such a funny name, Cordelia. Evelyn had wanted something more modern like Tiffany. But she didn't care. One name was as good as another.

The crying stopped suddenly, like an alarm turned off. She

222

debated getting back in the tub, but it required too much effort. Night shooting was a strain. She had to get some sleep or it would begin to show on her face.

She wished Max had never started the film or that she had been committed to another project. Except he would have just waited for her. She hated her part, Hester Prynne. It didn't do too much for her image. Hester Prynne, an adulteress.

She hated being in this house, in this town. She hated the whole thing.

Naked, she walked over to the wall of mirrors lighted softly from above, dragging her robe behind her and unpinning her hair from the top of her head. Not bad. She'd exercised constantly and all through the pregnancy had rubbed cocoa butter on her disgusting belly. The doctor was amazed at how little weight she'd gained, she remembered proudly. She looked at herself closely. Unless you were as familiar with her body as she was, you'd never have noticed the difference. But there was one tiny wrinkle that would not go away and a slight slackness around her navel. When Max had discovered she was pregnant, she'd agreed to have it. Only no more. And there wouldn't be any more. She'd see to that. She couldn't plead exhaustion forever, but she could be careful—very, very careful.

She slipped on the thick, velvety soft terry-cloth robe and let it slide down over one shoulder, revealing one perfectly formed breast. She struck a pose, tossing her head, moistening her lips. Not bad for her age.

And what that was, not even Max knew for sure.

CHAPTER 9

But the past was not dead.

THE FAIRCHILDS WERE MIDWAY THROUGH THEIR DAILY breakfast ritual. The baby was covered with cereal, its consistency suggesting Faith should quickly cut a strip of wallpaper and decorate her daughter. Ben was complaining that there were pictures of basketball players on the box but no cards inside. "No basketball players, either," his mother told him. "Now, please finish eating." He hadn't liked the answer and was staring off into space. Tom was doing whatever grown men did in the morning to get ready for work, which took roughly twice as long as most women. Faith had already poured and discarded two cups of hot coffee for him. When the phone rang, she reached for it as eagerly as a teenager.

"Good morning, Faith. Have you got a pencil and paper?"

It seemed an odd reason for Millicent to call, but it was always better to humor the woman.

"Why, yes. Right here." She reached for the pad and pencil from last night.

"Good, because I don't want you to forget to check any of these places."

"What places?" Faith was willing to play along. Anything beat chipping encrusted food from Amy, and she needed changing, too.

224

Millicent ignored the question. An agenda was an agenda.

"The problem is, I can't go into town myself, because—and this is quite shocking—the police are watching my house."

It was quite shocking and also quite unbelievable. Why would the police be staking out Millicent's Colonial? Surely they had come up with more likely suspects. Then it dawned on Faith. Of course. Dunne shot up a notch in her estimation. Follow Millicent to find Penny. He couldn't know that Millicent really didn't know where Penny was. And "places" meant places Penny might be. The game was getting better and better.

"So, you want me to go into Boston to look for Penny."

"Not you," Millicent corrected, "Pix and you. You need someone local to help you get around."

Faith didn't mind having Pix along at any time. And in this instance, she could be helpful negotiating the one-way streets all in the same direction that made up Boston proper, but it hurt not to be trusted to go it alone. She wondered why Millicent was bothering with her services at all and was about to ask when Millicent handily supplied the answer.

"You seem to be so much closer to the police force than dear Pix." It was not a compliment.

Still, Faith was more than happy to take on the task. If she could find Penny, she might be able to find out more about Alden, and then there was the whole issue of why Penny had run away. Faith did not believe it was grief. Penelope Bartlett must know something.

She had one more question, mostly because she was curious.

"Why are you so sure Penny is in Boston?"

"Besides the fact that I immediately saw the dog was in

225

his run outside and had food for a day or two, just her overnight case is gone. She wasn't planning to go far. I took the liberty of noting what was gone when Charley and I were going over the house—her toothbrush, night cream. . . . Obviously, she planned to stay somewhere. But from what I could tell, only her blue suit is missing from her closet. Remember, she was wearing a brown wool dress and a navy quilted down coat from Bean's?"

Faith had not remembered; had not even noticed, which tended to be the case with Penny's wardrobe. Millicent was a marvel. However, you wouldn't hear that from Faith's lips.

"She was carrying her brown purse, too. I hope you're getting this all down. When we're finished, I'll call Pix while you're getting ready. Perhaps it would be best to wear something, shall we say discreet—to blend in."

Was Millicent suggesting that Faith's normal attire set her apart from the madding crowd? She certainly hoped so. Yet it was a good idea and she'd leave her modish large-checked blanket coat at home and wear the preppy little black Lauren she saved for funerals instead.

"Here are the places Penny would be apt to go. Start at her club, the Chilton Club. Pix knows where it is. Her mother's a member. Penny might be having lunch there. But she isn't staying at the club, because I already checked."

Faith interrupted her. "But Millicent, would she go someplace so familiar? Someplace where she would be recognized?"

Millicent was indignant. "You don't think a member of our club would call the police about another member!"

Enough said.

"Shall we continue? If she's not eating there, she might be at the Museum of Fine Arts. In the restaurant, not in that little café with those spindly chairs outside the gift shop and certainly not in the cafeteria. You should also check the members' room. If it was Friday, our job would be simple, because Penny would never miss symphony. The only other thing I can think of is the flower show—in Horticultural Hall on Mass. Avenue. She never misses it and bought her ticket a month ago."

"Where do you think she might be staying? Does she have a favorite hotel—or friends in town?"

"Of course she has friends in town and I've already called them. And she assuredly would never have had an occasion to stay in a Boston hotel." Millicent's inflection made the two words sound decidedly seamy. "She has taken tea at the Copley, though. Add it to the list. Now you had best get yourself organized. That sounds like your child in the background, so I'll say good-bye." Millicent hung up and Faith was left to cope with her child, the crying one, as opposed to Tom's, who clearly never did.

As she took Amy upstairs to clean her, Faith made another list in her head. A "How Am I Going to Cater Tonight's Shoot and Take Care of My Children?" list. She started with Tom, who, surprisingly, thought going to look for Penny was an excellent idea. It would take his wife out of Aleford, away from further phone threats. Although Faith was pretty sure he wouldn't have been so keen if she was going by herself, but she'd take what she could get. She had been thinking about the call off and on since receiving it and had almost convinced herself it was Marta. The actress would have no trouble disguising her voice, and she might have decided her cryptic remarks at the Town Hall were not direct enough. Tom's voice broke into her thoughts.

"If Arlene can watch Amy this morning and give both kids lunch, I can work at home this afternoon. And today

227

young Benjamin will take a nap. I'm working on the eulogy for Alden and it doesn't matter where I write—it's a mighty task."

Faith was sympathetic. "You couldn't get someone else to do it? Like Dan Garrison? He was a friend of Alden's."

"Alden specifically mentioned me in the funeral arrangements he outlined in his will, the lawyer said. Perhaps I was supposed to feel honored."

"You never know, he may rise from his grave and correct your grammar. That may have been the intent."

She moved on to other things. "Could you call Arlene while I change my clothes?" She didn't have any round-collared blouses, but she'd assemble something demure. It was a challenge.

"Sure, give me the baby."

A squeaky-clean Amy gave her father a toothless grin. Daddy's little girl. It started early.

Before Tom could call Arlene, the phone rang. It was Pix. She told him to tell Faith to meet her in the driveway in fifteen minutes and to wear a hat and gloves. There was nothing like Pix for marshaling forces.

Faith threw on some clothes, enough makeup to maintain the natural look she cultivated, and searched for a hat. Since she was not a member of the Royal Family, the choices were meager: a broad-brimmed straw, a vintage fawn-colored man's fedora, or a large black velvet beret. She also had a light beige stocking cap, purchased when "grunge" meant grunge, and she wasn't wearing it until the fad passed and the word reverted to what it, and these fashions, were. She doubted any of the hats would meet with Pix's approval, but she chose the beret as the best bet. It matched her coat. Gloves were no problem. Now all she had to do was get ahold of Niki. The time had come to delegate with a vengeance.

"No problem," Niki said with obvious enthusiasm. What she had been waiting for day after day, maybe the lead would twist an ankle.

"Are you sure? We'll be back in plenty of time to set up tonight and you know what's in the freezer . . ."

"Boss, just go. Tricia doesn't have classes today. I'll get her to come in to help. We'll be fine."

"All right. And thank you!"

"You do pay me, remember. But I am also glad in my own tiny way to help further the cause of justice, or whatever it is you two are doing. Happy hunting."

Faith hung up. She would call them later.

Pix's Range Rover stopped at the end of the Fairchild driveway exactly on time, Faith climbed in. A spirit of adventure pervaded. Sitting high up in the car, she had the feeling they might be on the road to the Serengeti instead of Route 2 into Boston.

"Chilton, MFA, Horticultural Hall, and the Copley," Pix chanted, "and I've added another one—the YWCA."

"The Y? That doesn't strike me as Penny's style at all."

"After my father died, if my mother went to the theater or a concert and the club was full, she always stayed at the Pioneer rather than drive back to Aleford in the dark. Now, of course, she's not driving anywhere, thank goodness." Pix's mother was an indomitable eighty-year-old who had reluctantly turned in her goggles and duster the year before after backing over a favorite lilac bush.

"The Pioneer Y has been converted into apartments, but the Berkeley Street branch has rooms. Mother always says it made her feel safe to have so many women around, and I imagine Penny would think the same way. I know I would."

"But wouldn't someone be apt to recognize her?

229

Millicent was adamant her fellow club women would never turn her in, but these loyalties don't apply to the other places we're looking—or the streets."

"I'm sure that's why Penny went to Boston, if that's where she is. No one is going to notice her. Think about it. Sad but true, women of Penny's age are not studied with great care, and besides, she looks like a generic New England lady—somebody's mother, somebody's aunt. Around here, she'd stick out because everybody knows her. In the city, she's anonymous."

Pix was right. It was what Faith had recalled during her conversation with Millicent. Penny did not exactly stand out in a crowd.

The entrance to the Chilton Club was on Commonwealth Avenue, and since they didn't have a prayer of finding a parking space nearby at lunchtime, they went straight to the garage at the Prudential Center and walked over. For once in her life, Faith did not have a plan. Fortunately, Pix did.

"I'm not a member, but Mother is, so I'll say we're meeting her for lunch. You can be searching for a bathroom if anyone asks, which no one will, especially since you left that hat in the car. I'll stay at the reception desk and make a show of peering out the door and so forth, asking for a message and wondering where can mater be. This should give you enough time to look into the dining room. I can show you where it is from outside. It's got beautiful long windows."

Faith was impressed. Maybe she should give up catering and start a detective agency with Pix. John Dunne's worst nightmare come true.

The Chilton Club exuded a quiet elegance suggestive of monogrammed china and silver bowls of cut flowers atop a Chippendale chest. It was unmistakably a women's club.

230

The large living room just off the hall from the reception desk had butter yellow walls that picked up the background of the long chintz drapes. Comfortable sofas and chairs with needlepoint seats were arranged with a view both toward conversation and silent escape. The room was empty save for one lone lady deeply immersed in the *Wall Street Journal.*

In another direction, the buzz of conversation drifting from the dining room was definitely higher-pitched than that occurring some blocks away at the Somerset. Faith looked into the room hoping for first time luck. The windows *were* beautiful and there was a nice Welsh rabbit sort of smell in the air, although she did not actually spot the dish. She did not spot Penny, either. There were several Penny look-alikes, and Faith realized this would be happening all day in the venues they'd be casing. No one came over to ask her what she was doing there—too well-bred—so she double-checked the room.

She rejoined Pix, who was embellishing the story considerably and had obviously whipped her audience of the two desk attendants into a state of advanced concern for the elderly Mrs. Rowe.

When Pix saw Faith shake her head in a silent no, she suddenly looked at her watch—a watch so fully equipped as to tell the time and rate of exchange in Istanbul, among other things and exclaimed, "Goodness, something must be wrong with my watch. It says it's the twenty-second today." She tapped it speculatively.

"Pix," said Faith, catching on immediately, "It *is* the twenty-second."

"Oh, you're all going to hate me. I thought it was the twenty-third. That's when Mother's asked us for lunch!"

If anyone hated her, they were too polite to say so, or perhaps it was relief that Mrs. Rowe was not prone nearby in one of those Boston oxymorons, a pedestrian crossing.

They got out quickly and hastened down the stairs to the sidewalk. "You were brilliant," Faith congratulated her friend.

"Thank you. We can cross the Chilton off our list. After you left, I steered the conversation around to Penny. How Mother was so worried about her good friend and so on. They'd all heard about Mrs. Bartlett's disappearance and said no one had seen her."

"Car or MBTA to the Fine Arts?"

"Let's leave the car where it is and take the subway. If we don't find her at the museum, Horticultural Hall is two stops away. I have tickets for the show, by the way. Mine and the one I got for my sister-in-law, but this is more important. Besides, she's always saying she kills every plant she touches, and the sight of all those blooming successes might be too much for her."

A thorough search of not only the upstairs restaurant but the café and cafeteria at the Museum of Fine Arts—despite Millicent's imprecations, they had checked to be sure yielded nothing. It had been the old "having lunch with Mother" ploy again for the restaurant. This time, Faith went solo while Pix checked the members' room. Back at the entrance, they agreed their search had done nothing except make them incredibly hungry. Just as they were about to leave, Pix said, "We never checked outside! You know how nuts Penny is about fresh air. She might have taken a sandwich into the Garden Court to eat."

It was a sunny and surprisingly warm day for March. Not what Faith would call warm, but what all her neighbors, coats open, hats off, called warm.

"I suppose you may be right," she agreed, the idea of a picnic on a par with eating chilled vichyssoise in an igloo.

They retraced their steps across the museum's marble

floors and down the stairs to the cafeteria. The door to the courtyard was shut but unlocked, and, sure enough, there were people eating lunch at the wrought-iron tables surrounded by leafless branches and brittle ivy. A woman in a navy down coat similar to Penny's sent them racing across the garden. Halfway there, they realized she had a toddler in tow, and even if Penny thought the ploy would help her avoid detection, it was hard to think where she could obtain a child at such short notice, There were days when Faith could have helped her out, but this was not one of them.

Out on Huntington Avenue at the trolley stop, Pix wondered aloud whether the whole thing wasn't a waste of time.

"I'm beginning to think Penny hopped a plane for parts unknown. Disappearing from Aleford was such a strange thing to do that looking in her familiar haunts doesn't match up. At the least, we should be canvassing X-rated movie theaters or Frederick's of Hollywood."

"You may have a point," said Faith, moving from foot to foot, regarding her frosty breath and wondering where the train was. It was a peculiarity of Boston to take you from underground, above ground, and back down all in a matter of a few stops. "However, I am not going to be the one to tell Millicent we skipped some of the places on her list."

"Oh, I'm not suggesting we give up. I just don't think we're going to find her."

The train arrived, plunged underground, and deposited them at their spot.

They emerged from beneath the streets to face the turn-of-the-century facade of Horticultural Hall. It was a stately grandame of a building, brick, with a great deal of exterior decoration in the form of elaborate ornamental iron balconies and stonework. Over the entrances, three fruit-garlanded roundels in the style of Della Robbia welcomed those in search of flora. The middle one sported a nymph clad in trailing diaphanous garments, hands clutching bouquets, who floated high above the top of the globe, peeking through a blanket of clouds. Faith had never really looked at the building before and was impressed.

Inside, they could smell that ineffable combination of good soil and fresh flowers. The air was moist. It was tempting simply to wander through the hall, feasting their eyes on the beds of perfect posies, so far removed from the results of one's own backbreaking attempts.

At the center of the room, an entrant had recreated a Victorian-style conservatory with a glassed-in gazebo, suggestive of Kew Gardens, surrounded by flowering shrubs and masses of daffodils, tulips, and hyacinths. A wrought-iron courting bench had been placed beneath a weeping birch, and it was in this spot of romantic repose that, much to their surprise, Pix and Faith found Penelope Bartlett. All three stared at one another for an instant—Penny, eyes widening, assuming the characteristics of the startled doe, a period lawn decoration next to her. Had the deer been real, it would then have fled, and that's exactly what Penny did, plunging into the crowded aisles of gardening enthusiasts.

Faith and Pix followed in hot pursuit, but a garden club group, dressed by Smith & Hawken, momentarily blocked their way, "Some clematis like to be cut down each year. Some don't. It's important, ladies, to find out which variety you have."

Penny was moving right along. Walking her dog had indeed kept her in good shape. Faith and Pix shoved their way through disapproving stares and managed to keep their quarry in sight until they were once again thwarted by the sudden appearance of what looked like most of Boston's elementary-aged school population dead ahead. "Teddy, if I have to tell you once more not to touch the flowers, you're sitting in the bus!"

After that, it was hopeless. They completely lost sight of her. The navy blue coat was engulfed by the crowd waiting in the lobby to buy tickets.

Faith and Pix finally gained the sidewalk and looked up and down the street.

"She probably went straight down to the subway," Pix said.

"Damn, damn, damn," said Faith.

"I know. We almost had her. She must be terribly upset if she's running away from us."

"Or frightened."

"What now?"

"How far are we from the Y? After being spotted, she'll certainly go to ground, and this is the only possibility we have left. I doubt Penny would go have tea, knowing we were searching likely haunts."

"It's a bit far to walk to the Y," Pix said, which meant it must be several miles, Faith interpreted. "But we can take the subway to Copley and walk from there. If that's where she is, that's what she must have done, too."

Waiting for the train, Faith realized she should have stuffed some snacks in her bag. Even a granola bar would have been welcome.

Unlike her venerable sister, the Pioneer, the Berkeley YWCA was a modern building in the South End of Boston. The large lobby was attractive and warm; the security impressive. The woman at the desk greeted them pleasantly but firmly. What did they want?

"My aunt is staying here. She's expecting us and told us

235

to come right up. Her name is. . ." Faith had a sudden inspiration. "Mrs. Millicent McKinley."

"I can tell Mrs. McKinley you are here, but I cannot send you up without calling. Why don't you have a seat?"

There couldn't be two. Millicent McKinley aka Penelope Bartlett was at the Y. Faith shot Pix a triumphant look.

Five minutes later, Penny walked into the lobby. She did not look triumphant. She looked tired and extremely troubled.

"How did you know where to find me? No, don't bother. I've heard all about Faith's abilities. I suppose you're going to call the police now."

Faith had not really given much thought to what they would do once they found Penny. It had seemed so remote. But she certainly didn't intend to call the police, particularly not before she'd had a chance to talk to the woman. And first, she had to correct Penny's false impression.

"Looking for you in Boston was Millicent's idea. It was Pix's idea that you might be here, because her mother used to stay here." But mine that you'd be using your best friend's name, she thought, silently taking credit.

"Your mother's staying here is what gave me the idea, too," Penny admitted.

"Look, Penny, we've come because we've all been very worried about you. Why don't we go upstairs to your room and talk, then we can figure out what to do next."

Penny nodded. "All right, but the room is . . . well, a bit small. Two of us would have to sit on the bed. There's a coffee shop across the street where I've been taking my meals, although I could have them here. Why don't we go there?" Faith noticed Penny still had her coat on. She must have come in minutes before they had.

236

"Fine." Coffee sounded great. Food sounded better. Maybe it was some diamond-in-the-rough place where they baked everything themselves.

What it was was a perfectly adequate sub shop with a Greek accent. The three of them settled around one of the square Formica tables at the window, beneath a dramatic travel poster of the Acropolis at night. Penny chose a chair that placed her back to the street. She had only wanted a cup of tea. Pix ordered a Greek salad and Faith the same, with a slight glance at the large cheese steak another patron was enjoying. But this was not Philadelphia, and besides, it would be difficult to maintain the necessary investigative decorum required by the situation while dripping grease.

"I suppose you want to know why I left Tuesday night." Penny sounded vaguely hopeful that Pix and Faith might be there for another reason. Say, her recipe for mincemeat bars.

"Why *did* you leave?" Faith asked.

"This is not easy for me to talk about and it's something I have never told anyone, not even Francis. Not even Millicent." Penny said the latter as if surprised at herself—or at Millicent for not getting it out of her. "However, after I saw you at Horticultural Hall, I decided if you found me here, I'd tell you. But, I will not go back to Aleford until Alden's murderer is arrested. You'll see why."

Pix reached across the table and took Penny's hand. "You know that you can trust us. It's you we're concerned about, not anybody else."

Faith nodded vehemently. She wanted to hear what Penny had to say.

"Pix, you were young at the time, but you may remember I nursed my husband, Francis, at home the year

237

before he died. There was nothing that any doctor could do for him and we wanted to be together until the end. I hoped he could die with dignity, as they say, but there is no dignity in the kind of pain he suffered. The end was a blessing." She looked down at the tepid liquid in her teacup and took a swallow.

"He went to bed in August. It's funny . . . I remember it so clearly. There was a day when he just didn't get up. The day before he had. One day so different from the next. And I knew he would never get up again. I'm sorry to be rambling. Anyway, that fall a young woman who worked in his firm—I think she was a secretary, but not Francis's secretary. That was Mrs. Phillips. She used to bring him books to read and flowers until he didn't want to see anyone. But this other secretary called me and said she had something very important to discuss with me and would I meet her in town the following day. I explained Francis was seriously ill and couldn't be left. She said she knew and that was why she was approaching me. She didn't want to bother him, but she would if I didn't come."

"Did it sound like a threat?" Faith asked.

"It sounded as though she meant it, not exactly a threat. I arranged for a neighbor to come sit with Francis and went into town. We met at a restaurant on Newbury Street. When I walked in, she came over and greeted me by name. I'd never seen her before. She was quite pregnant, and after we sat down at a table, she told me she was carrying Francis's child."

Faith was stunned. "But wasn't that impossible?" she blurted out before thinking.

Penny allowed a shadow of amusement to cross her face. "Millicent told you, I presume. In fact, it was not a big secret, though we didn't announce it from the rooftops. We felt one's biological destiny or what have you is nothing of which to be ashamed. Yes, it was impossible. Francis was sterile. He'd contracted mumps in the army. I knew it when I married him and never regretted the decision for a single moment."

"Certainly you told this blackmailer that!" Pix was indignant.

"I did tell her, but she was very insistent. And you're right—she did want money. As she spoke, I began to realize that although the baby was not Francis's, he may have had a few foolish meetings with her. She knew so much about him, about us. I don't think it's uncommon for people, when they know they have very little time left in this world, to want to try things they've never done. Francis had been diagnosed the winter before. It's highly possible this woman was his way of assuring himself he remained alive and able to have an adventure of sorts."

Faith had always admired Penelope Bartlett. Never more than now. Still, it would have been better for all concerned if her husband had taken up skydiving.

"So, you paid her to leave Francis alone." It was very clear. What was not was what any of this had to do with the matter at hand.

"Yes, I did. I didn't want the time Francis had left to be complicated by ugly rumors. As I said, she was a very firm person and I have no doubt she would have continued to insist on the paternity of her child until Francis submitted to some sort of test. It was all too unpleasant to consider."

"But this was almost twenty years ago," Pix said, anticipating Faith's question.

"Yes, I know, except I have not been allowed to forget it. You see, Alden found out certain things."

Of course, Pix and Faith read each other's minds.

"I couldn't take such a large sum of money from the

239

bank without Francis's knowledge. We were a traditional couple by today's standards," she commented wryly. "He gave me plenty of money for the household accounts and clothing, but he controlled the rest. There was only one way for me to get it without telling him, and telling him was out of the question. That was to sell some shares in a family business in New Hampshire my father had left to me. Unfortunately, one of the conditions of the bequest was that they had to be offered to family members first, several cousins and Alden. I tried my cousins. They were not interested, so I was forced to go to Alden, who was. He never asked me why I needed the money and I thought all would be well."

"Surely this is not what he and Dan Garrison have been alluding to during the campaign? They kept talking about your taxes." Faith realized there must be more. There was.

"I did a very stupid thing. I didn't declare the income from the sale of those shares that year. Francis was still well enough in February to go over our taxes with Barry Lacey, who helped him prepare them. I never intended to cheat the government. I just couldn't let Francis be worried."

Faith understood completely. She would have done the same thing herself.

"Francis died in early September, a little more than a year after he had become bedridden. When I was settling the estate, I told our lawyer that, in the stress of Francis's illness, I had neglected to declare the sale of the shares to my brother and asked if he and Barry would straighten it out. I said I would pay the penalties. And they did. But during the course of all this, Alden must have discovered what I had done. He never said a word. Not until the debate the other night."

"Oh, Penny! What a terrible shock that must have been

for you." Pix empathized.

"It was. Alden knew there had to be some reason out of the ordinary that I was selling my shares. He was just biding his time. But I was darned if I was going to drag all this past history out into the open when it had nothing to do with the campaign. And, in fact, I *had* made amends and paid the fine. But hearing this alone without the whole story would have caused a ruckus. You know what sticklers people around here are about their—and more especially *your*—taxes. And I'm glad I didn't say anything. Especially since Francis can't be here to defend himself. I know this town, and there would have been more than one sly comment at his expense."

Something more was puzzling Faith. If Penny hadn't known until recently that Alden knew about the tax return, why didn't she speak to him?

"But what was it that led to the coolness between you and Alden? You haven't spoken to him for years."

Penny sighed. "I feel like that child with a finger in the dike. The difference is, I've taken mine out and now the water is pouring in from everywhere."

"This may not be something we need to know," Pix offered soothingly.

Maybe Pix would not make such a good partner, after all. Faith was about to say something to the effect that it might be a relief for Penny to unburden herself when Penny did so of her own volition.

"It's horrible to be glad someone is dead. When I heard the news, it was as if a huge weight had been lifted from me—a weight Alden put there when I was a child. My half brother was a very twisted individual. He had few friends, both as a child and as an adult. I was not surprised that he never married. It must have been difficult for my poor mother. She had to cope with Alden and was

241

pregnant with me almost immediately after she married my father. I think Alden must have hated her and hated me. Perhaps his mother's death caused whatever was good in him to die also, yet I think he would have been a disturbed person no matter what. When I was twelve years old, he tried to molest me. I escaped but was too ashamed to tell anyone about it. And frightened. He told me if I told anyone, he would hurt my mother, and I believed him. She'd been ill off and on since I could remember and I was in the habit of protecting her. I couldn't take the chance that he would harm her. What I did do was stop talking to him. He was in college at the time and our paths did not cross much. Most people probably didn't even realize it then. In my own childish way, I must have thought if I stopped talking to him, he would disappear.

Faith had one of Penny's hands; Pix the other. All three women had tears in their eyes.

"When I met Francis, I knew this was someone I could tell and I did. It was one of the reasons we had such a short engagement. My mother had died by then and I wanted to get out of the house. He confronted Alden, who denied it, of course, but Francis told him we would be watching his every move and if he ever tried anything like that again with anyone, we would go to the authorities."

"Do you think Alden stopped?" Pix asked.

"Yes, he threw himself into his work and we did watch—very closely. But I never spoke to him until I had to sell him the shares. He knew I must be keeping something from Francis, yet he didn't dare talk to him. He was afraid of strong men like my husband," Penny said with pride. "Then after Francis died, I would catch Alden looking at me with a knowing smile. How much he knew, I wasn't certain, but he never let me forget."

Faith sincerely hoped Penny was right about Alden's activities. She knew personally that he was given to lewd remarks, and there had been that encounter in the woods during the shooting of the nude scene. Perhaps he'd channeled his impulses in these directions.

"That's why I can't go back until the police catch the real murderer," Penny announced firmly. "It was clear as soon as Charley made the announcement. I would be the prime suspect."

"Because of Alden finding out about your taxes? And the very justifiable dislike you had for him? I doubt that very much," Faith assured her.

"That—and the fact that under the conditions of Daddy's will, I inherit everything he left to Alden, including the house. It's quite a bit of money."

Prime suspect sounded just about right.

They replenished their cups with hot tea and coffee. Faith and Pix took a few bites of their barely touched salads. No one said much. Faith was trying to figure out how to make the right thing to do coincide with what she wanted to do. Of course Penny should turn herself in to the police, but Faith's instincts also told her they might concentrate on building a case against Mrs. Bartlett, to the detriment of finding the real killer. Even Charley and John. There was the additional possibility Penny could be in some kind of danger from the murderer if all this had something to do with the Spaulding estate. The house alone, with its several acres of prime Aleford real estate, had to be worth over a million dollars. Faith tried to think of a tactful way of asking Penny the disposition of her estate without making it appear that she thought there was a chance Mrs. Bartlett could be receiving posthumous thank-you notes soon. Millicent had once mentioned that Penny's dog was like her child, so presumably there was a bequest in that direction, but unless someone at Angell Memorial had gotten wind of things and decided they had to have a new pet-care facility now, this line of thought led nowhere.

What was nagging at her? She'd hoped Penny's story would link the two murders. Sandra Wilson had been born in Boston. Could it have been her mother who approached Penny?

"Do you know what happened to the secretary after you gave her the money?"

"Oddly enough, yes. She sent me a postcard from Texas, I believe, thanking me and saying she'd had the baby—she didn't say boy or girl—and was moving to California."

It all fit. It being . . . ? If Alden had discovered that Sandra Wilson's mother had tried to blackmail Penny some twenty years ago—no wait, why would he want to kill her then? He'd want to keep her alive as evidence. All roads seemed to lead to Penny. She could have killed the girl. Why? Sandra was blackmailing her? Sandra really was Francis's daughter and the mumps thing wasn't true? She looked at Penny's honest face, less careworn than an hour earlier. Impossible.

But it was becoming more and more plain that if Penny came forward with all these stories, it would hopelessly divert the boys in blue from their job.

"Faith, I don't think it's absolutely necessary we mention to anyone except Millicent that we happened to bump into Penny at the flower show. We're going to be very busy with tonight's shoot and probably won't even see Detective Dunne or Charley." Pix had been going down the same road.

"I agree, but we do have to tell them somehow that something terrible hasn't happened to her. Penny, why

244

don't you write a letter saying you are fine and left because you needed some time to think or something like that? I can say it was in our mailbox, I know not how."

Penny was enthusiastic. "I can't thank you enough, and I'm sure they'll find out who did this soon. Maybe they have already. In the meantime, you know where I am. I think I'll stay indoors a bit more and eat at the Y for the time being."

"What about the election?" asked Pix. "I hope you're not thinking of withdrawing?"

"It did cross my mind. James would do a fine job, but it doesn't seem right when so many people have worked so hard."

She's afraid of Millicent, too, Faith thought.

"Of course, I can't stay at the Y forever," Penny mused. "I do hope the police will be quick."

The police, with a little help from their friend. Faith was sure she would be able to figure out who had killed Alden. The funeral was the next day. People in medieval times believed that the corpse would bleed again if the murderer walked by. She'd have to keep a sharp eye out for red drops on the blue chancel carpet.

Back in Aleford, Pix dropped Faith off at her front door and slipped Penny's letter in Faith's mailbox. There had been a convenience store across from the Y and Penny had bought some envelopes and a pad. "Such a shame I can't use this time to catch up on my correspondence. I owe so many people letters." She'd brightened at the thought. "Why not write them and mail them when I get home?" With that happily decided, Faith and Pix had left her to go home themselves.

Tom was in his study and miraculously both children were sound asleep, judging from the quiet that reigned.

Faith thought it a bit suspect to walk in carrying the letter, so she let it lie where it was. Better for Tom to find it when the mail came.

"Any luck?"

On the drive back to Aleford, Faith had agonized over what to say to her husband. Pix had a similar problem with Sam. They had decided to seek refuge in confidentiality.

"Such a funny word, 'luck.'" Faith stalled. "So much of the course of our lives is determined by chance encounters, lucky or otherwise."

Tom didn't mince any words. "So you did find Penny."

"I can't really talk about all this yet, darling, but the moment I can, you will be the first to know."

"And I'm supposed to take comfort from that?" He regarded his wife closely. "I hope you and Pix know what you're doing. In fact, I'd like to believe it. . . ."

"Here comes the *but*," Faith interjected.

"Forget the *but*—all the *buts*—and just be careful. Please."

"I promise," Faith swore. This was certainly the most confusing case she'd ever been involved in, yet she truly believed nothing posed any threat to her personally.

However, it was a little difficult to maintain objectivity when Tom came into the kitchen with the mail, the letter from Penny, stamp uncanceled, already opened.

"And what are we supposed to tell Charley about this?"

"About what?" Faith began, but it was her husband, after all. "Oh, Tom. You tell him you don't know how it got there, and you don't."

"*I* tell him. So that's it. If you're not there in person, there hasn't been any subterfuge."

"Something like that. Now I have to get going. I talked to Niki and everything is ready for tonight, but I want to

246

be there early to check. I hear Amy stirring, and Ben will not be far behind. I'll get the kids up and I've written down what's for dinner. They can watch Winnie-the-Pooh tapes on TV until then, which might not be according to Brazelton, but I'm beginning to think the reach may permanently exceed my grasp."

"Whoa there, I never thought I'd be saying these words to my spouse, but I'm going to give you twenty-four hours, then we go to the police and you and Pix tell all. I'm assuming there's a very, very, very good reason you're not saying where Penny is, because I'm afraid all this more than qualifies as impeding the course of an investigation."

Privately, Faith thought Tom was being a little high-handed with his time limit and three *verys*, but she agreed.

"All right, except give us until Saturday. I have the funeral tomorrow, then work. We may need a bit more time."

"For what?"

"I'm not sure," she admitted, "but it's not only time for us to try to figure out what's been going on. It's also to allow the police to track down the killer."

"Very gracious of you."

The eulogy must be going extremely slowly. Tom was almost never sarcastic. She gave him a big kiss. "Why don't you run the letter over to the chief while I get the kids up? I love you."

"I love you, too," he said ruefully.

One of the occupational hazards of being married to a minister was that one ended up attending a great many funerals. Over time, Faith expected to become inured to the solemn ritual and finality of the service, which always prompted fervent prayers of her own for the well-being of everyone she knew, but at the moment she was far from it.

Alden Spaulding's obsequies were no exception, and she sat in church the next morning reciting a litany, starting with Tom and the children and extending to Mr. Reilly, who brought fresh eggs from his chickens to the parsonage, along with pumpkins in the fall and pansies in the spring.

The church was filled to capacity, despite the bad weather. It was cold and a light rain was falling. Faith recognized many Alefordians, but there were also strangers, and she doubted if all were loyal workers from COPYCOPY come to pay their last respects. More likely, they were those odd individuals drawn to the spectacle by their own lurid imaginations, fed by the media. It was ghoulish, like those drivers that slowed down to get a really good look at an accident.

The organist was playing. Brahms, Faith thought. She was fairly good at classical music after years of listening to it at church and at home—Tom Petty and other heartbreakers of her adolescence had been relegated strictly to her Walkman.

The slow, sad strains sent her mind wandering pensively to an odd conversation she'd had the night before with Maxwell Reed during one of the breaks in the shooting. She'd been alone in the kitchen, preparing a new tray of sandwiches to take upstairs. He'd come to get a bottle of his Calistoga water. After learning of his penchant from Cornelia, she had stocked plenty for him and anyone else who wanted it. When he'd walked in with his request, Faith had wondered why the PA or someone else wasn't doing the fetching and carrying. He'd answered her unspoken thought.

"Wanted to get away for a minute and it's too damn cold to go outside."

He'd sat down in one of the chairs at the table and

248

Faith had gone about her business as silently as possible. But it was not solitude he'd sought. It was an audience, a small audience. He was in his ubiquitous corduroy pants and a crew-necked sweater over a turtleneck. The sweater had a hole in the sleeve. He hadn't shaved in a while and Faith could see there was a lot of white coming in. It didn't show so much in his blond hair, standing on end now as if he'd been running his hand through it all night. He looked rumpled but full of energy.

He took off his thick-lensed glasses and polished them on his sleeve. His eyes were fantastic—deep pools of blue in which a girl might seriously consider drowning.

"When I'm making a picture, nothing else matters to me, I don't think about anything else. If I could, I'd have everyone live on the set and shoot around the clock. I suppose this seems pretty callous in light of all that has happened."

Faith made an appropriate noncommittal murmur.

"It will hit me later. When it's in the can. I don't want to think about Sandra now. Or that old guy, whoever he was."

He'd gone to the fridge and taken another bottle of water, then returned to the table.

"Maybe I'm a hypocrite. Pretending what I'm doing is so God Almighty important that I don't have to think about other things. My wife. My kid."

The man had clearly been on the couch, and Faith was certain she was a stand-in. She nodded and asked a question. The role called for it.

"Your wife?"

"Yeah, Evelyn. We've been married for years. Going public is not good for her image or maybe for mine, either. But everybody knows."

Everybody did not know. Cornelia didn't and Faith was

sure Sandra Wilson hadn't known, either.

"Hypocrisy." Max was continuing to associate freely. "*The Scarlet Letter* is a story about hypocrisy—maybe that's what drew me to it in the first place. I never read it when I was a kid. I picked it up a couple of years ago and it blew me away. All the phoniness. All those people pretending to be something or someone they weren't. The townspeople. Chillingworth. Even Hester. She put the letter on, but she didn't feel guilty. She'd have done the same thing all over again, even though she was married. And Cappy, I mean Dimmesdale, he didn't get caught, but he was guilty—not so much for the adultery as for the cover-up. He didn't deserve her. Hawthorne knew that. That's why he killed him off. The governor's sister, the witch, is the only truth-teller. I see *A* as the perfect metaphor for the hypocrisy of our time—the Watergates, the Irangates, the fucking of a whole country."

It would be the rain forest soon, Faith was sure.

"And the environment. Yeah." He'd closed his eyes. "When we move up from Hester and Dimmesdale in the forest, we'll go high enough to show a dump or some nuclear power plant. Something toxic." He'd opened his eyes and focused his gaze on Faith for the first time. "Anything like that around here?" He hadn't waited for an answer, but bolted out the door. "Thanks for making me think of the idea—oh, and the food is great."

After he'd left, Faith considered once and for all abandoning' her Reed/Chillingworth theory. This was a man who would never have done anything that would get in the way of making his picture—unless, of course, he had an ingenue PA who could replace the star. Maybe Faith wouldn't totally give up on it yet. There was still the strong possibility Evelyn was the intended victim. If there was ever an example of an obsessive personality, it was

Maxwell Reed. If he thought Evelyn was having an affair with Cappy, that might have goaded him into thinking the picture would be even more of a masterpiece with Sandra. He might not actually have planned to kill the one he loved, just make her very, very sick.

Alden's last rites were moving right along. Tom had managed to get Dan Garrison to participate, asking him to read a psalm, Psalm 90. Dan read well and did justice to the beautiful words: "For a thousand years in thy sight are but as yesterday when it is past, and as a watch in the night." He continued on, soon reaching "Thou hast set our iniquities before thee; our secret sins in the light of thy countenance."

On the other side of the aisle, two rows ahead of Faith, Audrey Heuneman stood up when Dan said " 'secret sins.' " She was a petite woman with short light brown hair, always well dressed. She was standing very straight and very still. She looked taller. Dan stopped, momentarily startled, then went on with the reading. Audrey seemed about to speak. Sitting at her side, James's face was an enigma—was it pain, sadness, embarrassment? Perhaps all three. His wife reached for her coat and left the pew, walking rapidly down the aisle. James followed immediately. The front door closed with a bang behind them.

The thrill-seekers had gotten their thrill.

CHAPTER 10

It had the effect of a spell, taking her out of the ordinary relations with humanity, and enclosing her in a sphere by herself.

EVERY BONE IN FAITH'S BODY WANTED TO FOLLOW THE Heunemans down the aisle, even as her mind was sensibly alerting her to the further scandal that would cause. The funeral was already destined to join such other historic notables as Peter Smyth's—the casket lid fell off when the pallbearers tilted slightly to the left—and Susannah Prebble's—her daughter wore a crimson beaded cocktail dress.

Faith had a pretty good idea of what Alden Spaulding's "secret sins" might have been in regard to Audrey Heuneman. The Bartletts hadn't been watching as closely as they thought.

Instead of dashing off to test her theory, Faith had to remain where she was through Tom's eloquently circumspect eulogy, which segued from involvement in civic activities immediately to ah, sweet mystery of life—and death. By the time they all rose for the last hymn, "I Cannot Think of Them as Dead," she was ready to scream, not sing.

And there was still the burial service to endure before she could talk to Audrey. At least Faith didn't have to work today. The filming the night before had ended much earlier than Tuesday's, but Max had decided not to go on location until the afternoon. Apparently, he was going to spend the morning with Nils, going over the dailies and figuring out where they were. Despite recent events, the picture was on schedule. The producers would be pleased.

This meant no lunch, only snacks and the craft services table, which Pix and Niki were handling. Faith figured she could pick up Amy at the sitter's and then pay a call on the Heunemans. She'd already arranged for Ben to play at a friend's in case the funeral went past his schooltime.

The Spaulding family plot was at Mt. Auburn cemetery in Cambridge, thirty minutes from Aleford. The time to be in Mt. Auburn—for the living, that is—was in the spring, when its beautifully landscaped 164 acres were in full bloom. The venerable garden cemetery was the final resting place of many famous people, serving as a pleasant and—of course—educational outing for Cantabrigians and their neighbors. One of Faith's favorite spots was Mary Baker Eddy's grave, complete with an apocryphal story of a telephone to God on the site. Such a device would certainly make life easier, but even with call waiting, it would, no doubt, be impossible to get through. She drove past the impressive monument, following several cars behind the hearse and attendant limousine carrying Daniel Garrison, his wife, and poor Tom. A minister's lot was often not a happy one. Faith had insisted on her own transport and desperately hoped she could get out of going back to the Garrisons' for the baked meats after the service.

She parked and went over to the new grave. The press had been barred from both services, contenting themselves with exterior shots. And the interest of the ghouls at the church service had apparently not been sufficient for the drive to Cambridge. There were very few people to say the final farewell to Alden. Which made Charley MacIsaac and John Dunne stand out all the more. Faith was not surprised to see them and assumed they must have been sitting in the church balcony earlier, keeping an eye on things. Dunne had told her once that it was amazing how many murderers were unable to resist the temptation to attend their victims' funerals. Whether it was from a fear that they might not have done a thorough enough job, remorse, or simply to gloat, they came. Remembering this, Faith looked at the faces gathered around the elaborate coffin, heaped with mounds of gladioli, presumably by direction of the deceased, as was everything else save Audrey's performance—at the services. As Faith waited for Tom to find his place, she wondered whether she would like these flowers better if they were not so indelibly associated with headstones. It was one of life's many unanswerable questions—along with who among those gathered here this morning, heads bowed, hands clasped, might have picked up the two-by-four that irretrievably knocked Alden out of the running for selectman.

Faith eliminated herself, Tom, Charley, and John to start, then slowly examined the others. Most were known to her—parishioners—and it was hard to imagine what possible reasons they could have had for killing Alden. Disliking him, yes, but actually committing a mortal sin, no. Dan Garrison was not a member of First Parish, but again, why would he want to get rid of Alden just when the man might be at the point of attaining a position of power in the town? A position in which he might even be able to throw a little work in the path of his friend's contracting business.

The person emerging as a distinct possibility was not with them. She'd tried to sit through Alden's funeral rites and couldn't. Still, she hadn't been able to stay home.

Faith wished Tom weren't doing such a good job and would speed things up a bit. She wanted to talk to Audrey. Audrey, who just happened to bump a table, sending an urn of hot coffee Alden's way. Audrey, who had publicly declared that if Alden thought he was going to win the election, he was dead wrong.

And he was.

In the end, Faith knew better than to skip the Garrisons' post funeral gathering. The congregation might think she was neglecting her husband's duties. Once again, John Dunne and Charley MacIsaac were in attendance. They must be seeing a great deal of each other lately, she thought. Their friendship, dating back to Faith's own maiden voyage on the waters of detection, seemed to have increased markedly during subsequent investigations. They were sitting side by side in two chairs by the picture window in the Garrisons' 1950s split-level, which was not the one remodeled on "This Old House." Dunne's head was slightly inclined toward Charley, who seemed to be regaling him with the life histories of everyone in the room. Charley had a tumblerful of something other than fruit juice and Dunne was drinking coffee. A plate stacked high with spongy white-bread finger sandwiches sat on a table between them. The mound was steadily diminishing as each man systematically reached for another as soon as one passed his lips. They reminded Faith of Ben's book *Frog and Toad Are Friends*. The moment they saw her, they both rose. To save them the trouble—and because they looked so quaint, if that was indeed the right word— she went over and pulled up a chair.

She figured she could circle the room, thank the Garrisons, whisper something in Tom's ear, and be out in fifteen minutes. She'd kept her coat on, the black one, but unbuttoned it, revealing a dark gray Nipon suit. However, first she knew what was coming.

"We understand you've been getting some interesting mail lately," John said between mouthfuls.

Charley gave her a baleful look. "Come on, Faith, the stamp wasn't even canceled. How did you get that letter?"

"I suppose it must have been delivered by hand. We were certainly relieved to learn Penny was all right." She crossed her legs, considered a sandwich, and then came to her senses.

"I don't think the lady is telling us everything, Charley. Remind me of this the next time she wants to know something like whose fingerprints we found on the light switch in the Town Hall's basement."

He was so unfair. Maybe she could get Dale Warren to unwittingly spill the beans, because she wasn't going to— no matter what incentives they posed to reveal Penny's whereabouts.

"Why is it so important that you find Penny? She didn't murder Alden."

Charley and John exchanged glances. She was beginning to think they'd rehearsed the routine.

"How do we know when we can't talk to her?" Charley pointed out reasonably.

"Because you *know* Penny, even if John doesn't!" Faith retorted.

"Why did she run off?"

Dunne almost got her. She stood up. It was time to go.

"Mrs. Bartlett probably thought you'd arrest her and the real killer would remain at large."

So there.

They watched her work her way through the crowd.

"I'll have Sully put a tail on her."

"Good idea. Want some more sandwiches?"

It was an hour before Faith pulled into the Heunemans' sloping driveway in the Crescent Hill section of town. Amy needed changing and Faith had decided to also. The suit was a little severe. She stocked the diaper bag with toys, and the Snugli, in case Amy could be convinced to nestle quietly against her mother. She buckled her daughter securely into her car seat and received a cheerful smile for her troubles. "Amy," "beloved"—the name had been a good choice.

Faith was feeling cheerful. Much to her delight, she'd managed to get Dale to give her the information John and Charley had dangled tantalizingly in front of her. She'd called the station immediately upon her return and, as she hoped, he was the only one around. Charley was still savoring the feast at the Garrisons'. "Oh dear," Faith had said, "I think he wanted to get my fingerprints again—to eliminate them from the ones on the basement light switch."

"I don't think so, Mrs. Fairchild," Dale had reassured her. "We didn't find any prints on the switch. In fact, we haven't found any prints anywhere they should be. It was all wiped clean. Don't worry about it." Faith had thanked him profusely. Such a nice boy.

Crescent Hill had been the brainchild of a group of Cambridge architects about thirty years earlier. They'd purchased the large tract of land collectively and created a small community of unique houses, complete with a shared pool and park. Over the years, the group had gone on to greater fame and fortune. The houses were highly prized—not by people of Millicent's ilk but by everyone else. Most sold through word of mouth before they even reached the market. They were set far apart and now that the landscaping had matured, it was hard to see them from the road.

Faith located the Heunemans' by the name on the mailbox, turned up the drive, and parked in the carport. The house had a dramatic glassed-in entryway on one side, next to a small pond stocked with goldfish in the summer. The sun had burst through the clouds shortly after the funeral, and passing from the cold of March into the warmth of this solarium made Faith regret the lack of such an amenity at the parsonage. She rang the bell.

If Audrey was surprised to see Faith at her door, she did not show it. She asked her in, duly admiring the baby. James was nowhere in sight and had apparently returned to work.

Faith refused an offer of coffee. She sometimes felt she was swimming in it in Aleford, and it was never espresso. Somewhat awkwardly, she sat down on part of the large sectional sofa in the second-floor living room, which overlooked the yard, and unzipped Amy's snowsuit.

"I think I know why you left the service so suddenly this morning," she began.

Two bright red spots appeared on both of Audrey's cheeks. "It's really not something I care to discuss."

Faith felt she had to continue. She knew Penny would agree.

"I don't mean to push you into talking about anything you don't wish to, but I think in this case, it might make you feel better."

Audrey started to interrupt.

"No, please, let me tell you what I came to say and then you can do whatever you want. I have learned a great deal about Alden Spaulding since his death, and there is no question that he was a very disturbed individual, especially sexually."

Audrey breathed in sharply. She looked alarmed.

"He tried to molest his own half sister, Penny, when she

258

was a child. She didn't tell anyone until she got married and her husband confronted Alden, who denied it. The Bartletts thought their warning, and surveillance, would prevent any other attacks. But I don't think they were right."

"No," Audrey said softly, "they weren't."

Holding Amy on her lap, Faith moved closer to Audrey. The woman started to sob uncontrollably and Faith put an arm around her. The tears were streaming down Faith's cheeks, as well. It was only when the bewildered baby began to add her own cries that the two women pulled apart and Audrey, taking a tissue from her pocket, said, "You may not want any, but I have to have some coffee—or something else."

In the kitchen, with Amy comfortably ensconced in her mother's lap, daintily devouring the Cheerios Audrey had spread in front of her, Faith felt enormously angry—angry that she had attended this man's funeral; angry that she had been correct.

Audrey sat with her hands around a mug from Disney World. Her kids would be home from school soon, so she'd decided to go with coffee.

"You never stop feeling vulnerable. You never stop feeling afraid. When my girls were born, my first reaction each time was panic—how could I keep them safe when I hadn't been kept safe? It wasn't joy. He robbed me of that, too."

Faith wrapped her arms around Amy a bit tighter.

"My father was an early investor in COPYCOPY. The whole idea was so new and everyone connected to it was terribly excited. Eventually, when he made enough money, Spaulding bought everybody out, and they never got the big return he did, but they didn't do badly. My father was fascinated by the process and by Alden. The

259

two spent a great deal of time together, going over different systems and, when things got started, overseeing the stores. Mother felt sorry for Alden because he lived alone and she often invited him to dinner. Our houses were close together and he told me to come and play in his grounds whenever I wanted."

Her voice became dreamy. "You can't imagine how beautiful it was. I would take my dolls and have all sorts of pretends. It was my private, special place. I was eleven. Then one day, he was waiting for me and he made me do things to him. Horrible things. I screamed, but no one could hear me. It was impossible to get away from him. He told me if I told anyone, especially my parents, he would take all my father's money away and we would have to leave our home. That I would have to go into an orphanage."

"He was a monster!"

Audrey nodded. "I didn't believe the part about the orphanage, but I did about the money. I was an only child and a bit old for my years, in spite of my dolls, and I knew what this business meant to my father. He hadn't been particularly successful before. So I never said anything. I was very careful never to be alone with Alden, and I never went back to my special place, but he forced himself on me three more times—once in my own bedroom."

"Oh, Audrey, how horrible!"

"The day Daddy said he'd accepted Alden's offer and would no longer be involved in the business was the happiest day of my life. I thought we wouldn't see each other anymore, and gradually that is what happened. Yet from the first moment he made me touch him, I swore I would get even."

And how did you do that? The question hung in the air. It was difficult to imagine this small woman, who looked more like one of her daughters in a pair of Guess jeans and a striped turtleneck, wielding a piece of lumber with such deadly accuracy, but years of rage may have granted her the power.

"I didn't kill him." She spoke almost wistfully. "I've thought about it so often over the years that it was what finally pushed me into therapy. I had told James. Told him even before we married. That's another thing Alden stole—years of sexual enjoyment. James wanted to go to Alden immediately, hurt him. But my parents were both alive—still are. Alden Spaulding had done enough. I couldn't have Mother and Dad find out after all those years. They would have felt so helpless and guilty. And now I'm the parent."

Faith shifted Amy. The baby was getting drowsy and becoming heavier as she relaxed.

"I thought of sending anonymous threatening letters to frighten him, except I was afraid he'd hire detectives and I'd get caught. So I did little things. Like the coffee urn. It's made me feel better. But the big revenge was the election. As soon as I heard he was running, I begged James to run. I wanted to see Alden lose. I wanted him to be humiliated. It wasn't rational. Probably, if anything, it was Penny's chances we were hurting."

"Actually, once Alden started his vicious campaign against Penny, it was a godsend James was running."

"I hadn't thought of that. Anyway, that's my story. I wanted to go to the cemetery and laugh at his grave, but I couldn't even make it through the service. And all I've done since I came home is cry."

Audrey was crying now. Crying for that little girl who was robbed of her innocence and the feeling of being safe that is every child's right. Crying for that adult woman whose sexuality and first moments of motherhood were

261

compromised.

"The kids are going to be home soon. I don't want them to see me like this." She grabbed another tissue. "I suppose you have to tell the police?" It was definitely a question.

And Faith didn't know the answer. Nor did she know the answer to the larger question: If Penny or Audrey hadn't killed Alden Spaulding, who had?

She reflected a moment. She didn't intend to reveal Penny's whereabouts until the next day. She also didn't intend to reveal what Penny had told them about Alden ever, unless it was absolutely necessary. Audrey's confession—which Faith had sought—fell into the same category.

"I don't think there really is anything to tell the police at this point. What happened was in the past. Maybe we can keep it that way."

Audrey looked enormously relieved. "I wasn't happy to see you pull up outside, but now I think you are a kind of angel. I'll be telling James everything when he comes home. We don't keep anything from each other, and it's possible he may look at this in another way, though I hope not."

Nice that the Heunemans shared so much, Faith reflected. It was an interesting approach to marriage and one she ascribed to in theory, but when fact in the form of the cost of one's clothing and a husband who thought all wardrobe needs were covered by a single Lands' End catalog entered into things, budgets had to be surreptitiously adjusted. In this case, hers, which came from Have Faith's profits.

The two women hugged at the door. It had been a long journey.

That night, the Fairchilds were uncharacteristically quiet at the dinner table. Partly because the children were eating with them, which limited topics, and partly because both Faith and Tom were fatigued—emotionally and physically.

Ben made a face at his bowl of lentil stew. "It looks yucky," he complained, and Faith realized she did not have the energy to explain to him that the lentils were the delicious tiny ones from France, the beef stock homemade, the carrots, mushrooms, leeks, onions, and garlic the choicest available—all simmered together for several hours. Instead, she put a spoon in his hand and said, "Eat it. It's good for you." Sensibly, Ben gauged the direction of the wind and dug in. Tom followed up with, "And none of these," pointing to the plate of hot, flaky Cornish pasties filled with ground beef and spices, "until your bowl is clean." Then he lapsed back into silence.

Faith realized, despite her thoughts at the Heunemans, she really did want to tell Tom everything she'd learned. It was too much to carry around by herself.

"Honey, did you ever consider that Alden may not have been what he appeared to be?" She spoke before she had time to consider.

"I'm not sure what you're asking. Was Alden Spaulding an alias of some sort? No, I don't think so. Did we know everything about the way he conducted his life? No again, so the answer would be yes."

Tom must be extremely tired.

"You don't have to work on your sermon tonight, do you?"

"Either tonight or tomorrow night, and that begins to cut things a little close."

Faith sighed. She missed him.

After the kids were in bed, she brought a cup of tea into

263

his study.

"Look, love," he said, "you're not very good at keeping secrets and I have the feeling these are not exactly run-of-the-mill. We've both been under a lot of pressure lately. You seem suddenly to have two jobs, besides the wife/mother stuff. And I have a new one, which is tying up all the loose ends. Why don't you just tell me what's going on?" He put the cup on his desk and pulled his wife onto his lap.

"Alden was a child molester."

"What!"

"I can't figure out how it connects with his murder, unless there's a third victim I don't know about and it was her husband, father, mother—or the woman herself."

"It was Audrey, wasn't it? That's why she left the service this morning. Dear God!"

Faith nodded.

"I wish I had known. I wish I could have helped her earlier—and James."

"They're doing all right—better now that Alden is gone. Perhaps, in some way, it's satisfying that he had a violent end."

"And the other is Penny. You don't have to break any confidences. I can guess."

Tom was very shaken. It was difficult for the shepherd to learn the flock had been suffering so.

"You still don't want to tell me where Penny is? You're sure she's all right?"

"I promised—and she is all right." Pix had been in touch with Penny and had called Faith. Penny's major concern of the moment was her dog, and when she learned Millicent was taking care of him, she was fine.

"I hope this will all be over soon." Tom tightened his arms around Faith, the same way she had around Amy earlier.

"I have a feeling it will. It has to."

It was hard for Faith to leave for work the following morning, even though she knew that the movie company would be in Aleford only for another week if they continued to stay on schedule. The rest of the movie would be shot in L.A. Whether it was because of what she had discovered about Alden or simply because she had had very little time with her family lately, her impulse was to stay put in her own nest. She dragged her preparations out as long as she could.

Tom had been unable to continue working the night before and they had gone to bed early, falling asleep close to each other. He had planned to spend the morning with the children, but then he asked Faith whether Arlene could take them instead. She couldn't. However, Samantha Miller was free. She came to the door as Faith was trying to leave. Amy and Ben greeted the sitter with such uproarious delight that it was all their mother could do not to pick up the phone, quit the job, and assume her rightful place.

As she drove to the catering kitchen, her arms ached slightly. Must be all the directions they are being pulled in, she thought dismally. She looked out the window as she passed the green, such a misnomer at this time of year. The "brown" would be more like it. Two weeks ago, they'd been shooting the scaffold scene here. Two weeks ago, Sandra Wilson and Alden Spaulding had both been alive. Life *was* beginning to imitate art, she realized with a sudden start. Max had intended the group of townspeople on the green and at Town Hall to represent the real sinners, as opposed to the people on the platform. Hypocrites, murderers, gossips—and child molesters.

Who had been acting and who had not?

Her crew was already busy packing things up and they were about to leave when the phone rang. It was James Heuneman.

"Tom said I might be able to catch you before you left for work. I won't keep you long."

"Is everything all right?"

"Yes, or more right than it's been for a long time. Audrey wanted to thank you. I do, too. Talking to you was a tremendous help. After you left, Chief MacIsaac called. I was home by then. I hadn't wanted to leave Audrey for long. He asked me why we had left the service so abruptly. He also seemed to know you'd been to see Audrey. I told him to come over. We decided to tell him everything. It's great to have it out in the open, not that we are telling the whole town, but we both thought the police had to be informed."

"I'm glad, especially if it makes things easier for Audrey. She's a lovely person," Faith said, inwardly fuming. So Charley was following her!

"And now we are on our way to see the Reverend. We should have taken this to him years ago. However, that wasn't my decision to make."

"Everything in its own time." Faith was glad they were going to see Tom. It would make everyone feel better.

"Well, I won't keep you. I just wanted to thank you—oh, I almost forgot. I'm dropping out of the race. I was doing it for Audrey and it's not necessary anymore. Penelope Bartlett belongs on the board."

Here was news. Faith only hoped Penny would be in the neighborhood to serve.

She hung up and went to tell Pix about Penny.

"This has been a very strange election campaign," Pix commented.

It was an understatement!

The next few hours were busy as usual. It seemed they had barely finished the morning break when everyone started showing up for lunch. Max was working at top speed, too. Maybe he was superstitious. Get as much footage before the newest catastrophe. Cornelia was being run ragged, she told Faith proudly. With Sandra gone, Max had only Ms. Stuyvesant to turn to for the gazillion details that made her life worth living. She was coming for his lunch tray now. "Remember, he doesn't like the Calistoga water too cold." Evelyn also wanted a tray, and Cornelia told Faith she'd come back for it after she delivered Max's.

"Oh, we'll bring it to her. Don't worry." Faith was feeling magnanimous. It would give Corny a few more precious moments with Max.

"Thank you! I won't forget this," Cornelia promised. Which could mean a fruitcake at Christmas or a job when Corny was producing her own Maxwell Reed movies—or a postcard of Sea World.

Evelyn wanted only a salad, some fresh fruit, and emphatically—plain Perrier. It didn't take long to prepare the tray. And Faith had a single perfect scarlet anemone to put in a bud vase. She looked around. Everyone was occupied, so she decided to take it herself. She'd never seen the inside of Evelyn's trailer, actually a huge RV, and she was curious. The trailer, with the star's bright red sports car parked outside, was placed well away from the house, barn, and the other trailers. Evelyn was manic on the subject of quiet when she wanted to rest. She didn't want to hear anything—or see anything.

Faith knocked at the door and heard Evelyn's slightly husky, very sexy voice: "Entrez." Balancing the tray on one arm, Faith turned the knob and went in. It was not

267

typical Winnebago decor: no shag carpeting and not a single La-Z-Boy recliner. Neither was there a dressing table or mirror surrounded by lights. The only thing that distinguished it as the abode of a Hollywood legend was Evelyn's Academy Award, standing shrinelike on a shelf on the wall. Otherwise, the room looked like one in an East Side town house decorated by Sister Parish—needlepoint carpet, exquisite chintz, and a well-chosen assortment of bibelots to give just the right finishing touch. Despite the tiny windows, the entire effect was of sunshine and light.

Much to Faith's surprise, Evelyn, ensconced in a comfortable-looking armchair, was giving Cordelia a bottle. Faith knew Evelyn had given birth to this exquisite little creature, but she had generally assumed all maternal responsibilities had ended with that colossal endeavor. Thereafter, the parental role was no doubt fulfilled by making appropriate comments when the nanny brought the suitably clad baby for occasional inspection. Evelyn's words made her preference clear.

"The damn nanny insisted on leaving the baby here. It's supposed to be our bonding time. Max read something about it and now the nanny brings Cordelia every day. Mary Poppins went to find some vitamins or whatever she left in the car and didn't want 'baby' to go out in the cold. Of course, the moment she left, Cordelia started screaming, so I gave her this, which seems to be working."

"I'll put the tray over here on the table. She's a beautiful baby. Is she sleeping through the night yet?"

Evelyn gave Faith a look of total uncomprehension. "You mean they don't? Anyway, I have no idea. The nanny takes care of that. And if she's not back soon, she's going to be an out-of-work nanny."

Despite her lack of familiarity with the role, Evelyn

looked like an old hand—or rather like a Botticelli Madonna with child.

"I'll come back for the tray in an hour. Will that be enough time?"

Evelyn looked at the food with marked uninterest.

"Sure, you come back in an hour."

Faith had started to leave, when Evelyn began to talk again. Her voice and entire demeanor assumed a somewhat vague tenor, as if she'd gone off somewhere.

"Babies, children, kids. Cornelia says you have a kid."

"I have two—a boy who will be four in May and a girl who's six months old."

Evelyn nodded. "A baby."

It didn't seem to require an answer, but Faith said, "Yes," just to keep the conversational ball rolling."

"Did you breast-feed it?"

Perhaps she had missed the word girl. "Yes, I did. Both children."

"I didn't. Wouldn't. Oh, Maxie would have liked it. Would have liked a sip himself now and then, but it would have ruined my shape." She shifted the baby away from her chest and pulled up the jersey she was wearing. She was naked underneath and nothing had impaired her "shape." Not even the suggestion of a sag—her bosom was perfect.

Compelling as Ms. O'Clair's mammaries might be, what caught Faith's attention was the large *A* sketchily drawn in red pen on her right breast. It looked self-inflicted. Evelyn followed Faith's gaze and slowly pulled her shirt down. The baby was still hungrily working away at the bottle.

"Max is such a stickler for authenticity," she said coyly.

There didn't seem to be anything to say after that, and Faith left, wondering whether the star was on something or simply a little loopy by nature. She hoped the nanny would get back soon.

An hour later, Faith decided to go back for the tray herself. Cornelia was nowhere to be found and it was time to pack up and go home. Lunch was over and the staff was busy cleaning up—even more efficiently than usual, since it was Saturday and everyone was looking forward to a break. Faith told Niki and Pix to leave with the rest of the crew as soon as they were finished. They'd both put in a hard week. Faith would drive the canteen truck back, making sure the craft services table in the barn was stocked for the rest of the afternoon. She was glad she had refused any other bookings until the movie was finished. The idea of someone's wedding reception or other festive occasion tonight was overwhelming.

Setting out for the trailer at last, Faith ran into Cornelia, who was coming from the house. They'd been filming a scene with Dimmesdale and Chillingworth all day, she told Faith, and it looked like they wouldn't get to the section with Evelyn. She was on her way to tell Ms. O'Clair now.

"She's going to have a fit, but I don't take any nonsense from her, and everyone knows it. That's why Max sent me."

That, and because it was the PA's job to do everything nobody else wanted to do, like confront a hotheaded leading lady, Faith thought.

"I'm on my way to pick up her lunch tray and I'd offer to tell her for you, except I have a family who needs me." Evelyn's temper was as famous as Max's.

"It's not necessary. I won't have any trouble with her. The first time she blew up at me, I politely and firmly told her that was not the way professionals treated one another and I didn't intend to stand for it."

"Did it work?"

"Well," admitted Cornelia grudgingly, "she still gets mad, but I don't pay any attention."

Faith remembered the discovery of the *A* when Evelyn had literally bared her breast.

"I would have thought Max would have used something that looked a bit less homemade for her tattoo."

"What are you talking about?" Cornelia asked impatiently.

"The *A* on Evelyn's right breast."

"Evelyn doesn't have an *A* on her breast."

"Yes she does. She showed it to me." Faith related her odd conversation.

Cornelia was seriously annoyed. "What is that woman playing at now? She's not supposed to have anything there. It will show through the costume and Max will be upset."

They were at the door to the trailer and it was plain Cornelia planned to open with this new discovery. She was seething. "Probably used permanent ink and I'm going to have to find some way to get it off!"

Faith hoped she could grab the tray and run, but no such luck.

Evelyn was lying down on a chaise. She wasn't in her Hester costume; instead, she was wearing the jersey, tight black jeans, and snakeskin western boots she'd had on earlier during the mother number. The baby and nurse were gone. Bonding time was over.

"The tray's in there." She waved in the direction of a small door. It led to a bedroom, somewhat like a stateroom on a ship, with everything, including the requisite dressing table and well-lighted mirror built in. The tray was on the dressing table. The bud vase, empty glass, and some cutlery were in place, but no plate.

271

Another door led into the bathroom, and the plate and a fork were in there. Evidently, Evelyn was up to her old tricks and had taken the food in with her to save time.

Faith could hear raised voices from the main room. She started to pick up the plate, then was distracted by the sight of the medicine chest above the sink. It was more temptation than she could ever resist and she opened the door to take a peek at what kind of toothpaste Ms. O'Clair used—and what she might be on. It was Pandora all over again. Vials, bottles, tubes, and boxes spilled out into the sink. She grabbed for a giant glass bottle of mouthwash just in time. Serves you right, Miss Snoopy Nose, she chided herself, thankful for the din from the next room that masked her misdeed. She tried to catch what they were screaming about but could only make out an occasional *bitch* and the frequent repetition of Max's name. She hastily began to stuff everything back in the cabinet, when she realized that a box of cotton balls seemed surprisingly heavy. A hiding place for Evelyn's jewels? She dug around in the soft contents. It wasn't diamonds.

There was a box of slides at the bottom.

The coincidence was too great. They had to be the slides missing from the storeroom, which meant . . .

Faith ran into the next room. The scene she encountered momentarily stopped her where she stood.

Evelyn was on her feet, cheeks enflamed, waving her Oscar threateningly in Cornelia's face.

"You could never get one of these. You couldn't even come close! Telling me what to do! You piece of shit! You fucking little PA whore. Oh yes, I know all about you and our sainted director. You've been in my husband's pants for years!"

Cornelia gasped and looked as though she might faint,

whether at the news that Max and Evelyn were married or at the accusation she could only wish was true.

She rallied. "If I was, I'd be a whole lot better than you! You don't understand him. You'll never understand him. You think only of yourself, you—"

"What do you know about me? Or my husband! Keep your fucking nose out of other people's business!"

Before Faith could stop her, the star brought the shiny golden statuette down on Corny's head with murderous intent. Cornelia dropped to the floor and Faith jumped between the two women to prevent Evelyn from landing another blow.

"Miss O'Clair, please!" Faith had heard it said that people would kill for one of these on their mantel, but kill *with* was an entirely different matter. "I know there's nothing going on between Cornelia and your husband. She's an old friend of mine. She just admires his work, and yours! Let's calm down, before someone gets hurt."

"Calm down," Evelyn screeched, "You're as bad as she is. Who the hell do you think you are telling Evelyn O'Clair what to do? The whole world thinks it can tell me what to do! Well, I fucking do what I want!"

She pushed Faith and seemed about to repeat her earlier action, but Faith grabbed her raised arm at the wrist and forced her to drop the Oscar. The prize hit the carpet with a muted thud.

Evelyn made a sort of feral cry and lunged for Faith, who quickly stepped to one side, hoping to grab the woman from behind as she fell forward, but Evelyn did not lose her balance. She was almost foaming at the mouth now and screaming obscenities even Faith had never heard.

There was a phone on a table by the chair Evelyn had been sitting in earlier. Faith had to get some help. She

273

obviously couldn't leave Cornelia, who was out cold, yet fortunately visibly breathing, in the room with this maniac. But would said maniac let Faith call 911? Not in the condition she was in at the moment. The situation was becoming more and more bizarre. If she didn't do something soon, Faith realized, she'd be locked in hand-to-hand combat with one of America's biggest box-office draws. She could probably take Evelyn, but she'd just as soon not try. If only Cornelia would come to and give Faith a hand, even if it were to find something with which to tie the woman up.

Evelyn had backed off for a moment, panting heavily, her hair covering most of her face. Through the tangled blond strands, her eyes glittered dangerously.

"Why don't we call over to the house and ask Mr. Reed to come and straighten all this out? I'm sure he'll be very upset. He can tell you himself that he has nothing but a work relationship with Cornelia." Faith employed the same tone as the one she used when Ben and a friend both wanted to play with the same toy. It seldom worked then and it certainly didn't work now.

As Faith spoke, Evelyn ripped the phone from the wall with such force that the multicolored wires sprayed out from the plastic casing. The woman was strong. It might not be so easy to subdue her as Faith thought.

"You're not calling Max!"

She regarded Cornelia and Faith appraisingly for a moment, then grabbed a bulky sweater and Gucci purse the size of a steamer trunk from a shelf and started for the door. Hand on the knob, she delivered her last line in completely controlled tones: "You ladies have been forgetting who I am."

It was an accusation. It was hurt pride. It was a wrap.

Faith moved, but not in time. As she got to the door,

274

Ms. O'Clair was already on the other side and doing a very thorough job of locking them in. Faith reached for the knob and turned, but it was too late. She pulled frantically at the door. It was a solid one and shut tight. Seconds later, the car started. Faith listened despairingly as Evelyn left them in her dust.

Dumb! Dumb! Why had she let Evelyn get close to the door!

Faith would be replaying this scene and scolding herself for months to come, but first things first. She had to take care of Corny and then she had to get a look at the slides, which she'd slipped into her pocket.

Cornelia was moaning slightly. When Faith bent over her, calling her name, she opened her eyes and responded predictably. "Where am I?" What with Evelyn's exit line and Cornelia's entrance one, life was fast assuming all the characteristics of a B movie.

"We're in Evelyn's RV. She hit you on the head, but I don't think it's serious. Don't move. I'm going to get a blanket." And a towel. Evelyn had not managed to sell Corny the farm, yet Ms. O'Clair had made a mess of her victim's hairdo. Blood was streaming out of a large gash in Corny's left temple.

"Faith, Faith! I'm bleeding!" She had discovered her injury and was panicking. Faith rushed back with the snowy white quilt from Evelyn's bed and one of her monogrammed towels. Irony, at any rate, was alive and well.

She managed to staunch the flow of blood. Corny was going to have a lump the size of the Matterhorn and a headache for a week, but other than that, she should be lording it over everyone as usual before too long. Her good health, and all the milk she'd drunk as a child, had resulted in fortuitously dense bone mass.

275

It wasn't exactly the time for a chat, yet Corny seemed unable to stop talking.

"She thought I was having an affair with Max! And they're married! I never knew! How could he! Oh, Faith!"

Corny had shut up for the moment and, snugly wrapped in the down comforter, had closed her eyes again. She hadn't passed out again. Faith had asked her.

It was time to look at the slides. Faith switched on a lamp next to the armchair and held the first one up. As she suspected, Alden had been photographing the forest scene and had zoomed in on Sandra, who did full justice to the high-speed Ektachrome Spaulding had employed. Faith assumed the box contained more of the same, but she held each one up to check. Near the end of the roll, Alden had happened upon another scene. It must have been before the afternoon shoot, when he'd returned to his post.

It wasn't in the script.

The slide Faith held up to the light captured Evelyn twisting a hank of Sandra's hair. Alden had caught Ms. O'Clair face on, and her expression was terrifying—full of fury, hatred, and, above all, threatening. The next four were similar, but the last one showed Sandra. It was quite a contrast. She looked defiant—and incredibly beautiful.

So Evelyn had killed her. Faith sank down onto the chair. Evelyn had seen the rushes. They were the frosting on the cake that had been presented at Max's birthday party.

It was unlikely that Max would have replaced his star with a complete unknown in the middle of a picture, but he, or another director, might soon have raised Sandra to stardom, a stardom likely to have eclipsed Evelyn's own career. While not waning at the moment, it wouldn't have been long, and Sandra's ascent would have hastened

Evelyn's descent. Good parts for women in Hollywood were scarce enough, and few actresses remained in the limelight past their thirties. Evelyn had clearly seen the wolf at the door—and Max's and the other men's obvious attraction to this sexy beast had added jealousy to fear. Alden must have gotten in touch with her and alluded to the photographs. He might have had some crazy idea that he could trade them for sex with her. The slides didn't prove that Evelyn killed Sandra, but judging from the camera angles, Alden must have heard what they'd been saying, too. After Sandra died, he must have put two and two together—and come up dead himself. Evelyn had had to kill him or risk exposure for the first murder. The second death—had it been easier for Ms. O'Clair? Had the first one been so hard? It was all becoming clearer—as was the fact that Faith had to get out of the trailer immediately and call the police. Evelyn had no idea Faith had found the slides. She wouldn't go far, but then again, she might.

And it had been Evelyn, not Marta on the phone. She had just used the same phrase while shouting at Cornelia, but without the disguise.

The star's trailer was as secure as Hester's prison cell. The windows were too small for anyone save Ben to crawl through. But they did open. Faith went to first one, then another, systematically shouting for help.

It was no use. The trailer was too far from the other buildings. Unless someone expressly came to get Evelyn, there was no way Faith could be heard. And no one would come. With out the car, it would be assumed Evelyn had returned to the house after getting the director's message that she wasn't needed that day. What's more—no one would miss Cornelia. However much she exalted her role, it was not critical. Faith's own staff would be long gone by

277

now and it would be hours before she was expected at home. Cornelia opened her eyes.

"Faith, I think I can get up. I'm certain I should go to a doctor and have some stitches put in. It's been dear of you to take care of me like this." But, implied Ms. Stuyvesant, let's get the show on the road.

"We can't. She's locked us in. No one is going to hear me from here, so it's pointless to shout. Plus, my crew has gone. I stayed behind to do some last-minute things. Face it—we're stuck."

Cornelia burst into tears. Faith had seen her maddeningly happy, in a temper, miffed, but never crying. Corny turned out to be one of the noisy, gloppy kind. Soon her sobs were hiccups and her nose began to run. Faith shoved some tissues in her old chum's hand to stem the tide. It had to be over Max. But it wasn't.

"You're being so good to me and I've been so rotten to you," Cornelia gasped.

"There, there. That was all years ago. Don't even think about it," Faith assured her. She ought to see whether Evelyn had any Tylenol in the bathroom for poor Corny's head.

"No, it wasn't!" Cornelia wailed. "Two weeks ago. I did it. I put the Chocolax in your black bean soup!"

"What!"

"Max liked you so much, and all he could talk about was how good your food was. It was school all over again. Everybody liked you better. You always got whatever you wanted. I thought people would just get a little sick and you'd be off the picture."

"Corny, you could have ruined my business! Not to mention how much pain you caused everyone."

"I know, I was sick, too, remember. I had to eat; otherwise, everyone would have known who did it. I also

278

put it in Evelyn's soup—which served her right—when I took her the tray, so there would be no question but that it was the caterer's fault."

The woman must have been mad. "And you set the fire?"

"It was a very little one. I was a Scout, you know. There was no danger."

Evelyn O'Clair, a murderer. Cornelia Stuyvesant, an arsonist and food poisoner. What a casting call!

"You were jealous of Sandra, too. It was you who put the drapery fabric in the barn. Admit it." Faith was really angry.

If Cornelia had been other than flat on her back, she would have hung her head.

"I felt terrible about that after she died. I only wanted to ruin her reputation, not hurt her."

Faith remembered something Corny had said about the other movie. "Was it you who upset that PA on the *Maggot Morning* shoot so she would quit?"

"No, that must have been Evelyn," Cornelia said speculatively.

The two were quite a pair.

Faith sighed. Cornelia's confession had cleared up some things, but it wasn't getting them out of the trailer—an impulse that had taken on additional meaning. Faith Sibley Fairchild didn't want to spend a moment longer than was necessary with her fellow alum.

"I'll look for something to help your pain and try to figure out how we're going to attract someone's attention way out here."

"See the problem? Why do you have to be so nice? It simply isn't fair!" Cornelia started to weep again.

"Would it make things easier if I smacked you one?" Faith had a moment's fiendish hope for a reply in the affirmative.

"No. And you may not believe this, but all I ever wanted when we were young was to be one of your friends and go to your house." Tears again. Faith hadn't thought things could get any worse, yet they were. Now *she* was feeling guilty.

"Just lie still. I'll be right back."

Evelyn seemed to have every medication known to man or woman in the cabinet under her dressing table. Many of the vials were from the clinic in Switzerland, and Faith had a hunch that was where Evelyn had obtained her lethal quantities of chloral. A trinket or two to the right orderly and Ms. O'Clair had her very own Rexall's. Faith passed over the Darvon, attractive as the idea of Corny passed out was, and went straight for the Tylenol. It was possible that Cornelia had a concussion, so Faith had to keep her conscious.

She looked around, trying to think of some way to let people know they were trapped. It was getting late and soon everyone would be leaving for the weekend.

All Evelyn's cosmetics were neatly arranged on the top of the dressing table. It took an enormous amount of effort to be so beautiful. Faith's eyes lingered on a large bottle of nail polish remover. She'd been thinking of smoke signals ever since Cornelia had mentioned her fire in the barn. There weren't any oily rags around, but Faith could make the equivalent.

She got a tumbler of water and gave Cornelia the pill, advising she remain as quiet as possible. Then she went back and started to ransack Evelyn's closet. It would be a sacrilege to burn some of these things—a lovely black Bill Blass evening gown, for instance. But Faith had no compunction about the Hester costumes—and flimsy rags they were. She put the stopper in the sink, stuffed the

280

garments in, and poured polish over the whole thing, leaving it to soak in.

Next, she had to find something for a torch. She planned to throw the clothes far enough away from the trailer to avoid incinerating it—thereby lessening alumni donations to Dalton by two—and needed something she could ignite. The latest issue of *Variety*, well thumbed, was lying on the floor by the bed. It would do nicely. Now all she needed were some matches. Evelyn wasn't a smoker—or was she?

The stash was in the bottom drawer of the built-in dresser in the other room, carefully concealed—by someone with a sense of humor, probably not Evelyn—in a hollowed-out copy of *The Valley of the Dolls.* There they were. Lots of nice neat little joints—and matches from Spago.

Laxatives, purgatives, emetics, uppers, downers, and everything in between—no wonder the woman was nuts.

Faith went back to her soaking garments and made a bundle that she fastened with dental floss so it wouldn't come apart when she heaved the whole thing out the window. She tied the *Variety* into a roll with more floss and dipped it into the puddle of nail polish remover left in the sink, then went into the other room. These windows faced the direction of the house and there were fewer trees on this side. Faith didn't want the whole town of Aleford blaming her for burning down the conservation land forest.

She opened the window and threw the clothes as far away as she could. Then she lit the torch carefully. When MGM EXECS NIX PIX WAS BLAZING, Faith pitched the paper out onto the pile of clothes. It took a very long minute, but the fabric caught and soon the crackling flames sent up a welcome column of dark black smoke. It wasn't as noticeable against the dull late-afternoon sky as she would have wished, yet someone was sure to spot it.

She realized that Cornelia had been oddly silent during this frenzy of activity, not even reacting to the strong smell of smoke and acetone permeating the trailer. Her eyes were closed. Desperately hoping she had merely fallen asleep, Faith grabbed for Corny's pulse and was immediately relieved to find it as slow and steady as one of her prize horses. Cornelia Stuyvesant was dead to the world, but not dead.

She tried to wake her and was rewarded with a mumbled response. Corny's eyes opened. Faith didn't want to shake her or try to move her to a sitting position, so she let her be for the moment.

Faith moved back to her post at the window to be ready to shout for all she was worth at the slightest indication of movement. To her horror, she discovered that the wind had blown her neat little parcel back toward them, where it was rapidly enkindling all the dry grass in sight. The flames were already starting to lick the side of the RV and the heat scorched her face as she leaned out for a closer look.

The plan had backfired.

Before anyone found them, they were going to be burned alive.

CHAPTER 11

"I must reveal the secret," answered Hester, firmly.

FAITH RACED AROUND THE TRAILER, DESPERATELY looking for a container to hold water. All she came up with was the bathroom tumbler and a small carafe. She filled both and emptied the contents on the raging flames. It was like peeing in the ocean.

Then she wet two towels and draped one over Corny's mouth, holding the other to her own. The smoke was pouring in through the seams around the windows and door. She coughed and gagged. The smell was horrible. She tried to rouse Cornelia and couldn't. Finally, Faith knelt by her friend's side and kept her fingers on Corny's pulse. If worse came to worse, she could try to resuscitate her, but the present conditions in the room made "in with the good air, out with the bad" a farce.

She tried to think where the gas tank on the vehicle was. Underneath somewhere, but where? Maybe the ground, shadowed by the RV, was too damp for the fire to catch. She began to pray. It was hopeless to do anything else.

Help arrived in the unlikely combination of Detective Sullivan and Marta Haree, garments flapping in the breeze, trailing behind him. Hearing their shouts, Faith jumped to her feet.

"We're locked in!" she screamed out the window. "Evelyn locked us in and drove away. You've got to call the police and stop her." Faith assumed with all the smoke in the air, someone had already called the fire department.

Marta nodded and started back toward the house. Her expression of concern had not given way to surprise. Oddly enough, it appeared she did not find Faith's words hard to believe.

Others from the movie were now running toward the trailer. Alan Morris sprinted ahead with a fire extinguisher. Max was calling Evelyn's name in the mistaken belief his wife was still inside.

"Go to the door. I'm going to get you out!" Ted Sullivan yelled.

Faith watched in horror as he dashed close to the flames. Soon she heard his voice on the other side of the door. She pulled Cornelia over as gently as possible and stood out of the way. Was he going to kick it in? But she'd forgotten about those oh-so useful skeleton keys cops carry, and he had the door open in a flash.

"Run!" he yelled, prepared to do the same.

"I can't! Cornelia is here and she's unconscious!"

"Run, damn it!" he said again. "I'll get her! This could blow any minute!"

She obeyed, looking back once she was clear of the fire, to see him following close behind carrying Cornelia.

Alan had trained the nozzle of the extinguisher at the heart of the fire. Max was still screaming for Evelyn. Pandemonium reigned. Safely away, Faith and Sullivan collapsed onto the ground. Sully rolled Cornelia off his shoulder. Coughing and gasping for breath, it was some time before either could speak, and Sully beat Faith to it. "You can thank Dunne and MacIsaac when you see them. I've been tailing you since yesterday. Those guys may just have saved your life."

Faith nodded solemnly. She knew it. But there was

284

work to be done.

She could hear the sirens that meant help was on the way and ran over to Greg Bradley to ask him to stay with Cornelia. Sully looked puzzled when she returned with Max's stand-in.

"We've got to hurry. Greg will keep an eye on Cornelia. I'll tell you all about it in the car."

Out of earshot, Faith quickly filled the detective in on the scene that had occurred in the trailer and her discovery of the slides, still tucked safely in her pocket.

"I didn't want to tell Marta why I thought the police should pick Evelyn up. Let everyone assume it's because she locked us in. It may be that she wasn't acting alone, although I'm pretty sure she was. In any case, Max or someone else might warn her before we could get to her."

Sully agreed. "So, we're on the way to the house they rented?"

"No, I'm sure that's where the police, sorry, where you guys will go first and there's no point in duplicating effort. Besides, I doubt she's there. The nanny and baby would be around and I don't think Evelyn's in a motherly mood. She may simply be driving around hell-bent for leather in that car of hers, letting off steam. As far as she's concerned, she's just had another tantrum and locked two obnoxious underlings in her very comfortable dressing room. She may even consider us lucky to be honored with a prolonged stay in a place most fans—and Entertainment Television—would give their eyeteeth to see. She has no idea we have the slides." Faith noted she must be upset to be using such clichéd expressions. She was virtually certain she'd never referred to *eyeteeth* or *leather* before. Sully noticed it, too.

"And if she's not driving around in the colorful manner you suggest, I'm sure you have an alternative." Sully had

285

definitely been around Dunne too long.

"As it happens, I do." Faith gave him a slightly reproachful look. Cynicism was such an ugly trait. "What do people with eating disorders do when they're upset? They eat. And what's less than a mile from here? Webbs, the homemade ice cream place.

"I can't say that I've ever been there, but your logic makes a certain amount of sense. Tell me where to go."

Webb's was several turns off the main road. It had originally started as a stand adjacent to the Webb farm and was open only during the summer months, but after being discovered by *Boston* magazine and listed in several guidebooks, business increased to the point where the Webbs built a year-round structure and expanded the menu to include lunch offerings. The main emphasis remained on the ice cream with its sinfully high butterfat content. Webb's was not the place for frozen yogurt aficionados.

Faith and Sully were rewarded by the sight of Evelyn's shiny red sports car, sprawled across two spots in the parking lot.

"She's here!" Faith wanted to leap from the car and drag the woman out, but she restrained herself and told the detective her plan. He gave her a look that could have been approval and stayed in the car while she went in the door.

There was nothing cute about the inside of Webb's, just simple booths, a long counter, and a calendar from a feed company on the whitewashed walls kept scrupulously clean by Mrs. Webb. The one concession to decor was red calico curtains.

Evelyn was in a booth at the rear. Faith recognized the back of her sweater. The star's hair was covered by a large kerchief, and when Faith got closer to the table, she could

286

see that Evelyn was wearing dark glasses. Whether the disguise had worked, or because the late-afternoon clientele, busy spoiling their appetites for dinner, had decided to ignore her in their own inimitable New England way, Evelyn was being left strictly alone. Alone except for the wreckage of several of the Webb's gigantic ice cream specialties. These confections carried names such as Danny's Dairy Delight and Myrtle's Mounds of Mocha—in honor of the cows or the children, Faith had never asked. Evelyn was attacking Bessie's Chocolate Dream—a bowl of several hefty scoops of chocolate ice cream with hot fudge, marshmallow topping, whipped cream, nuts, chocolate chips, and several cherries.

Faith sat down opposite her. Sully walked in the door, said something to the cashier, and casually strolled to a booth across the aisle.

Evelyn looked up from her ice cream. For a moment, she seemed not to recognize Faith, then hissed at her, "What the hell are you doing here? Can't you leave me alone!"

"I thought we might talk about these." Faith held the slide box up, then quickly returned it to her pocket.

Evelyn pulled off her glasses.

"Give those to me! They're mine!" Her voice was rising. "You took them from my trailer!"

"And *you* took them from the storeroom after you killed the photographer, Alden Spaulding. His name is on the box, not yours," Faith said calmly.

Evelyn stood up and reached for Faith across the table, sending the sticky contents of Bessie's Dream flying all over Faith's jacket, much to the sleuth's annoyance.

"Give me those slides, you bitch, or I'll kill you, too!"

Detective Sullivan pulled Ms. O'Clair away from Faith, thereby saving her face from possible damage.

"You have the right . . ." he intoned.

Faith was very thankful. She was thankful that Dunne had had Sully follow her. She was thankful Evelyn O'Clair's talonlike fingernails hadn't reached their target. And she was thankful to be in her own house later that night with some of the cast of characters sitting around the Fairchilds' big kitchen table devouring Chinese takeout.

It wasn't a chicken feet crowd or even a clams in black bean sauce one. What wasn't deep-fried or covered with red dye number something sweet-and-sour sauce was being rolled up in mu shu pancakes. And, like other similar establishments in the Boston area, far from their roots in Canton, the restaurant supplied bread along with rice. There were some six-packs in the middle of the table and a few bottles of Coke. It lacked the finesse of a Have Faith affair, but even the lady herself agreed, it was a banquet.

"Shove some more of those shrimp over to this side, Faith, and stop showing off with your chopsticks," Charley demanded. He'd placed the order and was busy mopping up some sauce on his plate with a hunk of good old familiar white bread.

It was absolutely lovely to bask in warmth created by friendship and an almost-adequate heating system. Faith had taken a shower as soon as she'd returned home, yet it wasn't until the food arrived that the smell of smoke finally left her nostrils. She was none the worse for the experience except for some vivid, paralyzing moments of anxious "what ifs." She doubted, though, that her suede jacket from Barney's would ever be the same again. Evelyn's damage had been far-reaching.

Cornelia was fine, too. However, to be on the safe side, she was being held overnight for observation at Emerson

288

Hospital, where she'd been taken when the fire department arrived. The cast and crew of *A* had managed to contain the fire and keep the RV from blowing up, but they had not put the blaze out. There was plenty for Aleford's finest to do. Greg Bradley had gone with Cornelia to the hospital and somehow had ended up in the Fairchilds' kitchen, entering with Charley.

Pix and her husband, Sam, had rushed over as soon as they heard. Pix had refused to leave Faith's side for a moment, talking to her through the bathroom door as she showered, abandoning the watch only to call Niki with the news. Niki was at the door twenty minutes later with some of the day's leftovers. Plates of cookies, doughnuts, and a large pan of pear crisp sat on the counter—the next course. When Greg had walked in, Faith had steered him next to her assistant. No obvious tattoos and with a job— Niki wouldn't be bringing him home for dinner, at least not yet.

Dunne had arrived at Webb's shortly after Sully had read Evelyn her rights and Faith had immediately given the slides to him with a brief description of what was in the box. Ice cream melted in dishes as one and all watched the star being led away, screaming for her lawyer and Max.

"I didn't make it up to get her to confess. Spaulding's name *was* on the box. It would have been a good idea, except don't they call that entrapment? Anyway, I realized the name might be on it when Sully and I were driving to Webb's. There was no way Evelyn could claim they were hers. What did she say at headquarters?" Faith asked eagerly.

Dunne leaned back in his chair, smiling expansively. It was the end of a case, two cases really. Good food—and it was his turn to speak.

"She got in the car and shut her mouth tight. I didn't

289

expect to hear another peep out of her, but after we'd gone a few miles, she suddenly went ballistic and wanted to know what was going to happen to her car. Didn't want it left out overnight. Her car! She's killed two people and she's upset about a piece of machinery. Anyway, I told her someone would drive it to headquarters and that quieted her down. Then she said that when we were through with her, someone could just drive her back and she'd pick it up! I mean, the woman had no concept that she was in any more than slap-on-the-wrist trouble.

"I told her that could be a long time and she went nuts. This is not someone who generally hears the word *no*."

Faith could well imagine.

"Then she gets all high-and-mighty. Did we know who she was? What she had accomplished? She even brings up the Oscar. I point out that she may be facing additional charges of assault with said prize and she acts as if she hasn't heard me. Wants to know if anyone in the car has one."

The entire table cracked up.

"It wasn't the kind of question that expects an answer."

"Rhetorical," Faith supplied.

"Thank you, and to think I once took freshman English. Anyway, after this, we couldn't shut her up if we'd wanted to. I started taking notes. I reminded her about her lawyer, but now she wasn't interested in waiting for him and used some extremely coarse language to describe what she thought of the breed. Sorry, Sam."

Sam Miller was an attorney. "Don't worry about it, at least she didn't take Shakespeare literally."

"Oh yeah, 'kill all the lawyers.' That was freshman year, too."

Faith was getting impatient with these digressions. "Did she think Max was going to replace her with Sandra?"

"She didn't say so directly, but she certainly hated the girl. Kept saying that Sandra wanted to be her, Evelyn, but that there was only one Evelyn O'Clair. It was actually kind of pitiful. She kept asking us to agree. 'I warned her, but she wouldn't listen,' she said over and over. Like it was the girl's own fault she died."

Faith found herself adjusting her image of Evelyn O'Clair. Once again, someone was not who she or he seemed to be—a perception repeating with alarming frequency of late.

"Do you think Max knew Evelyn killed Sandra?"

Greg Bradley answered this one. He had been following the conversation with an anguished look. "I think Max didn't want to know," he said bitterly. "Doesn't want to think about it now, either. Yeah, he liked Sandra, and maybe he even thought she had a brilliant future ahead. But essentially, she was just another PA and there would be a new one to take her place the next day. He knew Evelyn wanted Sandra off the picture, but Maxwell Reed doesn't like people telling him what to do, even, or maybe especially, his wife. He didn't stop to think what might happen to Sandra—oh, I don't mean that anyone would have suspected Evelyn of being capable of murder. It's still a shock, but she could make things very unpleasant for people, and Max knew it."

If Max Reed had fired Sandra Wilson, she would be alive today. It was a horrible conclusion.

"Evelyn may simply have meant to frighten Sandra," Greg continued. "I saw her talking to Sandra that morning before the filming. Evelyn was clearly telling her to quit and Evelyn may have been threatening her."

"Which explains why Sandra looked terrified on the footage. It was real fear," Faith said to Dunne, then asked Greg, "Did Sandra ever mention Evelyn's threats to you?"

"Yes, she said Evelyn had told her to quit or Max would fire her. Sandra didn't believe her, and sadly, I agreed with her. Anyway, Sandra would have done anything to stay on the production with Max. I sensed that she was uneasy; there may have been threats she didn't mention. It's weird. I never suspected Evelyn, though it's all obvious now. She didn't act any differently after Sandra died. A normal person would have been eaten up with guilt, but with Evelyn, Sandra was gone and that was what she, Evelyn, had wanted. On with the show." He choked a bit on the words and Niki patted his shoulder companionably.

"The operative word here is *act,*" Faith pointed out. "Ms. O'Clair may well be one of the world's great actresses. Think about that night at the Town Hall. She delivered a performance, whipped downstairs for the slide show, which must have been prearranged, killed Alden, and was back in time for her next cue."

"That's pretty much what seems to have happened from what we've been able to piece together," John said. "She left the auditorium when Reed was doing retakes of the scene between himself and Camson. She was alone in the back. Alden had his slide show all set up in the basement. He must have phoned her to tell her what he had—and what he had heard. She hasn't said what he wanted in exchange, but it may not have been money. I think he wanted what Cappy was getting on the slides. She must have strung him along and maybe agreed to meet him the next day or something. Then as they were leaving the room, she let him have it. The first blow must have stunned him, then she finished off the job when he was lying on the floor. She had to have brought some other kind of weapon along, but the lumber was handy and easier to get rid of."

Dunne spoke. He sounded a bit stunned. "Do you mean Alden Spaulding was blackmailing her for sexual favors?"

"I think we can tell everyone what Alden was like without getting too specific," Tom suggested. Faith and Pix agreed. They summarized Audrey's and Penny's stories. Dunne was even more astounded—and upset.

"I wish the victims had come to the police. We wouldn't have let him get away with it."

"What else did Evelyn say? Why did you say the piece of lumber was easy to get rid of?" Many questions remained unanswered, and to her annoyance, Faith was getting sleepy. She was also getting a headache from the MSG.

"The woman was incredibly lucky. You know there are many murders that only get solved because the murderer tells someone about it. Can't keep it to himself or herself. Evelyn didn't blab. If Faith hadn't found the slides in the trailer, we'd still be wondering who killed Wilson and Spaulding. There was no evidence to link the two crimes and we've been kicking around the two killers theory all week. But getting back to the weapon. After O'Clair killed him, she put the piece of wood in her car, which was parked just outside. Later, when she got home, she burned it in the fire that she knew would be conveniently set for her arrival."

"I'm sure Alden never thought he was in any danger from Evelyn, a mere woman. She definitely had the element of surprise working for her," Faith commented.

"But she must have had a nasty moment when Faith arrived," Niki said. "Thank God you didn't see her!"

"She was wearing a long, dark hooded cloak—used it to open the door and switch the lights on and off, by the way—and it made her virtually invisible in the dark. Her only worry would have been that Faith might hang around too long and the people upstairs would start to wonder where their star was. When we went over the footage, we never noticed she was missing, because the camera at that time was either on the stage or the audience. We knew Alden was gone and Reed and Camson were there. That's all."

"It almost was the perfect crime," Faith said.

"Is anybody going to pass those cookies around?" Charley complained.

"How about me?" said a cheerful voice at the door. "I knew you'd all be here."

It was Millicent. There was going to be little rest for the weary tonight, Faith concluded, then perked up as she realized that Penny Bartlett was at Miss McKinley's heels. There had no longer been any need for secrecy, so Faith had told Detective Sullivan right away where Penny was, then promptly forgot about her in the rush of other events. Faith was very glad to see her.

Everyone jumped up and embraced Penny, even Niki, who had never been actually formally introduced to the woman before. Settled next to Charley MacIsaac, who was trying to adopt a stern manner toward the runaway, Penny declared happily, "You have no idea what it means to be home! Not that the people at the Y weren't absolute angels, but I've been missing Piggy—and the plants, too." Piggy was the totally unsuitable name of Penny's darling Irish terrier.

"Would you like something to eat?" Faith asked automatically, surveying the wreckage spread out on her table a few sad bamboo shoots floating in a pool of congealed sauce, half a container of rice, one egg roll. It was not very appetizing, but Niki had put the pear crisp in the oven to warm.

"No, thank you. We went out to dinner to celebrate. That's why we're so late."

"It was like something out of the movies. I was in my room working on some patchwork I'd fortunately remembered to pack, when Millicent called from the lobby and said, 'The murderer has been unmasked. Pack your things and make yourself tidy; we're going to the Ritz for dinner.' I don't suppose they hear many messages like this at the desk."

Faith had to hand it to Millicent. She possessed an ineffable sense of style. The Ritz-Carlton was the perfect choice. Two old friends tucking into their baked scrod or whatever in that elegant dining room overlooking the Public Garden. Two proper New England ladies: one a former fugitive from the law; the other, her accomplice.

"Now"—Millicent had determinedly wedged a chair between Pix and John Dunne—"what have I missed?"

Tom dished up the pear crisp while Niki added a generous amount of whipped cream to each serving. Those at the table took turns relating the story so far.

"How did you know it was all right to get Penny?" Faith asked, digging into the portion of what she knew to be a scrumptious dessert. She had assumed that after the police were informed of Penny's whereabouts, they would have picked her up.

"Well, we heard the woods near the Pingrees' were on fire and Ed Hayes, who's one of the volunteers, called his wife from some sort of phone in his car he seems to think he needs in order to be a good plumber. He told her you'd been locked in the RV and had set the fire to get somebody to let you out, which was extremely foolhardy, I must say, Faith. You *know* that's conservation land." Millicent actually shook a finger at Faith.

295

Faith had known it would come up sometime. She hadn't thought it would be so soon.

"You were tampering with a protected area. Thank goodness merely a few alders and some brush were destroyed." The way Millicent was talking, one might have assumed this particular area was the last remaining stand of virgin timber in New England. In fact, it was a reclaimed swamp.

"So, we all knew something was going on and I went down to the police station. Dale told me this actress had been arrested, and I went straight to Penny."

Pix, God bless her, hastened to direct the subject away from another tirade regarding protected areas that seemed to be swelling from Millicent's direction. "It's wonderful to see you, Penny. Have you heard? James has withdrawn from the race, so we should be toasting you as Aleford's newest selectwoman."

Penny looked very surprised. "Why on earth did he do that?

Faith did not have the heart—or the strength—to go into the subject at the moment. "I'll tell you tomorrow," she promised.

Millicent beamed. This was a victory party. *Her* victory party.

The actual election victory party Faith attended was a quiet, extremely select one, held at the Town Hall after the ballots had been counted.

The police chief had ceremoniously unlocked the old wooden box and the town clerk started the count promptly at eight o'clock. Aleford, typically, was one of the Massachusetts communities that still clung to its paper ballots. Who would be so madcap as to put all one's trust in a machine? Even though there was no race, the

296

electorate had turned out in full force to cast their votes. It didn't matter how many candidates there were. Voting was a sacred civic responsibility. The predictable result was a landslide for Penelope Bartlett with three write-ins, obviously the work of some of the younger members of the voting population: two for Jason Priestley and one for Mr. Ed.

Penny had asked the Fairchilds to come watch the count, then return to her house for coffee. Having exhausted all available baby-sitting options, they were forced to refuse. Tom convinced Faith to go for a little while, however. "I know you want to, honey. See the thing through." She'd kissed him gratefully and walked over—just for a minute.

An hour later, she was sitting in the Town Hall's kitchen with Charley MacIsaac. He'd brought a bottle of champagne to celebrate Penny's victory and perhaps to make amends for the dressing-down he had given her in private on Sunday for running off and not calling on him. Penny had taken a sip, given him a hug, then dashed off with Millicent to put out the coffee cups for the supporters she expected at her house. Charley had motioned to Faith, "I've got to lock up here, but let's kill this bottle first. Phone Tom and tell him I'll see you home."

Tom was amused, and grateful for the call. He was pretty jittery about his wife's whereabouts these days. "Don't you and Charley start stealing street signs or whatever. Remember the old saying, 'Burgundy makes you think of silly things; Bordeaux makes you talk about them; and Champagne makes you do them.'"

"Remember it! I told it to *you*," Faith said. It was one of the gastronomist Brillat-Savarin's oft-quoted remarks.

The champagne wasn't prompting them to particularly

outrageous behavior, although it certainly had loosened their tongues. There were no proper champagne flutes in the Town Hall's cupboards, but Faith had unearthed some dusty *coupes*, washed them, and put aside the jelly glasses Charley had set out.

She held her glass to the light and regarded the pale golden sparkling liquid intently. "These were supposed to be made from a mold of either Helen of Troy's breast or Marie Antoinette's. I've always favored the latter legend." Faith pronounced the last two words very distinctly. "Helen was more of a mead drinker, I'd say. Marie probably had champagne coming out of the taps of her bath."

Charley thought the whole thing was very funny. "I never thought I'd been sitting in the Town Hall's basement listening to a slightly tiddley minister's wife tell stories about historic bosoms."

"Life is like that," Faith said solemnly. "I never thought I'd be locked up in a burning trailer by a crazed, Oscar-wielding murderess. I've been saying to Tom ever since this thing started that it was getting pretty hard to draw the line between art and reality. If you filmed all this, Siskel and Ebert would definitely turn their thumbs down." Faith demonstrated with hers after carefully placing her glass on the counter. "Two thumbs down. Totally implausible."

"I agree." Charley was infinitely more sober than Faith but was having just as good a time. "Still, it is an amazing coincidence that Reed was filming a movie all about jealousy and meanwhile another story with the same theme was going on right in front of all our noses."

Faith had been right all along with her theory, she thought to herself. She'd simply miscast.

"You are so insightful, Charley." Faith was impressed.

298

"Professional jealousy and sexual jealousy—a real double whammy."

"I'm going to escort you home now, Mrs. Fairchild, before you start seeing double. The night air will do us both good."

"Good. That reminds me. I was good, wasn't I? Admit it. You and John were stumped."

"You were not good. You held out on us—but yes, we were stumped."

"Thought so." Faith smiled. She knew her feeling of well-being was not due to the moderate amount of champers she'd imbibed. It was because Penny had won, Evelyn been caught, Have Faith's black bean soup forever vindicated, and her current job over. Max was going to shoot the rest of the movie in California, making even further alterations in the story line to account for Hester's abrupt disappearance. Faith would be able to become reacquainted with her family. She had a great deal of quality time to make up.

But what was really making her want to crow out loud into the quiet of the night as she and Charley walked past the sleeping houses along Aleford's green was the realization she was getting better and better at this detection business. Not that she was going to go around searching for bodies, yet if another one happened to come her way . . .

"What are you looking so darned pleased about?" Charley asked. "No, wait, I don't want to know, do I?"

"Probably not," Faith Sibley Fairchild concurred. "Probably not."

It wasn't foggy. It wasn't an airport. It wasn't Casablanca. But she took Charley's arm, anyway.

Cha

CHAPTER 12

f sages were ever wise in their own behoof, I might have foreseen all this.

ALAN MORRIS HAD BEEN TO MORE ACADEMY AWARD ceremonies than he cared to remember, and mostly they were a bore. The real action was at the parties afterward. He'd start at Swifty Lazar's and go on from there, depending on his mood—and who had won. A lot of business took place at those parties once it had been established on worldwide television who was in, who was out; who was hot, who was not.

He hated the whole idea of getting all dressed up so early in the day before the sun went down. It felt unnatural. He'd decided to get his own limo for the drive to the Dorothy Chandler Pavilion. He hadn't felt like riding in Max's or the producers', and now he was sorry. First, he had to listen to the driver tell him that he'd never driven a loser, the same thing the guy said to every occupant every year. Then he had to face the prospect of stepping out alone in front of a huge throng expecting Richard Gere—or Cappy Camson.

It was taking forever. They had only moved an inch or two in the last fifteen minutes. L.A. was one vast acreage of stretch chrome.

He might not be famous, but at least his tux was perfect. Made to measure last time he was in London. It fit him like a glove. When he finally arrived, the thought cheered him enough to see him through the shrieking crowds. Shrieking crowds for the stars to the front and rear of him. "Who's that?" he heard one woman ask her friend as he walked past. "Nobody," was the firm answer. Army Archerd, the outdoor master of ceremonies, was introducing gorgeous Geena Davis, who had on a pretty crazy dress. Neither of them noticed him, either.

He found his seat. Max and the rest of them weren't here yet. "Nobody." He was getting just a little bit tired of being "Nobody." Of being ever so slightly in the shadow. One that was never angry. Never tired. Never without a solution. Never without the right word.

Last spring had pushed him to his limit. He'd watched Evelyn spinning further and further out of control. Max was always out of control when he was filming a movie. Living each film twenty-four hours a day. It was clear from the first moment in that hick town—what was it called? Aleford. Yeah, from the first moment on the set, he'd known that a whole lot of things were not going to work. Sandra, Evelyn, Caresse Carroll. But Max hadn't wanted to hear about it. Not then. Not later. He had had his plans. Nothing else had mattered. Not even life or death. The film came first.

And maybe it would today. Come first. Best Picture, Best Director, Best Screenplay, Cappy and Max both nominated for Best Actor. They'd be competing against each other. Evelyn had not been nominated for Best Actress. There had been no hushing up what had happened in—Aleford. Why did he keep blocking on the name? He knew why. So, no more Oscars for Evelyn. No more anything for Evelyn—save a nice padded cell or whatever the equivalent was these days. Caresse was nominated for Best Supporting Actress, though. People were calling her the next Brooke Shields. Marta should have been nominated. And they said these weren't a popularity contest. But maybe Caresse deserved it. She'd given a hell of a performance after Max rewrote the thing and had her acting as Hester in all those flashbacks to England. Chillingworth watching the child blossom, biding his time. The lust on Max's face was both pathetic and obscene. Maybe he deserved the award.

A had been a huge box-office success. The publicity surrounding the murders, as well as the big names, had attracted record-breaking audiences. The film had legs like a centipede and the producers were dancing all the way to the bank.

Here they were. Act normal, Alan old boy. You've been doing this for years. Nobody has to know how much you hate them. Hate all of them. What was it Max was always quoting from Hawthorne—something about in the end love and hate being the same thing? Love and hate. Then there was that other quotation. Max worked it into the script: "No man, for any considerable period, can wear one face to himself, and another to the multitude, without finally getting bewildered as to which may be the true."

Alan put on a face. He couldn't slip tonight, of all nights. He'd been doing it so long, so well. He was sure he could keep it up. For one more night. He put out his hand to Max, who shook it vigorously and slapped him on the shoulder.

"Great to see you, Alan. Have a good vacation?" Max was clearly uncomfortable in his tuxedo and even more clearly nervous about the awards. His forehead was already sweating slightly. "Why do they always keep this place so damned hot?"

Marta was next to him. She took a handkerchief from her purse and handed it to him. She looked terrific in a beautifully cut tuxedo with a skirt slit up the side instead of pants. Her hair was piled up on top of her head. Caresse and her mother were on the other side of Marta.

"When are they going to get started?" Caresse whined. She was not happy at Max's insistence she wear a duplicate of the film's dumb red velvet dress he'd had made for her. She thought it made her look like a baby.

Her mother smiled nervously. The rows behind and in front of them were filling up. People could hear—the ones who didn't have their cellular phones glued to their ears, that is.

"Any moment, darling. And your category will be early!"

"I told you not to mention it!" Caresse wanted the award so badly, she had barely been able to concentrate on anything else since the nominations had been announced. She'd told her mother not to talk about it to her. She didn't want anything to jinx her chances.

Jacqueline flushed. Max had been urging her to take a firmer hand with her daughter. She'd agreed. She'd agree to anything the man said, she realized. When he'd taken off those ridiculously thick glasses the first time they'd made love and looked at her with his persuasive blue eyes, she just said, "Yes"—and "Yes" again.

There was an empty seat beside Max. Alan had left it for Cappy. He knew the game. The star arrived next. The producers, Kit Murphy and Arnold Rose, after that, and then they were all there.

All except Evelyn.

Billy Crystal strolled onstage to wild applause. These things had improved since he'd started hosting them, Alan

303

thought to himself. Crystal told a few jokes he wouldn't tell on-camera and then they were off and rolling.

Caresse didn't win. The Oscar went to a legend, who had unaccountably never won the award before, for an admittedly lackluster cameo in a disaster film. The Academy was nothing if not sentimental.

"That old hag," Caresse fumed.

"Shut up," her mother whispered in her ear. "You're on-camera!"

Caresse shut up and smiled. A gallant little trouper, the press would say.

Next time. Next time. Next time, she chanted to herself.

It was late and they were getting to the good stuff. Alan didn't know whether he wanted the picture to win or not.

It was time to announce Best Actor and a clip from each film was being shown. There was Cappy, much bigger than life, in his final scene. Max had constructed a platform just like the scaffold on the village green and set it in the middle of a busy downtown L.A. intersection. He had Cappy make Dimmesdale's final confession to a crowd of commuters—Everyman and Everywoman, Max had called them. At the climax, Cappy rips open his shirt, showing his gorgeous chest, which the director had agreed to oil a little, with a hideous, scab-encrusted letter *A* carved over his heart. It was always one of those "Ooooh" moments in theaters across the country. The audience at Dorothy Chandler didn't "ooh." Most of them had seen it before, but they clapped loudly. Cappy didn't have too many enemies.

I wonder if he was in Evelyn's pants? Alan thought as the two presenters played cutesy games with the envelope. Max thought so; he could barely tolerate working with the guy. Evelyn must have told Max. She liked doing things

304

like that.

"And the winner is: Caleb Camson!"

Max and Cappy hugged like blood brothers. Up on the stage, Cappy captured a few more million hearts with his self-deprecating ways. He thanked his parents, Max, the producers, on and on, even Alan. Then he paused. "And I'd like to take a moment to remember someone who is not with us tonight. . . ."

"Evelyn, of course. I wish he'd said something about Sandra Wilson. I'm sure the studio never had a service for her, either. Then there's poor Corny. I'll bet Max has completely forgotten about her. She told me she'd invited him to the wedding and didn't hear from him. Alan Morris called to say Max couldn't make it. I wonder what he sent for a present?"

Cornelia Stuyvesant's family had taken a dim view of an industry in which employees were rendered unconscious by trophy-armed lunatics, and they'd whisked young Cornelia straight from the hospital to Bermuda. Not at all coincidentally, the eminently eligible son of dear friends happened to be sailing there. It was love at first tack, and if Cornelia was watching tonight's hoopla, it was on a wide-screen TV in Connecticut.

"Oh, come on, after the commercial, it's going to be Best Picture. You can't not watch!" Tom was reading Larry Bird's *Drive: The Story of My Life*.

"Yes, I can or can't. Whichever means I'd rather read my book." Tom had been ready to go to sleep an hour ago and had trouble understanding why Faith was so insistent on watching the rest of the tedious show. "You can find out tomorrow," he'd said.

"It's not the same. Besides, I like to see what people are wearing," she'd replied. And here they were, still up in front of the tube.

"All right, if it means so much to you." He put the book away and slung his arm around his wife's shoulders. "At least can we neck?"

"After, I promise."

"That's what all the girls say."

"Sssh, here it is."

A few minutes earlier, the screen had been split to show the reactions of the nominees for Best Director. Along with viewers all over the globe, the Fairchilds were able to catch Max's joy at winning. Now the screen was divided again. Max was holding Marta's hand.

"I'm sure it's going to get Best Picture, since Max got Best Director," Faith told her uninterested husband.

"Millicent never had any doubts. You could have trusted her and we'd be in bed by now."

Much of Aleford had been quietly taking credit for the picture's success during the last months. It had been tacitly assumed that of course their movie would win. And Aleford was right.

Max's acceptance speech was brief. He opened by saying, "There is someone who should be on this stage with me, and if I didn't think Billy would kill me for getting us off schedule, I'd have him up here."

"Him?" Faith said. "I thought it was going to be Evelyn again. Oh, I know, he's going to thank Nathaniel Hawthorne."

"I'm sure Nate would have appreciated that," Tom said sardonically. "And, by the way, would you mind telling me how Hawthorne would join Max onstage?"

"Sssh! I can't hear what he's saying!"

"He's my right hand." Max flung his whole arm out dramatically. "Maybe even the right side of my brain. All I know is, this picture could never have been made without

306

him. Alan Morris, my assistant director."

Alan was floored. Cappy jabbed him to stand up and he did, bowing slightly as the audience applauded wildly. For him. Maybe just one more picture with Max. Love and hate.

Clutching this best of all Oscars, Maxwell Reed closed by acknowledging the town—as was only fair.

"Some of those watching know that we went through a few tough times on this film and the good folks of Aleford, Massachusetts, were there for us. I'd like to thank them for their generous help and for providing the perfect landscapes." He chuckled and waited for the slight laughter to die down. "The individual people are too numerous to mention."

The camera was panning along the faces of *A*'s cast as Max spoke these last words. Alan Morris had tears in his eyes. Cappy looked relieved. Caresse smiled her famous smile. Jacqueline had moistened her lips. It lingered on Marta, who looked directly into the lens—directly at Faith.

"But," continued the director, "you know who you are."

And Marta winked.

EXCERPTS FROM

HAVE FAITH IN YOUR KITCHEN
By **Faith Sibley Fairchild**

A WORK IN PROGRESS
[Design]

It was marvelous to observe how the ghosts of bygone meals were continually rising up before him; not in anger or retribution, but as if grateful for his former appreciation and seeking to reduplicate an endless series of enjoyment, at once shadowy and sensual.

UNADULTERATED BLACK BEAN SOUP

1 pound dried black beans
2 ham hocks or 1 ham bone
2 medium onions, 1 red and
1 yellow

7-8 cups water
1½ teaspoon salt

¼ teaspoon freshly
ground pepper
1 tablespoon dry
sherry or Madeira
(optional)
sour cream
chives

Pick over the beans, rinse, cover with cold water, and bring to a boil for 2 minutes. Remove from heat and let stand at least 1 hour. (Or soak the beans overnight.)

Rinse the ham hocks. Peel and quarter the onions. Bury hocks and onions in the beans.

Add 7-8 cups cold water and bring to a boil. Turn the heat down and simmer 1½ to 2 hours. Be sure the beans are soft.

Remove the hocks or bone and strip any meat from them. Add the meat to the soup and puree the mixture in batches in a blender. (Note: a food processor sometimes leaks with this much liquid). Put the pureed soup in a clean pot; warm, adding the seasonings and wine, if used. Serve with a dollop of sour cream and finely minced chives. For a special party, put the sour cream in a pastry tube and pipe two concentric circles on top of the soup. Take a sharp knife and pull it through the circles, first toward the center, then away, for a nice spiderweb effect.

This soup tastes better if made a day ahead. Serves 8 to 10—more if served as a first course.

NORWEGIAN MEATBALLS

½ pound ground veal
½ pound lean ground beef
½ cup bread crumbs
1 egg, slightly beaten
½ teaspoon salt
¼ teaspoon freshly ground pepper
1/8 teaspoon ground nutmeg

3 slices of salt pork (or slab bacon), 3 inches square, rendered

Sauce:
2 tablespoons butter
2 tablespoons flour
1¾ cups beef stock

Combine the meats, crumbs, egg, and seasonings into balls 1½ inches in diameter, using as little pressure as possible. Cover and let stand for 1 hour.

Brown the meatballs in the pork fat.

In a separate pot, melt the butter and add the flour, whisking together to make a roux. Slowly add the stock, stirring constantly. Bring to a boil and add the browned meatballs. Simmer very low for 1½ hours. Serve over egg noodles and garnish with finely chopped parsley. Serves 4 to 6.

PEAR BRIE PIZZETTE

Dough
1 cup warm water
1 package granular yeast (not rapid-rising)
1 teaspoon sugar

2 tablespoons butter
1 tablespoon olive oil
2½-3 cups all-purpose flour
cornmeal

Pour the water in a bowl and sprinkle the yeast on top. Add the sugar, salt, olive oil, and mix until the yeast is dissolved. Add 1½ cups of flour, stir, and add 1 more cup. Combine thoroughly and turn the dough out onto a lightly floured surface, adding the rest of the flour if the dough is too sticky. Knead for 5 minutes.

Put the dough in a lightly oiled bowl and let rise in a warm place until double in bulk—about 1 hour. Punch down and divide into two pieces for pizzettes. Let the dough rest for about 15 minutes. Using a rolling pin or your hands, shape into two rounds.

Topping
3 large yellow onions
1 tablespoon olive oil

2 large ripe pears
(comice are especially good)

1 tablespoon unsalted butter
1½ tablespoons sugar

1½-¾ pound ripe, but
not runny, Brie

Preheat the oven to 450°.

Slice the onions into thin rings and sauté in the melted butter and oil until limp. Cover the pan, stirring occasionally. Cook slowly for about 15 minutes. Uncover the pan, sprinkle the onions with the sugar, turn up the heat, and cook until well browned. Stir constantly. The sugar caramelizes the onions. This will take 15 to 20 minutes. Set the onions aside.

Peel and slice the pears.

Brush the tops of the pizzettes with some olive oil and spread the caramelized onions over each. Arrange the pear slices on top and dot with slices of the Brie.

Bake for 15 minutes on a lightly greased pizza pan on which you've sprinkled cornmeal. The dough may also be baked on a cookie sheet and cut into squares. Serves 4—more if served as a first course.

DENOUEMENT APPLE/PEAR CRISP

This recipe can be made with pears or apples. It is especially delicious with a mixture of apples, such as Empire or Delicious (sweet) and Macoun or Macintosh (slightly tart).

1¾-2 pounds apples or pears
juice of ½ lemon
2 tablespoons maple syrup
6 tablespoons unsalted butter

¼ teaspoon salt
3 tablespoons brown sugar
¾ cup flour

Preheat the oven to 375°.

Peel, core, and slice the fruit. Toss it in a bowl with the

311

lemon juice to prevent browning.

Place the slices in a lightly buttered baking dish. Drizzle with the maple syrup.

Put the flour, salt, sugar, and butter in the bowl of a food processor fitted with a metal blade and process briefly. Or you may cut the butter in with a pastry cutter or two knives. The mixture should be crumbly.

Cover the fruit evenly with the flour mixture and bake for 45 minutes or until the juices are bubbling.

Let sit for five minutes and serve with whipped cream, vanilla ice cream, or crème fraîche.

LIZZIE S SUGAR AND SPICE COOKIES

¾ cup unsalted butter
1 cup sugar
1 egg, slightly beaten
¼ cup molasses
2 cups flour
2 teaspoons baking soda

1 teaspoon cinnamon
¾ teaspoon cloves
¾ teaspoon ginger
¼ teaspoon salt
sugar

Preheat the oven to 375°.

Cream the butter, sugar, egg, and molasses together thoroughly. Sift the flour, baking soda, spices, and salt together. Add to the butter mixture and stir.

Roll the dough into balls, 1 inch in diameter, and roll the balls in sugar. Set approximately 2 inches apart on a lightly greased cookie sheet and bake for 12 minutes. Let cool on brown paper or racks. Makes approximately 4 dozen.

For an elegant tea cookie, make ½-inch-diameter balls and reduce the cooking time to 9 minutes. Makes approximately 8 dozen.

AUTHOR'S NOTE

I apologize to all of you who have been asking for recipes. I should have done them sooner, but when I wrote my first book, *The Body in the Belfry,* I thought it might seem I was borrowing more than a cup of sugar from the late Virginia Rich, one of my favorite authors. I was also afraid recipes might distract readers from the plot. You would be so busy deciding whether to put Spanish or Vidalia onions in your soup that you'd miss a red herring. However, here they are at last. I hope they will give you as much pleasure as they do my family.

Faith is a purist. I am not. People in fiction seem to have a great deal more time than the people I know in real life, with nine-to-five jobs, gardens to weed, and wash to do (plus that stack of books next to the bed). These recipes will all taste fine with modifications such as a good canned beef stock, instead of homemade, for the meatballs (although not canned bread crumbs) and already-prepared pizza dough, like Boboli, for the pizzette. You can also make the cookies ahead and freeze the balls, baking a batch when you need—or want—them. The point is to end up with something tasty to sit down to with the latest Faith Fairchild mystery propped up next to your plate. *Santé!*

Dear Reader:

I hope you enjoyed reading this Large Print mystery. If you are interested in reading other Beeler Large Print Mystery titles or any other Beeler Large Print titles, ask your librarian or write to me at

> Thomas T. Beeler, *Publisher*
> Post Office Box 659
> Hampton Falls, New Hampshire 03844

You can also call me at 1-800-251-8726 and I will send you my latest catalogue.

Audrey Lesko chooses the titles I publish in Large Print. Our aim is to provide good books by outstanding authors—books we both enjoyed reading and liked well enough to want to share. We warmly welcome any suggestions for new titles and authors.

Sincerely,